THINGS HE NEVER KNEW

Sarah Haynes was born in Surrey and grew up in Berkshire, attending the Abbey School in Reading. Looking after her ponies and writing stories took up all of her spare time. After completing her A-Levels she studied Law at Southampton University. After graduating she married and now lives in Hampshire with her husband and two daughters. Sarah writes full-time; *Things He Never Knew* is her first novel and she is currently working on her second.

THINGS HE NEVER KNEW

Sarah Haynes

THINGS HE NEVER KNEW

Olympia Publishers
London

www.olympiapublishers.com
OLYMPIA PAPERBACK EDITION

Copyright © Sarah Haynes 2010

The right of Sarah Haynes to be identified as author of this work has been asserted in accordance with sections 77 and 78 of the Copyright, Designs and Patents Act 1988.

All Rights Reserved

No reproduction, copy or transmission of this publication may be made without written permission.
No paragraph of this publication may be reproduced, copied or transmitted save with the written permission of the publisher, or in accordance with the provisions of the Copyright Act 1956 (as amended).

Any person who commits any unauthorised act in relation to this publication may be liable to criminal prosecution and civil claims for damage.

A CIP catalogue record for this title is available from the British Library.

ISBN: 978-1-84897-089-2

This is a work of fiction.
Names, characters, places and incidents originate from the writer's imagination. Any resemblance to actual persons, living or dead, is purely coincidental.

First Published in 2010

Olympia Publishers
60 Cannon Street
London
EC4N 6NP

Printed in Great Britain

For my sister, Kim. In recognition of her endless help and encouragement, and genuine faith in my writing.

Extra thanks are due to my husband, for making it possible for me to pursue this career at all.

And to those who have encouraged me – you know who you are.

And particular thanks to my daughters, Molly and Alice, for providing lots of inspiration.

CHAPTER ONE

Paris in 1996 was busy; far busier than she'd expected. She hadn't done a huge amount of research – there hadn't been time – but it was loud, noisy and thronging with people. Mostly chic businesswomen as far as Steph could tell. She longed to join their ranks and dress like they did, to wear her hair in a neat chignon and carry a tasteful leather bag. She glanced down at her own battered jeans and t-shirt. One day, maybe. However bad the outlook was at the moment.

She looked around herself, hoping Theo would hurry up. He'd said he wouldn't be long. Steph threw down her rucksack and just as she was about to sit on it, a phone box caught her eye on the corner of the street. It was only a few strides away and it was empty. God, she needed to speak to him. Even just for a minute, it didn't take long to say those two words. Should she risk it? And it was a real risk – if Theo overheard... Steph hesitated, torn between sense and longing. Then she grabbed her rucksack and ran, two seconds down to the corner and slammed the phone box door behind her. Carefully with shaking fingers she dialled the international code and then Ed's number.

"Hello?"

Her voice froze for a second and Steph swallowed hard, "Ed? It's me, Steph."

A hard silence.

"Ed? Are you there?" But her voice crackled into the line, it broke and split with static and reverberated back at her. "Hello? Hello?" She couldn't be sure he'd heard her at all. Then the deep purr of the dial tone hit her ear. *Shit.* For a moment she considered ringing back but then she saw Theo walk past looking for her and she had to leap out of the phone box quickly.

He smiled his wide, generous smile when he saw her, "You OK?"

"Yeah, fine."

"Ready to go?"

"Yes. Let's." She slid her hand into his and they walked together towards the Metro. Steph didn't look back.

****

"Twins! What are you doing up there? Come on, five minutes or you'll be late. And don't forget your violins." They'd only just received their violins as a reward for working so hard at mastering the basics on the school ones. Mia and Tilly had been delighted; the violins were bright pink. Being able to choose your own colour was a new design initiative for 2007.

"Mummy I hate the violin," Mia groaned.

"No Mia, you don't. And your lesson is today. Come on. Have you got yours Tilly? Good girl."

"Mummy, Mia poked her tongue out at me!"

"Ignore her. Mia, *stop it*. Come on or we really will be late."

"I don't care. It's spellings first thing," Mia pouted.

"I care, I don't want a late mark," Tilly said, looking worried.

"Hop into the car then!"

Steph grabbed her new handbag – a thoughtful birthday present from Theo – and pulled open the door of her car to throw two violin cases into the back. It was Monday; that meant Mrs B was coming and the bins needed to go out. Damn. Why could Theo never remember? She hauled the recycling bin out between the iron gates and onto the street, taking a moment to admire their new house name sign. "*Touchstone*" was etched in a charcoal colour onto a piece of varnished pine. Simple, but it looked good. And it hadn't been cheap either. But then nothing that came from Raggy Rose was cheap. The latest design company in Churchwell had come straight from London with quite a following. And, as someone who had once had interior design aspirations, there was no other company to use.

The white iron railings of the St Catherine's School for Girls became visible the moment they rounded the corner. The girls grabbed their rucksacks, water bottles and violins without being told, and clambered out.

They were so grown-up at ten; Steph could hardly believe the difference in the last few years. Even Theo had been moved to comment that they were less annoying than they had been. Having twins had been hard at first, especially because the pair of them had been so young, frighteningly young, but now they were truly beginning to reap the rewards. Steph walked slightly behind Tilly and Mia, watching their identical blonde ponytails bobbing up and down.

Life was good. Settled, relaxed, organised. Now that the girls were older she and Theo had even been able to claw back a little time for themselves too. They had no family nearby, their relatives were all back in Tinford, a forty-five minute drive away. They didn't go back often, there were too many lingering memories and awkward feelings seemed to hang around every familiar corner. It was easier to stay away.

"Mummy! Come on, we'll be late!" Tilly had turned around from outside the school as pupils in their matching blazers hurried inside. Obediently, Steph sped up a little in her Carvela heeled boots. A bit OTT for the school run but they were just so fabulous, and as someone who was only 5'2", she needed all the help she could get in the height department. Vertiginous heels weren't her thing, but an extra couple of inches didn't go amiss.

It was almost half past eight, Tilly was quite right; another couple of minutes and the bell would have gone for morning assembly. And Steph prided herself on always being on time.

"All right, all right. Off you go then. Have a lovely day." She pecked them both quickly on the cheek and straightened Mia's tie out of habit.

"Muuum! It's already straight," she grumbled.

"I like to make sure. Right I'll see you later." The twins disappeared through the wide, wooden door into the depths of the school. As always, Tilly turned and gave her a quick wave at the door – slightly less certain, less confident than Mia who never bothered. Steph smiled at her and waved back.

She was reminded every morning of her own school days as she waved goodbye to her girls. Of course her school – or rather, hers and Theo's and Edward's school – wasn't a patch on St Catherine's. It hadn't been in a nice part of a smart town with its own playing field and large playground. It hadn't had six science labs, language labs, two main halls, labyrinthine corridors and a boarding block. Tinford Junior School had basically been one, smallish building, into which six years of thirty children each were crammed. Its one saving grace was that it had backed onto endless open fields, which had given a false illusion of space.

Taking Mia and Tilly to somewhere so upmarket still intimidated Steph slightly. Having never been to an independent school herself, she had no idea what life was like behind that big, white, wooden door. Besides occasional forays into the school for parents evenings and sports days, she never went near the place. It was her girls who were metamorphosising into the accomplished, confident young ladies that St Catherine's eventually turned out, and Steph wondered exactly how much they would achieve in their lives that she hadn't. A lot, she suspected, but then that wouldn't be hard.

Not that anyone watching Steph would think that she was insecure. Her groomed appearance belied her manner. A casual observer wouldn't know that she was often anxious as to what others thought of her for no obvious reason. She was young, pretty, approachable (she thought) then she wondered if perhaps they were actually hindrances rather than blessings. She remembered feeling embarrassed on the girls' first day at St Catherines, her and Theo had been so young. The youngest of all the parents there. She'd hung her head as they walked briskly through the school, whilst Theo strode on confidently. But no one would know that to look at her now. She stood at the white railings and waved goodbye vigorously to the twins; so pretty, so neat with their matching rucksacks, pulled-up beige socks and polished, brown shoes. She was careful though, not to catch the eye of any other mothers; she wouldn't know quite what to say. They were all older than her and all had flourishing careers. At least she assumed they did judging by the speed at which they accomplished drop-off, and the amount of nannies around doing pick-up. She sort of wanted to be part of the in-clique and sort of not, she didn't know yet if she would fit in. Her compromise last term had been to join the parents committee, colloquially known as Cath's.

When she thought about it, Steph felt very grown-up knowing she was the mother of eleven year old twin girls. Slightly too grown-up. A tiny part of her thought that shouldn't it still be someone taking Steph for spelling tests and double maths? Where on earth had the time gone? How had she gone from the Steph she was then into the Steph she was now? It wasn't what she had envisaged for herself at their age.

And the twins did remind her so much of herself sometimes. It seemed only yesterday that it was Steph trailing her satchel through the playground – no rucksacks in those days – checking to see that her shoelaces were done up and hastily refastening her dark plait. Mrs Hunter had been strict about appearances. Steph smiled as she re-traced her route back to the car and unlocked it. She could still remember Mrs Hunter telling Theo that his hair was "almost long enough for a ponytail". That had been the very first, fateful, day of school. The same day that she had met Theo and Edward.

Ed.

****

It was 1983 and they had all been nearly five. Steph couldn't remember much about her life before she started school, but walking into that building for the first time had left a huge impression on her mind. She'd been walking past it with her mother for years. And her mother had pointed it out to her as she got older, "Look," she would say, "you'll be going there soon." What for, Steph had no idea. But she knew something important was happening when new items of unfamiliar clothing were bought for her and her feet were measured for new, stiff, red leather shoes. "For school," her mother kept saying. "You're a big girl now."

And there hadn't been room for any worry. Steph was so proud of her uniform and the neat plait with its ribbon hanging down her back, she hadn't even thought to be nervous. And it wasn't until they approached the playground on that first morning that she began to feel a little odd and unsettled. But there had been twenty-five other children all new and equally unsettled, and her new classmates fascinated Steph. She'd never been in the company of so many other children her age before. They had been put into smaller, more manageable, groups on that first morning and Steph's had been called the "Star Group", which she was pleased about as they all got to wear bright golden stars. With her had been two girls and two boys. She couldn't remember the names of the girls, but the boys had been Theodore and Edward. Theo with the long, scruffy hair and glasses, and Ed with fine, blond hair and pale skin.

They'd shared their milk and biscuits together at break time, and played together at lunch on that first day. And that was really all that Steph could recall from early on. After that she could just remember them all being friends. Because that was the way it was. The way it had always been. Until it ended.

****

"Steph! Steph!" came the shout from behind her, and she was jolted from the past. She swung round to see Katie waving at her. She stopped and waited. Katie had obviously hared around the corner from St Luke's Boys School, she looked all red and completely out of breath.

"Hi! Hi, sorry to screech at you. I was late, Jack couldn't find his shorts and – well, never mind," she took a deep breath, "it's just that it's Monday morning and I've got every task under the sun waiting for me at home, including some really grim ones, and I was wondering if I could talk you into having a coffee with me to delay things a bit?" She grinned broadly at Steph, her flame-red curls dancing from her freckled face in the wind.

"Well I was just off to the gym," Steph smiled wickedly. She hadn't been, actually. Briefly, she had considered going down to the stables to see if she could get Archie in for a quick session in the sandschool, but she'd decided against it.

Archie was a riding school horse but rarely used because of his habit of bucking and Luke, the owner of the yard, didn't mind if Steph rode him. She always left him some money and, "It's probably more than he'd make me otherwise," Luke had joked in the beginning. It worked out well for both of them. Steph had watched the twins learn to ride with a mixture of pride and envy. She'd been a competent horsewoman years before and one day Luke had asked if she fancied having a lesson herself. It had spiralled from there and now she often rode when she felt like it.

Katie groaned at the thought of exercise, "Oh no, really?"

"You could always come with me?"

"No, I would, honestly, but I'm so unfit I think I'd probably die."

"Well we can't risk that. Coffee it is then. Where? Luigi's or mine? Yours sounds like a bit of a non-starter."

"You are welcome but I wouldn't," Katie shrugged theatrically. "I still haven't quite cleared up after Sunday lunch would you believe."

"Are you serious?"

"I know, I know, it's just that I had two glasses of red and before I knew where I was I'd agreed that Jack could get the Warhammer out and it was all downhill from there."

"What about Tom?"

"Oh, online. As usual, eBay I think. Then it was Midsomer Murders and then I was too tired."

"Sounds like mine it is. Let's go." Morning coffee sessions with Katie were something Steph loved. Katie was almost a polar opposite of herself; loud, confident, funny and no insecurities at all.

"Is your divine Mrs B coming in today?"

"Yep. She's going to tackle the bedrooms and the girls' playroom this morning."

"A playroom! I'm so jealous. A room with a door I can shut all the mess behind is my fantasy. Aren't I sad? No firemen for me."

Katie's red-brick terraced house with its workshop out the back for her sculpting was gorgeous, with a little front garden, wisteria trailing round the front door that she was always trying to tame and overgrown window-boxes, but it looked a mess even before you stepped inside. It was usually a fair approximation of clean, but always looked to Steph like two dogs had had a squabble in there.

Steph kept her home meticulously neat, even though there was a great deal more of it and she had two children instead of one.

"That doesn't count though," Katie had objected one day. "You've got two *girls*. That's like having half of one boy." Steph had laughed and allowed her to get away with it.

Walking back to the car, Katie admired Steph's jeans, "I love them. Where did you get them?"

"Little boutique in Peppard. Fab place, all designer brands but the nice stuff, without the shit. No snakeskin."

"What are those?"

"Seven For All Mankind."

"*God*. My brain wouldn't even let me dream of affording those."

"I can cast them off to you in a few months if you like," Steph offered.

"Yeah, like I would ever fit into them."

Steph was as slim as a reed and dressed exquisitely in her gorgeous jeans, cashmere sweaters and expensive heels. Today Carvela, but tomorrow could be Manolos. She even had a separate shoe closet where each pair was stored in their original box. Katie had wondered for a long time if perhaps Theo had a shoe fetish, but no, it had turned out to be just how organised Steph was. She didn't even leave the house without straightening her long, dark hair, which was shot through with honey-coloured highlights. Katie, looking at her, was reminded of a fairy. Everything about Steph was so light and ethereal. She was usually smiling her wide, coral smile and her teeth were improbably white. Together with tall, dark, tousle-haired, bookish Theo, who had long reverted to his glasses, and identical twins Mia and Tilly, who still had the stunning white-blonde hair of young children for some reason, they looked a picture-perfect family. Katie quite often thought that they should be on the front of some catalogue or other. Mini Boden, perhaps. She had suggested to Steph that the girls do some modelling, they were so cute, but Steph had recoiled in horror. It would be her nightmare to have her girls faces featured everywhere; too risky. "Oooh let's get inside. It's freezing out there." It was only October but there was a distinct nip in the air. "Looks like we've beaten Mrs B to it. Excuse the mess." Two cereal bowls, two water glasses and a teacup were sitting neatly by the dishwasher to be stacked. Katie snorted in derision.

"Sit down, I'll make some proper coffee. If it's just me I have the cheap, Sainsbury's own brand stuff, but I'll get the Colombian coffee and percolator out for you." Steph grinned at Katie and pulled her long hair off her face impatiently. "So, what's been going on with you guys then since last week? Any gossip I should know about?"

"Hardly. Oh, except I do have a new order for ten of those statues, you know the ones?"

"Really? That's amazing! Well done you." Katie was an extremely talented sculptor and ran her own small – very small – business. The profits were almost nonexistent, but Steph had often admired her for having the conviction to follow her dream; if only she could have been as brave. And Katie was seriously good; it was just a case of waiting for the right break at the right time. Katie dreamt of contracts to supply national chains of garden centres with her sculptures, as well as local shops, but there was a dearth of opportunities at the moment. There were rumours that a recession was looming.

"Yes, a friend recommended me to someone high up and, well, that was it. It's only a one-off, but still."

"No, that's brilliant. When's the deadline?"

"Three months. Enough time to put the effort in without rushing too much."

"Well if you need any help with Jack you only need to ask."

"Thanks. I might do."

The door clicked open and Mrs B appeared, "Morning both."

"Morning Mrs B. How are you?"

"Oh you know, mustn't grumble." Steph hid a smile; she'd never known the woman anything other than fit and well.

"What did you have in mind for me today dear?" She unwound a long knitted scarf and placed it carefully on top of her capacious bag on the gleaming worktop.

Steph glanced around, "Well, after the girls playroom, I wondered if you'd run a duster round the spare room at the back for me? And give it a quick vacuum? I've a decorator coming in later to look at doing it up for me."

"The cream room? Why?" Katie asked, looking up from the newspaper. "It's gorgeous as it is."

"I know. But the thing is, Mia and Tilly are beginning to get sick of sharing a room so I'm thinking of moving one out into the bigger guest room. They are ten and a half now and they're only going to end up with more rubbish and clutter. They could do with a bit more space each."

"Ooh, I foresee fights over who gets the new room and new stuff for it."

Mrs B kept quiet, knowing what was coming.

"Well... actually, I'll probably end up redoing both rooms. It's only fair that way." Steph felt herself blush to the dark roots of her hair. She felt awful, as though she were flaunting their disposable income – which she definitely wasn't – but what else could she say?

Katie rolled her eyes in mock exasperation, "Oh how the other half live." She didn't mind though, Steph knew she didn't.

"Right you are, I'll get on with that then."

"Thanks Mrs B," Steph said gratefully. "I'll bring your coffee up in a minute."

"So that's going to leave you a room down then?" Katie said, swirling her third biscuit around in her coffee.

"Yes, I suppose." Steph hopped up onto a kitchen stool next to her and pulled her cup close. "Not that it really matters. We've got our room, Mia and Tilly will end up the other end of the house together with that small bathroom down there to share and Theo's study, and the box room will be in the middle. And what we'll do is somehow squeeze a bed and chest of drawers into the box room for guests."

"It's hardly a box room!"

"It is compared to the spare bedroom at the moment. I mean, the girls could always share again temporarily if we had an important guest or one that stayed for a long time, but how often does that happen?"

"Never in our house because they'd have the choice of sharing with me and Tom or Jack, and I don't know which would be worse to be quite frank."

Steph laughed. "Right, I'm taking Mrs B's coffee to her. Help yourself to more biscuits, they're in the cupboard."

"I shouldn't, I'm on a diet, but God – Monday morning..."

"That's it, have another biscuit, live life on the edge why don't you."

"Ha bloody ha," Katie poked her tongue out and watched Steph disappear out of the wide kitchen door and up her stairs. Living life on the edge, like she would know anything at all about that.

CHAPTER TWO

Much as Steph adored her twins and loved the chaotic whirlwind that accompanied them, she enjoyed her house when it was quiet. She often walked the length of the long upstairs hallway when the girls weren't around, appreciating the peace and knowing that if she polished something it would stay polished, and put-away things would stay put-away without endless nagging. Her house was decorated in neutral tones; magnolia, cream, rose pink for the girls' room. The bathrooms were a very pale duck-egg blue, which Steph thought she could get away with without making the rooms feel cold because they were bathrooms. Like now as she climbed the wooden staircase, she could smell the beeswax polish Mrs B used on the front hall floor and hear her humming in the distance. Noise couldn't penetrate the fiercely double-glazed windows but everywhere smelled fresh and aired. Relaxing. That's what this house was. Peaceful and relaxing. Welcoming. Steph adored it; knew they were lucky to have it.

They hadn't always had the luxury of a beautiful home. She shivered every time she recalled the squalor of the small flat they had been forced to rent just after they left Tinford when they were eighteen. It was all that had been available on their joint income at the time, and the grottiness of it stuck in her mind even now. The whole place had been damp with peeling paint and wallpaper, the bathroom had been covered in mould and the kitchen was quite obviously visited by rats. It was cold and had smelled. They'd been horrified, going to view it, but the landlord had leaned against a wall and shrugged his shoulders, "It ain't no palace but it's all you're likely to get for what you're paying."

Even that sum was a fortune to them. It had been Theo who had spoken, "It's fine. We'll take it," he said, quickly sliding his hand into Steph's and squeezing it tightly. It had been just before their travelling and had they known about the twins then Steph doubted whether they would have been so brave.

They'd moved their belongings in quickly – "before we change our minds," Steph had joked – and more swiftly than they'd anticipated they had got used to the flat. But they didn't go back to it after their travelling. Thank God Theo had got his business off the ground when he had or who knows what might have become of them? Steph shook off her gloomy thoughts as she reached the top of the stairs, the shadows of her past seemed to be stretching uncomfortably towards her today. Perhaps that was what happened when you got old.

"Mrs B! I've got your coffee," she called. "Wow," she stopped in the doorway, "that looks better already." Mrs B had flung the windows wide open to air the room and polished every surface until it shone. The blinds were pulled up and there was a beautiful view out over their garden.

"It's a lovely room, that's for certain. Thanks dear. Whichever one of them monkeys gets this is a lucky girl. Well, they're both lucky girls in my view."

"Absolutely," Steph agreed. "It'll be lovely as a bedroom. I'm thinking pink, or lilac or maybe a primrose yellow. Curtains to match, but in a contrasting tone. Maybe even chocolate brown blinds if we went with pink walls," Steph said thoughtfully. "Bit out on a limb for the girls I suppose, what do you think?"

"Sounds nice. Keep the double in here will you?"

"No, I shouldn't think so. Either a canopy bed or one of those cabin things, with a desk underneath. It's almost time they started doing their homework in their room. Or it will be next year. Easier for them to concentrate."

"Only, I know my Mike is on the lookout for a good quality double. If you were thinking of getting rid I might know of a home for it."

"Oh, OK. All right. I'll have to ask Theo, we haven't really discussed anything like that yet. But it won't fit into the box room," she said. "OK, I'll see. Anyway, thanks Mrs B."

"That's a pleasure dear."

Steph lingered a minute to try and imagine the walls painted a shade of lilac perhaps, or maybe even a slightly deeper pink. She glanced round at the furniture, what was in there was solid, serviceable pine but she rather thought she'd like to pick new bedroom furniture for them both. John Lewis had a gorgeous range. It would be such a fun project, especially now Mia and Tilly were old enough to have sensible opinions and she could discuss colours and designs with them. And besides, once the rooms were done that would be it for years and years. Five or six at least. It was more of an investment. That's how she'd present it to Theo anyway.

Steph poked her head tentatively around the girls' current bedroom door; not too bad today. Duvets were half-hanging onto the floor, their bedside lights were on despite the blazing sunshine and two nightdresses were scattered across the floor along with a few pens and bits of paper. It would only be the work of a moment to clear that up, and once Katie had gone Steph would have quite a few free moments. She sometimes wondered guiltily if she were doing enough with her life; if she were *quite* satisfied, but she always stopped herself immediately. Theo would be horrified, say she was ungrateful – he wouldn't understand. It wasn't that she was dissatisfied, she just sometimes wondered whether there were more in store for her or whether she would keep house and look after her girls forevermore. She'd once had different aspirations, but they were long-buried. And she did take a deep pride, deeper than most, in housekeeping and child-rearing. Every school holiday was planned with military precision so that the twins would be neither lonely nor bored. It usually ended up as a chaotic merry-go-round of friends to play, picnics and visits to the swimming pool. But when Mia and Tilly tumbled, worn out, into bed at the end of the day, Steph would convince herself that it had all been worth it. Theo thought they should spend more time entertaining themselves.

"We never had all of this," he gestured widely with his hand, "we had to amuse ourselves and we learned a lot because of it."

"Theo," Steph said, appalled, "you cannot be saying that our village childhood is preferable to what the girls have?" Images of picnics and ball games flew to mind. Fine every once in a while, but the summers had seemed hot and endless.

"Not in every sense, no. I'm just saying that they don't need to be entertained every second of the day. Leave them to write stories and paint pictures once in a while."

"I do."

"No, you organise them into an activity. Leave them to come up with the ideas themselves. God knows they're organised enough at that school. I want them to learn a bit of self-sufficiency."

He had a point, Steph thought, but she wasn't sure if she agreed. They were ten, but that was still little in her eyes. Katie had laughed at her when Steph repeated the conversation.

"I wouldn't worry if I were you. Soon enough you'll be sick of catering to their every whim. Jack's lucky if I organise one day out every holiday."

Steph thought she was probably joking.

She wandered back into the kitchen, sheepskin slippers slapping on the tiled floor, "You look like you're miles away," Katie said. "What are you thinking?"

"Oh, just about what Theo said, you know, about the girls entertaining themselves more."

"Still bothering you?"

"No. I just wonder who's right."

"Fifty-fifty I'd say. That would be a fair compromise. Why? Are you two not getting on?"

"Yes, of course we are, you know us. In fact," Steph hesitated, letting her hair swing over her face, "he's come up with a rather novel idea for making sure I have less time to devote to the girls." She hadn't been sure whether to say anything or not; this was a bit of a gamble. Her heart started to quicken.

"He's never suggested you get a job?"

"Hardly, you know what he's like about being the breadwinner. No, it's um… that is – I…" Oh God, was she doing the right thing?

"What? What is it?"

"Well – he wants us to have another baby," Steph said quickly.

"A baby!" Katie said incredulously. "Seriously?"

"Yes. What's wrong with that?" Steph had not expected this.

"Nothing. Nothing at all." There was silence for a moment. "It's a lovely idea, it's just that I didn't see you two with another child. I don't know," Katie said slowly, "you just seem so happy, the four of you. Nice big house, life of luxury, neat 2.4 children, you with a great figure. I just thought you'd be keen to hang onto all of that."

"We haven't decided yet and I guess I'm less keen than he is to be honest. Theo's always wanted a bigger family, a child for every room he says, and he feels that now is the ideal time to do it."

"And you?"

Steph sighed, "I agree that another baby would be nice. At some point. Probably. But I worry about the impact on the girls, the disruption. Stuff like that. You're right, I love my neat, ordered life and another baby would turn it upside down. Besides, I'd have to take a very deep breath before I flung myself back into sleepless nights and dirty nappies again. Plus," she hesitated, "I don't know if I want to spend all my young adult life having children. It wasn't what I originally planned, after all. Sometimes I do think about catching up career-wise, getting a bit more out of life."

"More?"

"No, wrong word. I think about taking my life in different

directions."

"Such as?"

"I don't have new ideas, it's just that I still think about interior design from time to time." She felt foolish just saying it. It had been her original plan, before she left school. A highly-cultivated dream. And that was what it had stayed, a dream.

"I bet you were shocked when you found out about the twins then." Katie commented.

Steph flushed deeply, "Why would you say that?"

"For the same reasons you just said. If you had glamorous career plans." Katie peered closely at her. "Sorry, I didn't mean anything by it."

"No. Well, I suppose I was. In a way. It's a long time ago though, I don't really remember." She busied herself with stacking the chrome and steel dishwasher.

There was a pause, then, "So what do you think you're going to do?" Katie asked curiously.

"Talk about it a bit more first off. Then we'll see."

"Good plan. Ooh, how exciting! Baby number three. Girl or boy? A boy would be nice. I wonder how much it would look like the twins."

Steph kept her back turned, "Well, quite."

****

Steph was standing at the kitchen island chopping ginger when Theo arrived home. She heard his key slide into the lock and the clunk as he turned it, then the familiar clatter of his keys into the enamel bowl that sat on the hall table. He didn't call out because he knew the girls would be in bed. Instead he put his briefcase down by the hat stand, loosened his tie, slipped his shoes off and went into the kitchen to find his wife.

"Hi gorgeous," he wound his arms around her waist and nuzzled into her neck. "Mmm, it's good to be home. Nice day?"

"Not too bad." Steph put her knife down and swivelled to face him, loving as she always did her first proper glimpse of her husband. When he left for work she was usually still snuggled underneath the duvet. "I've poured you some wine."

"You're an angel." Theo pulled his tie completely off and dumped it on the side.

"Don't do that," Steph said automatically.

"Why not?"

"Because it gets in my way, it'll get stuff spilled on it and the kitchen is not the place for ties. Take it upstairs with you when you get changed."

"You're never happy are you?" But Theo was smiling as he headed out of the kitchen and towards the stairs. Somehow, the hallway always smelled more of whatever Steph was cooking than the kitchen did.

Theo walked soundlessly down the upstairs corridor on the solid walnut floor. It had been the most extravagant thing about their house, apart from the Poggenpohl kitchen with its three-ring Aga, but they both loved it. He pushed the door of the twins' room open and peeped in; they were already fast asleep. They lay sprawled across their duvets, face down, Mia still clutching a Barbie and their soft nightlight on. Theo tiptoed across to take the doll and paused between the beds as he did so. He wasn't sure about Steph's new plan to move one of them out into another bedroom. He loved being able to come in and see them both lying so close together like this; it was now that he was most able to imagine them as one entity; one, single egg somehow split into his two, miraculous, girls. On his other side Tilly stirred suddenly and Theo backed out of the room hastily. Steph would be cross if they woke up, and blame him. Much as she adored her girls, she was adamant that evenings were for adult time. It was a bit of a shame as it meant that Theo didn't get to see as much of them as he would have liked, he rarely got home before their bathtime, and, like tonight, sometimes even later. And he rarely got time to play his beloved golf. What had started as networking tool for corporate reasons had turned into a passion. It was the one thing he did away from Steph. But that was the way life was at the moment. Theo had plenty of plans and dreams for the future and was mostly impatient at having to wait, but, "don't wish your life away," Steph was always warning him, and he supposed she was right.

"So, tell me about your day." He took his seat at the table with its antique candelabra in the centre, and picked up his fork.

"Not much to tell. Katie came for coffee this morning."

"How is she?"

"Fine. She was avoiding her housework. I felt a bit guilty sitting here with her as Mrs B whizzed around doing mine, but," Steph shrugged as Theo frowned.

"Don't feel guilty," he said. "That's what she's here for. You aren't responsible for Katie's lifestyle any more than she is for yours."

"No, I know, it's just... I do feel bad that we have almost every luxury while she has so few."

"Steph, that is not the way to view it. Katie's your friend, enjoy her friendship. Don't worry about what we've got that she hasn't."

"I don't. Not really. Anyway," she said hastily, "how was your day? Anything exciting happen?"

"No, nothing." He was never keen to talk about his day. Work was to be relegated the minute he walked through the door as far as Theo was concerned. It was time for his wife and children. "Same old, same old and more tomorrow I imagine."

"Well, that's good." A pause. "I've had the decorator in to look at doing up the spare room."

"Oh yes?"

"The quote was what we thought, depending on what we go for obviously. It would only take a couple of days. Seemed quite easy."

"Good." Theo listened as he ate his noodles.

"Yes, and I was thinking about getting new furniture from John Lewis."

"Uh huh."

"What do you think?"

Theo shrugged, "Fine, I suppose. It's as good a place as any."

"Katie thought it was a good idea."

"Oh well then, that's it." Theo smiled his wide, generous smile and Steph pulled a face.

"Don't be like that. I can make decisions on my own."

"I know you *can*. Anyway, what would we do with the bed?"

"Ah. Mrs B said Mike might want it if we don't. I can't see it fitting into the box room though."

"No, it wouldn't. Well it could but there wouldn't be room for anything else." He took a mouthful of wine. "And besides, we may not need a bed in there."

"What? Why not?"

"If it was turned into a nursery then we wouldn't need one. Cots take up much less space." There was a twinkle in his eye.

"Yes. They do."

"You sound hesitant." Theo watched Steph looking at her plate.

"Well – no, I'm not hesitant, it's just that I was talking to Katie this morning."

"Of course you were." He'd nearly finished eating.

"Well I was! And she sounded surprised that we were thinking of a third."

"Why?"

"I don't know."

"It doesn't matter what she thinks. Look Steph," Theo set his cutlery down, "I get the feeling that I'm talking you into this a bit. And that's not how it should be."

"No, no, you're not," Steph twisted her napkin agitatedly, how could she explain this? "I think another baby is a great idea. Fab. The best. But I'm worried about the girls, how it will be for them." She couldn't tell him about her interior design work dreams, he'd see it as a slight on his earning power.

"Oh Steph," Theo reached over the table to grab her hand. "Is that all? That's normal. That happens to everyone I bet. It probably will be tough at first, sleepless nights, a newborn screaming in the house, you tired and with less time."

"Theo – you're not really selling it to me here."

"No listen – what you have to focus on is the end result. The bigger, stronger, happier family that we'll end up with if a brother or sister comes along for them. Siblings are so important."

"Yes. You're right." Steph stared at her wine glass in the flickering candlelight for a second in silent contemplation. "I do want to do it. I'm just nervous. You'll have to bear with me."

"That's fine. I can cope with nerves. Darling, that's brilliant." His smile nearly split his face. "Fantastic. Another baby! That would mean the world to me. Three beautiful children of my very own." He raised one eyebrow, "And how long do we have to wait to get started on this process?"

"Oooh, give me twenty minutes to clear up?"

"Done."

But later Steph made an excuse to send him up on his own as she sat in the darkened kitchen with its neatly drawn blinds, shining surfaces and eco-friendly household cleaner smell. Everything she had said to Theo over dinner was true. She did want another baby, she was worried about the girls, but there was something else too. Something she couldn't possibly explain to him. It was the way the old shadows reached for her in her dreams, still somehow able to smash her new life into smithereens, despite the protective walls she'd built. The gnawing fear every time Theo mentioned babies, the tightness of panic in her chest that had been gone for so long after she'd lulled herself into a false sense of security. It was her secret. She stared sightlessly ahead into the dark. Don't be silly, she told herself, clutching her glass a little harder. It will all be fine. It has to be fine.

Nothing can happen because no one knows. Unbidden thoughts flew into her mind of awkward, medical conversations, things written on her maternity notes – stop, she told herself firmly. Just stop. And think what you'll finally gain from it. Think how perfect things could finally be. One more, that was it, that was all there needed to be.

She took a few deep breaths, swallowed the last of the wine and slipped off the stool. One last look round at her darkened kitchen and then she closed the door quietly and made her way upstairs.

CHAPTER THREE

They had all been born in 1978. Steph only had hazy memories of their early years at school, that first day aside of course. It was all rolled into one, distant memory now of pencils, small chairs, milk bottles and hopscotch. She, Theo and Ed had quickly become best friends, and that was how it had stayed. Now, her recent memories of Theo had overtaken the older ones. He was a different person now. Well, he belonged to Steph, which he hadn't done then. Not by a long shot. Memories of Ed were different. Darling Ed. So eager and yet so awkward. He didn't have that many friends as he got older. Steph had looked at him sympathetically and thought that she could understand why. He wasn't really rude, just slightly stand-offish. Made you feel as though he didn't really want to be talking to you, which was never the case. Well, hardly ever. He was just shy and a bit awkward. He'd always stand staring down at the ground if he could and rarely smiled. It was like he didn't know how to behave, like he was still biding his time and making up his mind about what he thought. It was only when the three of them were alone that Ed really relaxed. Then his whole demeanour transformed; no longer quiet and sulky, but rolling around on the floor hooting with laughter. He could make Steph and Theo laugh until their sides ached with his impression of Tina Turner. Steph often wondered how no one else ever saw it. She was always telling her girlfriends how great he was but they'd look at her disbelievingly, "Ed? Edward Osborne? Yeah, right. I'm sure."

"No, he really is," Steph would protest. "He's just shy." But no matter how many times she said it, they never believed her. Ed was simply the sullen one.

By the time they had got to fifteen, friendship groups had been firmly established, and Steph, Theo and Ed were one unit. That was the way it was. There were other friends too, such as Kirsty with whom she rode, long, rambling hacks in and around Tinford with ponies borrowed from the riding school in return for chores. It was on these rides that Steph felt at her most relaxed and calm, her mind fell into tune with the pony's gentle rhythm. And then there were Mark and Grace of course, there were lots of peripheral friends around, but regardless Steph sometimes thought she would have been lost without Theo and Ed. She used them to judge her outfits and new highlights, recommend good CDs, books and films. Looking back, they'd been like countless other teenagers of course, nothing special at all. Until it changed.

Which it had when they reached sixteen. Ever so slowly. Steph gradually became aware that she was looking more to Theo for company than Ed. She found that she could tire relatively easily of Ed's company, and hardly ever of Theo's. But of course by then Rachel was on the scene. She was a pretty, quiet girl from the year below whom Theo had met the year before in the library.

"The library!" Steph and Ed had shrieked. "Are you for real?"

"Well, yes," Theo looked slightly miffed. "What's wrong with that?"

"It's boring? And weird?"

"Well, she's neither. And if you're both going to be like that then you can't meet her."

"Oh no, let us, let us. We'll be good, we promise."

And yet, even then, Steph had felt a pang of something strange. Not jealousy exactly, just a sense of losing something that had previously been hers. It was a little harder to confide in him, knowing that he had things which were necessarily secret from her. She imagined their whispered, private conversations, saw them holding hands, pictured their first kiss. Wondered what else they did.

In confusion she turned more to Ed, and one drunken night after a party, they had kissed. That was all, but Steph felt it was a dreadful mistake and waking up the next morning with mascara smudged around her eyes, she had barely been able to face her reflection in the mirror. Apart from the fact that there was Peter, Steph couldn't quite believe that it was Ed that it had happened with. She'd always imagined her and Theo out of the group if anything like that was going to happen. Not with Ed. Poor Ed. But just – no. Was this the kind of person she was? Was this what she wanted?

Luckily, Ed obviously felt the same way as he never mentioned it again and it was quite soon after that when his obsession with Kirsty began. Seeing Theo so happy with Rachel – serious Theo – made Steph both happy and sad at the same time. She didn't think that she was that happy with Peter. Peter was great – partly because he was two years older than her – and she was happy to go to the cinema and stuff with him, but he wasn't really her dream boyfriend. Perhaps most importantly he was better than nothing though and she was loath to be single while Theo was so loved up.

She discussed it endlessly with Ed.

"Why does it matter?" he'd asked, genuinely confused. "Why do you need someone just because of Rachel?"

"Because I don't want him to think that I'm single and lonely."

"You don't want him to pity you?"

"No it's not that, it's just embarrassing."

Rachel was always suspicious of Steph and that made things ten times more difficult. She could never accept their friendship at face value and was always accusing Theo of preferring Steph to her, which eventually had the result of Theo saying: "At least she doesn't nag me like this." Steph felt slightly mollified when Theo recounted this tale, apparently unselfconsciously, even if he then did ruin it by saying "She just can't see she's The One."

The One? Steph had sloped home that night feeling lower than ever. Rachel couldn't be The One. That wasn't how it was supposed to be at all. She'd lain in her pretty, pink bed that night, tossing and turning, eyes wide open in the darkness and thinking. By dawn she'd made some decisions.

****

"Do I ever tell you how much I love you?" Theo wrapped his arms around Steph.

"Mmm. You mention it from time to time. Get off! You'll ruin the cake." It was Sunday morning and Steph was standing in her kitchen in her Cath Kidston apron attempting to make a chocolate sponge cake.

"What for?" Theo had asked, dipping his finger into the mixture. "It's no one's birthday."

"For guests and things." She didn't particularly enjoy baking but it made her feel very worthy. Like she was earning her keep.

"I thought I might take the girls down to David Lloyd later for a swim." He glanced out of the window at the pouring rain. "I can't see much else to do today. Do you fancy it?"

"Oh I wish I could but I'm going to make a start on looking through those catalogues, I haven't got anywhere with it yet. I've got to ring Jim back tomorrow."

"Jim?"

"The decorator."

"I thought you did that yesterday?"

"No, I was riding yesterday." She adored slipping off on her own for a couple of hours and getting into the countryside around Churchwell. She could think whatever she wanted to think while she was riding; there was no danger of anyone guessing her thoughts, it was just her and Archie.

"Oh right. OK." Theo was slightly disappointed. He loved having his family all together and watching his beautiful girls swim with his beautiful wife. He loved the way her hair became so dark when it was wet and how her cheeks flushed when she swam up and down. Her peachy skin was one thing Theo adored about her appearance; she always looked so healthy and happy.

But Steph had serious amounts of planning to do and not just for the decorating. Yesterday morning she'd had a call from Julia, a fellow parent at school whom she didn't particularly like. A tall, determined lady, always claiming to be juggling ten different things, Julia had wanted to speak to her about the upcoming term, and, more specifically, what help Steph could add to Cath's committee. For some reason Julia expected her to have all the free time in the world to dedicate herself to the cause of St Catherine's. Steph suspected it was because she didn't work. She didn't mind helping out but she was constantly evading suggestions of what more she could do, Julia seemed determined to overwhelm her with tasks. If there was ever a cupboard that needed to be sorted or some obscure wishlist item to track down, she'd volunteer Steph. Which was odd, because when she'd first joined the committee at the back end of the summer term, Steph could have sworn that Julia was very cold towards her, as if she didn't like her for some reason. But over the summer holidays she seemed to have thawed a little. She wasn't to know that Ian – fellow parent and treasurer of Cath's – had ordered Julia to be a little nicer, "She's young and keen," he'd told Julia, "and we don't want to put her off. We need all the help we can get this term. Please try to get on with her, she's nice really."

"I don't know what you mean," Julia had replied, big eyes wide with innocence. "I've always been nice to her."

"Julia..." Ian suspected that Steph's looks and comparative youth had worked against her in this instance. Julia was ten years older than Steph and it showed. And she aspired to be a wealthy, bored housewife, without managing to achieve any of those aims. Steph's young, happily married and moneyed status irritated her.

"And now it's the autumn term, there's so much going on," Julia had trilled down the phone to Steph. "We've got the Murder-Mystery dinner-dance in November, the Christmas Fayre to organise, as well as all the usual events for the children. That's Halloween, firework night and their Christmas disco. Do you think you might be able to lend a hand?" Plus the other one, my feet, all my fingers and toes and other body limbs that she can see, Steph thought grimly.

"Yes of course," she said soothingly. "I'm sure I can spare some time. When's the next Cath's meeting?"

"Thursday night. We'll all be there. Oh that's great Steph, such a relief I can't tell you. Another body on board makes such a difference. Tell you what, if you could look up a list of caterers before Thursday, perhaps get some quotes, then scale down to a shortlist that would be amazing."

"I..."

"I know you're handy with the Internet, that's probably your best bet. Super, you're an absolute star. I must dash, see you at pick-up maybe? Bye."

Steph was left staring at the phone in her hand. She had no doubt that she would see Julia at pick-up, but seeing was all she'd be doing. Julia was one of those people who only spoke to you if she wanted something, and faked an interest in your life to seem chummy. But it could be worse, aside from the driven career women, there were a lot of blonde bimbos on the arms of wealthy, much older men. Plus Julia had recently separated from her partner of twelve years, which must be tough, Steph had sympathised when she heard. To cover her mortification at being a single mum, Julia had leant in closely and whispered, "Actually darling I don't mind losing him, it's the money I'm going to miss." Followed by a guffaw of laughter so Steph knew she was joking.

Steph sighed loudly in the empty house and looked longingly at her magazines. She supposed they would have to wait. She loved flicking through *Homes & Gardens* or *Period Living* and creating a mental mind-map of all of her favourite designs and brands. Just recently she'd been thinking about adding a conservatory to the back of the house, off the kitchen, it would go perfectly and then they could eat in there. But she wasn't sure about losing the space on the patio.

She picked up her mug of hot chocolate and went into the study that opened off their spacious living room. It was the only room that seemed to be a constant mess; Sophie Kinsella and Marian Keyes books spilt across the desk, DVDs were stacked in an out-of-kilter pile, wads of paper, some with notes, information and some just scribbles dumped on any available surface. Steph had no one to blame but herself; this was kind of 'her' room, she spent a lot of time in here. Either reading or daydreaming or sometimes online research when the house was empty and she could pretend that she wasn't just Mummy.

Google quickly found a list of local caterers for her and Steph wrote down their details on the pad of paper next to her so she could call them tomorrow. Five quotes, that should be enough. It would help if she knew what she was asking them to quote for, of course. Three courses? Service? Silver service? Knowing Julia, four courses and gold service. As she was debating what to write in her email, a link Katie had sent her for Facebook caught her eye.

"It's terrible," she'd complained. "I'm trying to work and pitch for contracts and I keep getting distracted by Facebook. It's addictive. You can practically stalk people. Old exes, friends, enemies. You should sign up."

"What for?" Steph had asked. "I'm not interested in talking to people online."

"Just do it. Trust me. It's great!"

So where was the harm? Steph clicked on the link to open the site. Maybe it would be fun to keep in touch over the net, certainly easier than texting people. She could even look up Kirsty and – or maybe not. Best not go there, Steph had always been stupidly scared of Kirsty meeting the girls – just in case. But it would be handy for the Cath's Committee. They all used it, she knew for certain. Her mouse hovered over the sign-up button for just a second before she clicked and filled in her details quickly.

Steph fired off a couple of quick notes to caterers that accepted online requests for quotes and then shut down the computer. That was quite enough for one day. It was still pouring with rain outside, that was what living near the coast did for you. Precipitation, was that what it was called? At least the girls would be having a nice time. She shoved her feet back into the fluffy sheepskin slippers that Theo laughed at and padded into the warm sitting room. Her magazines and catalogues were still there, in their comforting pile. She'd better get on and get this bedroom designed then, if things went to plan, it looked like she'd be having a lot less free time fairly soon. Besides, wasn't paint supposed to be toxic for pregnant women?

****

She didn't tell anyone how she felt at the time. It had come as quite a shock to her back in those days, she wasn't sure that she could cope with explaining it and justifying it to anyone else simultaneously. All the advice in Just Seventeen seemed to be to evaluate her feelings carefully before telling Him. Telling Him? The idea was appalling. She'd be so embarrassed. She couldn't imagine what he'd say. So instead, Steph did what the magazine told her not to and withdrew almost completely from Theo. Firstly it was easier than confronting the issue, and secondly she couldn't bear to see him all lovey-dovey with Rachel.

"What's going on?" Ed and Kirsty had asked repeatedly, bewildered. "What's happened?"

"Nothing," Steph had snapped. "Nothing at all." She had let things with Peter drop off too.

"Such a shame," her mother had tutted. "He was a nice boy." How did mothers always know the least helpful thing to say?

To make up for it Steph saw a lot more of her girlfriends. Suddenly, she was the first one suggesting a night out, the last one to go home. Most of the time she had Ed with her, he was always around somewhere, waiting for Steph. If she hadn't been so bound up in her own feelings Steph supposed that she would have seen what was going on a long time before she actually did.

It had taken ages for Theo to cotton onto the fact that he never saw Steph any more. In typical teenage boy style he'd blundered along in his life, anchored by the twin concerns of his schoolwork and his girlfriend. Rachel was his life at that moment, they were almost literally joined at the hip. If they weren't together they were writing little love notes to one another. That left him almost no time for noticing Steph wasn't around as much. They still glimpsed each other at school, exchanged quick smiles across the dining room – but that was it.

"Want to come round to mine later?" Theo offered periodically and Steph would smile a regretful smile and shake her head.

"Oh I can't sorry, I'm playing netball," or "I'm going out with Ed" or "I'm seeing Grace." It hurt like hell but Steph didn't fancy the alternative, which, as Just Seventeen informed her, was confronting and dealing with her feelings.

****

The girls came bouncing in from swimming with washed and dried, but unbrushed hair. Typical Theo. Or perhaps that should be typical man? Steph grinned at her husband as Mia and Tilly leapt on her, "Mummy! Mummy! We missed you!"

"The pool was *freezing*!"

"Oh dear, was it?"

"Yeah, it really was. You should have felt it. It was like an *iceberg*."

"Not prone to exaggeration at all are you Mia?"

"Not what to *what*?" Mia wrinkled her nose.

"She's just like you Steph," Theo remarked. "You know what she asked me at David Lloyd? 'Daddy, did you remember the ghds'? I told them I didn't even have a hairbrush, never mind that jiggery-pokery."

"You should have come Mummy, now we look like scarecrows."

"Rubbish, you both look beautiful." Steph clambered to her feet. "Fancy making some pizzas for lunch?"

"Yes! Yes!"

"Did you have a good time?" she asked Theo.

"Yeah, missed you though," he put his arms around her and snuggled into her neck.

"Oh well, you lived," she smiled at him. "Mum rang by the way."

"Yours or mine?"

"Mine, for a change actually. It was just a pit-stop phonecall to let me know that they're back from the Netherlands, and that they're flying out to Egypt tomorrow."

"Really, whereabouts?"

"Sharm el Sheikh, apparently. Well, you know what John's like, he can't stand the cold can he? He wants the beach, sun and sea. They're planning on going diving."

"Good grief."

"I'll make you a bet right now that it'll be Christmas before we see them."

After lunch they went for a walk in Merryacre woods. There was a distinct chill in the air, it was cold enough for coats, and the leaves were beginning to scatter on the ground.

"Your comment earlier made me think, it really will be Christmas before we know it," Theo said.

"Oh don't," Steph groaned, sliding her hand into his. "What a performance that always turns out to be."

"Does it?"

"Yes," Steph turned her head in surprise. "You know it does."

"Do I?"

"Yes! How can you forget? Your mother always refuses the invitation and then changes her mind at the last minute, my mum and John always want to do a hideously inconvenient Christmas Eve meal and the girls are so worn out by excitement by lunchtime on Christmas Day that they turn into wailing banshees all afternoon. And we're too tired by the evening to do anything but flop by the fire and drip-feed your parents with alcohol."

"Sounds familiar," Theo mused. "Would you change it?"

"Change Christmas? Maybe. I'd cut out the hassle, the endless cooking and entertaining. I mean, I love seeing everyone but I'd rather do it on my terms."

Theo stopped and pulled Steph to face him, "Well I'm serious. We can change it. Have it on our own this year. Calm everything down. I can't have you stressed, I mean, you might be pregnant by then. It's only – what – two and half months away."

"Don't count your chickens Theo," Steph warned.

"I'm not. I'm just saying you might be."

"Yes, I might," she conceded. "Nothing stopping it."

"Look at how quickly you fell pregnant with the girls. They weren't even planned."

"Mmm, yes," Steph said quickly and pulled away from him, "come on, speaking of which, let's catch them up." She began to jog gently up the path. Theo stopped and watched her as she ran, God, she was gorgeous. His tiny, delicate Steph. He didn't think he'd ever loved her so much before as right now. Apart from when she was pregnant with Mia and Tilly maybe, he'd felt a fabulous protective love towards her then. Seeing her bump grow and grow, knowing two tiny pieces of himself were inside – it had been an amazing time.

"Come on slowcoach!" Steph was yelling. "We're getting bored waiting."

The rain returned during their walk, drenching them all and meaning that Mia and Tilly had to be re-bathed before bed, much to their disgust. But eventually they were both tucked up, washed and scrubbed with poker-straight blonde hair neatly plaited. Steph looked at them with pride from their bedroom door, each girl in her bed under a pink duvet with a Famous Five book to read.

"Twenty minutes," she warned. "That's it."

"OK Mummy."

Downstairs, she poured herself and Theo a glass of red wine and pulled a kitchen barstool out so she could perch on it, jean-clad legs not quite reaching the floor.

"Were you serious about Christmas?"

Theo looked up from his laptop, "Christmas? What?"

"Changing it. Doing it our way."

"Oh. Well, yes, of course. I'm not doing anything you're not happy with."

"Really? Even if it meant not having your mum?"

"Really."

"You're amazing, you know that?"

"Actually, I do."

"What are you doing online?"

"Emails. Work," Theo said apologetically. "Just to get an idea of what I'm going into on Monday morning. I won't be long."

"Oh," Steph suddenly remembered. "You know what I did earlier?"

"Let me guess – straightened your hair? Made another cake?"

"Ha ha. No, far more exciting. I joined Facebook."

"You? Why? I thought you hated those places? You don't like the idea of people being able to look you up."

"It was a whim. Julia called yesterday and wanted me to look up caterers for the Murder-Mystery thing."

"What?"

"Don't ask. Anyway, I was in the middle of doing that when I saw a link for Facebook and thought I'd join. All the Cath's people are on it," Steph shrugged. "It might make keeping in contact a little easier. And a little more remote. It'll be easier to say no online."

"If you say so."

"I do. Katie's always raving about it."

"Yes, I know a lot of people who use it."

"Are you on there?"

"No. But I might have a look."

"Fair enough." Steph pulled open the fridge. "Now, what shall we have for dinner?"

****

His voice had been very quiet, she remembered that. Low, and alarmed. "Steph, you have to tell me what's going on."

"What do you mean?"

"You know what I mean. I'm not stupid. I have noticed that you don't want to talk to me, or see me or be around me."

"You sound sad."

"I am sad, Stephanie. You're my best friend. I want to know what I've done to upset you so much."

"Who says you've done anything?" Everything about her screamed defensive, she knew. She stood, arms folded across her chest, long fringe falling across her face, staring down at the ground.

"I must have done something, otherwise you wouldn't have changed." His voice nearly killed her; it was so gentle.

"I can't tell you." She couldn't lie to him, that was beyond her.

"Why not?" He moved towards to hold her hands but she pulled away. "Steph! Please!"

"What?"

"Please tell me. We've been friends for so long. I need to know."

"Honestly, Theo – really nothing."

"Stop saying that!"

Steph's eyes filled with tears, "Sorry Theo – I have to go."

"But..."

But she'd gone. She ran all the way to the stables that day, feeling the pent-up sobs catching in her chest and the tears begin to fall. If this was what being a teenager was all about then life was shit. She took a feisty pony out over the cross-country course and leapt the wooden jumps and ditches as fast as she dared. All she wanted was to feel the wind in her hair and forget the pain Theo was causing her.

She found herself clinging to Ed more than ever. He was so kind. He didn't bother her if she didn't want to talk, like Kirsty and Grace did. He seemed to know when she did want to talk, and he'd often come round bringing chocolate or a tape he'd made for her, which no one else ever did. She found herself looking at him in a different way, she'd never known that he had it in him. Had she misjudged him? Surely not. She still noticed Theo watching her, always from a distance. But he never came over. Well – that must be it. Friendship over. Every time she thought that tears rose to her eyes and she had to swallow hard to get rid of them.

"Have you still not sorted it out with him?" Kirsty asked, one bitter winter morning as they groomed the ponies.

"No. There's nothing to sort. I like him, he doesn't like me, he's got Rachel, that's it."

"How do you know he doesn't like you?"

"He's got Rachel!"

"He might dump her for you."

"No. I'd hate that. So would he. Theo's a really loyal kind of person. I wouldn't want to make him to do anything he didn't want to."

"So you're stuck moping around then? God, you're so annoying. Mind you, at least you've got Ed." Kirsty winked.

"What?" said Steph, startled.

"Oh come on, you must have seen those big, puppy-dog eyes looking at you all the time."

"Er – hang on – it's *you* he likes, not me. We're just friends."

"Yeah yeah, and I'm Batman. Come on Steph, don't be blind. He adores you!"

"He so does not!" Steph blushed deeply, horrified.

All the same, it made her think.

****

"Right, is everyone present and correct?" It was Thursday evening and the Cath's committee had come together for their AGM. It was held in the Senior Common Room at St Catherine's, buried deep within the grand old building.

"Are you going to take a register Julia?" Ian joked, and caught Steph's eye.

Julia glared, "I hope I don't have to. Now, I know I've spoken to all of you individually so you all know what your tasks are. Have you all managed to get at least a bit done? If not, are there any problems? Steph, perhaps you'd like to start." Julia sat down heavily, not looking at Steph.

"Ah – yes. Right. OK," Steph stood up, slightly nervously, and flicked her hair over her shoulder, aware of the cool stares of some of the committee. Stay-at-home mums weren't always popular. If you weren't juggling a full-time job and three kids with no nanny then you were seen as a bit slack.

"I've spoken to a few of the local caterers regarding the arrangements for the November dinner-dance and I've got some quotes. Assuming that there will be about 200 parents, most of the figures I got back were almost £1000, for a three or four course meal with staff."

"I think four, don't you?" Julia said, looking round expectantly. There was a murmur of assent.

"Some were a bit taken aback at the short notice."

"Short notice!"

"Well, yes. It's only eight weeks away. And it's quite a big booking."

"I'm surprised, for this area. Carry on."

"And then of course we have to sort out a paying bar. And a license for it. It doesn't take too long but we would need to get on with it. Julia, I've collected all the quotes together, whether you want to go through and pick the most suitable one?"

"Certainly," she said graciously. Then, "Thank you Steph," through gritted teeth. "Ian, did you get anywhere with the after-show entertainment?"

"I did, yes. Assuming the Murder-Mystery thing takes between two and two and half hours, we'll have at least two left to kill, excuse the pun. There's a few options, although again – I came across the short notice problem."

"Really? I must say, I am very surprised. Perhaps we should have got on with it earlier. I don't know why we didn't. Anyway," she gave a tinkling laugh lest anyone think she was criticising, "do carry on Ian."

"As I was saying." Steph caught his eye and grinned. "Our options are a standard disco and DJ combo. You all know the sort of thing. Fairly cheap, popular, easy, lots of drunken dancing. Or a steel band. Bit novel. Or a travelling casino if we don't want music."

"Oh I think we do," Julia interrupted. "How else will we dance off all that champagne?"

"If the budget stretches to champagne Julia," Ian warned, in his role as treasurer.

Idly, Steph looked around the room. She'd expected more parents there. Especially seeing as it was a new year, she'd thought more new parents would come along. But there was only her, Julia as Chairwoman, Ian as deputy-chair and treasurer, Ruth as secretary, Marian as something non-specific and then a couple of parents higher up the school whom she didn't recognise. It was Steph's first AGM, and Ian had warned her Julia could be a bit of a handful.

"Very power-hungry," he'd warned. "Can't bear it if anyone knows more than she does. She works hard for Cath's, to her credit, but she demands recognition for it. Don't be fooled into suggesting something new, you'll be gently swept aside, all new things have to come from Julia."

"OK. I'll bear that in mind."

"Secretly, I think a lot of people are waiting for her to step down, she's been in the position a while, there's a lot of fresh blood waiting in the wings but no one who's willing to try and oust her. It wouldn't do to make an enemy of Julia."

"No?"

"No. What Julia wants, Julia gets and woe betide anyone who stands in her way. Ah look – speak of the devil and she shall appear – Julia my darling, how *are* you?"

Steph stood back and watched this false little display. Was this something that corporate people were trained to do? Did Theo do this? Genuine, lovely Theo? When Steph's turn came she greeted Julia politely and air-kissed her once. It was as well to stay on her good side.

After the meeting Julia didn't stay, but dashed off, pleading babysitter problems.

"You know how it is, single mother and all that," she said ruefully and lowered her eyes.

"Don't believe a word of it," Ian hissed to Steph. "She's after the sympathy vote."

"I didn't realise what a social minefield I was getting involved in. Silly me for thinking I was just going to be an extra pair of hands."

"Oh no, everyone's a pawn at St Catherine's. I'm surprised you haven't popped up somewhere before."

"Why?"

"You're a prime target. Young, pretty, big 4x4, personalised plate. All the major attractions." Ian smiled. "And obviously clever."

"Thanks for saying so, but I'm not sure it's very PC for a married man to call me pretty."

"For any other man it wouldn't be. But I'm married to Penny and no one can top her," Ian beamed.

"Right," he said loudly. "All done? Anything anyone want to say behind Julia's back?" There was a murmur of laughter and a few small snipes which Ian pretended not to hear. "Good. Let's get this Murder-Mystery evening rolling then. It's going to be a big one Steph, hang on!"

CHAPTER FOUR

For a long time Steph had blamed Theo completely. Looking back, she was mortified, but she had been young and immature. Her view had been – *if* he hadn't been with Rachel, *if* he hadn't insisted she tell him what the matter was and most of all, *if* he hadn't just stormed off and left her. Why hadn't he told her the truth? Why pretend she was nothing to him? It had taken a very long time before Steph saw that she had no one to blame but herself. The conversation itself had, in retrospect, been very short for something so momentous.

It had been a dark, cold and stormy night. The kind where murderers and ghosts jostle for position in the shadows and you can't be sure which is worse. Steph had been wrapped up in her pink, fluffy dressing gown, listening to Duran Duran and being glad that she didn't have to go out, when the doorbell rang. Cursing her parents for being out at a village event she'd shuffled downstairs and answered the door. Theo had been standing there, drenched and wearing his thin jacket that Steph knew didn't keep him warm.

"What are you doing?" she'd exclaimed without thinking. "Come in, you'll freeze!"

"Thanks."

They'd stood, facing each other, in the hallway.

"So."

"So." Suddenly Steph was acutely aware of her dressing gown, scraped back hair and no make-up. To Theo she looked so sweet and young. So Steph.

"Why are you here?"

"Steph – I – what's going on? I hate this. What's happened to us?"

A step backwards, "Um, Theo, I think you've misread something. Nothing's going on."

"Why the body language then? Look at yourself."

Steph stared down at her tightly-folded arms. A hot flush began to creep up her neck, what was she supposed to say? Oh, for some Just Seventeen advice now.

"What are you doing here? You could have rung."

"But you wouldn't have talked to me. I was sitting at home, feeling lonely and wondering why, then I realised – I was missing you. I was listening to that song, you know?"

"Lonely? But you've got Rachel." The words were out before she could help it.

"Ah." A small pause. "I thought she might figure somewhere."

"Sorry, I shouldn't have said that."

"Is that all? Is she all this is about? You're sulking?"

"No!"

"Well what then? I miss you so much Steph, I want you back. How can I make things better?"

"We'll always be friends Theo. You know that."

"I know that, but I want more than friends."

"Do you?" Hope shimmered in the distance.

"Yeah, I want best friends. I want to be close, share things, have a laugh."

There was another short pause, "I'm sorry, I just don't think I can." To Steph's horror, tears began to rise.

"Why not?" Theo's face was wracked, he'd taken a step towards her, held out his arms.

"Stop it! Theo, can't you see." Then, suddenly, there it was – "I love you."

"I know Steph," he'd said impatiently, "I love you too."

"No, not like that. Not like friends. Theo – I love you properly."

His face had fallen and he'd stepped backwards this time, "What?"

"You heard." Steph had turned away, not wanting to see his face, not wanting to see his disgust. God, she was sad. How could she have just done that?

"So… all this time… you mean – this whole thing?"

"Yes."

"Oh my God."

Silence. He sounded appalled.

"But…" Theo said.

"Yeah, I know," she just wanted him to shut up. Horrible, crimson shame was rising fast in Steph. Only his size prevented her from bundling him out of the door and shutting it firmly. Silly really, when all she wanted was to grab him by the hand, lead him upstairs, undress with him, lie down and never let him go again.

"I have to go."

"What?"

"Sorry Steph, I really am but – God, this is…" and he'd gone. Practically turned round and run, leaving Steph staring after him through an open door. At least her parents weren't around, she thought irrationally. They'd love this little drama.

She hadn't known it was possible to feel so much pain. And it was worse than before. Before, it had been her secret and she could pretend everything was fine, but now he knew. Now she could never look him in the face again. What on earth had made her say it? "I love you properly", the words replayed themselves time and time again. It was such a cringy thing to say, apart from anything else. She stared wildly around her room. The four walls that had before seemed so comforting were now unbearable. Hastily, she pulled on a tracksuit and trainers, grabbed her keys and left, slamming the door behind her. No note, but sod that, they'd have to worry.

She jogged the ten minutes to Ed's house, through the wind and storm, her mind racing. She wasn't sure why she was going, but she also sensed that didn't matter. Ed was as surprised to see her as she had been to see Theo, "Steph!"

"Hi," she'd pushed past him and shaken the rain from her hair. "I know, I look a state, don't say anything."

"What's up?"

"Nothing," she said miserably. "Who's in?"

"No one, they're all out at that village hall thing. Seriously, what's the matter?"

"Oh, just Theo. I don't want to talk about it." She knew she was being difficult and hated herself for it, but she couldn't change it. "Have you got any wine?"

"Yeah, of course." Ed was slightly taken aback, Steph was usually so calm and collected, this was way out of character.

"Can I have some?"

"Sure." Ed fetched a glass, took some wine from the bottle in the fridge and handed it to her, "there you are."

"Thanks." She drained it in one gulp and held it out for more.

"Really?"

"I know. Shut up."

"OK." Filling hers and one for himself, he grabbed the bottle and ushered her upstairs, the last thing he wanted was for his parents to come home and find her standing in their kitchen drinking their wine. It would not look good. Feeling bemused, Ed flicked his bedroom light on and closed the door.

"Going to talk to me?"

"No. Sorry Ed, but I just can't."

"OK, no problem." Except there was, he didn't know what to do. Unnerved, he pressed 'Play' on his CD player. Nirvana filled the room.

They drank in silence for a bit, listening to the heavy beat of the music, until Steph's head began to swirl pleasantly, and she felt less like wanting to kill herself. She even began to feel sorry for Ed, sitting there, looking so anxious, just waiting. Waiting for what? Her, she supposed.

"What shall we do?" she asked him after a bit.

"Do? Talk, listen to this."

"Have you ever been in love, Ed?"

"No."

"Lucky you."

"Why lucky?"

"It's crap. If the other person doesn't love you back."

"Are we talking about Theo?"

"No. We're talking about me."

"You and Theo?"

"There's never been a 'me and Theo'."

Ed gave up and refilled their glasses. He lay down next to Steph on the floor, his feet by her head.

"You don't need him, Steph."

"Is that you giving advice?"

"Stop being such a bitch."

"Sorry."

"I'm serious," he propped himself upon one elbow and looked down at her, gently stroking her leg. "You're so great, so sweet, why moon about after him?"

"I am not mooning about!"

"You are a bit."

"Shut up." She giggled suddenly, "Oh who cares about stupid Theo? He can keep that dowdy bitch Rachel forever as far as I'm concerned."

"That's the spirit."

"Yeah, they can be serious and study together. They can get married in a study." For some reason that was hilarious. Ed laughed until tears ran down his face.

"I don't need him."

"You don't."

"More wine?"

"Here you are." Ed managed to get most of it into the glass but a few drops spilled onto the floor. Steph wondered if she were drunk.

"Ed, have you – you know – ever had sex?" she asked out of the blue.

Ed was taken aback, "Er – not exactly."

"Not exactly?"

"No."

"Well what have you done?"

"Stuff." Ed squirmed. "Why are you asking?"

"Just wondered."

"Have you?" he asked shyly.

"No."

"Want to try?" It was meant and said as a joke, but once the words were out the mood changed.

"Maybe." Steph had said softly, and that was just about the last sensible thing that she could remember.

If someone had asked her ten years later what she could recall, she would have listed: dim lights, Nirvana, the taste of wine on Ed, a flurried tangle of limbs and clothes and groaning and utter surprise. Surprise at what she was feeling, surprise at the pain, swift though it was, but most of all surprise at herself that she was doing it at all.

****

"A little bird tells me that Julia has finally got you into her clutches."

"Really? Who's that then?"

Katie shrugged, "Oh, general gossip mill. I couldn't even tell you where it originally came from. Jeanie told me." The gossip often spilled over into St Lukes.

"Yes, it's true actually. She asked me to help on the Cath's Committee to plan that Murder-Mystery evening."

"And you agreed? That's it, you've signed your life away you realise."

"Happily not," Steph turned from the teapot. "And besides, this way at least I can help make sure that it's a decent evening. Plenty of dancing and booze. I hope you're coming?"

"I should think so. Even if it is Tom's birthday that day and I'm not technically a parent there."

"Oh – bollocks to that. And is it really Tom's birthday?"

"Yes, he's going to be thirty-five," Katie grinned wickedly, "I keep telling him it's all downhill from here. Forty next, then fifty then sixty and then you're dead before you know it."

"Katie!"

"He knows I'm joking. I'm a lot happier going to this dinner dance knowing you're on the planning committee. What has Julia delegated to you then?"

"It started with food, caterers and staff. And spiralled into food, caterers, staff, seating plans, table decorations," Steph smiled ruefully, "etc."

"That's the bit that would worry me."

"Yes, I know. I don't mind, but it's an awful lot of pressure to get it right. If there are any mess-ups it's going to be down to me."

"You won't mess up," Katie said confidently. "I know you. You'll make a success of it."

"Well I really hope so."

"What does Theo think?"

"Not much. He's more concerned about me resting and eating healthily and not drinking too much. I tell him I've got to stock up for when I can't drink anything."

"Oooh yes, baby number three plans! So exciting, how are they coming along?"

Steph shrugged, "You know how it is. You haven't a clue what's going on until the end of the month."

"When's that for you?"

"About a week."

"Excited?"

"Yes, a bit. I must admit, the idea's grown on me a lot. I like the idea of completing this family with one more baby. A little boy maybe," Steph smiled determindedly. "One that looked the spitting image of Theo."

"You think? I always prefer it when the boy looks like the mother – so sweet."

"No," Steph said firmly. "Like Theo. Now, do you want to come and admire Mia's new room?"

"Mia's?" Katie hopped down from her stool.

"Yes… Mia decided that she wanted to be the one that moved and so," Steph spread her hands, "that was what happened. You know what Mia's like. But Tilly didn't mind," she said, climbing the broad stairs, "she was happy to stay put."

"She's so biddable, that child," Katie said. "Wow! I love it," she stared wonderingly around the room. It was painted four different shades of pink, with heavy, white curtains and a border of subtly designed, sparkly flowers around the top of the walls. A small set of coloured fairy lights decorated the window. "It's not as OTT as I thought the girls would choose."

"Actually, I was surprised too. But I did warn her that I wouldn't be redecorating in a years time, so she had to choose something that she was happy to live with for a while."

"Fair enough. No, it's lovely. Why is the double bed still in here? I thought that was going to Mrs B?"

"No. Theo and I decided in the end that it would be silly to get rid of it. In case we have guests because we're going to use the current guest room as a nursery. So if we keep a double bed in here then if we ever do have people – don't ask me why Theo thinks that's going to happen – then we've got a nice room they can sleep in."

"If they like fairies and mermaids."

"Well, yes. There is that."

"And what did Tilly decide for her room?"

"Nothing yet. She says she likes it as it is."

"She reminds me so much of you, you know."

"Really?"

"Yep. Quiet and unassuming. Placid. Lovely character but with personality."

"And Mia?" Steph raised an eyebrow.

"Stronger. Tougher. Streak of steel through that girl. Wonder where she gets it from?" Katie mused. "Neither of you are like that. Mind you, genes can stay hidden for generations can't they? Mia's probably got an identical character to your great-grandpa or something."

"Yes. Something. Anyway, can I persuade you to stay for lunch?"

"AFraid not, pot-painting awaits me."

"Ah yes, the master craftswoman. I saw your very slick advert in the paper. I was impressed."

"Thanks. I've just got to make good on the promise now."

Steph smiled, "You'll be fine."

****

"Darling?"
"Here."

"Where's here?"

"Playroom."

Theo stuck his head around the door, "God, what happened in here?"

"Paints and clay. Don't ask." Steph rubbed her nose, wiping a streak of orange paint onto it. "Anyway – hi darling, how was your day?"

"Good thanks. But I need a drink. Fancy some wine?"

"Red or white?"

"White."

"Sauvignon?"

"You're on. Give me two minutes." Steph scrambled up from her knees feeling exhausted. The girls had been more demanding than usual that evening; lots of squabbling and tears, hence why Steph had eventually resorted to the use of paints and clay together to calm them down. It was days like this when she wondered how a third baby would fit into the house. But then again – lots of people did it. It must be possible.

When she reached the kitchen, Theo was pulling his tie off.

"Don't." Steph said automatically.

"What?"

"Dump it on the side."

"Would I?"

"Hmm, you know I might just give you the benefit of the doubt this time Theo Hammond." She wrapped her arms around him and snuggled into his chest. "Thousands wouldn't, but I'm not thousands, I'm just one."

"A very special one." Theo kissed the tip of her nose affectionately. "Now move out of my way woman so I can get a drink."

"The girls might still be awake, you could say goodnight."

"Really? This late?"

"It's been a hectic evening."

"I gathered. Oh, I knew I had something to tell you," his back was turned to her, unscrewing the cork from a bottle of wine. "You will never guess who rang me today?"

"Won't I? There's some post here for you." Steph busied herself sorting some paper to recycle; the council were getting so hot on it. You could be fined if they found paper in your normal refuse bin.

"No you won't guess."

"Well go on then, who? Cheryl Cole?"

"Nooooo, I should be so lucky. Ed. Edward Osborne. You remember?"

A bolt of adrenaline shot through Steph. She felt her fingers begin to tremble and her face flush. "What, Ed? Really?" she tried to keep her voice calm.

"Yeah. Bit of a blast from the past. I felt a bit bad talking to him to be honest."

"Bad? Why?" she could hear the shaking in her own voice.

"I know it's been a long time, but," he hesitated, "I still can't forget what we did to him."

"Oh come on, it wasn't that bad. We left, we moved on. We grew up. I'm sure he's over it by now." Her tone was disdainful. Theo was surprised.

"Er – well, he sounded fine."

"What did he want?" Her heart seemed to be beating a hundred times faster than normal and her legs felt weak and shaky. She grabbed a stool and hoisted herself up onto it.

"Just to catch up. Actually, he mentioned that he found us through Facebook. He must have seen your profile there. He tracked down our number and decided to ring."

"Hang on, how can he have seen my Facebook profile?"

"Why not?"

"He'd have to know me, be my friend – you can't just see people like that." Steph explained impatiently.

"Oh well, I don't know then. Maybe I got that wrong. It was only a quick chat; I've invited him round for dinner on Friday for a proper catch-up."

"*What*? Friday? Theo, what were you thinking?"

"What's wrong with that?" he stared in surprise. "Steph, you're being really odd. What on earth is the matter with Ed? He's our oldest friend."

"We were all friends once, years ago," she snapped, "almost twelve years ago."

"Eleven."

"Whatever. Ages ago. We've got nothing in common any more."

"How do you know that?"

"Oh come on, you and I were always close. He was the odd one out."

"I remember you two being very close. Round about the time of Rachel."

"Yes, as two sixteen year olds! God Theo, I have no interest in seeing him now!"

"Steph, why are you so angry? I thought you'd be pleased," Theo sounded bewildered. "I was telling him about the girls, he wants to meet them. Wants to see you. I thought it would be nice. Especially for Mia and Tilly to meet one of our old friends."

Jesus. Steph's heart felt like it would explode out of her chest and her nails gripped the marble-effect surfaces tightly.

"No Theo, I'm sorry. I really don't want to see him," she said with an effort.

"Well – OK. That leaves me a bit stuck, to be honest. I've already invited him."

"So un-invite him."

"It's not really that simple darling. I can't ring him up and cancel all the plans with no reason."

"I don't care how you do it, just do it!" It was more panic than anger, but Theo couldn't fathom it at all.

"Mummy?" Steph's head whipped round, Mia was standing in the doorway, blonde hair tousled, eyes sleepy, "Mummy, I can't sleep. Can I have some milk?"

"Yes of course darling," Steph instinctively drew her daughter close to her and held her as she poured milk into a cup for her and heated it in the microwave. She deliberately avoided Theo's eye.

"I'm going to get changed," he said eventually.

Christ, this was bad.

Seriously bad.

A nightmare.

Would he walk in and be able to tell? Would the genes leak information by osmosis? Those that had them would just know? It couldn't be done, it couldn't happen, she couldn't just let him stroll on in here and – "Mummy? I'm tired."

"I know darling, I know." Steph found herself stroking Mia's hair rather harder than she'd meant. "Come on, up to bed." She shepherded her small daughter out of the room and up the wide staircase.

"I love this house," Mia said, apropos of nothing.

"Really? I'm glad. Here we are."

"Mummy, I don't sleep here any more."

"Yes, of course." The new room still smelled of paint; Steph hoped it didn't matter. It wouldn't be toxic would it? She couldn't bear the thought of anything bad happening to the girls. Either of them. Oh God, oh *God*, what was worse – mental harm or physical? They were probably the same. No, this could not happen, she just couldn't let it. She felt shocked to her core.

"Night darling."

"Night Mummy, I love you. And Daddy. And Tilly a bit too."

When she got downstairs Theo was pulling the cork out of a bottle of red wine. He looked up guardedly as she came in.

"Mia OK?"

"Yes, fine."

"Want a glass?"

"Just one." Steph watched his big, strong, capable hands as he poured the liquid. Theo's hands, *her* hands. Their wedding rings were the same. She felt dazed and confused. And outraged. How the hell could Ed have just strolled back into their lives as if it were the easiest thing in the world?

"Steph," as he spoke the phone rang, loud in the silence.

"I'll go," Steph said quickly and strode out to the hall. "Hello?"

"Steph? It's me, Katie. How are you?"

"Oh fine, yes, you know."

"You sure? You sound a bit odd. I haven't interrupted something have I?"

"No, honestly. What's up?"

"Just rang for a chat really, and the latest gossip from Camp Julia."

"I'll have to disappoint you I'm afraid, haven't seen her for days."

"Oooh, maybe there's a new man or two on the scene?"

"Could be. Actually – Katie, do you mind if I call you back? Tomorrow? Theo's just got in and…"

"You don't have to tell me – a night of passion awaits you!"

"Not exactly."

"Have you done an early test? Has Baby 3 been made?"

"No. I don't know." What a hideous thought. "I'll speak to you tomorrow." She could see through the glass door into the kitchen; watched Theo moving about, opening drawers and putting glasses away.

"OK, OK, I get the message."

"Sorry, sorry. It's just – I – oh, I can't talk now."

"What's up?"

"Nothing. Listen," Steph turned her back to the kitchen so Theo wouldn't be able to see her lips moving, was this what paranoia did to you? "Do you fancy a coffee tomorrow? Not here, in town somewhere." She felt desperate to get away from the house, she didn't want to think these mind-whirlingly negative thoughts in her home.

"Sure, no problem. What time? I've got a client coming to collect at 2 but any other time suits me."

"OK, let's say 11? I'll meet you at Starbucks."

****

"That was odd," Katie said slowly.

Tom looked up, "What was?"

"Steph. She sounded strange."

"In what way?"

"Worried. On edge. Like something was bothering her."

"It probably is."

"Thanks! I can work that out. But what? What's she got to worry about?"

"Who knows? The latest colour change in her living room? Not being able to ride that horse?"

"I don't think so somehow. Odd. Oh well, I guess I'll find out tomorrow."

"Do let me know."

"Sarcasm will get you nowhere."

****

"Theo – I am completely against this idea."

"I gathered that much. Why for God's sake? I just don't understand." Theo rubbed his chin in bewilderment. He looked tired.

"We've all moved on. We used to be friends, I don't think we'd fit into each others lives now," Steph said firmly.

"What's that got to do with anything? I'm not suggesting he moves in! All I'm saying is let's get together for dinner, what's so hard about that?"

"The fact I don't want to!" She was getting angry now, Theo could tell when she was angry, her lips became thin and drawn. "I am so busy right now, with this Cath's stuff, the girls, Christmas is coming, the baby plans," she knew what that would do to him.

"OK, OK, shush, calm down," Theo went to hug her but she pulled away. "How about drinks then? How about we have him round for a glass of wine?"

"Oh yeah, I can really see that being enjoyable! Good old sociable Ed – have you forgotten how awkward and quiet he used to be? And that's when we saw each other every day!"

"He sounded fine on the phone." Theo said defensively.

"So you keep saying." Steph looked away.

There was a moments silence, "I'm sorry Steph, but I really do want to see Ed," Theo said at last. "I was pleased to hear from him and I would enjoy a catch-up. I didn't think you'd react like this but that doesn't change things for me. I'm not doing anything wrong."

Steph didn't say anything.

"How about I cancel dinner on Friday and meet him on my own? Would that be all right?"

How could she refuse? Theo was clearly being so reasonable. And if you took the complications out – he was right. But she could hardly do that now.

"OK, fine."

Theo sighed, "I'll email him then."

"Email? Why not ring?"

"I don't have a number for him – does it matter?"

"No, I suppose not."

"You still don't sound happy."

Careful, Steph, careful, you don't want to make him suspicious. "No, I don't mind. I'm not up for all being best friends together again, but you go for a drink if you want."

Theo leaned over and kissed her nose, "I don't think I'll ever understand you."

Steph smiled weakly, "I'm a woman, you're not supposed to."

"Let's hope the girls are more me than you, eh? At least I might stand a chance with them."

Steph could have vomited on the spot. "Yes," she said. "Yes."

Keen to change the subject, Theo waved the TV listings at her, "There's a Poirot on at nine, fancy watching that?"

"OK, sounds good. I might run a bath first though."

"Good idea, relax a bit." He grinned at her. "What day are you now?"

"22."

"When can you test?"

"28."

"Do you feel pregnant?"

"Oh Theo, you are not going to help by nagging me!"

"I'm not – sorry. Sorry. But you fell pregnant so easily with the girls I can't help thinking we might have done it again this time."

"Mmm." A sickly pause. "Don't get your hopes up. But who

knows? I'll see you in a bit."

Steph felt sick walking up towards their en suite bathroom. Another baby into this mess was unthinkable. An awful idea. She wanted a relaxed, trouble-free pregnancy this time, and she wouldn't get it the way things were. The past had well and truly come back to haunt her. Why now? She put the taps on full and sat on the edge of the bath, why now? Things were so perfect, she was so happy – and bloody Ed could ruin it all in one fell swoop, just like he'd done before. But it was too late for this month, she could be pregnant already. Steph put her hands against her taut, flat stomach, honed from months of Pilates. Theo's baby could be in there right now, a tiny, small seed of a thing taking up residence, ready to grow into something undeniably Theo's. His DNA could have fused with hers and made some incredible little thing. A perfect little boy or girl to join their distorted family. Such a little baby that could give away such a big secret. Steph felt her heart quicken as clouds of steam rose around her and filled the bathroom. She felt as though she were trapped in some terrible nightmare – if only she could run away. But she'd done that before. And there were so many other 'if only's', if only she hadn't had that fight with Theo; if only she hadn't decided to sleep with Ed; if only she hadn't fallen pregnant; if only she'd told Theo at the time. It was quite a list. But she didn't have those options now, all she could do now was keep Ed as far away from his children as she possibly could, hope he got the message and pray for some damage control.

Steph took a deep breath and stepped into the boiling bath feeling slightly calmer. Yes, keep Ed away, don't panic and this mess could well just sweep on past. All she needed was an iron-tight grip on her life. Hers and Theo's. And the girls'. And she must not relinquish it under any circumstances.

CHAPTER FIVE

Ed selected an Il Divo CD from the neat stack by his BoseWAVE music system and slid it into the player. A strong, crisp sound filled the room. Ah, perfect. He sat down heavily on his black leather recliner and dimmed the lights with his remote control. A glass of Meusault sat at his elbow on the oak occasional table and a smell of freshly polished furniture filled the apartment; Ana had been in to clean today. If he craned his head just slightly to the left he could see through to his fridge, which he knew was well-stocked by Ocado, but sod it – what was the point in paying for the kitchen to be cleaned if he was just going to mess it up again? Chinese it would be tonight. His kitchen was the smallest room in his apartment, little more than a galley kitchen really, but Ed had thought that was fair play when he bought the place, considering it was going to be the room where he spent the least time. The living room was open plan and spacious, with deep, soft wall-to-wall carpeting that led out to the hall in one direction and to the balcony in the other. He sometimes stood out there to enjoy a late-night whiskey.

He let his head fall back against the sofa and the music wash over him gently. What a day, what a bloody day. It was Monday, but it still been a hellish one. What was it with Counsel, why were they always such bastards? It was as if every single one of them disliked him personally, and that could hardly be the case. It was already nine o' clock and the wine was making his head pleasantly fuzzy. And Jenna hadn't stopped calling, emailing and texting, why hadn't she got the message that it was over? Christ, she was a secretary for God's sake, it was never going to be anything serious.

Just about the only decent bit in his day had been speaking to Theo Hammond again. It had taken Ed a while to decide whether or not to call him, after seeing Steph's Facebook profile. That had been a shock and a half that morning. He'd hardly been able to believe it when he'd seen her name against his old mate Julia's profile. 'Steph Hammond', bold as brass. He'd thought it must be a different Steph Hammond but peering closely at the picture had told him otherwise.

How the hell did those two know each other then? Ed and Julia went way back, they'd been at Bristol Uni at the same time. She'd been the only mature student in his halls in first year, studying Business Management if he remembered correctly, while he'd been doing Law. Crazy days.

He'd thought for oh – at least a second or so about adding Steph to his Facebook page and contacting them that way, but instinct had guided him against that. Not that she wouldn't be pleased to hear from him or anything, if anyone was pissed off with anyone it should be him with them. No, he'd considered talking to Steph but decided against it. Theo was safer, men were more balanced, and besides, James Mears had very handily provided him with a number for Theo so Ed had spent a couple of hours weighing up the pros and cons, but he'd been pleasantly surprised when he had called. And who would ever have thought that would be the case? After all that drama ten years ago. But no, Theo had sounded like a decent guy, pleased to hear from him. He'd even invited him over, "Come round, have dinner, meet the girls."

"The girls?" Ed had asked blankly. How many wives did he have?

"The twins, our daughters. Mia and Tilly." Theo said proudly.

"God, mate, I didn't know you had kids." Ed had been genuinely astonished. And appalled. Who wanted kids?

"Yes, indeed. They're ten now."

"Ten?! That must have happened just as you…"

"Quite. But they're very grown-up, you don't need to worry about them puking all over you or anything."

"Great. That's great. I'll look forward to it."

"And Steph will be pleased to see you too." Theo was sure of it. Ed wasn't too certain, but a moments thought made him see well, why not? A silly teenage liaison ten, no, nearly eleven years ago can't still be playing on her mind. Never mind what she'd said at the time, she'd been young and upset.

"It sounds good mate."

"Does Friday suit you? It's short notice I know, it's just that I know we're free that night. Any other and I'll have to go home and check with Steph. Which I can do if…"

"No, Friday's great. It'll get me out of the post-work drinks where we're all supposed to lick the bosses' arse."

"And er – will you be bringing anyone? Is there any significant other?"

"Christ, no. Not anyone significant in any way. Just me really."

"Shall I tell Steph just one extra for dinner then?" Theo had sounded amused.

"Yes, absolutely. That'll be great."

There hadn't been a lot more to it than that. They'd exchanged email addresses and had a little bit of chat about their careers; Theo expressing surprise that Ed had gone into Law. "Corporate, mainly," Ed had explained. To his surprise, he felt smug. He known all along what Steph and Theo thought of him – an outsider, loner, awkward, shy. Never going to amount to much. It had been nice to tell Theo that he was now working towards a partnership in one of the county's leading corporate law firms. He'd bet his bottom dollar that he was doing better than Theo. He would've before, but especially with two kids, that couldn't be cheap. Ed wondered vaguely what Steph looked like now, heavier he'd bet. Babies did that to you. Would she look older? Wrinkles, grey hairs? Somehow he couldn't imagine Steph looking like that. She'd always remained eighteen in his mind; slim, pretty, delicate.

A shrill ring from his iPhone jerked him from his thoughts. Ed reached over and glanced at the screen. It was Jenna again, well, she could bugger off. He silenced the ring and settled back into his chair. Idly he considered watching a film but he was too tired. He couldn't be bothered to eat properly either. He got up and walked across soft, plush, Cappuccino-coloured carpets to his kitchen floor with their heated tiles; that had been one good investment. He slid a piece of bread into the John Lewis toaster and set the dial on the side to two minutes so it was well-browned. His kitchen was full of gadgets that he never used, the coffee machine was the only thing that saw regular use. Even his three Le Creuset saucepans had only ever been used once. They'd been a gift from Eleanor, his devoted girlfriend before last. Attractive, he remembered, big tits, nice waist but a bit puppy dog-ish, always hanging onto his every word, he'd tired of her after six months. But at least she'd left without a fuss, unlike Jenna who was proving a bit of a nightmare.

Ed yawned widely and ate his toast standing up in the kitchen, no plate to keep the mess down. He stuck the knife in the dishwasher to join that morning's coffee cup and tonight's wine glass and switched it on. His mother would tut at him about wasting energy but there was no way he was going to do a full day at work and then start washing up. He flicked the light switch off and headed towards his tiled shower room. His laptop sat in the corner of the room, unopened tonight.

After saying goodbye to Theo, Ed had realised that he'd given him the wrong email address and he'd meant to let him know the right one, but that could wait as well, he'd do it tomorrow.

****

It wasn't until she was untacking Archie in the yard that Steph changed her mind. She had kind of, half been considering telling Katie. But as she'd gone through her mundane routine with the horse, undoing the girth, pulling the saddle off, picking out his feet and leading him out to the field, she had realised exactly how much she would hate anything to change. She stood at the gate and watched Archie amble away. She loved her life, she loved her family, she loved her friends. If she admitted to anything the axis of her world would shift; a little bit more knowledge could skew the whole thing. She'd done so well at hiding it for so many years, not her intention at the start, but that had quickly fallen by the wayside. It was all very well for other people to judge what she might have been thinking but how could they ever know? Steph kicked at the mud with her booted foot; she didn't even want to hint at there being a reason why peoples' opinion of her would alter.

Katie was at Starbucks ahead of Steph, which was unusual, but it had taken longer to get home and showered than Steph had anticipated.

"Hi," Steph unwrapped her Hermes scarf, showing her pale, slender neck, just made for diamonds Katie thought wistfully. "Sorry I'm late, I sneaked in a quick ride this morning."

"No problem. I got lattes."

"You're a star," Steph sank gratefully into the seat opposite Katie. She had dark rings under her eyes and she looked worried.

"Are you OK? What's up? I was a bit worried after our conversation yesterday."

"Really? Why?"

"You sounded odd, like you were worried about something."

"Me? No, not really." Her new resolve stuck firm.

"Not really?"

"Well," she cast around for a reason. "Theo's putting a lot of pressure on me about this baby, which is both nice and not nice. I'm pleased he's so enthusiastic but he's making me feel like it's got to be this month, there's nothing relaxed about it. And constantly checking I'm all right, telling me to relax," she smiled, "I know I'm lucky, loads of women would kill to have a husband like Theo, but it's making me tense." Steph felt anew her desperation not to shatter Katie's illusion of their perfect marriage. She still couldn't believe it was actually her in this situation; Steph Hammond wasn't supposed to have this sort of life.

"Oh sweetheart, he just cares about you, that's all. And don't listen to him about it having to be this month – it could take ages yet. And it's nice that he cares so much," she added.

"I know, I know. Ignore me, I'm probably hormonal. How's Jack? He hasn't been for tea recently, he must come soon, the girls love seeing him."

"Because he's such a devil, that's why. Nothing to do with genuine affection. You've raised two lovely girls and in bowls my one hideous boy, leading them on into all sorts of naughtiness."

"That could be why," Steph admitted. "Although Jack is not hideous, he's sweet. But seriously, how about Friday? Theo was meant to be having this friend over but he's not now so we're free." It was amazing how she could transmute Ed, this figure of her nightmares, into 'Theo's friend' in conversation.

"Friday's fine. Shall I pick them all up from school and stay for a glass of wine? Or are you not drinking at all?"

"No, no, I'm still drinking," as a last bastion of support, Steph thought guiltily, "until I get that big, fat positive blue line I'll be drinking. So yes, that would be nice. Might relax me a bit." She glanced down at her tightly entwined fingers.

"Are you sure that's all that's up?" Katie asked doubtfully, following her gaze. Call her suspicious but there was something that wasn't adding up here. She drained the last of her coffee.

"Positive."

"OK. I believe you. So tell me," she leant forward eagerly over the table, green eyes shining, "the Murder-Mystery and Julia saga, how's that going?"

"Oh it's wonderful. I keep being warned off Julia left, right and centre – surprise, surprise. No, she isn't that bad. And my bit's done and sorted, except it's two weeks away on Saturday and we've still got tickets to sell. Julia's on the case though, as you can imagine."

"They'll sell," Katie said confidently, "it might be a last minute job but they'll sell. I'll put the word out anyhow. Why don't you put it on Facebook and see if any of your non-school buddies are up for coming along?"

"I could." Steph said vaguely and glanced at her watch. "Damn, got to run, sorry. I've a man coming."

"Oh yes?" Katie raised an eyebrow.

"About a dog. No, I'm joking, it's about the hallway, I was thinking about having it redecorated. I know, I know, don't look like that, it's just there's this fab little interior design company that have just opened up down the road, they're based in London, and they're supposed to be amazing." Steph knew full well what she was doing; had known the minute she'd done a panicked online search. Distraction, distraction and more distraction.

"What about the man that did Mia's room?"

"Oh he was just a decorator, we designed that ourselves. I'm talking about a company who will come in and have a perfect vision of my hallway. Raggy Rose they're called, they have a fabulous reputation in London. Quite low-key at the moment, now's the time to grab them. They did our house name sign."

"Why don't you do it?"

Steph actually laughed out loud, "What, have a vision of my hallway?"

"Yes. What's so funny about that?"

"The fact that I have no idea what I'm doing?"

"Don't be so down on yourself. You'd have the best idea of what you want and I remember you telling me about your career plans."

"Oh Katie, that was absolute eons ago. I couldn't even dream of following up on that now."

Katie, looking at her, saw that Steph truly believed this to be the case. She held her hands up and grinned, "OK fine, pay others to do it then.Good luck."

"Thanks, see you Friday."

Katie watched Steph's departing back in its Hobbs coat and thought that she could well be being overly suspicious, but she could swear that Steph was hiding something. The tried and tested method of time and wine would get it out of her for sure. And Tom was right – what on earth could Steph Hammond have to be worried about?

CHAPTER SIX

It wasn't until they were both watching the girls swimming lesson at David Lloyd on Thursday evening that Steph finally asked Theo whether he'd cancelled Ed.

"Yes, of course I did. I emailed him two days ago."

"And what did he say?"

"Nothing. He didn't reply." Theo had been a little upset about that. He'd thought Ed sounded like he'd turned into a nice guy, and yet his request to change dinner into drinks in the pub had been ignored. Ed might have been pissed off, he supposed, but why? Blokes weren't like that.

"So you aren't doing drinks either?"

"Doesn't look like it," he said stiffly.

Steph reached for his hand, filled with a passionate desire to explain. Theo was such a good, decent man and this was out of character for her. He knew that and that was why he was treating it with such respect. Steph wanted to tell him that she wasn't just being a difficult bitch, but there were no words. Not now.

"Thanks for doing that."

"No problem. It looks like they're coming out, shall I go or do you want to?"

"I'll go, you stay and finish your coffee."

The girls had come out of the water arguing about something and they were both grumpy by the time they got to the showers.

"I'm not sharing with *her*."

"Mia, please, darling,"

"*No*. I want my own shower."

"Mia, you know that makes it difficult, we've only got one shampoo and shower gel," Steph pleaded, avoiding the sympathetic glances from the other mothers. Who were they to judge? In a minute they'd be going home to their easy lives, faithful marriages, uncomplicated parenting. Sudden guilt made her shout, "Mia! For God's sake, will you just behave for once?"

Two shocked little faces looked back at her. Mummy didn't

shout, not ever. Not even when they were really naughty.

"Sorry," Steph muttered after a minute, "sorry girls. Let's just get washed and dressed shall we?"

A subdued trio emerged from the changing rooms fifteen minutes later. Theo thought he could detect a hint of redness around Mia's eyes.

"Anything the matter?"

"Mummy shouted."

Theo glanced at Steph in surprise, "Really? Well, what had you done?"

"Nothing."

"Just leave it Theo, it doesn't matter," she said wearily.

"OK. More coffee or a spritzer?"

"Neither. I'd rather just go home actually, I'm quite tired. If you don't mind."

"No. Not at all."

She was being very strange, Theo thought as he drove home through the wet November roads. Not like Steph at all. Snappy, distracted – could it be hormones already? A surge of hope rushed through him. He wanted to suggest an early pregnancy test but Steph had been quite short with him when he'd raised the idea before and he didn't want anything to stress her. Not now, this was too important. He looked over at her in the passenger seat, "What are you thinking?"

"About the Murder-Mystery."

"Oh yes?"

"Just plans, what needs doing. Nothing exciting."

"Are you nearly there?"

"I wish. It's Friday tomorrow and I have to have a file collated for Julia by Monday about the catering, table layout, seating plans and glass hire."

"Who's in charge of the entertainment?"

"Ian."

"Ah. Good man. Well I can help you if you want?"

"I can manage you know."

"I didn't mean that. I know you can. I just wondered if – never mind." Theo took a deep breath and concentrated on the road and yellow lights around him. "Seeing as we don't have any plans tomorrow now, how about we go out?" He tried a different tack. "Get Katie over to babysit and go to Kuti's or somewhere?"

"Actually, Jack's coming over to play and Katie's staying for a drink when she collects. Sorry, forgot to mention it."

"No problem. Another time then." He was so easy-going, Steph thought. So laid-back he was nearly horizontal. What she wouldn't give for some of those relaxed vibes right now. *Your fault*, a little voice taunted her, *your fault – your fault*. With an effort she pushed the thought away and turned to face the girls in the back.

"What do you girls want for tea tomorrow with Jack?"

****

She had meant to go home, she honestly had, but somehow it hadn't happened. She'd woken on the floor at seven the next morning, sun streaming through Ed's window straight into her eyes. A vicious headache pounded in her head, she swallowed and her throat was like sandpaper. Oh *God*. Last night. She raised herself up to glance at Ed but he was asleep in his bed. A single pillow and duvet had formed her bed on the floor. She flopped back down and closed her eyes. This was seriously bad. Had they…? Oh yes, her memory confirmed, they had. For her very first time. After at least a bottle of wine. Shit, where were his parents? Had they been into the room? Had they seen anything? A wave of nausea rose in Steph's throat, not entirely alcohol-induced. She was at least wearing her knickers and bra and her jumper.

Steph lay on her side, trying to filter the information that was seeping back and process it bit by bit. Theo had come round. She'd told him that she loved him – *bugger*. A wave of shame washed over her. She bit her lip. So she'd come to Ed's, they'd talked and then – what then? Who had instigated what? She remembered the sex; it had hurt. It hadn't been like she'd always expected sex to be. Had he even used a condom like you were meant to? What was she supposed to do if he hadn't? She couldn't properly recall the end of the sex or what, if anything, had happened after that. And now, she was here. In Ed's room. Awake, and horribly hungover.

"Ed?" she whispered. "Are you awake?" A gentle snore told her he wasn't. Carefully and slowly she climbed out of her makeshift bed and pulled on her trousers. Her head spun unpleasantly; she needed water. She tiptoed across the floor, out of the door and down the stairs, praying that it was too early for anyone else to be up. Her prayers weren't answered.

"Morning dear," Mrs Osborne was standing at the sink washing dishes. "Sleep well?"

"Yes, thanks."

"Cup of tea? You look tired. I don't expect that floor was very comfortable."

Oh God, she'd been in. "No," Steph managed, "not really. Actually, can I just get some water?"

"Help yourself. Oh and don't worry about your parents, I let them know you were here when we got back."

"Thanks." Steph had stayed over so often at Ed's that she hadn't even got round to worrying about that.

"Can I get you any breakfast?"

"No, no, I'm fine thanks," Steph drained her glass. "Actually, I'd better be off. I've got a lesson at ten and I need to get home and showered and stuff," she shifted awkwardly. "Will you tell Ed goodbye from me?"

"Yes, of course dear. You can shower here if you want?"

"No, it's fine. Thanks anyway." Steph gave an apologetic smile.

"Any time, dear. Any time at all. Take care now."

The walk home in the fresh air cleared her head slightly. That of it that could be cleared anyway. What on earth was she going to say to Theo? There wasn't that much that could follow a declaration of love, and she suspected Just Seventeen would be all out of advice for this situation. He'd looked pretty shocked anyway, perhaps he wouldn't want to talk to her. Her heart plummeted and she realised that would be the worst possible outcome.

Her mum and John had left for work by the time she got home and the house was clean and quiet. She shut the front door behind her and took a deep breath. Now what? She did have a lesson at ten like she'd told Mrs Osborne, but she had no intention of going to it. A shower, more water, tea and her bed was all she wanted. And a lot of sleep, hopefully her brain could work through this mess without her active participation. She left the kettle to boil and went upstairs to clean her teeth and wash her face. Her reflection in the mirror did not impress her. Her face was white with dark circles and smudges of mascara under her eyes, but she could hardly expect anything more.

The kettle had just boiled for her to fill her mug to the brim, when the doorbell went. Damn. Steph glanced up at the clock, late enough for Ed to be at school and early enough for the postman. Mum had probably ordered some clothes again or something. She ambled down the hall and pulled the door open, not bothering to look through the peephole. Theo stood on the doorstep, shoulders hunched, hands shoved deep into his pockets. His face was pale and worried.

"Oh. God."

"Thanks. You're that pleased to see me?" He tried a smile but it came out more as a grimace.

"Sorry. I – it's – I wasn't expecting you."

"No. Did I wake you up?"

"Um, no. Not really."

"I waited for you, you weren't at school."

"Not today."

"Shit, it's because of me isn't it?" Theo dropped his head. "Steph, look, we need to talk. Seriously. Is your mum in?"

"No, both parent and step-parent are at their respective work. Luckily, or else I would be at school."

"Can I come in then?" he asked urgently.

"Yeah, of course." Steph stood back to let him in, then closed the door behind him. This was one conversation she wasn't going to like. When she turned around, Theo was standing right in front of her and before she knew what was happening he'd pinned her arms to her sides and his lips sought hers insistently. He kissed her long and hard, her back pressed against the door, and mind too shocked to comprehend properly what was happening. His lips crushed hers, his body pressed hard against her. It was totally unfamiliar and yet slotted so perfectly into place.

"I love you too Steph. I love you too. I'm sorry, I didn't mean to do that, I just couldn't help it. I've had such a hard night. After you said that – after you said what you said I didn't know what to think. I certainly thought it could never happen, me and you, it's never been like that between us, and I couldn't think of what to do. But I knew I had to. And the more I thought about it, the clearer it became. I don't know what I've been doing all these years Steph, it's you I've wanted."

Silence. Steph tried to think of something to say, and failed.

"Why aren't you saying anything?"

"I don't know what to say."

"I thought you'd be happy. I couldn't come back till now, I had to talk to Rachel."

"And tell her what?"

"That it's over."

"So why have you only just realised now? How you feel I mean?" Her mind was so muddled.

"I haven't. I've always known. I just haven't always told myself."

"Theo – this sounds, like, really *weird*. No offence."

"Like you don't believe me?"

"A bit."

"Well, you can. Really, Steph, I think you're amazing. I always have. I've missed you so much."

"Really?"

"Really. I know, I can't believe it either. It sounds so stupid, but when I thought about it – it's always you I want to be with, it's always you I miss when you're not around. I've hated these last few weeks, not knowing what I'd done. I thought you hated me, I thought I'd upset you. I couldn't tell you how I felt, there was Peter – and Ed – and…"

"What's Ed got to do with this?"

"I've seen the way he looks at you. He's crazy about you."

"Shut up."

"He is Steph, he is. Hasn't he said anything?"

"No!"

"Well – just trust me. Anyway, then I came round here, desperate to sort things out and you said you loved me – I couldn't believe it," he finished simply. "I could not believe it."

"So where does Rachel fit into this cosy triangle?"

"That hasn't been going so well for ages. But I had to finish with her before I said anything to you. I couldn't do that to her."

"Good for you."

"Aren't you happy?"

"I don't know Theo. This all seems so sudden and – unexpected. What did you imagine? That I'd fall into your arms and we'd live happily ever after?"

"No. Not exactly."

"This is too sudden."

"Too sudden for what?"

"For me to take in." A vestige of a headache still clung around her temples and she felt terribly tired. "I need to think."

"OK. OK. That's fine. I just wanted to come here and tell you that I feel the same."

"OK. Thank you."

"Shall I go?"

"Yes. No."

"Which?" And it was then, as he stood in her parents doorway looking so downcast and yet hopeful, so open and eager and so – *hers*, that she realised the way it had to be. The way to get rid of all this mess and claim what she wanted for herself, forever.

****

It had been a long time since she'd had to apply herself so diligently to something so boring. Steph thought she could put a figure on it – about ten years ago. History A-Level had been pretty dull. But then again, she stared at the sheets of paper in front of her, perhaps committee stuff could rival even European history.

She'd been dreading sitting down to do this ever since she dropped Mia and Tilly at school this morning. It was worse than going back to the housework. It was silly really, only planning; stuff that most people did in their spare time, but knowing that Julia would probably rip it apart made Steph resent doing it. But – if she was serious about being on this committee, it had to be done. This was her first event, she had to pull her weight, prove herself. And she didn't even have a job of any sort. If she failed at the first hurdle, she could just imagine what the others would say about her.

Gritting her teeth she fired up her laptop and logged onto Google to search for silver tablecloths, her neatly ordered file beside her. The 'to-do' list seemed to be breeding. Katie had warned her; but back then Steph had brushed off her concerns, it had been before all this Ed nonsense had started. No, she thought firmly, I will not dwell on that. Theo had sorted it out, it was fine. She even felt a bit sorry for him, at his obvious disappointment that Ed hadn't responded.

Three hours and two phonecalls later, Steph was a little happier. They had all the characters cast – first tick in the box. Ticket sales were slow but steady, which was better than it could be. They needed sixty to make the event happen at all, eighty to break even, one hundred and fifty in an ideal world and two hundred and thirty was full capacity – which nobody was expecting or wanting. Steph felt a little guilty that she'd only bought two tickets for herself and Theo, but really, who else was she going to take? It was hardly a social highlight of the year, unless you were on the Cath's committee at St Catherine's, that was.

Steph looked down at her list again; silver tablecloths done, centrepieces for the tables done, catering company booked and confirmed, Murder-Mystery pack bought. Ian had found that online, it was an eight character thing called 'Murder at St Cakes', and happily she'd got out of an acting role; she didn't much fancy dressing up as a caretaker.

Her gaze wandered through the open study doorway and into the hall, and a test patch of paint she'd put on the wall. Raggy Rose had quoted an astronomical amount to redecorate just the hallway; even Steph had been shocked.

"I don't know what you expected," Theo had shrugged. "They're an up-and-coming interior design company, they've got a good client base in London – they can afford to charge top whack."

"I know, I know. I did choose them based on their success."

"Do you want the hallway done that much?" Yes had been the answer at the time and the answer she'd given Theo, but now – she wasn't so sure. There were far better things to spend the money on. Steph clicked onto her email account and typed out a quick email to Raggy Rose telling them she'd come back to them in a few weeks. There was spare paint in the original colour for the hallway in the garage, she was sure.

The house was empty and silent – and clean. Mrs B had done a good job this morning. It was two o' clock, she didn't have to collect the girls for another two hours. It was at moments like this that she could imagine herself sitting quietly in a nursery, feeding a baby. Or pureeing sweet potato. Or catching up on her sleep after a broken night. Her mind wandered back to the twins' early days, but things had been different then. A smaller house, less money, less Theo; he'd always been working so hard. She'd been in far closer company with the truth of course, but she'd had so much else to think about, it had meant less. Were skeletons bound to jump out of your closet?

Her mobile trilled its irritating tune, making Steph jump.

"Hello?"

"Steph, darling, it's Julia. How *are* you?"

"I'm fine, thanks. Just working on the Murder-Mystery stuff actually."

"Good, good. How's it coming along?"

"Fine. I'm done on the tablecloths, decorations and caterers. What I thought we'd do is..."

"How about you drop me an email? That would be fab. Any movement on the seating plan?"

"Yes, it's done."

"Would you be an angel and speak to Mike for me?"

"Who's Mike?"

"Our guy who does the disco. He's done the last three events. He's not the youngest and always needs a playlist – you might have a think about that too – but he's got all the equipment, he's reliable and knows how we work. I wouldn't ask but I've got this blasted reunion,

I'd forgotten all about it."

"Reunion for what?"

"Uni. We usually do a Christmas thing but everywhere's so packed and overpriced that we thought we'd shift it forward this year and it's the weekend before the Murder-Mystery event. Typical timing! And guess who's got lumbered with the arrangements? That's right – muggins here." Julia gave a tinkling little laugh. Steph wondered if she knew how horrendously hypocritical she was being.

"What Uni did you go to?" Steph asked, a little wistfully. She'd never made it in the end.

"Bristol."

"What did you study?"

"Business management. I was a mature student though so I didn't get up to the usual shenanigans. Listen, must fly, thanks for the help, really appreciated. Catch you in the week, 'bye."

"Bye." But she was speaking to a dial tone. Steph sighed and grabbed the mouse; baby daydreaming was going to have to wait.

****

By the time Theo got home that evening, the house was utter chaos. The playroom was a tip, DS Lite games, clothes, pens, cars and Polly Pockets were scattered the length and breadth of the house, and the children were playing some game that involved screaming blue murder.

Steph and Katie had sought refuge behind a closed door in the kitchen with two glasses and a bottle of wine.

"Let them get on with it," Katie shrugged. "It's Friday. No homework or early bedtime."

"It's not your house they're ripping apart!"

"Surface damage. Don't be weak. Let them work off their pizza and E-numbers, it's only fair."

"I suppose they might sleep in tomorrow," Steph yawned and stretched.

"Hard week?"

"Something like that." There weren't really any words that could cover the nightmarish ups and downs of her week.

"It would have to be the something in your world."

"What do you mean?"

"I'm just teasing. Did the decorator not turn up?"

"No, actually I changed my mind. Decided it was too expensive."

"Really?"

"Yes, why do you sound so surprised?"

"You don't normally pay attention to piffling little details like money."

"Hello girls." Theo came up behind Steph and planted an intimate kiss on her neck. "I see our house is hosting World War Three."

"What gave it away?" Katie smiled at him.

"Hello darling, good day?"

Theo shrugged, "Same old. You know."

"God, there's nothing like enthusiasm for your work!" Katie said.

"If I were still enthusiastic about it when I got home, that would be worrying. I would be questioning my status as a bona fide family man."

"Never, Theo Hammond, never."

"Drink?" Steph slid off her stool and Theo caught himself admiring her *derriere*, encased as it was in tight jeans with a wide leather belt wrapped around her slim hips. Her hair had got surprisingly long; when she tilted her head back to reach up for a glass it fell nearly all the way to her waist, in its dark, gentle layers.

"Well?"

"What?"

"Do you want a drink? Come on, wake up!"

"Sorry – yes, whatever you girls are having. I was too caught up admiring your beauty my darling." Theo grinned and leaned in to kiss her.

"Corny! Corny!" Katie screeched. "And if that's after ten years or so of marriage, I dread to think what you must have been like at school."

"Oh I wasn't the favoured man at school."

"Weren't you? That's funny – I could have sworn…"

"Enough of school, Katie doesn't want to hear all about our halcyon days at Tinford Secondary Modern," Steph said firmly, "come on, let's brave the children and go and sit in the sitting room. We may not have an open fire, but the woodburner comes a close second."

They removed the children from the sitting room – "You've got two bedrooms and a playroom, scram!" – and cleared a space among the clutter to sit down.

"Is it only seven?" Theo said in surprise. "It feels like nine."

"That's what a full day at work will do to you," Steph said.

"The expert speaks."

"If you don't think running a house and looking after twins…"

"I was teasing, only teasing, calm down."

"Mind if I help myself?" Katie reached for the wine bottle.

"No, go for it. Are you driving?"

"No, I walked tonight. Doubtless Jack will moan but it'll do him good. So I'm free to drink!"

"We were thinking of a takeaway later," Steph said, tucking her knees up underneath herself, "feel free to join us if you'd like?"

"Good idea. I'll have to check with Tom though; sod's law tonight is the night he's decided to cook me a gourmet meal. The chances are slim to none, admittedly, but I wouldn't want to risk it." Katie grinned wickedly.

"Invite him too," Theo suggested.

"Could do. I'll give him a ring in a bit."

Gradually, the woodburner crackled through its logs, the wine bottle emptied and the noise from upstairs lessened. Theo stuck his head out of the door, "You know, I think they've put a DVD on."

"What, Sleeping Beauty? Jack'll be having a whale of a time," Katie snorted.

"Don't be ridiculous. Sleeping Beauty was a favourite when they were seven. It's all about High School Musical and Hannah Montana now."

"I can't see Jack leaping at either of those, to be honest. Wall-E or Bridge to Terabithia, maybe."

"As long as they're quiet…" Steph said mildly. She was feeling a little bit drunk. It wasn't often that she drank more than two glasses of wine in an evening.

"Fair point." Katie leaned forward to grab a crisp from the small bowl that sat on the coffee table. "What are these?"

"Vegetable crisps. Slices of parsnip and beetroot, deep fried. Theo hates them, I love them."

"Do they count as one of my five-a-day?"

"Sadly not, I don't think. Theo? What do you…"

The doorbell cut through their conversation like a knife.

"Oh – that must be Tom," Steph said, putting her glass on the table. "That was quick."

Katie frowned, "I didn't ring him. That's good sixth sense!"

"Or guesswork," Theo stood up and winked at her, "whichever you prefer. I'll let him in shall I? Rather than leaving the poor man on the doorstep."

"Go for it." Steph settled back comfortably against the big white cushions, and Theo thought again how beautiful and angelic she looked; her petite frame melted into the Jaspar Conran sofa, face slightly flushed with wine.

"I will." It was nice, Theo thought, striding towards the front door, how they had the friends to be able to do this kind of impromptu thing. Needing no arrangements, no discussions, just an easy, quick simple decision that they were all free, all fancied an Indian on a Friday night and hey presto – there they were. Except, opening the door, the face didn't fit. It wasn't Tom's dark hair and rugged looks that greeted him, it was someone blond. Very blond. Who was wearing a suede jacket and carrying a bottle of Veuve Cliquot in each hand.

"Good evening. I'm not early, am I?"

CHAPTER SEVEN

Before that Friday night, Katie had read a lot of books where people were described as having all the colour from their faces 'drain away', but she'd never witnessed it herself. From her position next to Steph on the sofa she was in the best position to watch her friend's face turn from healthy pink to deathly white.

"Er…" Theo had come back into the room almost guiltily.

"What?" Steph turned in anticipation.

"It wasn't quite who we all thought…."

"What?" but a different-sounding 'what?' this time. Then – "Oh my God," and the loss of colour.

"Sorry," said the blond man, looking perplexed. "Have I got the wrong night?"

"Sort of," said Theo. "Did you get my email?"

"What email?"

"Ah."

"Shit, you sent an email? Mate, I'm so sorry, I gave you the wrong address. I was going to tell you but I didn't think…"

"No, no, it's fine."

"Obviously not."

"No, really. No problem." Small, awkward pause. "Can I get you a drink?"

Katie glanced at the blond man; she'd have been melting with humiliation by now, but not a bit of it from him. He simply held out a bottle of champagne and said, "Cheers. Great to see you both. And you as well," he nodded at Katie.

"Yes, nice to meet you," she replied automatically. What was going on?

When she glanced curiously at Steph, her face looked set. White and set and her knuckles were clenched tightly round the stem of her wine glass. She looked like she'd seen the proverbial ghost.

"Theo – shall we get some glasses?" she said quietly, and they both left the room.

"Well, I'm Ed. Edward Osborne," he said to Katie. "In the

absence of any other introduction."

"I don't think they were expecting you."

"No, doesn't look like it, does it?" Ed paced the room idly, examining a couple of ornaments as he went. "I expect that was what the email said, 'sorry, ten years is too long, we've changed our minds.' Shame I didn't get it."

"Ten years?"

"Yes, I'm an old school friend. And you are?"

"Sorry – I'm Katie, Jack's mum."

"Jack?"

"A friend of the girls."

"Oh yes, the twins."

"Mmm. Gosh, ten years is a long time."

"Yes. We haven't really stayed in touch, calling Theo was a bit of a shot in the dark. That's why I brought the champagne, thought it'd ease the tension a bit."

"I'm sure it will." There was an uneasy silence. Katie dreaded to think what was going on in the kitchen. Steph hadn't looked happy, that was for sure. What was wrong with – Ed did he say his name was? He was quite attractive, whoever he was; tall, very blond, with a strong jawline and just a hint of stubble.

"So," Ed threw himself down onto the sofa next to her, "how long have you known these guys?"

"Oh, about six years. Since they all went to pre-school really."

"Jesus," Ed shook his head, "I still can't get my head around them having kids. I mean, it's great, but…"

"You didn't know?"

"No. As I said, we didn't stay in touch," he said, a touch stiffly.

"Oh. Well, yes. Twin girls. Mia and Tilly, they're great."

"Sure. I don't really have a lot to do with kids."

"No?"

"No."

The door opened and Steph and Theo returned, complete with an open bottle of champagne and four glasses. Steph looked more composed but still pale and her mouth was set in a thin line.

"Ah – count me out," Katie got to her feet, "thanks for the offer but I think I'd really rather be getting Jack home."

"Oh no Katie, do stay." Steph's eyes pleaded with hers.

"Thanks, but I can't. Tom's going to wonder where I am. Besides, it sounds like you three have a lot to catch up on."

Steph's heart was pounding so hard she was sure the others could hear it. She swallowed; her throat was dry and she felt dreadfully sick. "Are you sure?"

"Perfectly. I'll speak to you in the morning anyway." She headed for the door and stuck her head out, "Jack? Jack! Come on, we're going."

"It's OK," Steph practically leapt to her feet, "I'll go."

"Don't be silly, he'll come down. Jack! I mean it. One... two... three..."

"Muuuum," came a distant grumble. "For God's sake."

"Don't say that. Come on, we've got to go, it's late, and Steph and Theo have got a visitor."

Steph closed her eyes in silent helplessness and acknowledgement of what was about to happen.

"Ooh, who? Who is it?" came two excited shouts, and seconds later the living room door was filled by two identically flushed faces, framed by long, blonde hair in Hannah Montana pyjamas. "Who is it Mummy? Is it someone we know?"

Ed stood up, "Hi."

The girls looked him up and down, "Oh. No, it's not. Come on Jack, let's go and hide."

"Er – girls – that is not very polite. Come here," said Theo sternly and the girls slunk back into the room. Theo took a hand of each, "Ed, these are our daughters," he said proudly, "Mia," he raised the left hand, "and Tilly," he raised the right.

"Hello Mia and Tilly." He could have picked them out in a crowd as Steph's children, Ed thought. The same fine features and full mouths. Same mischievous eyes. "Nice to meet you," he said.

They giggled, "Mmm, yes," one shot a glance at the other and they wriggled on the spot. Theo sighed, "Go on then girls, off you go – to bed."

"Noooo!"

"Yes, it's late. Sorry," he directed to Ed, "it's a bit chaotic here this evening, sorry to drop you straight into it. If we'd known..."

"No problem."

"I'll take them up," Steph said quickly, and before anyone could object she'd swept them out of the room, shutting the door behind her. Ah, peace, Ed thought as a swell of silence descended.

"Here you go mate," Theo handed him a glass of champagne. "Look – really sorry about all that, we seem to have our wires crossed a bit. I hadn't exactly cancelled, just changed the location, but when I didn't hear from you I assumed you couldn't make it."

Ed took a sip from his glass, crystal, he noticed. "Yeah, I gave you my old email. I should have given you the work one. I didn't think it would matter."

Theo shrugged, "Doesn't really. Anyway – cheers! Great to see you again. Where have you been hiding all these years? Sit down, sit down."

Upstairs, Steph wondered if she were in the grip of a panic attack. Her chest felt tight, her heart was racing and her mind whirled. She felt totally disorientated. This just should not be happening to her.

"Mummy, can we read? Pleeeeease?"

"OK, five minutes." Steph said automatically, picking up crayons and toys. This could not be happening. It couldn't be true. The figure from her nightmarish dreams had just casually turned up on her doorstep like some ghastly horror film. Why hadn't she guessed this might happen? Why hadn't she prepared herself even slightly? And why was he here? He couldn't, surely, have put two and two together, could he? Heard about the girls, done some sums... Christ, *no*.

"I cancelled like I told you," Theo had hissed at her in the kitchen, "he just didn't get the email."

"How very convenient."

"It's true! Why on earth would I lie?"

"Oh – who knows? Because you wanted him to come and I didn't?"

"Steph, please, not now. We'll talk later," he'd said, and left the room, leaving her staring after him. She'd taken a minute or two to compose herself before she followed. What the fuck was she supposed to say to him? How quickly could she get him out? God, this was a nightmare. Worse than she had ever envisaged. He had to be kept away from the girls, he had to be. Steph felt panicked tears prick at the back of her eyes.

"Mummy! Tilly's got the book I want to read!"

"Well find another."

"But I was reading it," Mia scowled.

"Never mind. Just find another one or go to sleep." She left the room and leant her forehead against the cool wall outside, taking deep, calming breaths. It's OK, it's fine, she told herself. He was here, but so what? He was hardly going to guess, was he? Neither was Theo, the thought wouldn't occur to them in a thousand years. Didn't need to occur to them. Theo was the twins' father. In every way. Except the most important. Shit. All Steph needed to do was keep calm, keep quiet and keep Ed the hell out of their lives.

"Steph!"

"Yes?"

"There's some very nice champagne down here getting flat waiting for you."

"I'll be down in a minute."

She went into their en suite bathroom and switched the light on to look in the mirror. God, she looked awful, pale and with mascara smudged under her eyes. Very reminiscent of the morning after – no, don't think that, I will not think that, Steph willed herself. She splashed a little cold water on her face and added some blusher to her alabaster cheeks. She wiped under her eyes carefully and reapplied her mascara. A touch of lip gloss, she fluffed out her hair and then she was done.

"Hi," she walked back into the room as casually as she could. "Sorry about that, they're in bed now. Hello Ed, good to see you."

"And you, you look wonderful." He jumped up and gave her a quick peck on the cheek. She was wearing a nice, light perfume.

"Thanks." Steph sat down and reached for her glass, wondering if anyone else could tell her hands were shaking.

"Ed's been filling me in on the last ten years," Theo said, grinning at her.

"Oh yes?"

"Mmm. He's a lawyer now. Almost partner apparently."

"Well, I wouldn't say that, but I'm confident I'm on the right track."

"Fantastic." Steph said politely.

"Isn't it?" replied Theo. "I was saying to him, I would never have put him down as a lawyer. And a corporate one as well."

"And I wasn't sure whether that was a compliment or an insult."

Steph smiled. "So whereabouts do you live?"

"Not too far from Tinford actually. I still see your mum occasionally."

"Really? She hasn't said."

"No, I mean literally see her. Walking that dog, usually."

"Oh, right." Steph couldn't help herself, she sat there drinking in his every feature, eyes roaming over his face, studying his mouth, lips, nose, eyes and hair. Trying, and not trying, to see the similarities between this stranger and her precious girls. Were his hands like theirs? The shape of his face? It had been so long since she'd seen him, and she'd ripped up every photo she'd ever had, that she'd forgotten what he looked like. She watched him almost fearfully, petrified that she would see a resemblance that would ricochet the truth into her conscious mind. That somewhere there would be an inextricable link forged, a line drawn between them – and him. It was a strange juxtaposition of desperately wanting to and desperately not.

Ed watched her watching him. He couldn't remember absolutely but he thought the last time he'd seen her was the night they'd slept together, all that time ago, however long it was. She was looking at him very intently right now. And she was looking good herself, better than he'd expected. He wasn't quite sure what that was, but definitely someone a little heavier, not quite so well-groomed as this Steph was. And she hadn't changed, she still had that delicate, ethereal quality to her that made her so appealing. Quick, light, graceful movements. Her eyes looked charged with something, he couldn't tell what. She caught his gaze for a minute, then quickly looked away. She couldn't still hold a candle for him could she? No, he dismissed the thought as soon as he'd had it. That was ridiculous.

"Top-up?" Theo proffered the bottle.

"Yes please."

This was nice, Theo was surprised to find himself thinking. Ed seemed like a thoroughly decent chap – even if he was a lawyer. He was straight-talking, intelligent and witty. Good company. Theo wondered briefly why he had no girlfriend, then thought perhaps he had more than one. He seemed the type. And he wasn't at all what Theo had been expecting, not what he'd thought Ed would turn into. This tall, confident, well-educated stranger bore no resemblance to the awkward, geeky teenage boy he and Steph had known. He was better. A better version of Ed. He'd grown up and matured and made some good decisions along the way, apparently. It was a nice surprise.

Theo topped up his own glass; Steph hadn't finished hers. Too terrified of getting drunk, she drank her champagne in tiny sips. How very ladylike, Ed thought approvingly. Steph tried to tune out of their conversation and concentrate on calming her thoughts.

"I hope you don't mind Ed, but we'll be looking at a takeaway tonight," Steph heard Theo say.

"That's fine. But honestly, if it's a problem, I can take myself off–"

Theo held his hand up, "No, not at all. Won't hear of it. Would Indian suit you?"

"Sounds great."

Steph's heart sank further, this evening was turning into a never-ending nightmare. Tension coursed through her veins, making her jumpy. She could feel her teeth gritted and her muscles taut as she perched on the edge of the sofa.

And surprisingly, some new emotion was making its unwelcome way into her mind; gently but insistently probing against her barriers. Because it was all very well being scared that Theo would find out, but when that fear had receded a bit, she could sense a nasty guilt waiting in the wings to pounce. Over time she had almost managed to turn Ed into a fairytale person, alive in her mind but not in reality. He had receded so far into the mists of time that she could almost live comfortably with the truth. But having Ed sitting in front of her for the first time in ten years had brought her up sharply – he was a real person. And more than that, she really had done that awful thing. The events of ten years ago had become so distant and fuzzy that it was fairly easy to pretend that they'd never happened, or shove them to the furthest recesses of her mind at least. But with Ed here, he was The Truth – in technicolour. He was real, it did exist, things were not as she had made them out to be. God, this was horrible.

"Steph?" Theo was looking at her, his deep, soft eyes searching hers.

"What?"

"Ed was asking how you fill your day."

"Oh – sorry, miles away. I, er, look after the girls really. And the house. School runs, washing, cleaning, that kind of thing."

"A kept woman?" he grinned at her.

"I suppose."

"And you've got your committee work," Theo said loyally.

"Truly a kept woman." Ed was surprised, he hadn't expected to see dynamic Steph as a paltry housewife.

"Oh no, she does some important stuff, don't you darling? What's that thing that's coming up the weekend after next?"

"The Murder-Mystery night, Cath's Committee fund-raising thing."

"Murder-Mystery?" Ed said with genuine interest. "I did one of those years ago at a corporate event, it was great! The actors were good and everybody really got into it. Fabulous. How are the plans coming along?"

"Really well, fine."

"You should have a good night."

"I hope so."

"Guess it gives you something to do, so you don't get too bored as well. Some housewives do, don't they? Not that there's anything wrong with being a housewife though, a nice, solid family base. Very traditional of you Theo."

"We like it, don't we darling?"

Steph nodded; her heart could have melted with love for Theo in that instant. So kind, so genuine, so uncomplicated. Just a good, honest, caring man. Husband. Father. And what was she? Steph couldn't go there. It was too dark, too unexplored.

After a few attempts at engaging Steph in conversation, Ed gave up. She was resisting all his efforts, she wouldn't even laugh at his jokes. What was up with her? He considered mentioning Julia at one point, but it was years since he'd seen her and then the moment had passed, and to be honest he was just enjoying catching up. It was such a long time since they'd all been in a room together. Quite surreal really. They were obviously all a lot older and wiser and slightly more jaded, the buzz of youth had vanished, but that was good. That was fine. Now they could form a more adult friendship.

Once or twice Ed had found himself nearly stumbling onto the subject of Steph and Theo's moonlight flit from Tinford, but he had refrained from it each time. It made him feel a little awkward. Old wounds didn't heal quite as well as he'd expected. It wasn't that he minded still, but when both your best friends just buggered off without telling you, it was bound to be a bit sore. They'd even sent him a postcard from Vannes that summer, promising they'd call when they were back, but they hadn't. Hadn't bothered, he'd supposed – both at the time and now.

When the bottles of champagne were both finished and dinner ordered and eaten, Ed eventually rose to his feet and phoned for a cab.

"Or stay, if you like. We've a spare room," Theo offered generously. Steph flashed him a glance of unadulterated horror.

"No, it's fine. I've overstayed my welcome as it is."

"No, you haven't."

"Ed probably wants to wake up in his own bed," Steph said.

"It's been great though, we should do it again. Maybe you could both come to mine? Except I don't really cook. Or we could go out? How about that? A nice meal somewhere?"

"Oh, well, the girls…" Steph said swiftly.

"Oh yes, I forgot. No, that's no good."

"You're more than welcome here," Theo said, "and to be honest it's probably easier for us."

"I think I heard your cab." Steph was holding the living room door open for him.

"Look – thanks, both of you. I'll be in touch."

She followed him to the door in a gesture of courtesy and he leant in to kiss her cheek but she ducked her head at the last minute.

"Seriously, that was a great night. It was good to catch up."

Steph found herself staring straight into his very blue eyes. "Yes, wasn't it?"

"So we'll do it again sometime?"

"Of course, of course."

"Thanks for the evening. Take care Steph." And with a quick wave, he was gone.

Steph closed the front door behind him and breathed a huge sigh of relief. Thank the gods that was over.

"Nightcap?" Theo offered.

Steph shook her head, "Not for me, I'm tired."

"Did you have a good time?" Theo came to sit next to her on the sofa. "I thought he was great."

"Yeah, it was all right."

Theo turned to look at her, "Just all right? Steph, we used to be best friends! He knows us inside out, it was fantastic to catch up, I thought he'd turned into a really decent guy."

"Theo – we knew him years ago. Ten years. We've moved on. Yes, it was an OK evening, but I didn't think that much of him and I'm not bothered about seeing him again." Careful, Steph, careful. Play it well.

Theo stared, "I can't believe you can be that nonchalant about it."

"Why not?"

"I thought... Oh never mind."

"I did tell you I wasn't interested. Look, all over now. Done. Shall we go to bed?"

CHAPTER EIGHT

Before she'd thought it was like a nightmare, but she was wrong. Nightmares vanished once you woke up. But when Steph woke the next morning the truth crashed over her again, so tangibly that she was surprised it didn't wake Theo. But it didn't, he lay on his side snoring gently. The thick, floor-length curtains locked out all the light and Steph lay flat on her back, fists clenched and heart racing. Panic and guilt raced around in her chest and her stomach felt tight. This was horrible. She was close to tears and it wasn't even seven o' clock in the morning.

Ed was back in her life. The unthinkable had finally happened.

How could she remove him? How had he even found them? In all the shock of last night Steph hadn't even thought to ask how he'd got their number. It was a bit random after all, ten years had passed, they had no mutual friends. Had he been stalking them for years? Did he secretly know everything about them? She truly felt herself to be in the wilderness of paranoia.

"Theo!" she turned over and shook his shoulder, "Theo, are you awake?"

"I am now," he murmured sleepily and not completely happily.

"How did Ed get our number?"

"What?"

"How did Ed get our number?" she repeated urgently.

"I've no idea. Why are you asking me now?"

"I think it's weird. He wouldn't have had it, not after eleven years. How did he get it?"

"James gave it to him. Steph, please, it's early and I'm tired." He burrowed further under the duvet.

"James who?"

"James Mears. From school. I did some business with him a couple of years ago and he's friends with Ed."

"Why didn't you tell me?"

"Tell you what?"

Good point, Steph thought, and lay back down. OK, so that was a partial explanation. But why now? What had prompted him?

"Why now Theo?"

"Why now *what*? For God's sake Steph," he said pleadingly, "what is this all about?"

"I just think it's odd, why he's suddenly come back onto the scene ten years later."

"I think he said he'd seen your Facebook profile or something."

"But he can't, he's not my friend."

"Don't start that –"

"I mean on Facebook. He'd have to be my friend to see my profile, I'd have to accept him and I haven't."

"Well, I don't know then. I'm going back to sleep now."

Steph slipped out of bed and pulled on her dressing gown. Ed had lied. Why? What was the real reason? Could it be the girls? But he'd barely reacted when he'd seen them, despite her illogical fear that their shared genetic information would ring a silent, unshared, alarm for him.

Downstairs looked the same. Doors shut, curtains drawn but no lingering scent of Ed. Her fear receded slightly.

"Mummy." Tilly, like a little ghost, suddenly appeared in front of her.

"Gosh, you frightened me! Good morning darling. Sleep well?"

"Yes. Mia's not awake."

"I expect she's worn out from last night." Steph filled the kettle and slid it onto the Aga. Tilly slid onto a bar stool, "What are we doing today Mummy?"

"Not much, I don't think. We'll wait till Daddy wakes up and see."

"Maybe the cinema?"

"What's on?"

"High School Musical 2."

"Maybe," said Steph vaguely. "Weetabix or Cornflakes?"

"Pancakes?"

There was a sudden beep from Steph's mobile, '*Hi,hope hvnt woken u.want 2 knw all abt Ed.coffee later?*' Oh Christ. That was all she needed, Katie was like a dog with a bone when she wanted to know something.

'*Nothing 2 tell*,' she texted back.

'*Rubbish*' came the reply. '*I reckon he's an ex!!!!!!*'

"Mummy? Pancakes?"

"What? Oh, I don't think we have enough flour."

"Yes we do," said Theo behind her.

"Bloody hell!" Steph nearly jumped out of her skin and dropped her phone. Hastily she recovered it and deleted the text.

"Morning to you too. What's made you so edgy?" Theo asked curiously as the kettle began to boil. "Teabags or tea leaves?"

"Teabags. Nothing, God, why is everyone nagging me this morning? I thought you were asleep actually."

"No, you woke me up."

"Mummy says there's no flour for pancakes."

"There is, I saw it yesterday. Top shelf in the pasta cupboard."

Should she answer? Should she tell her? Should she admit half the truth? All of the truth? None of the truth? Steph stared wildly at her phone. '*OK, coffee l8tr.*'

'*Luigi's, *buck's, yours or mine??*'

'*Luigi's.*' Steph thought back briefly to their last shared coffee; she hadn't wanted to shatter Katie's illusion of their perfect life then. But now it looked like Ed had done that all on his own.

Theo slid an arm around her waist and gave her a gentle squeeze, "You OK?"

"Yes, I'm fine."

"Who are you texting?"

"Katie."

"Why?"

"She wants to have coffee later."

"On a Saturday?" Theo frowned.

"Yes, what's wrong with that?"

"Nothing. It's usually a weekday thing, that's all."

"Well not this time. Is that OK?"

Theo looked carefully at his wife. She seemed snappy and not her usual self. Maybe she was tired. Or hormonal.

"I know, why don't you go and have a bath?" he said at last. "I'll make some pancakes for the girls and you have a nice, long soak. How about that?"

Nice idea – why did he have to sound so patronising? But – "OK." Steph glanced at Tilly but she was engrossed in a comic.

Upstairs in the mirror her reflection gave her feelings away. She looked white and drawn. And she felt a bit sick. But she refused to let herself imagine what that set of symptoms might mean. She could not be pregnant, that was unthinkable. It was bound to be the stress. Steph felt so stretched by tension that she thought she might snap at any moment. She ran a rose-scented bubble bath and slid under the water gratefully.

****

Katie looked up to see Steph weaving her way through the tables towards her. Being a Saturday morning, it was busy in Luigi's. It was a family-run, Italian café, full of dark-haired brothers and sisters shouting unintelligible, urgent, foreign things at one another. It reminded Steph of something out of the Sopranos, the soap that was 'so over', according to Katie.

Steph wore her usual high-heeled boots and Hobbs coat, same gorgeous jeans and close-fitting cashmere sweater, Katie noticed, but her face was very different. She looked pale and worried, very tense. Even expertly-applied make-up could not disguise the dark circles under her eyes.

"Morning," Katie looked up and smiled.

"How are you?"

"I'm fine. You?"

"Fine."

"I got you a caramel latte."

"Thanks."

"You look tired."

"I didn't sleep so well last night." Steph pulled off her scarf and worried at it with her fingernails.

There was a small pause before Katie decided to cut to the chase, "Steph – what's going on?" she asked gently. "You seem so – different. Not yourself. Is something worrying you?"

Steph looked at her; how could she even begin to explain what was worrying her? That her whole life was built on a heap of lies that could come crashing down any second. That everything she held so dear was too fragile to rely on, that somehow she'd lived this same life for ten years and only now was the true precariousness of the situation apparent to her. She felt embarrassed, guilty and to her horror a pushing sensation in the bridge of her nose warned her tears might be about to fall.

"*Steph*," Katie reached over and took her hand, "God, what is it?"

Steph fought to control her trembling lip, "If I told you, you wouldn't believe me."

"Try me."

"I'm serious. You think you know me but you don't. You know a version of me, but not the real me. The Steph you think you know would never do what I've done." Two tears fell into her lap.

"What are you talking about? Here." Katie reached into her handbag and pushed a wad of tissues at Steph. "Is it something to do with Ed?"

Her head shot up, "Why would you ask that?"

"Because until he showed up, you seemed fine, and now you're sitting here crying. Whatever it is, I'm not going to judge you sweetheart, honestly."

"You think I've been sleeping with him don't you?"

"No. Have you?"

"No," Steph sniffed, "well, not recently."

"Were you with Theo at the time?"

"God, no."

"Well what's the problem?"

There was a long silence. Steph stared down at the table, half-distracted by the noise around her and half-locked into her own world. She didn't – couldn't – meet Katie's eye.

"The problem is…" she exhaled a long breath, "is worse."

"Worse than what?"

"Worse than infidelity."

"Oh." What could be worse in Steph's world than being unfaithful to her kind, adoring husband? But before Katie could properly process the thought, Steph spoke. Her mouth was so dry with nerves that her tongue clicked audibly against her palate with every word.

"Ed is the twins' father. Not Theo." There – the words were out.

There was no response from Katie and after a long, long time Steph looked up at her. Shock was written across her face, "You aren't joking are you? *Jesus* Christ. Shit. That is – that is really – I don't know what that is."

"It's true."

Katie's face creased with confusion, "What… *how*?"

"It's complicated. We were eighteen, it was our first time, we were drunk and – I got pregnant. That's all there is to it. I was so unlucky. It should never have happened, Ed and I were friends. I got together with Theo shortly after. The day after, actually, and we left Tinford then. I assumed I could put the whole mess behind me, Theo didn't know anything, but then I found out."

"Why didn't you…?"

"Have a termination? I couldn't. I just couldn't." Steph pushed the fear to the back of her mind.

"So you just… carried on and didn't say anything?"

"What could I say? I was mad about Theo, had been for ages. If I'd have said anything he'd have left me. I couldn't risk that."

"And you'd rather *this*?"

"Well I didn't know that then did I? I was eighteen for God's sake, a child."

"Is there no chance you could be wrong?"

"No. Theo and I didn't – not for a while."

Katie sat back in her chair. "I can see now why you were so horrified last night."

"I never in a million years thought Ed would worm his way back into our lives. Never. We were never as close with him as he would have liked, it was always me and Theo. We left him behind when we left Tinford, I didn't think he'd bother to come looking for us eleven years later."

"I can see your point. What are you going to do?"

Steph shrugged, "What can I do? Keep quiet, keep calm and keep him as far away from us as I can. I'm terrified he'll guess."

"How would he guess?"

"The girls are blonde, neither me nor Theo are. There are bound to be resemblances as they get older. Maybe Ed will guess, maybe he'll come back and it'll just click into place, he'll somehow know. Maybe Theo will get suspicious, maybe I'll get drunk and say something stupid." Her fears came tumbling out, the words falling over themselves to be released first.

"Hey, hey – calm down. Nothing even near to that is happening, and I think you're lucky in that they look extraordinarily like you, actually."

"Maybe. But I can't rely on that."

"No. Have you thought about telling Theo?"

Steph felt like vomiting, the idea was abhorrent. Katie saw her face turn ashen. "OK, maybe not," she said quickly.

"Believe me – I have thought about all the options. I got myself into this hideous mess, it's mine to deal with," she said sadly, shredding a paper napkin.

"You've got me," Katie said sympathetically.

"Thanks, I appreciate that. I just cannot believe that this is me – that this is how I have to live my life. I'm the luckiest woman around, happily married to a husband I adore, two beautiful children, gorgeous home – it should all be so perfect, but there's an ugly, gaping wound across the whole lot."

"People make mistakes," Katie tried.

"Not usually this bad. I thought – I thought it was all behind me, to be honest. It was all so long ago, it was like a bad dream. I never, *ever*, thought we'd see Ed again. I thought I could forget about it. I was stupid, so stupid. And naïve."

"And young."

Steph bit her lip, "I guess this is the price I have to pay. I guess this is what happens to people like me."

"You're not *like* anything," Katie mustered together a coherent thought. "You got caught in something you couldn't cope with and made a risky decision. That doesn't make you a bad person."

"But that's not how it feels!" Steph burst out. "My husband – my children – every day I'm deceiving them. The girls are so innocent and I'm exploiting that, Theo is so trusting and I'm exploiting that too."

"Steph, I'm no expert, not by any means, but there is an argument that says what they don't know won't hurt them. Either that or come clean. Those are your two options."

Steph stared, "I can't tell him," she said finally. "I just can't. It would kill him. I never meant for any of this to happen."

"You've only got one option then."

"I know."

"Can you do it?"

"I'll have to," Steph said without conviction.

"No, don't say it like that. If you want to – you *have* to. If you want to save your life the way it is, you *have* to. This is serious, no half-measures here Steph."

"I can do it. Keep him away, stay calm, it'll be fine."

Katie shrugged, "It sounds simple but that's pretty much it. There's no reason for anyone to suspect is there?"

"No."

"Not even Ed?"

"Rationally speaking, I doubt it would even cross his mind. Subjectively speaking, I'm terrified he might just guess. Just by looking at them or something."

"Good, that's good. Don't forget that the rest of the world operates on a rational level as opposed to your subjective one, so that's really good. God, Steph – I can't believe this," Katie shook her head. "I really can't. How have you kept this a secret for so long? Does anyone else know?"

"No one, I swear. It's been a secret for so long because… when it's something this bad you can't think about it every day or it would drive you mad, you kind of push it to the back of your mind. It doesn't become part of your everyday life. And even when I did think about it, which was almost never, I got such a stab of guilt that I soon stopped. And over time it doesn't stay being the truth, it becomes something that doesn't matter any more. And it would have been fine, all of it, if only bloody Ed hadn't rung."

"Well he did, and now you have to manage. But don't panic, that's the important bit. Stay calm, like you said, stay normal. I'm sure there are hundreds of women in your situation."

Steph's head jerked up hopefully, "Really?"

"Yes – probably. There must be. You won't be alone."

"I feel alone, I feel dreadfully alone."

Katie wanted to say that she knew how Steph felt, but she didn't. Of course she couldn't.

"Not any more you're not."

"Excuse me – more drinks?" A waitress loomed up between them, shattering their privacy.

"Er – no, thanks. We're fine." Both mugs were untouched. Steph looked at her watch, "I should go. I've been gone an hour, Theo will be wondering where I am, it's the weekend. I'm sorry if I've shocked you?"

"A bit. But it isn't that bad, really. Don't worry, you can trust me. And talk to me, if you ever need to. Any time."

"Thank you," Steph smiled gratefully, winding her scarf around her neck. "I really mean it. You're great." She bent down and gave Katie a hug.

"Don't be too hard on yourself."

Steph shook her head, "I'll try."

Katie watched her walk away, like she'd watched her approach the table an hour ago. What had happened in an hour... she almost couldn't believe it. But for the state of Steph, she wouldn't believe it. That perfect little family unit was a sham. Theo wasn't their dad. It was too huge for her mind to process properly. Katie could feel her brain whirling with shock. Of all the things she'd ever thought Steph might say, that little revelation had to be right down in the 'no way, no chance, not ever' category. How could someone live like that? How could Steph live within that enormous lie? OK, so she hadn't actually lied to Theo, Katie doubted whether he'd ever questioned his paternity, but she had allowed him to labour under a bloody big false illusion for ten years. Her mind wandered; what sort of person did that make Steph? Not the one Katie thought she knew, certainly.

****

Theo and the girls were playing some raucous game when Steph got back.

"Hi darling, nice time?" Theo yelled into the hall.

"Yeah, it was good. What's going on in here?" She appeared in the doorway, looking pale, but more composed than before.

"Barbie versus Tinkerbell, to see who's the strongest."

"Ah."

"Join in?" he suggested, grinning at her from his prone position on the floor.

"Maybe in a minute."

"How are you feeling?"

"What do you mean?"

"You looked tired earlier."

"No, I'm fine."

"Mummy, guess what?" Mia said.

"What?"

"Daddy said Tilly and I could do an own-a-pony day at the stables. In the holidays. Maybe with Bethany and Jessica."

Theo groaned and rolled over to hide his face, "Mia! That was a secret."

"Did he now?" Steph tried to look stern, but couldn't. "That'll be a treat. I was saving that," she muttered to Theo.

"I'm sorry," he jumped up and encircled her with his arms, "they've begged and begged all morning and High School Musical 2 was booked out, so I didn't see why not."

"You could have asked me."

"Sorry sweetheart, I just couldn't resist my girls."

The words stabbed at her unkindly, "No problem. We'll have to organise some jodhpurs for them now."

"We can do that. Hey," Theo consulted his watch, "it's almost lunchime. Who fancies TGIs?"

"Me!"

"Me! Me! Me!" Two blonde heads jumped and down, pulling at Theo's jumper. "I want to go Daddy, I do, I do."

"Yes, I think I got that Mia."

"Me too, I want to. Can we have Coke?"

"I should think so. Are you feeling up to it?" he asked Steph.

"What do you mean?"
"Not too tired?"
"No."
"Or sick? Or..."
"No Theo, I'm not anything. OK? Let's go."

It was in the car on the way there that he finally said something, and Steph didn't see it coming at all. That was his way; placid and malleable 99% of the time, but with a will of iron for the other 1%.

"So – good to see Ed last night."

A fraction of a second pause, "Yes." Deliberately casual.

"When do you fancy getting together with him again?"

White-hot panic shot through Steph, "We've been through this," she muttered. "I'm not bothered to see him again."

"No, but I am. And you don't *mind*, do you?" he glanced at her curiously. "If I invite him over for a drink, or go out or whatever. You don't actually mind?"

What could she say? "No. No, I don't mind."

"Good. Oh, Julia rang for you this morning. I told her you'd ring back later." Conversation over. *Fait accompli.*

"Who were you talking about Daddy?"

"The man who came over last night. He's an old friend and he's called Ed. He was our friend at school, before you two were even born. Can you imagine that?"

"Your friend from school?" Tilly wrinkled her nose. "He must be really old."

"Not that old."

This is hideous, Steph thought, completely hideous. And yet a part of her wanted to laugh, it was so absurd. She felt dulled, her senses so overworked of late that they no longer reacted as they usually would. I am sitting in the car, she thought, listening to my husband discuss the biological father of my children, with my children, and none of them know. But I do. You couldn't make it up.

****

Ed threw the newspaper down onto his coffee table and lay back on the sofa in his hotel, hands settled comfortably behind his head, Cappuccino in front of him. Ahhhh, eleven o' clock on a Saturday morning and nothing whatsoever to do for a couple of hours. Perfect. Thank God he'd driven down the night before, very sensible idea. For a second he contemplated ringing Jenna for an exploratory chat, but swiftly decided against it. That would tie up his whole weekend and she'd only just let up in her persistent calls and emails. What was it with women? Why could they never be happy with just sex? Why was it always the whole kit and caboodle? It made things very difficult.

It was a oft-debated concept, but Ed reckoned his perfect woman would be tall-ish (but not taller than him), slim (without being skinny), large-ish tits (without being overwhelming, say a C-cup or so), long hair, definitely long hair, and definitely brunette. Perhaps surprisingly, he didn't much go for blondes. Probably something to do with being a blonde himself. She'd also have to be pretty, nice mouth, intelligent (without being fierce) and definitely no feminist-types. In fact, Ed realised, his perfect woman would be a lot like Steph Hammond. Except taller and not married to Theo of course. It had been good seeing them last night, Theo was a nicer bloke than he'd remembered. Sort of more rounded and worldly. As he would be, being ten years older. Steph and Theo had been kind of snippy at school sometimes to him, a bit close and giggly between themselves. Even when Steph had gone off Theo and spent more time with Ed, he'd never truly felt involved with her. But last night had been good, good to catch up and see old friends, and they'd been pleased to see him too – he thought. Although Steph had definitely been a bit funny. Off, not as open and friendly as he'd remembered. She'd looked worried all evening too, Ed wondered suddenly if she'd ever told Theo about sleeping with him. Probably, married couples told each other everything, didn't they? It was one of the – many – things that put him off marriage. That was probably why she'd been funny, because she hadn't seen him since. Women were like that. Or maybe she'd finally realised what she'd missed out on. Ed had waited long enough for that moment.

CHAPTER NINE

It must be sod's law that all the most important things in life happened at the most inconvenient time, it really must. There is no way that this could be a coincidence. It was six thirty on Monday morning, the Monday before the Murder-Mystery party when there was a very important, last-minute meeting and the Monday when the girls had to be in school extra early because they had a violin lesson at eight o'clock. And that made it a bad morning in itself, it was hard enough trying to get Mia out of bed as it was without the added problem of violin. It had also transpired to be the Monday morning when Steph's period decided to start.

She hadn't quite been able to believe it when she had seen the streak of blood in her knickers, it had been such a shock. She didn't know why, it was hardly unusual, it was just... she'd thought... deep down she'd thought that she and Theo might have done it. It would have been such a perfect thing at such an awful time that it seemed perverse that it hadn't happened. She'd been semi-dreading it, and now she didn't need to. Steph was faintly astonished. And her first thought was for Theo. Poor Theo, he was going to be so disappointed. He'd tried to hide it, but Steph had seen how much he had pinned his hopes on her becoming pregnant this month. She sank down onto the lid of the toilet and tears blurred her eyes; poor, poor Theo. She couldn't even get this right for him. Was it karma? Could a foetus tell when it wasn't wanted and refuse to implant? Roughly she wiped away the tears, it wouldn't look good to turn up at this meeting with red eyes. There was a sharp tap on the door, "Steph? You nearly done?"

"Yes, yeah, nearly finished. Hang on."

"I've got to go in twenty minutes. Want a coffee?" there was a burbled exchange of voices. "Mia says she feels sick."

"Tell Mia she's still doing violin," Steph called back, hastily gathering her clothes and a couple of tampons. She'd think about this later, not now. It could wait.

They managed to be only five minutes late in the end, and the twins went one way while Steph hurried in the other.

"Coffee?" Ian said, looking up as she entered the library.

"Please, that would be great." Steph sank into the only free seat. There were ten of them there, Ian caught her looking and leant over to mutter, "Glad to see you attending the three line whip."

"Who…?" but the question was left unfinished as Julia swept in.

"Morning, morning, thank you all for coming. Sorry I'm late, I was flapping a bit, I've been away all weekend and I couldn't find my file anywhere."

"Anywhere nice Julia?" Ian asked politely.

"A Uni reunion in Cardiff, so it was nice. Good to catch up with people, as you can imagine."

"Yes, absolutely. See any good friends?"

"One or two." A slow smile spread across her face. "In fact, you might all be meeting an old friend of mine; I've invited him to the Murder-Mystery."

"That's nice. Plenty of tickets left."

"Really? How many?" She was instantly alert.

"No, it's not a disaster, don't worry, I'd say we've got fifty left in total."

"Oh, OK, that's fine. It allows for last minute revellers. Now, do you all have your notes with you? Good, good. Right – where do we start? Does anyone have any problems or any queries? Excellent, confidence – that's what I like. Now as you all know this is *the* event of St Catherine's year. The focus point, the gala evening, the glittering night to show how well we can entertain." Steph wanted to point out that they were talking about a school, but Julia was in full flow. "No holds barred, pull out all the stops! Ian – have you sorted out the bar?"

"Yes, everything's done. I'm going to go and pick up the alcohol on Friday morning. We're getting it from the supermarket on a sale or return basis, unopened bottles obviously. Or else anyone can buy leftover wine or beer to take home."

"Excellent. Who's running the bar?"

"One of the fathers, ex-barman I believe. He volunteered."

"A father?" Julia said sharply. "I hope he's going to look professional?"

"As I said Julia, he's ex-barstaff. He'll be fine." Ian said patiently.

"OK. All right. Marion, did you get all the decorations in?"

"Oh yes. We've got leftover tinsel and things in the store cupboard, but I've organised drapes to cover the walls."

"Sounds good, what colour?"

"White."

"Okaaaaay," Julia ran an eye down her list. "Seating plan? Who was doing that?"

"Me," Steph said. "I was."

"And?"

"And it's done, it's here," Steph passed her a piece of paper. Julia didn't even glance at it before she tucked it into her file. "I'm sure it's fine. I'll look at it later. And caterers? They're all done?"

"Yes, they're coming in at 6pm on the night and they'll be in the kitchen from then on. I don't think they're doing major end-to-end cooking in there but I'll speak to Denise anyway about to how to leave it on Friday."

"But they will be ready to serve by 7.30pm?"

"Yes."

"Good. And drinks on the door? Who's doing that?"

"Um – that wasn't me."

"No? But I thought – who is it then?"

"Actually Julia, when we first started planning this last year you said you were going to ask Paul to do it?" Ian said gently.

"What – my Paul?" She looked genuinely astonished.

"Yes."

"Oh, crap. Are you sure?" She looked pale all of a sudden.

"Fairly. Look, don't worry, it's only a small job, I'm sure we can find someone. Last minute thing."

"But that's what I didn't want, no last minute things! It's so important that everything runs smoothly on the night and whoever's doing the drinks on the door is going to be the first face that people see, it's terribly important. We can't have just anyone doing it."

Steph glanced round the table, everyone was looking down or fiddling with their notes. Specific roles like this were not popular, they tied you to the spot too much and prevented you from joining in like a real guest.

"Does anyone have any suggestions? Know anyone who might be up for doing it?"

"No."

"Er – don't think so."

"Not really."

"Couldn't say."

"I'll do it," Steph said, surprising herself and feeling her face turn red.

"You?"

"Yes. Why not? My bit's over now, I've nothing to do on the night, bar just turning up. I know most of the parents, they'll know me..." She felt a twinge of pain in her abdomen.

"Yes, I think that's a good idea," she said firmly, dragging her attention back. "Ian?"

"Yes I'm fine with it. No one else wanted to do it did they?" There were a lot of shaken heads and murmurings. "OK, that's it then. Steph, you are the face of Murder-Mystery Night 2008."

"Hardly, I'm just handing out glasses of – what am I handing out glasses of?"

"Oh – Cava. We couldn't stretch to champagne in the end," Julia said regretfully. "But that's a relief. Just make sure you look presentable, hair and clothes and so on. I'd do it myself but I'm overseeing general co-ordination so I can't be held down to something so specific, you know how it is. It's a very important role though."

"Don't worry, I'll be fine."

"I'm sure. Oh and Mike, did you get hold of him?"

"Yes I did, and I think Helen was going to do a playlist?"

"I've done it Julia, I'm seeing him on Thursday so I'll give it to him then."

"Well done, well done."

Her bit over, Steph sat back and allowed the rest of the meeting to wash over her. It rumbled on endlessly; guests, tables, plans, bar, tickets, fund-raising, dress code for the Cath's, last minute licence check. Her stomach ached uncomfortably, she thought vaguely of what she was going to say to Theo tonight. She couldn't just tell him that she'd come on and leave it there, she needed to tell him more. Explain that she wanted to postpone the baby plans. Except she wasn't sure how she could explain that to him when she didn't really understand fully herself yet.

****

Ed didn't get in from work until late on Monday night, there had been an awkward last minute hitch with one of the contract clauses.

"Bloody Jack Higgins," he muttered to himself, throwing his suit jacket onto the chair. It was ten-thirty and he was starving and shattered. He grabbed a phone and dialled the number of the local Thai place while he made himself a strong coffee. He still hadn't shaken the hangover from Saturday night.

God, but that had been a weekend. Exhausting, but the best fun he'd had in ages. Cardiff wasn't the dive he'd expected either, and his old mates hadn't let him down. Starting with pints at twelve they'd steadily drunk their way through fourteen hours. Pub after pub after pub then back to the hotel, which was where Julia had joined them, glasses of champagne in the hotel bar, quick shower then off to the Indian for a curry and bottles of Cobra. More bars and then finally they'd ended up in a strip club; and to her credit Julia had stuck with the boys all night. The rest of the girls had peeled away at about ten, pleading tiredness, but Julia had stuck by Ed's side all night. He smiled at the memory, it had been like having one of his exceptionally clingy girlfriends with him, whenever he'd looked round, she was there.

But there was no doubt that Julia had been the biggest surprise of the night. He remembered her as older from Uni, she'd been a mature student mixed in with a load of eighteen year olds. He hadn't taken a lot of notice of her, she'd floated peripherally in his social circle, always somewhere on the fringes. And after they'd moved out of halls in the second year he had only seen her occasionally. She'd been very driven at Uni, working hard for her degree. And after they'd all graduated he hadn't stayed in touch with her, it was only when she'd popped up on Facebook that he'd given her another thought. But now – well, wow. She was stunning. Tall, with long, dark, glossy hair, curving red lips and oozing all the glamour and confidence that only an older woman could. Ed wondered how he'd bypassed her all those years ago. Perhaps his tastes had changed. By the end of the night Ed had definitely fancied her and before he knew what he was doing, in a bizarre twist of fate he'd agreed to accompany her to the Murder-Mystery thing that Steph was organising next weekend; Christ, he wasn't sure how good an idea that was in retrospect. At the time it had seemed fine, but he'd spent all day wondering if he should get himself out of it, take her out for dinner or something instead. Firstly, it would be hellishly awkward with Theo and Steph, and secondly, he wouldn't actually get to see that much of her. Julia's face when she'd realised that Ed knew Steph had been priceless.

"What, Steph Hammond? From St Catherines?"

"The very one. I was wondering how you knew her." It was a bizarre conversation; conducted while a young blonde cavorted around them, half-naked. Ed found it hard to concentrate.

"She's a fellow parent at the school. LA Steph, we call her," Julia giggled.

We? "Really? Why?"

"She's very *good*. Very Lick-Arse. And worthy. And always on time for drop-off and pick-up. And she looks fabulous most of the time too, like she's stepped out of LA. Fake tan, fake nails, highlighted hair. Expensive jeans, Kurt Geiger heels, big Volvo 4x4. She's a real yummy mummy." There was just a trace of bitterness in her voice.

"Yes, we had a catch-up last weekend. She looked like that then."

"Goodness, I am amazed. What a small world. Were you good friends? At school?"

"The best. We all got on really well. Until she married Theo, we weren't quite so close then."

"Ha ha! No, you wouldn't be. Well, gosh." A small pause, and Julia leant in so close to Ed that he could feel her breasts resting on his arm. It was distracting him from the blonde. "Well, that's perfect then," she purred at him. "I was going to invite you anyway, but knowing that you're friends with Theo and Steph makes it so much easier."

"What are you talking about?" The noise and music and chatter and alcohol were making Ed feel slightly dizzy.

"Next weekend. We're having a big bash at the school, and I thought you could be my plus-one. We could have a proper catch-up."

"I don't know; schools aren't really my scene these days. How about I see you another time?"

"Oh come on, it'll be fun. I mean Amy, my daughter, will be there but doesn't need to be a problem."

"I don't know?"

"Tell you what, just say yes now and you can think about it properly tomorrow. When you're sober. How's that?"

"OK. All right."

"Excellent. As long as you don't spend all your time talking to Steph."

Ed put a hand gently on her leg, "Of course not. We're barely friends any more, I wouldn't worry if I were you."

"I'm not worried. She's no competition. More champagne?"

Engrossed with watching the blonde girl as she removed her stockings with her teeth, Ed missed the jibe at Steph.

And now he had to think about whether this really was a good idea. Steph hadn't exactly been overjoyed to see him the other night. He seemed to make her feel awkward for some reason; he pondered vaguely on what it could be. There were two likely options – either she felt bad about what had happened all those years ago, or the fact that they'd slept together was still bothering her. Perhaps she and Theo had even been together at the time. No, Rachel had still been on the scene then, couldn't be. His mobile rang, "Hello?"

"Ed? It's Julia. How are you darling?"

"Good, thanks. I was going to call you actually."

"And I've saved you the bother, clever old me. I'll be quick, I just wanted to let you know that I've sorted out your ticket for Friday. It was a bit of a hassle, the office claimed they'd all sold out but I managed to convince them to sell me one from the emergency stash."

"Oh." She'd gone to a lot of trouble then. "Are you sure this is wise?"

"Of course, why not? There's not a problem is there?"

"Er – not a – not a problem, exactly."

"Good, I had to reorganise our table plan to get you seated next to me too. That did not go down well with Steph, I can tell you."

"Really?" He didn't like the thought of upsetting her. "Well perhaps in that case I'm better off not coming." He tried to sound firm, these plans were making him feel distinctly uncomfortable.

"But I've done it now," she sounded perplexed. "Don't you want to come?"

"Well yes, it would be lovely to see you of course."

"Excellent. That's sorted then."

So there he was. All ticketed-up for this gala event on Saturday. He wondered briefly about phoning Theo to tell him that he was coming, but decided against it. It would sound too much like asking permission. Far better to just go and get on with it and they could make of it what they liked.

****

"Steph – Mia's only got one tap shoe," Theo called down the stairs.

"Really?"

"Yep – said the other one's at school 'somewhere' and it's her tap class tomorrow."

Steph gritted her teeth, "Tell her she has to find it then," she shouted back. "She's old enough to look after her stuff by now."

Theo appeared on the landing, face rueful. "I tried that. She says it's not in Lost Property and she doesn't know where else to look."

"That's not good enough."

"But Mummy," Mia appeared beside Theo. "It's not fair. Tilly gets to do tap and I can't."

"Tilly hasn't lost her shoe."

"How do you know she hasn't lost hers and taken mine?"

"Have you asked her?"

"Yes, she says they're both hers. But I haven't lost mine!"

"You'll have to find it Mia, or not do the class."

"But that's silly when you've already paid."

Theo hid a smile.

"Mia – your things are your responsibility," Steph said firmly.

"But it's not *fair*!" Mia stamped a foot.

"Life's not fair."

"No – you're not fair!"

"Mia! I will not have you speaking to me like that."

"Hey – look – shush-" Theo intervened. "Mia, go back to your room and get into bed. We'll talk about the shoe in the morning," and then he shot Steph a concerned glance. As well he might, she supposed. It was very unlike her to snap at the children, she usually had infinite patience. But it was harder when she was as tense as a coiled spring, her stomach had a dull, dragging pain in it and she had an unpleasant conversation to look forward to with Theo. And when she could recognise that Mia's argumentative streak definitely came from Ed. He could be as tough as old iron too.

"Are you OK?" Theo mouthed from the top of the stairs.

"I'm fine."

He came into the kitchen ten minutes later as Steph was stacking the dishwasher.

"Sure you're OK?" He ran a hand up and down her back.

"*Yes*." She stepped away from him.

"All right."

Steph looked at the blue plates stacked neatly side by side, and felt despair begin to well up inside her. Before she could control it, an image of a long-ago day rushed unbidden into her mind. She'd been young, perhaps ten, and home early from school.

"Hi Mum," she'd skipped into the kitchen to find Mum bent over the dishwasher. "Guess what? Mr Robson was ill so we got to come home early. I'm starving, is there anything to eat? Can I watch TV?" There was no response. "Mum?" and it wasn't until she'd gone close up that she'd seen her mother's face contorted with agony. Sheet white, lips pressed together, knuckles gripping the sideboard. "Mum, are you ok?" Steph had been alarmed.

"Yes, yes, I'm fine," her mother had managed to say. But she hadn't been. Steph had run and got Mrs Davies from next door because John was at work, and she had put Mum into bed. Then, later that night, Mum had had to go to hospital. The bleeding had got too much and she needed the doctors, Mrs Davies had explained. Bleeding? No one had said anything about bleeding to Steph. The bleeding that means you aren't going to have a baby, Mrs Davies said. But – that didn't make sense, because Mum was going to have a baby, she'd told Steph herself. She was going to have a little baby. And she'd knitted a blanket for it.

Steph had seen Mum as she hobbled out to the car, bent double and clutching at John who had rushed home. Her face had looked really different and Steph had been frightened.

"It's OK," she'd said. "I'll be back soon." And she had been, by the time Steph got home from school the following day, Mum had been back and looking cheerier. But the baby had never arrived. When she'd got older she'd asked questions of her mother, and she'd been told that the baby hadn't been well enough to live. Mum and John had loved the baby, but it had been ill. And there was never another one. Steph knew that she'd never forget the cold horror that came from looking at Mum's face that day. Never. Miscarriage, stillbirth, whatever it was – it was something to be feared, that was clear. And it was another few years again before Steph could link that awful day when Mum had lost the baby to her own inability to have a termination.

"I'm going to the sitting room," Theo was saying to her back.

"What?" It took her a few seconds to re-orientate herself. It's not then, it's now, Steph told herself firmly. You're here, in your kitchen, with your husband. You didn't lose a baby. She took a deep breath.

"I asked if you were going to sit down with me."

"Oh, right. Actually Theo, there was something I wanted to talk to you about."

"What's that then?"

Steph poured them both a glass of wine and gestured for him to sit at the table, "I'm not pregnant," she said, not looking at him.

"You mean... Ah."

"Yes, it started this morning. Sorry."

Theo put his glass down and came round to her, "Hey, it's all right. No problem. Don't apologise."

"I am sorry though," – *sorry that you want it so much and I don't.*

"Don't be silly," he said firmly, tilting her face towards him. "It's only one month, there are plenty of others. We can try again."

"Um – about that too – why don't we give it a rest for a while? Try again in a few months?" She tried to sound nonchalant, but Theo wasn't fooled.

"What?"

"I just think that maybe now isn't such a great time. The girls – the house – Christmas coming up. How about we leave it till January or February?"

"The girls? The house? Steph, what are you talking about? This doesn't make any sense. Why are you calling it off?" He sounded so hurt.

She couldn't meet his eye, "Like I say, I think there could be a better time, that's all. What's the big deal? I'm not saying never – I'm saying not now." She wanted to tell him so much – *when Ed's gone again, when I've achieved something for myself, when I'm not so stressed, when I'm secure that you won't leave me, when I know that our precious baby won't give away my secret* – but she couldn't. Of course she couldn't. So – "I'm sorry Theo but I'm not changing my mind on this." Even to her it sounded so harsh.

Theo watched her dark hair swing over her face. He couldn't really make sense of what she was saying. OK, so it had taken a few weeks for her to get used to the idea of another baby but he thought he'd convinced her. No, not convinced, that was the wrong word. Shown her – that was better. Shown her what an amazing thing it would be to have another little brother or sister for the twins. It was like Steph was slowly withdrawing from him. She wasn't as happy as she used to be. Or as open. Or as – as – anything. She was different.

"What's going on Steph? Why are you so different?"

"What do you mean different?"

"You've changed."

"In what way?"

"That's just it, I'm not sure."

"Well what are you asking me then?"

"You seem distant – a bit moody – unhappy, just not your normal self and I'm asking why, what's going on to make you feel like that?"

"God Theo, this is a bit deep all of a sudden!" Steph gave an uncomfortable smile.

"Steph you've just told me that you don't want another baby with me, what do you expect?"

Again, she looked down and didn't meet his eyes. "Look if it's such a problem we'll just do it OK? Carry on trying?" she snapped. "Would that make you happy?"

"*No*. It wouldn't. I want this to be a special experience. We didn't have this with the girls, they were suddenly just there. I wanted this time to be different and special. I certainly don't want to go ahead with your attitude like this."

"I'm sorry. I really am. I want to give you what you want, but it isn't right for me now," Steph said in a low voice.

There was a small silence. "When will it be right?"

"I don't know. Soon. Hopefully."

Theo smiled a brave smile, "Well that's fine. Soon is fine. I just wish I understood you a bit more."

"*Mummy!*"

"Me or you?"

"You're Mummy."

Theo sat on the kitchen stool and raised his glass to his lips thoughtfully. Steph had never been like this in all the years that he'd known her. Edgy, irritable; confused almost. And if she wouldn't tell him what was bothering her then there was nothing to do but ride it out. He just wished that he didn't find it so disturbing.

CHAPTER TEN

OK, *think*. This was important. Hair done? Check. Make-up perfect? Check. Nails painted? Check. Un-laddered tights? Check. Funky dress? Check. Well, half-check. Steph had agonised over her choice of dress for a week. Nothing too tight or short or revealing. But also nothing too boring or old, she needed to get the balance right here. She needed to be young and trendy without being tarty. Initially she'd thought probably her black, strappy Karen Millen dress, but at the last minute she'd seen a gorgeous Lipsy cream lace shift dress and gone with that instead. In the shop it had looked perfect but right here and now in the bedroom – might it be too short? Steph turned in front of the mirror trying to examine herself from every possible angle. It was long-sleeved and high-necked, just enough room for a necklace, but it really was very short. She was wearing nude, shimmery tights and silver heels. It looked nice, with her long hair reaching most of the way down her back, but...

"Gorgeous."

"Oh!" Steph spun round to see Theo standing in the doorway. "Do you think? Or is it too short?"

He took a minute to look his wife up and down; she was clearly unsure, she was chewing her bottom lip and her big eyes looked wide with indecision. "No, I think it's perfect. You look amazing. A million dollars."

"Flatterer."

"It's true. In fact," he crossed the room in three big strides, "if we didn't have to go out in precisely five minutes, I would be suggesting pulling that dress up."

She put her hand out to stop him just as – "Daddy? Mummy? When are you going?" They looked up to find Tilly standing in the doorway.

"Five minutes darling, why?"

"Because Lisa says we can start watching the film when you've gone."

"Ah – OK. We'll be out of your hair as soon as possible," Theo winked at her. Lisa was fifteen years old and the daughter of a neighbour.

"Is that what you're wearing Mummy?"

"I think so, yes."

"It's really nice. Hey Mia, come and see Mummy's dress."

Mia appeared in the doorway, "It's nice," she said thoughtfully, "but I don't really like it."

"Why not?" said Theo.

"The colour. It's too boring. I prefer blue or pink."

"Lucky it's not yours then," Steph squirted four blasts of Pure Poison by Dior onto her neck and wrists and leant forward to kiss the girls. "Be good," she warned. "No messing around, don't go to sleep too late and do as you're told."

"We will," they chorused.

"Come on," Steph tugged at Theo's arm, "we'll be late."

It felt like she'd been preparing for this night forever. It had taken the Cath's Committee months to plan it all out properly, paying attention to every tiny detail and making sure nothing had been forgotten. There had been a last-minute hitch when Ian had discovered that they were ten chairs down, but the gardener had risen to the challenge and found some old ones in a disused shed at the bottom of the tennis courts. Scrubbed up and repainted, they were fine.

When Steph had left St Catherines on Friday afternoon, the set-up was well underway and looking amazing. The entrance hall was to be used as the venue. Steph had expressed surprise when Julia told her, but, "We thought about using the dining hall, but it's so big, we could virtually go all evening without seeing everybody, which isn't what we want, so we've gone for the hall. It'll be cosy, but that's the idea." For her and her loverboy, whoever he may be, that was possibly true, Steph thought. But for the rest of them, it might be nice to have some space. "And besides," Julia had continued, "you have to be sure you can see and hear everything clearly, otherwise you might miss vital clues."

Oh yes, Steph had been so focussed on this as an event, that she'd forgotten there was a game as part of the evening. In fact, she hadn't given any thought to it whatsoever.

"I might even advise people bring pencil and paper to jot things down," Julia had mused and Steph looked at her in surprise.

"Really? Are people going to be that into it?"

"Oh I would hope so. The actors have gone to a lot of trouble to get their characters just right."

"You don't think there's a chance people will just have a few drinks and relax and join in without taking it too seriously?"

"Perhaps. But we can rely on the committee to hold things together, can't we?" Julia replied gravely.

Oh great – so as well as all the planning and serving drinks on the door, Steph now had to be on the ball enough to hold the Murder-Mystery together if required. Theo had suggested she get blind drunk and thus sabotage Julia's plans.

"No," Steph had groaned. "This isn't really going to be a social occasion for me, I don't think. I feel like I'm being put to work."

"Well, you shouldn't. You're no more reponsible than anyone else."

"Except this is the first event I've been involved in and I'm going to look bad if I duck out of any responsibility."

"We are just going to go along, have a few drinks, enjoy this Murder-Mystery, have a dance and come home. How long do you have to be giving out drinks for?"

"Until everyone's arrived. It's only one glass as they come through the door."

"That's OK then. Relax, enjoy it."

"I'll try."

And now, it was finally here. In a way Steph was looking forward to having it over and done with. She grabbed her black wrap and sequinned handbag, gathered the girls into a hug to say goodbye and hopped up into the passenger seat beside Theo.

"You know," he remarked as he reversed the car out onto the road, "it's been ages since we went out together like this."

"No it isn't, we went for dinner last week."

"No, I meant literally like this. Us and our friends. I'm looking forward to seeing Katie and Tom."

"We're not sitting with them, did I tell you?"

"No, but never mind. We might have someone amusing to sit with. Or old men with bimbo wives."

"Mmm, you might see a few of those."

"Par for the course."

They parked down the road from the school and walked the last few hundred yards. It was early, not quite seven, but pitch dark and freezing cold. The entrance hall lights of St Catherine's were dimmed and the front door locked.

"Damn, we'll have to go round the side to the pupils entrance." There was a covered walkway up to the side door, decorated with tiny fairy lights, and Julia stood at the top, fiddling with her phone.

"Steph darling!" she cried when she saw them approach. "And Theo, how wonderful to see you." She grabbed them and air-kissed them both; one for Steph, two for Theo.

"Julia – hi, is everything OK? All running according to plan?"

"Absolutely. Not a hitch yet." She was dressed in a clingy, purple, wraparound dress with a plunging neckline and high, black heels.

"Where do you want me?" Teeth chattering and arms covered in goose pimples, Steph desperately hoped it was not at this doorway.

"Inside, if you go to the far entrance of the hall where the coat stand is, you'll find the first tray of glasses waiting to go. A couple of people have arrived, but hardly anyone. Your job will be to hover around the doorway and just hand out the glasses as people go through. Ladies first, obviously," Julia gave her irritating, tinkling laugh.

"Obviously."

"Will you be OK then sweetie? Ian and Marian are here if you need anything."

"I'm sure I can cope."

"I must dash then, got to collect from the station. Ciao." She teetered off on her vertiginous heels.

"She must be nearly six feet in those," Theo murmured. "She's not small, is she?"

"No, she isn't. But it's all part of her character," Steph said loyally.

"It's bloody frightening is what it is. Where did she say she was going?"

"To collect someone from the station. Her friend, I think, she was talking about him in a meeting the other day."

"What friend?"

"Oh I don't know. Some bloke from Uni. Right, come on, let's go inside, I'm freezing."

Someone had done a spectacular job with the hall. Noticeboards and paintings had been artfully concealed by decorative swathes of white material, candelabras were dotted around and the tables were simple scrubbed pine with placemats and namecards, the idea being to achieve the effect of a school dinner without making people feel like they were actually at one.

"Ah, Steph, there you are," Ian hurried up. "Hasn't Penny done amazingly well?"

"Did she do all this? It looks great."

"Not on her own. Helen helped."

"I wouldn't recognise it," Theo said.

"Really? That's good. You must be Steph's husband?"

"I am yes," he reached across to shake Ian's hand. "Theo Hammond."

"Ian Davies, nice to meet you. You have lovely daughters."

"Thank you."

The words sank, razor-like through her defences. Steph swallowed nervously; it had to get everywhere didn't it? One occasion when she'd thought there would be nothing to remind her and ten minutes in she was already being pulled up sharply. Your fault, she reminded herself, your fault.

"Steph? Shall I take your coat?"

"Suppose. Oooh I'm freezing though!"

"Drink that," Theo handed her a glass of white wine. "That'll warm you up."

"Right – OK – I'm going to get into position, will you be all right?"

"I'll be fine, don't worry. They teach us corporate types to mingle professionally."

"There's nobody here."

"Then I'll pounce on the first guests like some desperately sad, lonely bastard."

"Don't you dare, people know I'm your wife," Steph grinned at him.

Theo was right; the wine did warm her up and relax her. There turned out to be nothing to handing Cava to people; why had she build this into such a huge thing? They came down the corridor, hung their coats up, passed through the doorway where Steph was proffering her tray, being replenished every so often by one of the catering staff, took a glass and continued into the hall. It was lit only by the candelabras and a couple of lamps; the whole atmosphere was warm, heady and intimate.

Someone came up behind Steph and put their hands on her shoulders, "You look amazing. I lurrve that dress."

"Katie."

"The very same, hello," she gave Steph a quick hug. "Seriously, that's gorgeous, where did you get it?"

"Lipsy. I like yours too." Katie was wearing a blue dress, cut low and tight with a high waistband and a big skirt that fell almost to her knees. "You look gorgeous. Where's it from?"

"£18 in the H&M sale."

"It looks fabulous. I'd love a cleavage like yours."

"You wouldn't love the weight that goes with it. How's your duty going?" She took two glasses off the tray.

"Fine, actually. A doddle. Theo's buggered off somewhere."

"Probably with Tom."

Steph rolled her eyes, "Men! And to be honest it's looking pretty packed in here, I think I must be nearly done."

"And how many glasses have you had?"

"Ooh, one or two…"

"Good for you girl. I'm going to go and find our seats. Where are you sitting?"

"Ah well, if you look the tables are named after cakes so there's Victoria Sponge, Currant, Lardy – can you believe! – Fruit, Fairy and Eccles. Theo and I are on Fairy."

Katie pulled a face, "God I'd better not be on Lardy, that's awful. Who did the names?"

"Guess."

"Um – her highness Queen Julia?"

"Spot on."

"Where is she? Not sitting near me I hope."

"I've no idea, around somewhere. The last I saw of her she'd gone off to the station."

"OK. All right, well I'll go and hunt and gather my husband and I'll see you in a bit." She gave Steph a quick kiss and disappeared into the ever-thickening crowd. They must have sold over a hundred tickets, Steph thought, looking around. The tables were getting full, the library where the temporary bar was set up had a steady stream of people going in and out and she couldn't even see the DJ at the far end of the hall through the crowds. Steph tried to remember who was playing a part, and failed. She was sure someone had told her. Or had they? Perhaps it was a secret.

"Order! Order!" Someone was banging a wooden mallet on a table. "Can I have order in St. Cakes please!" The chatter died away to a hush and Steph stood on tiptoe to see who was shouting. It was one of the fathers. "I am your Headmaster this evening, Mr French, and I'd like to take this opportunity to welcome you all to St Cakes." There were vague murmurings and muffled laughter. "I am very proud of my school and I can assure you that you are in for a wonderful evening, lots of good food, fine wines and of course – plenty of fun!"

Cue more raucous laughter. "Could I ask you all please to make your way to wherever you are seated so that we may proceed with the meal."

There was a slightly urgent bustle as people moved towards their tables carrying ice buckets and with bottles tucked under their arms. Steph grabbed another two glasses off her tray and was on the point of deserting her post and heading over to Fairy table when a familiar voice spoke loudly behind her, "Not quite finished yet are you Steph?" Julia was coming down the corridor at quite a speed.

Steph turned with gritted teeth, "Actually, I thought I was."

"Well I will have a glass – thank you very much – and I'll take one for-"

And before Steph could open her mouth to ask after Julia's mysterious companion, he came around the corner. Dressed in a dinner jacket with a smart white scarf dangling round his neck, his blond head suddenly looking horribly familiar.

"Sorry Julia, I had to take that call…" he began to say and stopped as he caught sight of Steph's horrified face.

"I would introduce you two," Julia said, smiling slightly, "but I think you know each other?"

Steph's chest constricted suddenly, her face flamed red and her hands went ice-cold, "I – yes –" she managed to say. It was Ed. He was here. How could that be?

"Evening Steph," Ed leant over casually to give her a kiss. *No*, her head roared but her face stayed frozen still.

"How do you…" were they together? Had he come with Julia? Had she found him loitering outside somewhere? Was he following her? "Why are you here?" she asked eventually.

"I'm with Julia," Ed had the good grace to look somewhat ashamed.

"*This* is my old friend from Uni," there was a hint of malice about her words. "I thought I'd mentioned it to you? I knew you were friends. Goodness, did I forget to tell you? How awful. Yes, we go back donkey's years, not as far as you two obviously, but a good way all the same. Ten years or thereabouts would you say Ed? We were in halls together."

"About that. Look Steph, I hope you don't mind me just turning up like this, I did think of ringing." Ed began awkwardly.

"Of course she doesn't mind, what a thing to think. Why would she? Come on, we'd better sit down." Julia grabbed his hand and pulled him after her. Steph couldn't take her eyes off him as he disappeared into the throng, he was really, actually here. In this hall, near her, near her girls, in her territory, in the heart of their life. How could this be? He was friends with Julia? She struggled to process this appalling information. Think, Steph, think. Who did she say she was bringing? A friend from Uni. An old friend. Not a boyfriend. Someone she'd met at a reunion. So they went to University together? How could she not have known this? Julia did. Why hadn't she told her? A nasty, sneaking feeling crept up on her; Julia hadn't told her deliberately. Julia knew – what did she know? She knew something. She couldn't know... the truth? Somehow? For some ghastly, unthought of reason?

"There you are darling, come and sit down, we're about to begin," Theo was standing behind her. "God, are you all right? You look very pale." Her lips were bloodless.

"He's here."

"Who is?"

"Ed."

"Ed? Our Ed?"

"No someone else's fucking Ed! Of course our Ed!" she hissed at him.

"How can he be here? Who's he with? He hasn't come on his own?"

"He's with Julia."

"Julia? Does he know her?"

"Order! Order! Can I have everyone seated please!"

"Come on, let's sit down, tell me there." Theo grabbed her hand and pulled her along on shaking legs to their table. Steph barely registered where they were sitting, she was just grateful to sink down into a chair. On auto pilot she unfolded her napkin and laid it across her knees with trembling hands as Theo solicitously filled her wine glass. Their soup was served and Theo turned to her again, "So how does he know Julia then? This is very strange. Didn't she say anything to you?" He broke off a bit of bread roll and offered it to her.

Steph shook her head, "No."

"I wonder why." Steph hadn't got to that part yet; the fact that they knew one another was bad enough. As subtly as she could, she scanned the room to try and see where they were sitting. They weren't on her table, nor on Katie's. God, Katie. She hadn't noticed yet, but she was going to love it when she did. This was undreamt-of drama. Another bolt of adrenaline shot through Steph, might Katie say something in an unguarded moment? A wave of nausea so intense swept over her, that she thought she might actually vomit. Abruptly, she put down her soup spoon.

"Are you OK?" Theo whispered.

"I'm fine. Just a bit surprised, that's all."

"Well yes, me too. Very odd. We'll have to seek him out and have a chat later."

Steph thought she'd rather die.

"Ladies and gentleman, I am going to make a speech," Mr French had stood up again. "We are very proud to be here tonight celebrating the fiftieth anniversary of our wonderful school..." Steph rapidly tuned out, and kept her attention firmly focussed on locating Julia and Ed. It didn't take long, they were sitting three tables away on the right. Sandwiched between the Headmistress and some very wealthy parents. Of course, Julia would have put herself there in what she imagined was the most influential spot. Steph felt a sudden surge of anger towards Julia. The woman was inhuman. Fancy doing this to someone. It was unthinkable. Steph watched Ed swivel his head surreptitiously. Well if he was looking for her he'd be out of luck, he was sitting with his back to her.

"...And now, having welcomed you all, I'm going to indulge in one of my favourite cakes," Mr French, rather theatrically, reached forward and picked up a slice of cake. "Mmm, this is good. Just what the doctor..." and with a crash he fell forward onto the table, apparently dead.

CHAPTER ELEVEN

Theo watched Steph covertly, but carefully. She hadn't been right since she'd realised Ed had arrived, she was being very strange. Yes, it had been a shock to them both, but it was more amusing than anything else. An unbelievable coincidence, talk about small worlds. But she was behaving like it was an almighty disaster. Theo felt a twinge of annoyance. Why couldn't she just pull herself together and be normal towards him? She was the one who kept going on about how grown-up they all were now, yet she was the one behaving like a teenager. Except – except – she'd seemed to like Ed more when they were teenagers. If he thought about it, which he rarely did these days, Theo remembered Steph and Ed being quite close. Very close in fact. As a sixteen year old he'd long suspected them of being more than just friends, but whenever he'd asked Steph she'd cut the conversation short, claiming a bad memory. But no, he was sure there must have been more to it, they'd always been together and sixteen was a very hormonal age. Not that it mattered now, of course. It was a different life. Theo couldn't say that the concept sat easily with him, this was his beloved wife he was thinking about, but neither could he say that he minded. He felt a sudden feeling of unease sweep through him and wished fervently that he hadn't. He took a deep sip of his red wine. Don't be silly, he told himself. You're overreacting to nothing at all; you're just on edge because of how unsettled Steph's been over the last few weeks, that's all. Don't start reading things that aren't there.

****

Christ, she looked fantastic. Ed glanced quickly around him as he sipped his soup. Leek and potato, ugh. The wine was pretty dodgy too, but Steph – wow. She looked amazing. More amazing before she'd spotted he was there though. In that instant as she'd laid eyes on him she'd gone from relaxed and happy, smiling that wide smile, to looking desperate and trapped. Such a cliché but she really had reminded him of an animal in the headlights, a bit like that deer on the

A32 a few months ago. What the hell was her problem? He couldn't see where she was sitting, pity, he'd like another look at her legs in that dress. Ed felt marginally guilty for a second as remembered this was Theo's wife he was thinking about. But hey, he was only looking.

"You OK darling?" Julia nudged his elbow.

"Yes, I'm fine thanks."

"Good. Sorry, it's probably all incomprehensible to you isn't it? Must be years since you were in a school!"

"Quite a few."

"There's a good group of people here though," she lowered her voice, "that over there is the Head, Mrs Sheldon-Clarke, to my right are Mr and Mrs Butler; they're fabulously wealthy, they own thousands of acres in Scotland."

"Really?" This could get boring.

"Yep. They are the crème de la crème of County society."

"That's nice," he said politely.

"Don't worry, I can see you're bored. I'll introduce you to a few people in a bit and meanwhile you just relax and enjoy the wine. There'll be quieter time later," she winked at him. A sudden commotion made him look up, oh – there it was, someone appeared to have died. Four men came through the tables, lifted up the dead man and carted him out, to whoops of laughter and rounds of applause. Ed wondered if he were a popular man.

"So what's the deal here?" he asked Julia.

"Watch the drama unfold, some written clues will come round and the characters should make themselves available between courses too, to answer any questions you might have. But don't feel that you have to get involved if you don't want to."

"So we mingle between courses?"

"You can do," Julia said slowly, "or you can stay here with me."

She didn't want him talking to Steph, Ed realised. That should be easy enough, she'd practically run away from him. What the hell had he ever done to her? He felt indignant all over again, it was his place to be annoyed with her, not the other way around.

****

The clues were rubbish. Steph flicked through the pile on their table, but they didn't actually tell you anything. They'd nearly finished collecting the soup bowls; she'd go and speak to Ed when everyone started to move around. He had to be warned off.

"You OK?" Theo asked. "I'm enjoying this, it's good fun. The characters are really throwing themselves into it, it's nice to see the effort. Are we going to go and speak to Ed?"

That jolted her, "Why?"

"We're the only people he knows, we can't ignore him."

"He knows Julia." Even to her it sounded petulant. "But I thought I'd go and speak to him in a minute."

"I'll come with you," Theo folded his napkin and made to stand up.

"Ah – actually, I think they're a prefect short on this table." There was a lone, unclaimed sticker lying by the candelabra. "It's bound to be important, why don't do you do it? Here." Steph grabbed the sticker and pushed it firmly onto his chest. "There you are. And here are the sheets you need to read," she dumped the pile in his lap. "It won't be hard. Back in a sec," and leaving Theo looking slightly bemused she threaded her way through the tables. What should she say? Fuck off? Demand an explanation? No, no, nothing like that. The absolutely, utter worst thing in the world would be if Ed and Julia were somehow romantically linked. That would mean he'd be around all the time, near the girls and if anyone could whip up trouble, it would be Julia.

"Hi."

Ed turned to see Steph standing over him, "Hi." He wiped his mouth quickly and pulled out a chair for her, "Here, sit down."

Warily, she sat. Julia had turned the other way; hadn't noticed her. The room was busy and noisy.

Ed turned to face her, "Look, I realise that this might seem a bit off."

"I just wondered why you hadn't said anything to us," Steph said stiffly.

"Er – I hadn't known about it too long, it only came up last weekend at the reunion. And to be honest, I didn't think you'd actually mind." His very blue eyes stared at her. Steph blocked all familiarity from her mind.

"It's not a question of minding, it just all seems so strange. We don't hear from you for ten years, then you turn up on the doorstep and the next week you're at the children's school."

"Small world."

"You can say that again."

"Small world." And he smiled at her.

Steph felt a flicker of recognition pass between them, just an echo of what had once been there, and pushed it aside impatiently. Ed smiled cautiously, "Besides, it isn't so bad having me around is it?"

You have no idea, thought Steph, "No. Not bad. Just strange."

"It's been a long time."

"Ten years."

"Has it been a good ten years?"

Despite herself, Steph smiled, "Oh yes. The best."

"You look pretty happy."

"I am. How about you?"

Ed stretched back and folded his arms behind his head, "Yeah, it has been good. Never thought I'd be where I am now, but that doesn't mean I'm not happy. I've been very lucky, had a few good opportunities along the way."

"Is Julia one of them?"

"Look, if you're worried about me and Julia…"

"I'm not worried. Not at all. Just asking."

"It wasn't planned, she invited me out of the blue."

"You could have rung."

"As I said, I didn't think you'd mind," Ed took another mouthful of wine. "We were good friends once," he said defensively.

"Yeah, once." Steph looked around and caught sight of Katie approaching with a determined look on her face. Oh shit.

"Hi, I think we met last week? I'm Katie." She thrust her hand at him.

"Oh yes," Ed stood up, "Ed Osborne."

"This is unexpected. Who are you with?"

"Julia," Ed touched her shoulder lightly.

"What? Oh – hello you two, is everything OK? Steph, no disasters I hope?"

"Not that I've noticed."

"Have you all had a chance to talk to the characters? Mmm? Oh good, sorry, do excuse me," she was clearly torn between a socially-furthering conversation with Mr Butler and entertaining her guest.

"So how do you know Julia? That's a bit out of left field isn't it?"

Steph dropped her slightly spinning head into her hands. This was a bad idea, Katie was all over him, she wouldn't let up until she'd satisfied her extensive curiosity. Ed gave her a truncated version of his and Julia's association.

"Well gosh, what a coincidence."

"I did mention to Theo that I knew Julia, back in our first ever phone conversation. That was how I found these guys again, I noticed a Steph Hammond among her friends on Facebook and thought ah – I wonder if it could be – and it was. It prompted me to ring."

"Amazing." There was nowhere Katie could go from here without stepping into dangerous territory. Steph gave her a pleading look.

"Anyway, it looks like I'm about to get my chance to grill those people on their murderous intentions, so I'll say goodbye. I'll see you in a minute Steph."

Ed watched her disappear back into the crowd. "Is she a good friend?"

"Yes, we've known her a while."

"She said last week, since the kids started school or something."

"Yes," Steph said quickly. "About that." Not the children, not the children, anything but them. "So – no girlfriend then?"

Ah ha, Ed thought. "No, no one serious."

"Shame," Steph gave a quick smile. "I'd better get back, I left Theo taking on a prefect role." She stood up. "Nice to have a chat."

She felt disturbed, making her way back to Fairy table. No longer so frightened, no longer so antagonised, but it didn't feel right to be friendly with him, it really didn't. But it was hard to be so tough with him when he was so gentle and nice to her.

Guarded, that was what she must be.

****

In retrospect, it had taken Ed a staggeringly long time to realise that Theo and Steph had left Tinford for good.

He'd been very surprised that Steph had just gone home after that night. It had been such an event to him, that when he'd rolled over and opened his eyes to discover her missing, his first thought had been – what had happened to her? Because she couldn't have just pissed off, surely? But when his mum appeared with a cup of tea, he'd discovered that that was exactly what she'd done.

"She said she had a lesson at ten."

He felt slightly miffed but figured that he'd see her later at school. In the meantime, he rolled back over to consider what had happened between them. A surprise? Definitely. Appreciated? Certainly. Did this mean they were together? Well... Did he want them to be together? Yes. He knew it had been her first time, and you didn't just jump into bed with a friend for a casual first time shag. Except some people did, but not Steph. She wasn't like that. It must have meant something to her. Especially when you considered all the time they'd been spending together recently. They'd barely been apart. Ed had felt quite smug when he saw that Steph was shunning Theo in favour of him; he'd been waiting for that moment for ages. He'd always thought it might come, and eventually it had. She hardly saw Theo at all, except at school. Instead she chose him, Ed. It was him she'd hang out with, him she'd ring in the evening and now evidently him she wanted to sleep with. He smiled a wide grin to himself; that last bit said it all really. Wow. Amazing. Stephanie Oakton wanted to go out with him, no one would believe it. Now all he had to do was think up a romantic way to ask her out, make it official. She would be expecting it. Hmm… He'd waited for her after her ten o' clock lesson, but everyone else streamed out and not her. A casual enquiry revealed that she'd not attended at all. Weird. He'd waited until after lunch and when she still hadn't shown up, he'd tried her mobile. Switched off. After school he'd gone round to her house but although her bedroom curtains were drawn there was no answer. Ah, that was obviously it. She was sleeping off a hangover.

Disconsolately, Ed remembered kicking a football onto the Rec and hanging around to see if any of his mates would turn up, but they didn't. He considered going and knocking on Theo's door but felt a bit awkward. After all, he and Steph used to be really close. So he wandered back home and hung out in his room, wondering vaguely if she would turn up again that night. He really hoped so, seeing what had happened last time. Otherwise, there was always school in the morning.

It had been days before proper worry kicked in. She didn't come to school and no one had seen her. Phonecalls to her mother were answered stiffly and unhelpfully. No, she wasn't in and no, she didn't know when she'd be back. He hadn't thought to ask if she'd been back at all. Eventually he thought of ringing Theo. Strangely – in retrospect – he hadn't noticed if Theo had been around or not. He'd been so focussed on Steph and waiting for her. So he'd dialled Theo's number and waited, listening to the irritating *dring-dring* of the phone and then, someone had answered.

"Hello?"

"Hi Mrs Hammond, it's Ed. Could I speak to Theo please?"

"Theo? Oh, don't you know?"

"Know what?"

"Theo's moved out."

That did make him sit up a bit, "Moved out? Out where?"

"We don't know I'm afraid," there was a big sigh. "He went last week, left a note to say he'd be back to collect his things at a later date. I'm surprised you don't know, I thought Steph would have told you."

Total confusion, "What's Steph got to do with it?"

"Well she's gone with him."

It took a moment or two to compute the words; Steph had gone as well. Gone. With Theo.

"Thank you," he managed to say, and hung up. What the fuck? Where had they gone? And why? Neither one would answer their mobiles, though he tried from different numbers, and no one knew any more than Mrs Hammond. Theo and Steph had evidently packed a few bits and disappeared off into the sunset. The night he found out was the last time Ed remembered crying. His best friends, the girl he adored, had just buggered off and left him without so much as a fleeting farewell. He hadn't even been able to ask her out. The whole thing didn't make sense.

The summer had dragged on after that. Ed felt desolate and alone. Lost. Brokenhearted. He kept expecting them to turn up or ring or something, but they never did. It wasn't until that postcard from Vannes arrived that his world was properly shattered, '*Hi! Sorry we left without saying goodbye. Will explain later. Been travelling a bit, hot here! Ring when we're back, love from Steph and Theo xx.*'

Steph and Theo. There it was, in black and white. They were together. Steph. And Theo. Strangely, he didn't feel the jealousy and anger he'd expected. He felt let down and hurt and curiously numb. And completely confused, he just hadn't seen this coming at all.

In all his empty time he'd revised a bit harder, though he'd done his exams with no real interest and had been surprised when he scored three A grades. Right, he'd thought, this is meant to be. I've got the highest grades possible, I'm going to make something of my life. And he'd gone through clearing to get a place to study Law at Bristol. University had been exactly what he expected, lots of booze, women and hours in the library. And Ed had been in the thick of everything, no more shy, retiring, unpopular Ed, oh no. Here in Bristol he was Jack-the-Lad, drinking the most, shagging the most, partying the most and working the hardest. Blokes admired him and women adored him; hung onto his every word. He'd sauntered through three fabulous years with a hardened heart, reinventing himself and loving it. And he had never looked back. Until now.

****

The evening was winding down before Ed saw either of them again. The Murder-Mystery completed, amidst hoots of laughter and silly dances. The Spanish teacher was the murderer. The tables had been cleared away and a dancefloor created in the hall; music thumped (pity the poor boarders upstairs) and the library-cum-bar was full of parents, a lot of whom were dressed up as schoolgirls and keeping the photographer busy.

Julia had been drinking steadily and as a consequence became a little more relaxed. Less uptight, she was now giggling and letting her hair down on the dancefloor, leaving Ed alone. He didn't mind. He was quite enjoying being able to sit back and observe this world, this very different world. They were lucky girls, Mia and Tilly, to go to this school. Just by looking around he could tell it was a very nice place to be. Large classrooms, roomy corridors, plenty of facilities, nice furniture. If you were educated in a place like this, did you just absorb class? He could quite imagine the girls as posh, braying eighteen-year-olds going off to study Economics at LSE or something. Was it just that bit easier if you were born into this life? Presumably you didn't have to wait until your life was trashed before getting off your arse and doing something about it. Not that their lives would ever be trashed, Mummy and Daddy wouldn't allow it.

"Hello stranger," jolting him from his thoughts, Theo sat down next to him, beer in hand. "Sorry I couldn't chat to you earlier. I didn't mean to just say hello and go off but Steph got all competitive on me about deciphering the clues."

"No problem.

"Having a good night?"

"Yeah – yeah. It's a bit surreal to be honest. Julia asked me last weekend if I wanted to come and, I have to be straight, I didn't actually realise I'd said yes. But then she rang me on Monday and told me she'd bought the tickets. The last two, according to her."

Theo laughed, "Doesn't surprise me. I don't know her personally but I've heard things, if you know what I mean. Obviously got an eye for you. How do you know her?"

"Uni, we were in halls together. She was a mature student. We didn't keep in touch, we'd hooked up over Facebook and then saw each other at this reunion and it went from there. She's great though, it's been a bit of a whirlwind, but a good one."

"I don't really know her to be honest, but good for you mate."

There was a silence and Ed realised he should probably explain a bit more. "I didn't ring you or anything about – you know – this night, because…"

Theo held a hand up, "It's absolutely fine. Not a problem. Your life is your concern. We hardly overlap that much, you don't need to explain. It was just a surprise seeing you here, it was the last place I'd thought you'd be."

"That's fair enough. Nice school though."

"We like it. Girls are doing well here."

Ed shook his head, "God, I still can't get my head around you two having kids. And not just kids, but old ones. Not babies, I mean. I still think of you at eighteen at times," he confessed.

"I can understand that. But yes, twelve next year. Between you and me, we're thinking of another, but Steph's not so keen."

"Christ, three kids? That's just a world away from my life. The only things fighting for position in my flat are the takeaway menus and the Wii and X-box."

"I'd love more, but again, Steph's not so sure. Which is fine, she's the one that's got to have them."

Speak of the devil and she shall appear; Steph whirled into view, her already short dress flying around and revealing a substantial amount of slim, toned thigh. Ed fought to avert his gaze, but Theo chuckled, "Epitome of decency, my wife."

"Hey mate, it could be worse, she could be a complete dog and flash her legs. That would be embarrassing."

"True, true. I can't see Steph being like that though, somehow."

"No, me neither." It was said with such conviction that again, Theo felt an uncomfortable sense of being missing from something. He wanted to know how Ed had gained this knowledge of his wife, where he had been at the time and what had gone on that he didn't know about. Too late to ask now, it wouldn't do anybody any good to go raking over old history. He should frankly be grateful that Ed seemed prepared to forge a new kind of friendship.

"So, you staying with Julia tonight?"

"That's the plan, but her little girl's there, Amy is it? And I'm not too sure about that yet. It's a bit soon. I'm planning on the train back, but," he spread his hands, "you never know if I'll be allowed."

"There's a bed at ours if you want?"

Ed looked at him speculatively, "Are you serious?"

"Absolutely. There's plenty of room. You might have to contend with the loud noise of two girls up and about in the morning, but that's it."

"Would Steph mind?"

"Why would she?"

Because she seems to hate my guts, Ed thought. But, "OK, you're on, that would be great, if you're sure."

"Never been more sure in my life, it's the least we could do." Theo stood up to go and find Steph, and Ed finished his glass of wine, feeling pleasantly mellow. It was like nothing had ever happened between him and Theo. Ten years had washed over them like water. The events of that summer might never have happened, as far they were concerned. Ed forgot momentarily that Theo knew nothing of his heartbreak, knew nothing of his feelings towards Steph, and possible even nothing of what had happened that night. Who knew?

Steph was where the problem lay, and for the life of him, he couldn't work out why.

****

Steph woke suddenly at 6am and was immediately, and painfully, wide awake. She'd read of that happening, apparently the moment the last vestiges of alcohol left your body you woke up, because your body was missing something. In her case she suspected it was nothing of the sort, it was the horrible knowledge that just a few feet down the corridor, her enemy slept.

She'd been furious when Theo broke the news to her. But nicely furious, because they were in a public place and that place was the girls school so decorum must be maintained at all times.

"What the hell do you mean?" she'd half-whispered, half-shouted. But over the music it hadn't mattered.

"He's coming back to stay. It's because of Julia, he thinks it's too soon to be spending the night there, that it might lead to false impressions or something," he shrugged.

"Can't he sort himself out?"

"No Steph, I've offered him a bed and that's it," Theo said firmly. "Stop being so bloody silly about him. There's nothing wrong with him."

Feeling completely impotent, and with nothing sensible to say, she'd just stood there gazing angrily at Theo, until Katie noticed and came over. They went to the loos as the only quiet place.

"What's going on? Why the scene?"

"He's invited bloody Ed to stay!"

"Oh..." Katie gave a low whistle. "I see. Why?"

"Apparently he was being kind, made the offer and Ed took him up on it. I don't really care why, I just desperately don't want him in the house!"

"Shhh shhh. Well, OK. Is he definitely coming?"

"Oh yes, Theo's had the last word," Steph felt tears rise up. Too tired, too drunk, she couldn't cope with the conversation.

Katie saw, "Hey, come on," she gave her friend a quick hug. "Don't worry about it."

"How can I not worry about it? When he'll be so close to the girls? I physically felt my nerves frazzling when he stood near them last time – a whole night and the morning after...." The door swung open and someone came in.

"Come on, let's go, you could probably do with some water."

Neither of them noticed that the end cubicle had been occupied. Inside, Julia slowly digested what she had just overheard.

Her head spinning, eyelashes clumped together with mascara and hair tangled, Steph eased herself out of bed with a groan. Slowly, she felt her way to the en suite bathroom and without looking in the mirror she swallowed a glass of water and two Nurofen. At least now she could try and sleep off this dreadful headache. Back in bed she tossed and turned fretfully under the covers, unable to get comfortable. Eventually she fell back into a dark, uneasy sleep.

****

Once the euphoria of having eloped from Tinford wore off, which didn't take long, both Steph and Theo were left feeling very uncomfortable.

Guilt reared its ugly head, "We've just left," Steph whispered to Theo in the middle of one rainy night. "Left school – our parents – our exams. What were we thinking?"

Theo raised himself up on one elbow to look at her, "That we love each other," he said simply. "That we want to build a new life together and the best place to do that is not Tinford."

"But our *exams*?"

"You weren't banking on using them for anything were you? I certainly wasn't. I plan to work my way up the career ladder, entrepreneur style."

"Well, kind of," her designing dreams still hung by a thread. "But anyway, that's not the point," Steph chewed anxiously on her fingernail. "We still should have taken them, whatever."

"Bit late now."

"Thanks, that's really helpful!"

"Babe, do you know in your heart of hearts that you've made the right decision?"

"Yes."

"Stop worrying then. We'll be fine."

"What about Ed?"

"What about him?"

"We've just left him behind. He'll be upset. He was our best friend."

"Two's a couple, three's a crowd. He was getting in the way," Theo said bluntly, not liking the affinity she was showing for Ed. But still Steph didn't tell him the real reason for feeling so guilty about leaving him; she hadn't even spoken to Ed after they'd had sex. They'd rolled apart, slept apart and when he had woken up she would have been gone. It seemed a cruel thing to do. She wished she'd had the courage to say goodbye at least. But she couldn't confide in Theo, he'd never forgive her for sleeping with Ed, and having so nearly missed out on their relationship she wasn't prepared to start sabotaging it now. No, it was for the best that Theo never knew.

Shortly after that they had decided to InteRail around Europe for a bit. They had saved while they lived in their grotty flat, and they planned to work as they went. Three weeks after they went abroad they arrived in the city of Vannes, on the south-west coast of France. It was in the middle of a heatwave and stifling hot. The city was beautiful, part of it facing onto a natural harbour where the most luxurious boats Steph had ever seen were moored. She and Theo used to stand on the waters edge looking out over the sea, "I'm going to have one of those one day," Theo would say.

"But you can't sail."

"So?" And Steph had loved him even more for his dreams and aspirations and absolute confidence that he would get there. They wandered around the dark, cool, hushed Cathedral and lit candles for long-dead grandparents. And one night they got drunk on vodka and decided to write postcards to everyone they could think of.

"Even Ed?" Steph had wanted to know. And yes, even Ed. So they'd scrawled a silly, blasé message on the back of a postcard of the harbour and sent it to him, never even thinking how callous a gesture it might seem. It was that night that they finally consummated their relationship.

A week after that Steph started being sick in the mornings. At first she blamed the heat, the food, the unfamiliar pattern of life, but when she counted back through the weeks and realised that she had missed not just one period, but three, she didn't need a test to tell her that she was pregnant. She'd cried for days; through guilt, through fear, through resentment. It was the end of the travelling, the end of the fun. They'd gone home, shocked and sober and pretended to be grown-ups. Theo had assumed the mantle of fatherhood manfully and found the best job he could and worked as hard as he could and ruthlessly climbed the corporate ladder.

When the twins were born, any life before that seemed nothing but a distant memory, and the fear that Steph would carry with her every day crawled into her heart and set up home. Her girls, her beautiful twin girls were the spitting image of Ed. She couldn't see how Theo didn't notice, their faces, their hair, the way they cried. But he was besotted; utterly, truly and totally in love with all of them. It had been just after that when Theo had proposed. Caught up in a post-natal haze and dazzled by her love for Theo, Steph accepted without explaining.

CHAPTER TWELVE

"Steph!" Theo hissed at her through the bedroom door, just cracked open a little bit.

"Yes? Careful, they'll see!" the floor was strewn with wrapped and unwrapped presents, rolls of Sellotape, ribbon and wrapping paper.

"Do you have any more pink wrapping paper left?"

"No, I don't think so, just tartan stuff. Why? We've done the girls." It was Christmas Eve and the house was chaotic. Theo's parents had arrived the day before, as they always did. It had become their custom to spend Christmas with their son and his wife; one which they had slipped into easily. It hadn't been so easy to mend the fractured relationships that Steph and Theo had both had with their parents after they left Tinford, in fact it had taken until the success of their marriage and Theo's job had spoken for themselves until things were actually back to normal. Their elopement was rarely mentioned now. They weren't a family who discussed thorny issues; Theo's parents in particular believed in letting sleeping dogs lie, and that there wasn't much that couldn't be cured by a good bottle of white. Which is what they were drinking right that moment in the comfort of the sitting room while the girls went wild with excitement.

"Yes, but I haven't exactly finished wrapping your presents."

Steph looked up at him from her position on the floor and smiled her wide smile, "Oh if it's for me then any paper will do. As long as you're using copious amounts of it."

Theo grinned back, took the roll she threw at him and jogged back downstairs.

Steph was looking happier again, which pleased him. She hadn't forgiven him for having Ed to stay after the Murder-Mystery night. He'd known of course that she wouldn't be keen, but she'd really let rip at him the next morning.

"I can't believe you did that!"

"Shush, he'll hear."

"No he won't he's upstairs and I don't care if he does anyway."

The glass door to the kitchen was firmly shut.

"Steph, this just isn't on. I haven't done anything! I gave an old friend a bed for the night because he needed one."

"Theo, you present it as if he had nowhere else to go when he could have gone with Julia or home, and apart from anything you don't know that I don't want him around. I keep telling you!"

"But I don't understand. What's so bad about him? If I understood perhaps I could change things."

Ah, and there he had her, "I feel awkward having him around," she snapped. "I can't forget that we ran off and left him behind, and despite you saying it was ten years ago and it's forgotten now, I still feel bad. The memory hasn't gone. And apart from that, I just don't want to be friends with him. I certainly don't want him in my house. My life's moved on, I've got new friends."

"But what about me?" his face was suddenly angry. "What about what I want? I'd quite like to see him socially, are you telling me that your feelings are so strong that they override mine? Or are you just dictating to me?"

"*No*. I'm not. But I'm saying can you please respect my feelings and not make me host him overnight?" They glared at one another.

Behind them, the kitchen door opened and the twins sidled in.

"Mummy? There's a man in the spare room. In the bed," said Mia, looking faintly shocked.

Steph turned to Theo, a look of fury on her face.

"Yes that's our friend, Ed. You remember? He came here once before." Theo deliberately didn't look at Steph.

"Oh yeah, we do, don't we?" Tilly nodded. "So how come he's here now?"

"He came along to the party last night, at the school. With one of Mummy's friends. And it was too far for him to go home so he stayed here."

"But how come he didn't stay with Mummy's friend?"

"He preferred it here. Now I think you two had better scoot back upstairs and get dressed, you're riding in an hour."

Steph waited until their footsteps died away, "Oh well that's a really great example for the girls," she spat at him. "For them to wake up on a Sunday morning and find a strange man sleeping in the spare room."

"It would be worse if he was in with us," Theo quipped.

"Theo! That is not funny and I don't know how you can think of joking about this."

"Sorry." Theo looked at her sadly; where had his Steph gone? The one who was always up for a laugh? Who had a funny, infectious giggle that filled the room and brought a smile to the saddest face?

"It's just not appropriate for the girls."

"They're fine, they understand. They have friends for sleepovers."

"They're ten!" It was at that moment that Steph was overwhelmingly glad that they'd had the Poggenpohl kitchen fitted; otherwise she seriously thought that she would have damaged something.

And unsurprisingly, that morning had sparked the beginning of an intensely frosty period between them. Theo was confused and upset; he didn't remember things ever being this bad. Theo had apologised to Ed for Steph's unfriendly behaviour, "I'm sorry mate, she isn't normally like this."

"Don't worry, it's fine, she's probably hungover," Ed said easily.

"Yeah but still…" Theo was obviously upset; Ed felt sorry for him.

"Listen, I'm going to head off anyway," he said cheerily. "I'm meeting someone at the gym. Cheers for the bed, it was good to see you guys again. Maybe we can meet up in the week for a drink if you're allowed off childcare duty."

"Absolutely," Theo said gratefully. "Give me a call."

In the following days Steph felt herself sinking into an all-enveloping pit of despair. She was trapped. She had only the flimsiest of excuses for not wanting to see Ed, but it was literally all she had. And she was desperate, she had to use it. But the more she kept reiterating it the more pathetic and childish she sounded, which she knew confused and irritated Theo. He couldn't understand her point because essentially she didn't have one. Only, he didn't know that she knew that. So she had to keep doggedly on with it. She knew that she was behaving in a way that Theo didn't recognise and she saw that he retreated slightly from her. He didn't talk to her about Ed, didn't discuss seeing him or what they talked about. It was a jaw-droppingly anxious time. She couldn't sleep properly, started to lose weight; the whole thing played on her mind constantly. She understood that by sticking to her guns she was backing Theo into a corner with Ed, but she couldn't stop now that she'd started. The only other option was to suddenly 'change her mind' but that would give him free rein to her house, her husband and her children. It was a risk too far. But the odd thing was, if she delved deep into her consciousness beneath all the knowledge and fear that was ever-present, crouching like some poised tiger, she found that if things were different then maybe she would quite like to get to know Ed again. She'd liked him. But almost as soon as she'd had the thought, her mind closed off that lane of possibility and it was gone. No. It could never happen. Would never happen. And she mustn't think it.

Theo and Ed had met up one night at a pub midway between the two of them. Steph hadn't been happy about it but then she couldn't complain as Theo was fitting in with her rules; not in the house, not with her and not with the children. She'd thought that if she made things as tight as she possibly could then he'd be so put off that he just wouldn't bother. But that had backfired badly. So now she saw that she was in the position where Ed had come between them twice, and the fuss that she was creating was just drawing them closer; re-igniting an old, close friendship.

"I just can't understand it," he'd said to Ed. "She seems to have a real bee in her bonnet about what happened eleven years ago, thinks we were unfair."

"Hey – look – it's really fine. Forget about it."

Theo shrugged, "I have. We were kids. But she can't or won't let go of it."

"Want me to talk to her?"

"Maybe. But she's a bit prickly at the moment, I don't think she'd appreciate it." Privately, he shuddered at the idea. "Leave it a while. I don't know how to get across to her that some things can be left in the past."

"Just keep telling her," Ed sipped at his drink. "Keep telling her and showing her. And at the end of the day, she doesn't need to like me. We could just let her be."

"I know but it frustrates me. I want her to see how silly she's being. We've been friends for eons and I want her to join in." Theo looked upset.

"Give it time. We've only got together recently, and to her it must seem like one minute I was on the phone for the first time in ten years and the next I was everywhere. The coincidence with Julia is almost unfortunate."

"I know," Theo sighed. This was awkward. "She doesn't like that either."

"It was a bit of a surprise to me. I'd never thought anything of her all these years, barely remembered who she was. And then – bang, she was there at that reunion." A smile drifted across his face, "And she's great. I really like her."

"She has a reputation for being formidable."

"I like that. She's got balls." Theo could see how that would appeal to Ed, though inwardly it made him shiver, "Well as long as you're happy," he said.

Ed flung one arm back along the chair, "Ah, who knows. It's early days, very early days. But I'm prepared to make the effort for a bit, see what happens."

"And what about the fact that she's got a daughter?"

"Not ideal," Ed admitted. "No offence or anything, kids just really are not my scene at the moment. But I think I'm mature enough to cope with it if need be."

"Children aren't the devils you think they are, you know."

"Yeah, I know. Just unexplored for me. I'll get there one day."

"You need someone to make an honest woman of first," Theo remarked.

A frightened look shot across Ed's face, "Er – I think you're committed enough for the both of us."

"Marriage doesn't appeal?"

"Not just yet."

"Funny – I always had you down as a loyal kind of guy," Theo mused. "I thought you'd be the first to find someone and walk down the aisle."

"Really? Why? You were the one with the steady girlfriend at school."

"You seemed on a steadier path than me. I could never decide what I wanted to do. The reason being that I never knew until it hit me in the face."

Ed understood what he was saying. "Well, there you go. No, I had a whale of a time at Uni, it was a whole new world. Opened my eyes."

"Do you ever see any of the old lot? Rachel or Kirsty or James?"

"I speak to James and Kirsty from time to time, she runs that riding school in Tinford now, you know? But not the other girls, no." He couldn't tell Theo that he'd blamed them for not telling him about Theo and Steph being together. They'd just watched him mooch around after her and never told him anything. It had left a very bitter taste in his mouth and he'd found it hard to trust girls after that. They were cliquey, always sticking together. It was better, he'd found, to keep his distance. Even in relationships.

Theo found Ed's company very easy. And somehow, very

familiar. There was no getting to know him or judging whether or not he liked him; it was as simple as just catching up. The old ties were still there, this was someone who had once known Theo very, very well. Theo knew that it was him who hadn't been keen on staying in touch at first but that had been just jealousy, he hadn't been able to cope with the idea that his precious Steph had at one time been so close to Ed. It wasn't as if he presented a threat but Theo hadn't liked it.

But now it was a different matter. They saw each other not regularly after that, but frequently. For a drink in the pub or sometimes a round of Theo's beloved but neglected golf. They chatted, exchanged views and opinions and slowly pasted over the past. It was almost like being at school again. The only thing missing was Steph. She was watching from the wings in horror as this whole, ghastly pantomime was played out in front of her. How would it end? It hadn't been easy with Theo seeing Ed. But there was nothing she could do. The ground rules had been laid down and that was it. But every time he disappeared out to see him Steph's throat constricted and heart raced – would this be the night? The only way she could cope was by not thinking about it. Any of it. Not her mother's miscarriage, not the pregnancy, not her deception. And definitely not Ed.

****

"Phew!" Steph flopped gratefully into an armchair by the woodburner and accepted a glass of wine from Theo's dad, "Thanks Paul." She was determined that Christmas would be different. Christmas would be good, she would be the best mother and the best wife. Even if it meant using all her energy to push her scary thoughts very firmly to one side and leaving them there. She didn't need to think about Ed or his encroachment on her family; he wasn't there and everyone else was.

"You're welcome, you've had a busy evening."

"I know, but the worst bit's over now," Steph brushed some hair out of her eyes. "The frantic wrapping and getting everything under the tree is done for another year. Now I just have to concentrate on the food tomorrow."

"Hey you've got me for that," Theo came up behind her and dropped a kiss on her head.

"I'll believe that when I see it."

"You'll be believing it tomorrow then."

"I thought lunch went well?" There were murmurs of assent. They usually did a Christmas Eve night meal with Steph's mum and step-dad, but that was so inconvenient that it had been transmuted to lunch this year, which had worked much better.

"Though John was looking pale," Maggie remarked in her soft, Scottish lilt.

"Was he?"

"Oh yes. Always does dear, looks a bit worse each Christmas."

"I hadn't noticed. Did I tell you that Katie and Tom might pop in tomorrow morning after church for a glass of something?" she said to Theo.

"No, but that's fine. The more the merrier."

It felt very festive, with the woodburner lit, candles dotted around and carols playing softly in the background. Steph got up and stuck her head into the hallway to listen for the girls; nothing.

"I think they may be asleep," she tucked her legs up underneath herself and found a hairband to secure her hair. "Ooooh, that has been a long day."

"Ah you'll reap the rewards tomorrow," Maggie said. "When those wee lassies come charging down in the morning..."

"At some ungodly hour," Theo put in.

"That's the way of youth. Enjoy it now, it'll be past soon. They're growing quickly, your girls."

"Indeed."

Please don't, Steph squeezed her eyes shut tightly. Please don't mention another baby. It hung in the air for a minute as a possibility but nobody spoke. Steph breathed again. Even the mention of babies made her nervous and uptight, aggravated the lingering guilt. She'd even felt guilty wrapping the girls' presents that night; how much of this is a sham? Because we aren't what we appear to be. How far does the truth go? *No*, I will not think like this now.

"Steph!" Paul was standing by the door holding a camera. "Come on, smile! Say cheese!" Maggie and Theo thrust themselves behind Steph's chair and grinned for the camera. "Perfect," Paul said, examining the photo. "Perfect family picture."

"Let's see." It was a happy photo; Steph looked tired, Theo a little dishevelled and Maggie a bit mad, but it was a good memento of Christmas Eve 2007.

"More wine anyone?"

"Oh me please!" Steph hopped up. She felt determinedly but

pleasantly relaxed after the chaos of the day. Most things were done, not much to stress about... she flopped back in the chair and idly considered what she might get for Christmas. Theo knew that she wanted a new watch, a Raymond Veil one was her brand of choice, though at £1500 she doubted that would be under the tree. New Ugg boots – maybe, from the girls. A new iPod, the malfunctioning state of her old one was her current excuse not to go to the gym. She just could not run without an iPod, she couldn't imagine what she'd ever done before they were invented. Well, there had always been something hadn't there, Walkmans, mp3 players. The phone rang suddenly, disturbing the gentle burble of chatter in the room.

"I'll get it," Steph said. "I'm nearest." She hurried out to the hall before it could wake the girls, "Hello?"

"Steph?"

That familiar bolt of shock, fear and guilt all in one. "Hi." How could she have thought that she would escape?

"How are you?"

"I'm fine, thanks. You?"

"Oh you know, same old. Looking forward to Christmas?"

"Yes thanks. Shall I get Theo?"

"Er, yeah. Listen, take care, have a great one."

She didn't reply; left the phone lying on the table.

"Theo?" he turned, and her heart jolted as she saw the love, laughter and expectation on his face. He thought she was going to say something nice, it was Christmas Eve after all, they were in their beautiful home with their gorgeous girls and surrounded by family, of course he thought it was going to be something nice.

"Phone's for you."

"Really? Who is it?"

Steph said nothing, she stared at the floor. Theo gave her a strange look and passed by her to get to the phone, "Hello? Oh – hi, how are you? Yes, yes, I remember, how did it go?" A pause. "Seriously?! She actually said that. No, not really. I..."

Steph shut the door quietly, not wanting to hear any of their friendly chatter about familiar topics. What a bloody time to ring, Christmas Eve of all days! Didn't he think about anyone else? It occurred to her that he didn't really have anyone else to think about. That he knew of. Oh *God*.

"Who was that on the phone for Theo?" Maggie asked curiously. "Strange time for a phonecall."

Shit. "It was – it was Ed. Edward Osborne, from school?" she hated saying his name, she didn't know what showed in her face but it was bound to be some telling emotion.

Maggie sat up a little straighter, "Edward? Oh yes, I remember Edward. You three used to be such good friends, until," a cloud passed over her face, "well, until that little drama." She patted her hair uncomfortably. "I didn't realise you and Theo had stayed in touch. How is he?"

"We haven't stayed in touch, it's quite a recent thing. He rang out of the blue and we haven't seen that much of him really."

"Gosh, what a nice surprise for you both. I remember you three getting on terribly well."

"Mmm," Steph busied herself tidying the coffee table.

"But an odd time to ring, no? On Christmas Eve?"

"I think it's different for him, he doesn't have a family yet."

"Did he know about the twins?"

"No."

"I'll bet that was a nice surprise. Did he sound surprised?"

"I don't know. It was Theo who spoke to him."

"Oh it's always nice when old friends have children. It reminds me of the circle of life, a bloodline perpetuating itself. Genetic material passing down generation to generation, maintaining that family line."

"Yes," Steph replied slightly desperately.

"And when the parents are two such good friends, I'll bet he feels quite proud to know you all."

"Mmm."

The door opened and Theo came in, looking a bit guarded.

"Theo dear, Steph was just telling us about dear Ed. How nice you're back in contact. How is he?"

"Oh fine. He's a lawyer now, did you know? Yes, quite high up in one of the county firms, on his way to partner apparently."

"Goodness now, that's quite dizzy heights for that small, quiet boy," Maggie sounded surprised. "I never thought he'd go on to that, he didn't seem the type."

"He seems to have had some sort of epiphany at University," Theo threw himself down into a chair. "Seen the light or whatever and decided that was the path for him," Theo shrugged. "Good for him, I say. He's having a quiet Christmas."

"Oh yes?"

Steph tried to close her ears, not wanting to hear, not wanting to know.

"Yes, he's spending it with his mum."

"No girlfriend?"

"No. He's been seeing a friend of ours actually, a fellow parent at St Catherines. He knew her from Uni but it's only recently that they've been spending time together."

"What?" Steph turned, aghast. "They're not together properly are they?"

"Well… not together as such, I don't think. But definitely seeing one another."

Fuck.

Steph lay in bed a short while later, wide awake, heart thumping uncomfortably and stared at the ceiling. That was it, the spell had been broken and the magic had vanished from the air. Her perfect Christmas was ruined. None of it mattered now, not the piles of presents downstairs, not the enormous turkey waiting to be cooked, not the boxes of crackers, not the carols in the CD player. None of it. Because these material things were little more than a smokescreen shielding her from the God-awful truth, and all she could feel now were the walls were closing in on her. Like a cage was being constructed where she, Mia and Tilly were on the inside, huddled together, and Theo, Ed and Julia were on the outside, prowling like lions. And every now and then they'd unwittingly shake the cage a little and Steph would wait to see if it gave.

****

"Well, this is a nice surprise." Ed said. It was Boxing Day evening and he'd been settling back for an evening of beer and his Christmas DVDs when his door buzzer had gone.

"Hello?"

"Hi," a breathy voice had floated up at him. "It's Julia. I was in the area and thought I'd pop by and say hello." He'd toyed with the idea of seeing her over Christmas but had decided against it, too early for that he'd thought. "Can I come up?"

"Sure." He pressed the button to let her in and hastily threw his dirty washing back into the bedroom and scooped up the plate and glasses that lay on the floor.

"Hi," he pulled open the door and kissed both cheeks dutifully. She smelt of a heavy, musky perfume. "How are you?"

"Oh you know, I get by." She stepped past without asking and looked around critically. "This is a nice place. Big for an apartment."

"You think? Can I get you a drink?"

"A glass of wine would be lovely."

"Sancerre?"

"Perfect, darling." She followed him into the kitchen and casually dropped her bag and fur coat on the side. "Sorry to drop in unannounced, *so* rude, but I couldn't resist. I was literally passing by."

"It's no problem, I wasn't doing anything."

"How was your Christmas?"

"It was fine, just me and mum. Quiet. How about you?"

"Oh you know what it's like with a small child," Julia rolled her eyes. "Manic. Up at 5am, wrapping paper everywhere."

"No, I don't actually. I've never had Christmas with a child. Come through?"

Julia went through to the living room, clutching her glass of wine like a trophy and perched on the edge of his cream, leather sofa, "There are no children in your family?"

"None that I know of. I'm an only child and all grown-up now," he grinned at her. "We have very civilised Christmases."

"I'm quite envious. Ours are hectic and always end up with an over-excited child who's eaten nothing but chocolate all day. I'm always shattered on Christmas Day night. There are no decorations up in here?"

Ed looked around, "Well, no. I've got a small tree in the bedroom but there doesn't seem much point in going the whole hog. I'm not here during the day to appreciate them."

"Different world here darling, different world. Anyway, I just popped by to have a little chat. I was going to do it over the phone but," she spread her hands.

"Oh, OK, what's up?" Ed felt the wine move through him in a warm glow.

Julia hesitated, "It's – it's a little delicate darling."

"What is it?"

"It's about – us. Us seeing each other I mean. I know it's all nice and casual and we've kept it low key but I'm concerned that we might be treading on some toes." She raised her eyebrows meaningfully.

"Treading on toes? Whose toes?"

"Your delightful friend Steph."

"You don't sound like you mean that word."

"Hmm. I am aware of some *contention*, shall we say. About us."

"Really? From Steph?" Ed looked disbelieving.

"Afraid so. It seems that she isn't the happiest little bunny about our burgeoning relationship." Ed blanched at that phrase but Julia carried swiftly on, "And what I was going to say was that if it's going to cause problems between you and old friends, maybe we should knock it on the head? It's absolutely the last thing I want to do, we're having such fun, but perhaps it's wise?"

"Hang on, has Steph actually said that she's unhappy with us seeing each other?"

"It's filtered back to me that that is her view, yes."

"But she hasn't actually said it to your face?"

"No, but that isn't how these things work. It's a lot more subversive than that." And Julia was using some artistic licence, but Ed didn't need to know that.

"But – it doesn't make any sense. Steph's not like that, and she wouldn't have a problem with us getting together every once in a while, I'm sure," Ed said doubtfully.

"I'm just repeating what I've heard. I'd hate to be the one to come between you."

"Really – I'm positive that –" Ed stopped. Could he be positive? Look at Steph's behaviour towards Theo over seeing Ed. She'd done her level best to keep him away from Ed; everything bar a full-on tantrum according to Theo. Might she not do the same thing with Julia? Could there be some truth in it? And why would Julia lie?

"This is all a bit strange, but I'm not sure we should let it affect our friendship," Ed said carefully.

Julia gave him a winning smile, "Are you sure?"

"It's nothing to do with her, it doesn't affect her at all, we aren't particularly close anyway."

Julia leapt on that like a hound on a fox, "Really? I thought you were the best of chums?"

"We were, but to be honest," Ed leant back with a sigh, "ever since we got back in touch she'd been very – funny about seeing me. She doesn't seem to want to. Theo's fine, but Steph's been a bit awkward. I feel disloyal saying that but I can't let you have some misconception about the way things really are between the three of us. I like Theo a lot, he's a good chap, and Steph too but she is being a bit odd. Going to all sorts of lengths to keep me away from her family and I don't know why. Anyway, it isn't important but what I'm trying to say is don't let her feelings bother you. I'm not sure what's going on but it shouldn't concern you."

"There was something else as well. I wasn't going to tell you but I considering what you've just said I think perhaps I should."

"What's that?"

"Well, at the Murder-Mystery night, I overheard something in the toilets," Julia hesitated.

"Go on."

"Gosh, I feel awful saying this - Steph didn't know I was there for a start, and she was talking to Katie, she said '*How can I not worry about it? When he'll be so close to the girls? I physically felt my nerves frazzling when he stood near them last time – a whole night and the morning after...*'" Julia repeated the words verbatim, softly.

Ed frowned, "She said that? Why? I don't understand."

"I heard her."

"She doesn't want me near the girls? Mia and Tilly? But why not? What have I done?" His face creased in confusion and Julia felt a momentary and uncharacteristic stab of guilt.

"Apparently not. I don't know darling, she didn't say any more, but it does tie in with what you said."

"Oh. Shit, Julia, I really don't understand this," Ed felt a sudden surge of anger. "Seriously, I haven't seen her for eleven years and she's doing her level best to keep me away from an old friend and she thinks I present some sort of threat to her children?"

"I'm sure she doesn't see you as a threat. Some women can be quite protective of their young, you know."

"But she doesn't know me!" He felt the injustice keenly. "She's treating me like a predatory paedophile."

"No, no, I'm sure she isn't."

"I'm going to have to speak to her about all this you realise?" he looked at Julia, sitting so guilelessly on his sofa.

"I really don't think that's a good idea," she said hastily, swallowing the last of the wine. "I'd rather the information was treated in confidence. Besides, don't you think it would make things a little awkward for Theo? You'd be opening a whole can of worms."

Ed sighed out of sheer frustration, "She is – she's treating me like an enemy. A threat to her family. What the hell have I ever done to her?"

"I don't know darling, really don't, couldn't possibly comment," Julia did a good impression of discretion. "But perhaps if us getting together every so often is aggravating the situation then it's best if we stop?"

"No!" Ed felt an overwhelming indignation; who the hell did Steph think she was dictating who he could and couldn't go out with? An invidious thought made its way slowly into his mind; maybe Steph was actively trying to destroy his friendship with Julia so he wouldn't be around Theo? It all felt a little incestuous at the moment but he was on new territory. And if that was the case then he could not allow that to happen, Steph couldn't have everything her own way. Julia was right, he shouldn't say anything, he must just be grateful that she'd felt able to tell him.

"There's a works' drinks party next Friday. Want to come with me?" His blue eyes gazed steadily at Julia. Despite herself, she felt her cheeks redden, "I'd love to."

Ed indicated her empty glass, "Want another?"

"I can't, I'm driving. In fact, I must be off, I was only popping by. But thanks for the drink and I'm sorry to be the bearer of bad news."

"It isn't your fault, don't think that. It's a complicated situation. But I think we must carry on as before."

"I'm happy if you're happy."

Julia let herself back out onto the dark street with a sly grin. That had gone perfectly; better than she'd imagined. Talk about a cat amongst the pigeons, a bit of reverse psychology always worked. And Steph's attitude would get her nowhere either, what a bonus. She hurried back to her car, Ed was a good catch; young, single, wealthy and no children. He was ideal and there was no way he was going to slip through her fingers easily, Steph Hammond or no Steph Hammond.

CHAPTER THIRTEEN

"I've got a solution for you," Katie announced.

"Call me cynical, but I find that unlikely." Steph looked up, rubber gloves in hand.

"No honestly, I really think I might. Don't rule it out; listen to me." She pulled out a chair at the kitchen table.

"OK, I'm all ears." Steph slid the gloves on and began scrubbing out the sink with bleach. She remembered a time when she'd been all eco-friendly and green and nothing had passed the threshold that wasn't environmentally friendly, but that had gone out of the window these days. She just wanted fresh and clean and scrubbed till no lingering stains remained. And if bleach was the way to do that, then so be it.

"Right. You've been talking for years about how much you love interior design, OK? About how that would have been your career, that was what you'd planned, dreamt of, etc.?"

"Yeees..."

"Well it's simple – you need something to take your mind off all this, it isn't healthy being so wound up about it as you are."

"Can you expect any less?" Steph said grimly, scrubbing the sink until it shone. No traces of any dirt could be allowed to remain.

"No, but listen to me. I think you should reinvestigate your dream career. The girls are easily old enough by now, you've got a lot of spare time. Your baby plans are on hold – it's perfect. You've always been into redecorating here, it's the ideal time for you to branch out."

"Branch out of what? I haven't even got a starting block! I have no qualifications, no experience, and believe me, I know that competition for those sort of roles is very strong. It's the clever, determined, young students that are going to get them, not me."

"You're running yourself down. Turn it around – you've got the desire, the ability and the determination. You must tell potential employers that your age – and let's face it, you're not exactly over the hill yet – is a bonus, an added extra because therefore you have the maturity to make wise decisions and the experience to better judge what a wide range of people may want."

"I'm not sure. What about qualifications? I don't even have A-Levels."

"So get them. Don't let that put you off. You could be studying and getting work experience at the same time."

"In order to what?" Steph turned to face Katie, her eyes looked weary.

"In order to forge a new interest for yourself! In order to have some sort of identity outside the home. To be able to move on a bit, like who you are, get some self-confidence. You're pretty low on that at the moment. Don't forget I've known you a long time," Katie raised her eyebrows. "I know you pretty well Steph Hammond and I've never seen you so unhappy."

"I don't know why you're surprised."

"I'm not surprised; I'm *worried*."

Since her coffee-shop revelation, Katie had repeatedly tried to draw Steph into more and detailed disclosures about her and Ed, but Steph hadn't been able to do it. It spurred her into guilt and made her feel even more disloyal to Theo and the girls. She'd given Katie the bare bones, but that was it. She'd gone back to being wrapped-up in her thoughts and insular. Only being able to watch from afar had been very difficult, Katie found. She wanted to be in there, supporting Steph, helping her to come to terms with it, but that wasn't where Steph was headed. She was frozen in fear, waiting to be discovered; living her life on a knife edge. Even New Year had felt farcical, trying to celebrate a new year in a shit life. And it shouldn't be shit, everything was so perfect from the outside; talk about façades.

"Because you need to remember," Katie was saying in a determinedly cheery voice, "that this is the worst it's going to get. This is the lowest. I mean, you don't seriously imagine someone's going to guess do you? Well, there you are. And you're hardly going to spill the beans so don't worry. And think about something that you'd like to do for yourself. That's why I thought about interior design. Here…" She sheepishly pulled a wad of pages out of her capacious bag, "I hope you don't think I'm jumping the gun or anything, but I thought you might be interested in these." It was a selection of printouts about interior design; courses, qualifications, advice for work experience applications, even details about Steph's company of choice, Raggy Rose.

Steph stared at them, appalled. "I can't do all this!" She picked up a piece of paper listlessly, "I mean, listen to this – 'Your work as an interior designer would typically involve meeting with clients to discuss their requirements and ideas (the 'brief') , developing a design that suits the needs of the client, the available budget and the type of building, preparing initial sketches for the approval of the client, advising on colour schemes, fabrics, fittings and furniture, working out costs and preparing estimates...' – I can't do all that. All I've got is a vague eye for colours and patterns that might compliment each other."

"That's what training is for, building on existing skills. Don't be so hard on yourself."

"You will need a high level of design skill," Steph read out. "In practice, this usually means completing an art- or design-based BTEC HND or a degree. I don't even have A-Levels! Several universities offer interior design courses. Other useful subjects include fine art, 3-D design and architecture. You will need a portfolio of examples of your design work to show to potential employers and clients – Katie, does this really sound like me?" Steph tried to sound light-hearted and failed. "I'm an archetypal housewife, I'm good at running my home and bringing up my children, I can't go out to work and do all this."

Katie met her gaze, "You can do whatever you want to," she replied. "The question is whether you want to."

Steph looked away and continued with her cleaning. And later, when Katie had gone, she bundled up the pages and shoved them into the bottom of the desk in the study. It wouldn't do for anyone to catch sight of those and go about getting the wrong ideas.

****

"I'm enjoying this new regime." Ed was flopped on a chair in the clubhouse after a particularly long game with Theo. "I haven't played this game in years; in fact I didn't think I'd be able to, but I've surprised myself. You were right about a New Year's resolution to be more fit."

"I hate to say I told you so. But no, for me it was a no-brainer. Long days in the office, too much wine at weekends, it had to stop. I'm not the spring chicken I once was."

Ed took a sip of his water and grimaced, "Don't. You feel old – I'm the quintessential bachelor, think how I feel. No wife, no children, just a flat, not a house."

"I don't think you need to worry yet. I quite envy you your freedom sometimes." That wasn't strictly true. From time to time

Theo had found himself wondering what would life be like if it had taken a different path. If Steph had chosen Ed, for example, married him, had children with him, what would have become of Theo then? Would he have been a contender for the Sun's 'Shagger of the Year' award? Be on his way to being a high-flying lawyer with a plethora of casual girlfriends? No, he didn't think so. Wasn't the type. He would probably be much as he was now, with a different girl. Some faceless Steph clone. But he wouldn't be as happy, he knew that. He wouldn't have been able to achieve the absolute, perfect contentment that he had now without Steph.

"Penny for them?"

"Just thinking about the game actually," Theo said hastily. "It's nice to be away from the people I work with, to be doing this with someone else."

"Oh God, tell me about it. That's mostly what made me do this. I know I'm a lawyer but honestly, they are a bunch of wankers. Always talking about negligence this, discharge of duty that. I want to tell them to shut up sometimes, that they can just chill out and have a coffee." Their occasional round of golf had suited them both as they eased back into a friendship and kept Ed away from Steph. Theo was no closer to getting to the bottom of that mystery, but he'd given up trying.

"Did you tell Steph that I'm going out with Julia?" Ed asked Theo.

"Oh yes, by accident actually, but yes I did. Over Christmas I think."

"And she didn't flip out?"

"Not at all." Second lie of the night. "Didn't take much notice if I remember rightly."

"That's good. Good."

"How are things going anyway? Both happy?"

"Yes, I think so. I'm still not sure about the daughter though. I haven't met her yet."

"Tell you what, come and practice on ours. I know they're a bit older, but that will initiate you gently. Eleven year olds aren't generally as full on as – how old is Amy?"

"Four, five, don't know."

"Well they're less intense than that. Seriously, come round."

"Mmm. What about Steph?" It was the quickest excuse he could think of to avoid a crash-course in childcare.

"I'll speak to her," Theo said firmly. "She'll understand."

"Not so sure mate, I'm really not."

"She has to come round to this sometime, may as well start now." There was a brief pause. "Do you think we'll ever get to the stage of going out as a foursome?"

"Yes, eventually." Ed didn't think any such thing but felt loathe to say so. He had to be careful where Steph was concerned. Theo clearly idolised her and Ed doubted anything negative he said about her would go down well, which was why he'd held back from telling Theo what Steph had said about the children. Bearing that in mind, he could not imagine she would be happy to have him practising his lack of skills upon the girls. "Perhaps we should aim for that first? Test the water a bit? A dinner somewhere, us four, neutral venue. What do you think?"

"I think it could work," Theo said slowly. "It isn't as if Steph and Julia don't know each other and it isn't as if us three are strangers. Maybe we should do that, force the issue a bit?"

"If you're sure forcing is the right idea?"

"I don't see many other options. Rumble on as we are, meeting every couple of weeks on our own. It's ridiculous, they must see each other every day at school to natter in the playground or whatever it is they do. Why shouldn't we go out and be sociable?"

Ed wasn't so sure. Privately Julia had reported that Steph was a bit of a bitch at the school gates, driving up in her great big 4 x 4 and swanning around faux-moaning about her stay-at-home status. Apparently she rarely deigned to speak to Julia. It was amazing how time changed people.

"Well, OK. I'll leave it in your hands then. Go ahead and organise it by all means, I'm sure Julia would be up for it."

"Great, I'd like that." Theo smiled happily, wondering if he were being a bit naïve. But surely Steph wouldn't let him down, would she?

****

"Coo-ee! Steph!"

Steph rolled her eyes and took a deep breath before she turned around. Damn, she knew she should have got here later. It was 3:35pm in the playground and the children didn't come out for another ten minutes.

"Hello Julia, how are you?"

"Absolutely tip-top thanks, busy as ever!"

"How's it all going?" Julia had been struggling for work ever since she split up from her partner. She worked as an events organiser, but without Paul to organise the clients, the stream seemed to have dried up a bit.

"Well, you know. Meetings all over the place. Most of the work seems to be in London, which is a bit of a pain."

"Yes, I can imagine."

"Oh to be a stay-at-home mum like yourself," she laughed her silly twinkly laugh, "with nothing more to do than catalogue the freezer contents and make the beds." Steph looked at her with something approaching real dislike. "I'm joking, of course darling. I'm sure you make a very worthy contribution to society."

"Mmm. Us full-time mums generally do, keeping the children out of prison and so on."

"Oh, I see. Yes, well, what I was going to say was – how does Villa Marina suit you?" Villa Marina was an upmarket Italian resturant not too far away, but Steph hadn't the faintest idea what it should be suiting her for.

"Um, I'm not sure I quite follow you?"

"You know, for our dinner?"

"Dinner? You've lost me."

Julia's eyes widened, "You mean Theo didn't tell you?"

"Tell me what Julia?" Steph said slightly impatiently.

"Oh dear – I hope I haven't put my foot in it. The boys have been cooking up a plan between them, a cosy dinner for four somewhere. Ed told me about it last week."

Steph felt her face flush with anxiety immediately, "Right…"

"You had no idea?"

"Clearly not." She struggled to think of something appropriate to say. Deep breaths Steph, deep breaths.

"Oh. Well it's not a problem is it? I thought it was quite a good idea. We know each other, boys know each other, you and Ed know each other. Ironically it's me and Ed who know each other the least!" Julia leant in close to whisper: "Although, we're changing that fairly rapidly, if you know what I mean," and she winked at Steph.

Steph closed her eyes briefly, oh the horror. She had an image of a runaway train careering out of control and plunging down an embankment. "No," she said. "It's not a problem, but let me speak to Theo about it before we firm anything up."

"Perhaps I should have mentioned before, I've taken the liberty of booking a table at the restaurant for the Friday after next. I hope you don't mind. And I had to give a £10 per head deposit," Julia shrugged, "doesn't sound like much I know but in my current state... I'd hate to have to cancel the table. I wouldn't have done it but Ed said that Theo was sure."

Then you shouldn't bloody well have booked it, Steph wanted to shout. But instead she willed herself to remain calm, "As I said, let me speak to Theo but I'm sure there won't be a problem."

The twins ran up, swinging their rucksacks, "Mummy! I'm starving, did you bring me something to eat?" Mia demanded.

"Is my DS still in the car?" Tilly asked. "Here Mummy, you carry this."

Suddenly Steph's hands were full of rucksacks, art aprons and sports bags. She turned to Julia, "I'll get back to you."

"Sure. Absolutely no problem darling, I look forward to it." She watched Steph walk away through narrowed eyes; flanked by her two blonde girls they looked like a model family if there had ever been one. God, she was so smug, she needed taking down a peg or two. Everything was so bloody perfect in her world; rich husband, nice car, perfect children. It would do her no harm at all to be a little jealous of Julia for once. Ed had mentioned dinner in an ultra-casual way and been very clear that Theo was in charge, but it was too good an opportunity to miss. Ah ha, at last, a chance to show Steph that she had something worth having for once. She obviously felt something for Ed, otherwise why the nerves about having him near the children? She was clearly afraid that by letting him too close to the family he might upset things, and how many reasons could there be for that? No, Julia was sure Steph still held a candle for Ed and the last thing she wanted was to see Julia happy with him, it would mar her perfect little world. Well poor Steph, what a shame. Gloves off, claws out – roll on dinner. Julia smiled a tiny, tight smile.

****

Theo could sense an atmosphere the minute he walked through the door. Same routine for him, jacket off, keys down, but there was no noise, no sound of the girls playing or watching TV, no music on in the kitchen while Steph cooked. The house was deathly silent.

"Hello?" Maybe they weren't in for some reason.

"Daddy! It's Daddy!" He heard one of them say upstairs and then scrambling as they leapt up and thudded down the stairs.

"Hello gorgeous girls," he wrapped his arms around them and gave them a kiss. "How are you?"

"Fine," they grinned up at him with their stunningly blue eyes.

"Good day at school?"

"Yeah, except cross-country, we hate that don't we Tilly?"

"Good for the soul, I'll have you know."

"I don't think so," Mia said.

"Rubbish, it's character building. Where's Mummy?"

"In the kitchen," Tilly told him. "But she's in a bad mood so we were upstairs."

"Why? What's happened?"

Mia shrugged, "Don't know. But she just kept snapping at us, didn't she?" Tilly nodded assent.

"Oh. Maybe she has a headache. Let's go and find out shall we?" With an arm round each girl, Theo opened the kitchen door, "Hello darling, what's up?"

"What do you think?"

"Sorry?" One look at her was enough to tell him that she was properly angry. He cast around for reasons why, "I'm sorry, I really don't know."

"OK, how about we talk later?" She gave him a meaningful look.

"Ah. Yes, good idea."

Both girls rolled their eyes, "We are old enough to know that you mean that you don't want us around," Mia said.

"Never you mind. Have you had supper?"

"Yep, we had jacket potatoes and fish goujons. Mummy made them, I love them," Tilly said happily.

"And carrot sticks, don't forget those. Mrs Hamper was explaining last week how important it is to eat five lots of fruit or vegetables every single day."

"She's spot on, it's very important." Theo kept one eye trained on Steph; she looked as she usually did these days, tired and a bit deflated.

"She made us make a list of all of our favourite fruit and vegetables, I was quite surprised by how many there were," Tilly remarked.

"Oh yes?"

"Yeah. I had loads. Not as many as Mia though, but I think she was lying."

"I was not!" Mia said hotly.

"So how come you said you liked spinach but whenever Mummy makes it you won't eat it?" Tilly said archly. "I saw your list."

Mia flushed, "You copied!"

"I did not!"

"Did too!"

"Girls, that's enough. Have you done your homework?"

"Yeeees Dad," Mia grumbled. "Can I play on the computer?"

"If you want to, only ten minutes though."

"Cool, thanks Dad."

"I'm going to read," Tilly announced.

Theo ruffled her hair, "Off you go then. But bed soon, I mean it." He waited until they'd disappeared, "She's just like you Steph, head always in a book. So what's up?" Steph was unusually quiet. And unusually dressed, he saw. Old jeans and a baggy jumper, and her hair was just scraped back. "Are you feeling OK?"

"Yes, why wouldn't I be?"

"Just wondering. You don't normally wear those clothes." Too late, Theo realised how that sounded. "I didn't mean it like that…."

"Well you obviously did. What are you trying to say? That I'm not making enough effort for you?"

"No, of course not."

"What then?"

"Never mind. What's up?"

"Do you really need to ask?"

"Yes!"

She regarded him for a moment, "I had a nice little chat with Julia today."

"Oh yes?"

"Where she informed that we are all going for dinner, you, me, her and Ed," she spat the last name at him.

Theo groaned inwardly, "No, that is not what's happening."

"It is according to her."

"*No*. What Ed and I agreed was that at some point it might be nice if we all went out for dinner, and we would go away and discuss it with our respective partners. That was all."

"I don't believe you."

"What?"

"I don't believe you."

"Steph – I swear, that is all that's happening."

"If it ever was, it's not any more."

"What do you mean?"

"I mean that she's booked the bloody table. Friday after next."

Theo stared, "You're joking?"

"I am not."

"Honestly Steph, that wasn't the plan. We hadn't even discussed a date, it was just a vague idea."

"Theo, I'm really not sure whether I believe you. Why would Julia think she had carte blanche to go ahead and book an actual table if Ed didn't tell her so?"

Theo spread his hands, "I really haven't got a clue. I don't know what Ed told her. When I left him the plan was just to raise it as an idea."

"Well I'm not going," she turned her back to Theo.

"Pardon?"

"I'm not going." She didn't even look at him this time.

Theo took a deep breath, "All right. You're not going. To something that I thought might be a nice idea, that we haven't even discussed yet. Do you have any idea how that sounds?"

"I don't care."

"You don't care?"

"No."

"I swear to God Steph, I have never, ever known you behave like this in all of our lives. You are acting like a spoiled child. It's a simple invitation to a nice dinner with two friends, why the hell are you behaving like you're five? I just don't know what is up with you these days! We aren't getting on, you're being stroppy left, right and centre, bloody demanding, you refuse to speak to Ed because of some petty, teenage grievance," he was shouting now, "all in all, I feel pretty let down by you of late. I never thought I'd say that to you, my wife, but I really fucking do." He was vaguely aware of a shape behind the kitchen door, but it withdrew. One of the girls, he realised, quietly going away, appreciating what was going on. They were so grown-up these days. "What happened to the nice, caring woman you used to be? Calm, unflappable, knew exactly what she wanted in life, wonderful mother, fantastic wife. You've morphed into this – this – sulky, moody, miserable person that I don't recognise. And this isn't a passing thing, it's been going on for months. Our parents said we wouldn't last," he said sadly, "maybe they were right."

Steph's face was white, shocked rigid. "What do you mean?" she mumbled through numb lips.

"I mean is this the beginning of the end? Because you sure don't seem happy any more."

"No, no, it isn't. Nothing like that," she forced from her mind the likely chain of events if Theo were ever to discover the truth.

"I mean it, I feel so let down. You've embarrassed me thoroughly in front of our mutual friend on many occasions, you refuse point blank to have him in the house or speak to him on the phone. I thought you were a better person than that Steph, I really did. I don't understand it and neither does he. There's no reason."

She didn't know what to say. "I am a good person Theo. I love you so much, I really do."

"If that's true, why the behaviour?"

"Because, because..." She looked down; no idea what she was going to say. "I suppose I was angry that things weren't going my way," she said finally. It was a thin, flimsy excuse, but it would have to do.

"*Your way?*" Theo looked faintly incredulous. "Are you being serious?"

"Well yes, I didn't want you to be friends with him."

"And that's it?"

"Yes."

"I can't believe you, Steph. You have allowed some pathetic, childish gripe to become between us, make us argue and fall out more than we ever have in the history of our marriage. The girls say that you're snappy and grumpy, they choose to be upstairs rather than down here with you – I am appalled. Appalled at your lack of judgement." Theo suddenly realised how angry he was. This wasn't getting them anywhere. "I'm going out. I'll talk to you later."

"Where are you..." the words died on her lips as he wrenched open the kitchen door, grabbed his keys and the front door slammed behind him. Steph watched fearfully, he had never stormed out like that before, ever. Not as long as she'd known him. She sat down to relieve her shaking legs and her eyes filled with tears, was all that true? Was she letting him down? Was she being a bad mother? It was a terrible thought.

Theo was gone a long time. Past the girls bedtime, which Steph endured with as much jollity as she could muster, carefully explaining their father's absence as work-related. Then past their dinnertime and past their bedtime. At 11:30pm, Steph gave up and went to bed, not bolting the front door, just in case. As she was in the bathroom cleaning her teeth, she heard it slam. Theo back, or a burglar. She wasn't sure which would be worse. He came straight upstairs and lounged in the doorway, watching her, "Hi."

"Hello."

"You OK?"

"Yes. You?"

"Yes. Calmer now. Sorry for storming out."

"It's OK." There was a huge gulf between them. Steph desperately wanted to cross the floor and throw herself into his arms, but she couldn't. Of course she couldn't. But there was one thing she could do.

"I'll do it," she said suddenly. "Theo, I'll do it, OK? I'll do this dinner. If that's what you want, if that will make you happy, I'll do it. I'll sit with Ed and Julia and make sparkling, polite conversation."

"It would make me happy, but that's not really good enough. I don't want to have to force you into it."

"You haven't, I've just," she hesitated, "seen that it's the right thing to do. That's all."

Theo nodded slowly, "Come here." He drew her into his arms. "I love you, you silly girl. I love you."

Too choked to speak, Steph just nodded.

As she lay in bed that night, after some incredibly tender lovemaking, listening to Theo's breathing slow down as he fell asleep, she realised something. This secret of hers, the impact of which came upon her in great, breaking waves with the calm troughs in between, would never go away. She could never, ever escape it. For as long as Ed and her girls were on the same planet, it would never leave her alone. And she wasn't quite sure how she would live like that.

CHAPTER FOURTEEN

Sooner than Steph had realised, the date of this dinner wasn't the 'Friday after next', it was just next Friday. Then six days away, five days away, four days away, and after that just too horribly close to think about. The date loomed over her, larger than she liked, the day had been marked on the family calendar with a black star, but no one had commented.

It was quite a horrible concept.

But after Theo's tantrum, which had shocked her more than she cared to admit, she could not back out, and neither could she be seen to be openly loathing the idea. Day after day she told herself that she must be calm, she must enthuse. His stinging remark had cut her to the proverbial quick. Her, letting him down? He'd never said anything like that before, never as much as hinted it. She refused to think about the marriage comment. It couldn't be true, could it? But Theo wasn't given to rash remarks. He must be truly hurt. And she would *not* let Ed come between them again. Not now. Not in this life. He would not win; she would.

As the day approached, Steph privately panicked and outwardly was calm and polite, choosing a dress, matching shoes and buying a new bag for the occasion.

"How much is that bag? Do you really want to spend that much on an accessory for one night?" Katie hissed at her in John Lewis.

Steph stared, "Yes. I'm not going to be bested by Julia."

"You know what she's like," Katie warned. "She'll pull something amazing out of the bag on the night."

"She can't pull a few years out of the bag can she? At the very least I can look younger and slimmer."

"Mi-*ow*."

Steph shrugged, "If she can play dirty, so can I."

"Is she playing dirty?"

"Do you genuinely expect me to believe that she's conveniently fallen in love with my old best friend?"

"Maybe...."

"You're a nicer person than I am, then. I'm sure she's doing it to annoy me."

Privately, Katie doubted that anyone would be able to pick up on the finer nuances of Steph's emotions, however much she might believe them capable. Steph was imagining things that simply were not there. Julia was pursuing a younger, wealthy man, that was all there was to it.

"So are you dreading this dinner then?" Katie asked over coffee in the café.

"Are you mad? Of course I am. Sitting at a cosy table for four surrounded by someone I dislike, my oblivious husband and the father of my children, it's not a recipe for a fantastic night is it?"

"At least you have your Lulu Guiness bag to soothe your woes."

"True. I can pack up all my troubles in my Lulu Guiness bag."

"If you're laughing about it, it can't be that bad."

"Oh, it can, believe me. The thing is, I'm just running out of fight. I feel weary. Isn't that awful? I've been beaten down by my emotions," Steph raised a mock hand to her forehead. "I have to go, Theo needs me to go and somehow I have to find the strength to sit through a bloody-awful meal, be on my guard and yet witty and polite. And look a million dollars."

"That's the easy bit. Shall I help you choose an outfit? I'll be there for the girls anyway. I could just come a bit earlier?"

"That would be great. And bring your armour – this is battle!"

****

"Why don't you wear the same dress you wore to the Murder-Mystery thing Mummy?" Tilly enquired, lounging across her and Theo's king-size double bed.

"Because you can't wear the same thing twice to events the same people are going to."

"Why not?"

"Because they've seen it."

"So?"

"It's just not the done thing," Steph explained, fastening huge diamond studs into her ears. Even to her it sounded ridiculous, but if she wore the same thing, Ed might think she only had one nice outfit.

"Well, I like that dress anyway." It was a backless halter-neck in midnight blue, with a ruched skirt. Steph liked the way that it was covertly sexy and displayed her back muscles, toned through her years of yoga. It had also had a short skirt, but by virtue of the high neck managed not to be tarty. Once again her legs were clad in shimmery tights and matching blue heels. With her new clutch bag, manicured nails and professionally blow-dried hair, Steph was filled with confidence.

"Well I don't like that dress," Mia said, entering the room.

"Mia! That's rude. Why not anyway?" Tilly asked.

"I like this one better," she rummaged at the back of the wardrobe and pulled an old, silver sequin dress to the front.

"Mia, that was a dress I wore to a nightclub years ago. It isn't a dress for going out to dinner."

"I just said I liked it."

"Who likes what?" Theo appeared in the doorway, glass of wine in hand.

Steph groaned, "Can I not get ready without an audience?"

"You look ready to me," Theo looked her up and down. "You look amazing. Come here." He went to grab her waist but Steph squirmed away, "Careful! You'll ruin my hair."

"And this the woman who resisted the dinner with all her might? Who is now titivating herself so carefully?"

Mia sniggered, "Did you hear Tilly? Daddy said *tit*ivating."

"Girls," Theo gave them a stern frown. "Go downstairs and find Jack." He sighed as the upstairs of the house almost shook as they thundered down the stairs.

"Seriously, you look wonderful. Beautiful. I shall be very proud of you."

"Flatterer."

"It's true." He watched as Steph squirted perfume on her neck, wrists and then into the air so she could walk through the cloud. She'd done him proud. He'd felt awful for guilt-tripping her into agreeing to come but his patience had well and truly snapped that night. And you never knew, perhaps this might be the push that she and Ed needed to kick-start their friendship.

"Do you like the make-up?"

Theo peered closely at the subtle foundation, smoky eyes and glossy lips, "It's a bit more OTT than normal, but yes. Good for tonight. Did you do it?"

"No, Katie. That's why I asked. She brought this massive load of stuff with her, far more than I own, and I asked for a bit of glamour and got this! She even put glitter eyeliner on me, I thought that was the preserve of teenagers."

"I wouldn't say so. Listen, the taxi will be here in ten minutes. I'm going to hunt out my shoes."

Steph could feel her heart beating faster than normal as they sped through the streets towards the restaurant, but the pre-dinner gin and tonic she'd downed had done its work.

"Good luck," Katie had whispered urgently in her ear. "Just relax and you'll be fine."

By looking at Katie's face she could tell that she didn't actually think that. "No, really, you will."

"It's a bit weird though."

"It's a lot weird, just don't let it get to you. Pretend it's all normal, two old friends of yours joining you for dinner."

"Not some apparently misogynistic man who is actually the father of my children and the worst of all the mothers at school?"

"It sounds like a cabaret act, but don't. Don't think like that. The girls will be fine anyway."

"Even if their mother isn't," Steph said grimly.

"Stop it! Go, enjoy it. Good restaurant."

"Yes, it is," Theo said from behind them. They swung round. "What? I've been reading comments on their website. Plus Michael Winner was in there a couple of weeks ago and wrote a rave review that's going to be published next week. Once that's out bookings will go through the roof so we're definitely going at the right time."

"Great," said Steph, gulping the last of her gin and grabbing her cashmere wrap. "Let's go."

And now, as they walked through the darkened restaurant, its tables lit only by candlelight and a handful of Italian waiters in improbably tight trousers dashed around, Steph's eyes strained ahead desperately trying to catch a glimpse of where Ed and Julia might be sitting, so she could prepare herself before she actually had to speak to them.

"Can I take your...?" a waiter interrupted her thoughts.

"Oh, thanks," Steph handed over her wrap absent-mindedly, only then realising how naked she suddenly felt. Theo put a protective hand on the small of her back and ushered her through the restaurant in front of him, like a trophy, Steph thought. And then she saw the back of his head, blond, hair immaculately combed, stiffly ironed collar just below. He stood up when he saw them, "Hello." He grabbed Theo's hand and shook it in an overly formal manner, "Great to see you, how are you? Steph, you look stunning, as always." He didn't quite meet her eyes and reached out to kiss her cheek. She couldn't move and acquiesced; his lips touched her skin for the first time since that night. They were warm and soft and his aftershave was evocative, a familiar smell that she couldn't quite place. Nice.

"Steph, darling!" Julia moved swiftly in on Ed's moment and took her arm, "Fantastic to see you. I love that dress," she said in a lowered tone. "It looks fab. Where's it from?"

"A little boutique a friend recommended to me. One of those things you don't leave behind."

"No, it's great. Gorgeous. Sit down, sit down. We've been waiting."

"Not long I hope?"

"No, just long enough for a little drink," Julia touched Ed's hand proprietorially.

The table was square, everyone sitting at their own side. Glancing around, Steph saw Ed and Julia next to each other, rather than opposite, which left her a choice of sitting next to either Ed or Julia. Neither appealed, but Theo made the choice for her by sliding into the seat next to Julia, trapping Steph between him and Ed. Deliberate? She couldn't tell. She gave Julia's outfit a once over, which was difficult while she was sitting down. It appeared to be a dress, quite a fitted dress with a scoop neck and she was wearing a long, gold necklace that carefully drew attention to her *décolletage* in an understated way.

"We took the liberty of choosing some wine," Ed said, clearing his throat. "We went for a Cote du Rhone, as there's a lot of red meat on the menu."

"Funny isn't it how there's no pizza?" Julia said. "You'd expect that in an Italian. It never matters though."

"I think the idea is that it's an upmarket Italian," Theo said. "So it's not your bog-standard Zizzis or ASK. The food is amazing here." He told them about Michael Winner.

"Do you come here often?" Ed asked.

"A fair amount. It's one of our favourite restaurants isn't it darling?"

"Mmm. It is. We haven't been here for a while though."

"When was the last time?"

"I think Fiorina and Tim's wedding reception."

"A wedding reception here?" Ed asked disbelievingly.

"Yes, Fiorina was an old friend of mine from the girls playgroup and her parents were Italian, so it made sense. They wanted an authentic feel to the evening, and you certainly get it here." Steph sipped at the wine, she wasn't a big fan of red but this was nice.

"I'll second that," Julia said. "On the few occasions I've been here the waiters are flirting with me the second I set foot through the door. Typical Italian studs!"

Steph considered pointing out that was their job but decided against it. Ed met her eye and lifted his eyebrows slightly, "Well I've never been here," he said, studying the menu. "But it all looks very impressive."

"Honestly, the food's great," Steph said. "And, if there's something you want that isn't on the menu, they'll still do it for you. Like, years ago they used to do a really nice carbonara and Theo loved it, didn't you? And then they stopped doing it but when we commented they said just ask, we'll still do it for you."

"Favoured customers obviously." Ed winked at her, Steph blushed. "Anyway," he raised his glass. "Cheers, nice to see you all." They clinked glasses.

"Very nouveau-riche," Theo joked.

Julia looked taken aback, "Really? I didn't know that."

"I think a little tap is OK," Theo explained kindly. "Just not a great big whack against someone's glass."

"Oh right. I see. Still, quite a social faux-pas I imagine? Not a mistake you want to make?"

"It depends what circles you mix in," Steph said wickedly. "Probably glass-clinking is acceptable among some."

Ed tried to hide a smile. "More wine Steph?"

"Thank you."

"Hmm," said Theo closing the menu. "I'm going to have *Pezzetti di pollo al funghi*."

"Funghi? That's mushrooms isn't it?" Julia asked slightly anxiously.

"Yes." Theo confirmed. "I love mushrooms. Steph and I went to Italy a couple of years ago and I discovered quite how much I love Italian dishes, with mushrooms in particular. They usually serve them with a creamy sauce."

"That'll stick to your ribs," Ed commented.

"Yes, true," Theo sighed, "but hey, if you can't have a good night out every once in a while…"

"Oh absolutely," Julia purred. "I couldn't agree more. You can't get too hung up on your figure can you?" She looked around expectantly.

This the woman who's constantly in the gym, Steph thought. But she didn't say anything.

"We must set an example for the little ones too," Julia continued. "Just the other day Amy was asking me how much she weighed. I was quite horrified."

"Really? I don't think the twins have any concept of weight, do they darling?"

"Actually, Mia does," Steph told him. "She asked me a few months back whether she was fat. I told her that none of us will ever be fat, we eat the right kind of foods. And they work hard on it at school as well, when was it the girls were listing their favourite vegetables and finding that they liked more than they realised?"

"Oh yes, I'd forgotten that."

"That's quite good then," Ed commented gamely.

"But Tilly's never mentioned weight," Steph continued bravely. It was quite funny to discuss a secret with people who didn't know that they were a secret. "They're very different girls though. And I was never concerned about my figure when I was younger."

"I was. I recall being concerned about my body shape at school, but the lack of muscles rather than anything else!" Ed said. Steph laughed obediently.

"There's nothing remotely low-fat on this menu," Julia commented. "Everything's full of cream and cheese."

"Let's not bother about calories tonight," Ed said, smiling at her and squeezing her knee. "Just choose what you fancy."

Julia wrinkled her nose, "I don't know. Perhaps the *tagliatelle gamberoni* then."

"Steph?" Theo asked.

"Oh, um, *anatra con miele*, I think. I'm not a big fan of seafood."

"No, me neither," Ed agreed. "What's *anatra con miele*?"

"Duck. Probably a breast and probably grilled. Miele is honey so with some sort of sweet sauce."

"How do you know so much Italian?"

"I don't really. Theo and I spent three weeks out there with the girls near Lake Como a couple of years ago and we picked up some of the language then, that's all."

"Lucky you. I'd love to visit Italy, but I haven't got round to doing it yet."

"I'd recommend it, go for a while if you can. Absorb the culture. That's what we decided to do, rent a villa for those weeks and then use it as base while we travelled about a bit."

"How the other half live," Julia said lightly, toying with her wine glass.

There was an uncomfortable silence, only alleviated when the waiter appeared.

"So, Julia," said Theo once they'd ordered, "how's things on the work front?"

Good work Theo, thought Steph. It was safe ground as a topic.

"Terrible if I'm being honest. Things seem to have ground to a halt at the moment. I mean, it was never going to be easy in this climate but I didn't think it would get this bad."

"But Julia, you're always meeting clients," Steph said.

"Yes, but they rarely go on to have a full-blown event requiring me. They come along, get a few handy hints for free and then bugger off."

"Maybe you should charge by the hour?" Theo suggested.

"But giving a free initial meeting is how we drum up interest. Without that, I doubt we'd get any clients. Obviously I always recommend my services."

"What sort of companies do you deal with?"

"Well, funny you should mention that actually Theo, because I was thinking…" she shifted in her seat towards Theo and Steph couldn't hear what she was saying. She couldn't be pitching for business could she? Not here? She glanced at Ed and he was frowing at Julia; she was! She was networking at this dinner. Steph choked back a laugh and lifted her glass to her lips again. Ed caught her eye and raised an enquiring eyebrow. Steph shook her head and broke the gaze, but with Theo and Julia occupied she had no one to talk to. An uncomfortable silence lingered for a minute.

"You might have to talk to me now," Ed said to her in a low voice.

"Sorry?"

"I said – you might have to talk to me now."

"I don't know what you mean," Steph's fingers froze around the stem of her wine glass.

"Sure you do," Ed said easily. He sat back slightly in his chair and watched her through narrowed eyes. "You go out of your way not to talk to me."

Stung, Steph didn't respond.

"Sorry, am I being unfair?"

"Yes. I don't go 'out of my way' as you so charmingly put it."

"OK. I like your dress, looks good."

"Thank you."

"It's a bit more conservative than what I remember you wearing."

"Really?" It was an oddly flirtatious remark. Steph didn't ask what he remembered, didn't want to know.

"Yes. But that was a long time ago. Ten years now. It's surprising how so much changes in ten years. Things that are so important then are so trivial now."

Oh God, Steph thought, but, "Yes, I know what you mean," she said non-committally.

"It was a lifetime ago that we were friends wasn't it?"

"Yes."

"And there's been ten long years in between where we haven't spoken, haven't known anything about each other."

"Ed, where are you going with this?"

"My point is that we're two different people now, and it's all right if you don't like the grown-up version of me. You're not obliged to."

Steph closed her eyes briefly, "It isn't that," she began.

"Then what? What is it? Because you've made it very plain that you don't want me around you, or around Theo. I can't have done anything so I don't need to apologise, I just wanted to let you know that it's OK if you simply don't like me." He wanted to add that he didn't much like the new version of Steph, the snotty stories that drifted to him via Julia were not appealing. It was funny though, she never seemed like that when he spoke to her. Steph seemed, well – *Steph*. Normal. Polite, firm, friendly.

"Well, thanks. It's good to know, but actually, that isn't the case."

"No? Then what is?"

Steph's breath caught in her throat. This was a moment, she could tell him. She could look deep into those unfathomably blue eyes and say those unspeakable words. But she knew before she started thinking it that she would do nothing of the sort. It was like being gagged, she couldn't ever envisage a situation where she would voluntarily speak those words. After all, what good would it do any of them?

"How about we just move on?" she said easily, and smiled. Chin up, bright smile, make yourself look at him. "Start again as it were?"

"I'm happy with that if you are."

He was still devastatingly handsome, she realised, looking at him. That fine blond hair, strong, chiselled jaw – such a cliché but so true. She made herself look away and felt a hand on her knee, she jumped, convinced it was Ed's but no – silly you, Steph, it was the wrong side. And what demented thought process had made her think that Ed might do something so intimate? She wrestled with the question as Theo's concerned, brown eyes looked at her, "You all right? Having a nice time?"

"Yes, it's lovely."

A plate of bruschetta was placed in front of them and Steph busied herself with arranging her napkin and side plate as Theo put a slice onto it for her, "There you go."

"Thanks." Why did she have a sense of a conversation being left halfway through? There wasn't anything more to say. But what would have been said if Theo hadn't turned at that precise moment? Steph felt a twinge of annoyance and was cross with herself, Theo was her husband for goodness sake. She raised a hand and raked it through her long, glossy hair. It felt odd to feel the weight of it on her back, like she were naked. The thought was strangely arousing, and she caught Ed looking at her with that intent look of his and was embarrassed that he'd caught her thinking such a private thing. Her face felt hot, and stomach tense. She didn't want to eat a thing.

"Don't you like it Steph?" Julia asked, more as a challenge than anything else.

"I do, yes. But I get full so quickly that I don't really eat starters. You guys go ahead." She saw clearly the irritation in Julia's face. As Steph had said it first, Julia could hardly claim the same was true of herself.

The conversation was easy, it flowed remarkably well. Even if Theo was the only one who was completely relaxed. In between talking to Theo about their mutual interests, of which they seemed to have racked up quite a few, Ed was doing a good job of putting Julia at her ease, showering her with compliments and taking interest in everything she said, which Steph couldn't help noticing was mostly about herself. No mention of Amy. And yet, Ed's faultless manners seemed a little false. It was like he was saying what Julia wanted to hear without actually meaning it, Steph had a sense of his mind being elsewhere. Where was it? What was occupying his inner thoughts?

"Do you want to know what I remember?" Ed asked, turning to her suddenly in the interval before their main course. He hadn't spoken to her for about fifteen minutes.

"In what sense?"

"I remember a silver dress, I think it had sequins, it was certainly spangly. It was a dress you used to wear out clubbing," he smiled.

"You probably don't remember but it was that dress I loved on you. Not the sort of thing you'd wear now, of course." He missed the expression of shock on her face.

****

"So," Julia was quite drunk. They'd drunk two bottles of the red wine and one of white between them and now the girls were drinking Baileys and the boys had whiskey. "So," she repeated with an effort, "I want to hear all about the good old days. Way back when. When you all knew each other and I didn't know one of you," she laughed. "You must have some stories to tell."

"Not really," Theo said. "I think we were probably quite boring in that respect. Just normal teenagers."

"Well quite. There must be tales of unrequited love and derring-do." She was speaking too loudly, and too insistently, her words punctured the cosy, fluid atmosphere. They were relaxed, sitting back in the chairs, napkins askance, legs crossed. Theo's hand trailed idly across the back of Steph's neck, stopping to caress it occasionally. But Julia's words made them all sit up slightly.

"No," Theo was casual, "I really don't think so. We were very civilised. Unless you count the time Ed got wasted on cider at a village fete and threw up in front of the mayor," he grinned.

Ed groaned, "Oh don't remind me. I think my mum's still cross with me."

Julia put a hand too close to the top of his leg, "I think your Law degree and five figure salary go some way towards extinguishing those memories don't you?" Her eyes were huge and drunk in her face.

Ed looked at her with confusion, "Not sure," he murmured, twisting the cloth napkin in his hands.

"Anyway, it isn't those sorts of tales I want, it's the gossip. *Real* gossip. Like who kissed who first, who fancied who, who fell out with who. I want bare bones, warts and all," she demanded.

Theo looked slightly taken aback, "Honestly Julia, I really don't think anything like that went on. Us three were just friends, until Steph and I left Tinford."

"Exactly. So where did it start? There must be a story behind that. And Ed, didn't you mind being left behind?"

Oh Jesus, Steph was mortified. She couldn't have picked a worse conversation. Ed cleared his throat, "No," he said. "Not at all. It was fine, not an issue. Their lives took them off in a different direction, I was never anything other than happy for them."

Brave, loyal words, Steph thought, but fundamentally untrue, and they had the feel of a party line to them. Only she and he knew exactly how things had been left, and not even a phonecall since to smooth it over. Her mind flicked back to Paris for a minute, when she really had tried to ring him, just once. Just to apologise. But she never had spoken to him, and now he'd said she didn't need to apologise. Yet he hadn't asked if the same were true of her.

"So you were never jealous Ed? You never had designs on Steph yourself?"

Fuck. She was dangerously hot there. Steph felt Theo tense beside her, "Nothing like that Julia." He said firmly.

Ed said nothing.

"Come, come, I can't think that's true. She's gorgeous now, she'd have been even more gorgeous then. What's not to like?"

"Er, I am here Julia," Steph cut in.

Julia looked at her in surprise, "I know darling. Oh, don't get offended. I'm just digging, tell me to butt out if you want."

"Butt out," Ed said. It sounded like a joke but Steph knew it wasn't.

"Well – it's nice you're all back in touch now. I bet you had a shock when you spoke to them didn't you Ed? Did you know they'd got married, about the twins?"

"No. But I could have guessed. The marriage bit anyway."

"Twins is a bit harder to picture! Gosh, you were young weren't you Steph?"

"I suppose. Eighteen," she said guardedly. "Not as bad as it could have been."

"Twins at eighteen… eleven years ago… just as you left home…" she mused.

Steph felt her hands literally slick with sweat, she could feel the connection still unmade in Julias mind but it wouldn't take much, just a few more awkward questions – "Can I get a glass of water?" she said loudly to Theo. "I think it's time we got the bill."

"Yes, you're probably right, Katie's waiting at home." He stood up.

"Katie? What's she doing there?" Julia asked.

"Babysitting."

"Katie? Really?"

"Yes, why?" Steph asked through gritted teeth. Her head was

beginning to ache unpleasantly.

Julia sniggered, "Don't know… bit of a strange sort of babysitter. Mind you, I've always thought she was a bit nothingy. Is that how she makes an extra few pence on the side?"

"Julia!"

"Come on, you should probably have some water too," Ed muttered in embarrassment.

"What have I said?"

"Just leave it, Steph," Theo murmured in her ear. "Come on, grab your wrap and let's get out of here. Nice to see you Ed, I think we're going to head off. Give me a call, come round next week?"

"Cheers guys. Sorry…" he gestured towards Julia.

Theo waved a hand, "Don't think anything of it. Happens to the best of us."

They walked the short distance to the taxi rank by the station.

"I can't believe that woman," Steph fumed. "I really can't."

"She was drunk, she didn't mean it."

"Oh come on, there's drunk and then there's drunk. And imagine saying Katie earns 'an extra few pence'! Fucking unbelievable. Even if that were all she was earning, it would still be more than Julia, what a bloody hypocrite!"

"Calm down. She was out of order, but she was drunk. And she's obviously desperately insecure."

"That's more insightful than usual for you."

"It's obvious. She hasn't got a kind word for anyone and she can't take a joke. It's not attractive, I don't know what he's doing with her."

"It's a bit weird. Ed could get women a hundred times better looking."

"Including you apparently."

"*Pardon?*"

Theo looked at Steph, "I'm not being serious. I just meant what Julia said, about him being bound to fancy you."

"Oh – right."

"Why did you react like that?" Steph's face looked tense and pale in the moonlight.

"I didn't react like anything," she said defensively.

"OK." But she had, her face said it all. And, more worryingly, Julia had clearly thought that there had once been something between Steph and Ed. She'd behaved as if it were completely obvious. And if it was obvious to her, was he missing something? Theo stared straight ahead at the moon, hanging low in the sky and shivered, pulling his coat firmly around himself. He was being paranoid, that was all there was to it. He shrugged off the nagging sense of doubt and turned to look at his wife. Ed was a nice, attractive guy but he had never been near Steph. Theo reached out to tenderly tuck a strand of loose hair behind her ear. Even if he had it would have been years ago. Eleven years. What could it matter now?

CHAPTER FIFTEEN

"Go on, grab that one there."

"This one?"

"Yup."

"It looks like the heaviest," Steph said suspiciously. The box was buckled at the sides already.

"It's an optical illusion, I can assure you. They're all the same weight, I packed them myself."

"OK. But remember – I'm doing this as a payback favour and if I break my back, I'll sue!"

"What, with Lawyers-R-US?"

"Something like that. I hate those companies that help people to sue, it's like 'oh I tripped over the pavement because I had my bloody eyes shut, you owe me thousands in compensation'." Steph reached into the deep back of Katie's Peugeot estate car and pulled on the last box. It weighed a ton. "How many statues did you say were in here?"

"Twenty. Is that the sort of law Ed does?"

"I don't actually know, he said corporate so I imagine not."

Katie's order for ten statues had become an order for fifty. It was for a locally-based hardware shop that was branching out into garden ornaments, and the owner had just taken second premises in a town fifteen miles away.

"You won't need your fitness class tonight, at least," Katie said. "You can feel virtuous and relax with a glass of wine."

Steph shuddered, "Ugh. I still haven't recovered from Saturday."

"Julia's company or the alcohol?"

"Both. She is a witch, that woman. Where do you want this?" Her arms were aching under the strain.

"Next to that pot, there, by the door. Yes, it doesn't sound like the greatest meal ever." She paused, and placed her hands on her hips. "But what I don't understand is why she does it. Do you think she doesn't realise how obnoxious she's being?"

"I've no idea, it was my first – and last – intimate social occasion with her."

Katie laughed, "No more cosy dinners a quatre?"

"Over my dead bloody body."

"It may well be exactly that if Julia gets her own way." Katie lugged her box into line with the others. "Just what is her problem?"

"No idea. The worst thing was when she started quizzing us about being teenagers and who had fancied who, etc. It was excruciating. Mostly because I couldn't look at Ed. It was only him and me who ever knew the truth." Somehow, it helped to be so candid. It brought the truth a bit closer, but it made it seem less scary for that short time.

Katie wiped her hands free of dust, "Seriously? You don't think anyone else ever suspected?"

"Oh you know what secondary schools are like, there's gossip all over the place about who fancies who and who's shagged who. Only half of it is ever true. God, that's it. I am done in. No more boxes ever, please."

"Don't be so negative, if I become rich and famous you can claim your part in my success. Was that a roundabout way of saying that people may have known, or suspected, but they couldn't prove it?"

"I really have no idea. I was never aware of any gossip about us, put it like that."

"Fair enough. I bet there was though." Katie thought for a moment. "Who were your best friends at school? Apart from the obvious I mean."

"Kirsty. Rachel was very close to Theo. Poppy was a good friend, Grace I suppose. And then a few peripheral ones."

"What about Ed?"

"He didn't really have that many friends."

"So he wouldn't have confided in anybody about that night?"

"Katie, will you stop? You're scaring me."

"Ah, hello," said a voice from behind them. "These must be my beautiful statues."

"Indeed they are," Katie grinned at the tall, windswept-looking man who had wandered out of the shop. "Fifty of my very best."

"Perfect, young lady, just perfect. Hopefully they'll earn me my fortune."

Steph liked the look of him, he had kind, smiley eyes.

"Sorry – Graham this is my friend Steph, Steph this is Graham, proprietor of this fine establishment."

"Hello my friend Steph," he reached forward and shook her hand. "And are you a fellow sculptor?"

"Oh gosh, no. Not at all. Not an artistic bone in my body, I'm afraid."

"That's not true at all," Katie said loyally.

"Perhaps you just don't get enough chance to practise your skills?" Graham said kindly. "Have a desk job do you?"

"No. I – er – don't work."

"Time and enough then to practise your skills."

"I'm not sure that's quite the word I'd use."

"Steph's good at picking colours and designing patterns and things like that. She has an eye for decorating, could be an interior designer if she put her mind to it."

"Katie…" Steph said, a little awkwardly.

Graham smiled, "I have an interest there myself. Fascinating subject don't you think?"

"Well, yes. It was always my aim to study and go into interior design, not sure which area. But somehow, I never got there."

"There's time left. Thanks for bringing those over then."

"No problem. Take care, see you soon. He's a lovely chap," she confided to Steph as she headed down the hill. "Really kind and ever so practical. Fiercely intelligent, I would say."

"What did you have to say that about designing for? You made me sound silly."

"In what way?"

"Like a kid with dreams."

"You kind of are. And what's wrong with admitting to aspirations? I tell you, I have far more time for people with aspirations than those who just sit on their backsides all day doing bugger all."

"Are you trying to say something?"

"No!" Katie peered at her closely. "Will you relax?"

Steph stared out of the window at the landscape rolling by, and wondered what it must be like to have that sheer confidence in yourself. To be so sure that you could tell perfect strangers about what it was you wanted to do and why you would be so good at it. Katie had it in spades, no wonder she was making a success of her little enterprise. What would change in Steph's world if she too had that naked ambition and the guts to do something about it? Probably not much, that was the trouble. She'd been so hemmed in by panic and lingering dark thoughts for so many years that it would require a sea-change to shift her way of thinking.

****

By the time Katie had dropped her back at home, it was lunchtime. The house was still and quiet when she let herself in. The garden was empty, no birds on the table today, or squirrels stealing their seed. Steph stood and looked out at her garden for a while. It was nice, quite long and rolled gently down an embankment, to the chagrin of the girls who were desperate for a trampoline. The flowerbeds were neatly tended every week by a gardener and it was – fine. Good. It didn't need her at all. It was the same everywhere she turned, Mrs B had been in and the entire house was spick and span. Washing neatly ironed and put away, floors dusted, carpets hoovered, bathrooms cleaned and beds made. There was nothing constructive for her to do at all. Maybe she should go riding, she hadn't been for ages, Matt would be wondering where she was. All of her old, active pursuits seemed to have fallen by the wayside recently. It was nice weather, she could go and get changed quickly – but just the thought of it made her feel tired.

Quickly, she turned and rummaged in the cupboard for a tin of soup. She heated it in a pan and sat at the breakfast bar to eat it, looking out at nothing in the garden. She tidied away the bowl and spoon and went upstairs to the en suite bathroom. Her reflection was the same as it had been for a while; drawn, pale and slight rings under her eyes, despite the layer of foundation. Steph brushed a bit of blusher across her cheek and redid her eyeliner, then she felt more poised. Womanly. On the spur of the moment she looked critically down at her clothes and then ripped off her drab polo neck and jeans and changed into a tight, knee-length, Dior skirt and a TopShop blouse, cinched in at the waist with a wide brown belt. Her long boots would look perfect with this outfit; she fell to her knees and searched through the bottom of her wardrobe. There. Her reflection when she looked again in the mirror was different. More elegant and she looked more sure of herself. She looked like a woman who had a purpose in life and a place to be, other than the playground gates at 3:45pm. What was that Katie had said about creating an illusion?

Steph couldn't bear the silence. It got to her too much and made her thoughts seem louder and unavoidable. She grabbed her car keys and handbag and hurried out to the car. One click and it was unlocked. She adjusted her mirror, waited for the SatNav to locate itself and pushed her Gucci sunglasses on. Nothing energetic but she would go for a drive somewhere – anywhere – just to distract herself. God, she was sad. She could never imagine any of her friends doing this. And yet, what friends? How many people could she genuinely describe as friends? Tears blurred her vision suddenly and threatened to streak her mascara.

"Steph – you sad, ungrateful cow," she said to herself. "There are literally hundreds of women who would kill to have your life, and look at how you're behaving." But your life isn't *your life*, a little voice screamed. Have you created it yourself? Have you made choices and descisions? No, you've gone along with what someone else wants, your life is a by-product of theirs. Someone else has shaped and chosen and caressed your life into its current state. There's nothing proactive about you at all.

"And yet, is that so bad?" Steph wondered aloud. "I'm not ill or dying or destitute. I'm not obese or anorexic or homeless. I've ended up with quite a tidy little lot. Gorgeous twin girls, loving husband, close family, lovely home. I'm lucky," she said, trying to convince herself. "I'm *lucky*."

She ended up at an out-of-town shopping centre. She found a space for her car and hopped out to walk briskly across the concrete to the lifts. It was sunny outside, but cold and Steph shivered in her thin jacket. Maybe she could buy a thicker coat. She had the money after all, a debit card and two credit cards sat in her purse, rarely used for anything other than standard expenses or bonafide needs. She went down to the ground floor and walked the few metres to the entrance of the shopping centre, enjoying the click-clack of her heels on the pavement. 'Clip-clops' the girls had used to call high-heeled shoes when they were little, "Mummy, I want to wear my clip-clops." Her chest tightened remembering their sunny innocence that she alone had the power to shatter.

It was a weekday and not particularly busy. The neon lights and white walls were barely disturbed by the few people that wandered along. Steph joined their ranks, not sure where she was going, and tried to guess who they were, why they were here. Mums with buggies were easy, either genuinely shopping or else just getting out of the house. Same with mums and small children, they would be escaping the monotony of Balamory and plasticine. Then there were old people, killing time before it killed them. Professional shoppers, sprinting from one storefront to the next, flicking through the cashmere in the Brora sale, flexing their plastic. Borrowed or earned? Steph didn't know. Had she earned money? Technically, no. Had she earned the right to spend it? Probably. If you counted school runs, hours of childcare, careful overseeing of homework, the making of nutritious meals. It must all add up. It wasn't the same though. Not the same as using your own carefully honed skills and receiving payment in return.

Listlessly, she wandered along the lower and upper levels, past River Island and Topshop, Boots, Monsoon, M&S, Waterstones, listening to the busy noise around her, the sounds of life. Chatter, babies crying, the rustle of bags, clacking of heels. She looked idly at one or two coats but couldn't muster the enthusiasm to be genuinely interested. Besides, she wasn't wearing her normal clothes, she wouldn't be able to tell if it were suitable or not.

Inevitably – or by chance? – she ended up in the coffee shop, sitting alone at a table, stirring a Cappuccino. What sort of person did she look like, she wondered. Would anyone be able to identify her? From her hair and nails and the fact she was in here during work hours they would able to tell that she was relatively wealthy, that she didn't work. But then, she might have a day off. But surely people with days off didn't wander around shopping centres alone? They would be busy, purposeful. Full of chores that only got done occasionally. But her clothes today were those of a professional. Ladies who lunched did not wear Dior pencil skirts and high-heeled, knee-length, leather boots. They wore Tayberry and Joules and Boden and Monsoon skirts and pure wool cardigans. Seven jeans perhaps. Her usual wardrobe in other words. But ladies who lunched did not sit alone in cafeterias. So just for today Steph could be an anomaly, she didn't fit into a category. An unpleasant thought stole into her mind – was it just for today? No, no, she was a mother. 'Full-time mum' was her stock response if anyone asked her what she did. 'Full-time mum and I'm proud of it' was probably what it sounded like. Back when the twins had been small Steph had often been asked if she were going back to work.

"Back?" Theo would guffaw. "She never started!" Steph hadn't minded, but the other people often had.

"You're not going to work?" they would ask with furrowed brows. "But why not? Won't you be bored?"

"Well no," Steph would explain. "I have my children to look after."

"But they'll be at school."

"Only for seven hours a day. I need to be there for the other seventeen."

And the person usually turned away at this point, having relegated Steph to the ranks of someone who probably burned her bra and did voluntary work for the Women's Lib. She hadn't minded that either, but sometimes afterwards she had wondered if perhaps they were right. Maybe she should be considering a job of some sort. If she ever raised it with Theo he would laugh and say, "But why? Tell you what darling, if we get into difficulties I'll send you out to work, how's that for fair?" He thought he was being kind of course, and Steph always let it go but there had been a nagging doubt; could she do more? Should she do more? Did she want to do more? What it would mean to have something that was truly and totally her own.

"Excuse me?" a voice cut into her thoughts. "Do you mind if I sit here?" A plump lady with a buggy was standing next to her table, her hair scraped back and face tired.

"Oh no, of course not. Here, let me." Steph jumped up and moved a chair out of the way so the lady could get her pushchair through.

"Thanks," she said gratefully. "I wouldn't ask but it's ever so busy in here today."

Steph looked around, she was right, it was. Perhaps everyone was in here rather than the shops in this time of rapidly approaching economic gloom. She couldn't help but glance into the pushchair as the lady wheeled it past. Nestled inside was a tiny baby. The mother settled herself into a seat and began unpacking a nappy bag. Steph looked at the baby longingly for a moment. "How old is she?" She asked hesitantly. "Sorry, you must be sick of people asking you."

"Not at all. Two weeks."

"Oh she's so sweet." Steph peered in at the minute, dimpled face and little clenched fists. Her eyes were firmly shut. "What's her name?"

"Maisie. Maisie Rose."

"Well congratulations, she's gorgeous."

"Thank you. She won't be in a minute when she wakes up and remembers that she's hungry. She's being a little horror at the moment, feeding every two hours."

"I remember it well. I have twin girls, but they're eleven now."

The lady looked at Steph properly for the first time, "Twins? Gosh, I don't know how you coped."

Steph shrugged, "Neither do I really. The first year is a bit of a blur."

"But worth it now I bet?"

"Definitely," Steph smiled, thinking of her two precious girls. Deep and thoughtful Tilly, bold and stroppy Mia.

"That's what I keep telling myself when my eyes are wedged

open with matchsticks at two in the morning. It will be worth it."

"It really will, I know it's a tough period, but it does pass."

"I don't mind really. I'm just grateful to have her," she peered into the pram and stroked the side of the baby's face gently.

"Of course."

"No – especially grateful," she hesitated. "She was an IVF baby."

"Really? How amazing. That must have been a strain for you." Steph said politely, sipping at her Cappuccino, feeling very groomed next to this new mother.

"Not really, it was the light at the end of the tunnel. We'd tried for years and years naturally so at least there was real hope with IVF. We were actually doing something constructive at last."

"Yes, I can imagine. Well, no I can't actually, but I know what you mean."

"Sorry, I thought perhaps your twins were IVF?"

"Oh – no."

"Lucky you." Oh, if only she knew. The baby stirred and the lady leant over and deftly plucked it from the pram. Maisie's tiny body curled as she brought her knees up to her chest and let out a loud wail. "There, there, shush now." She unclipped a bra strap and manoeuvred the baby under her voluminous shirt. "That's one benefit of constantly feeding, you get very nifty at doing it in public."

"Not so great for the sleep though."

"No, but when you've been trying for twenty years it doesn't matter too much."

"Twenty years? Gosh."

"Well," the lady settled back in her seat, "we just assumed it would happen one day. Twenty years later we realised it hadn't."

"I see." Except she didn't. "Where did you work?"

"We both work in IT. Whether I'll go back, I don't know," she gazed down at the tiny, dark head. "We'll have to see how it goes."

"Yes. I suppose. It's good you got there eventually, she must be very special."

"In the end we decided IVF was the only way. I don't know why I'm telling you all this, blame sleep deprivation."

Steph looked at her, she did look quite tired. And reasonably old actually, definitely forty plus. She hoped fervently that they didn't get onto the subject of ages.

"It's fine, don't worry."

"And it just goes to show, we use donor sperm, first round of IVF and bingo – I was pregnant."

Donor sperm...? The significance filtered through. "So, excuse me for asking, but does that mean the baby is genetically your child but not your husband's?"

"Yes, that's right."

Steph's heart started banging painfully hard, "And he's OK with that?"

"Oh yes – it was a small price to pay for having our own child."

That was a contradiction in terms, Steph thought, and realised her hands were shaking. She shoved them under the table to hide it.

"Because, if you think about it," the woman continued, "it isn't so much whose genetic material is responsible, it's who loves them and brings them up. That's what we believe anyway."

But you'd have to, if that was your only way of having a child. You couldn't allow yourself to believe anything else.

"Yes, I suppose," Steph murmured.

"Just look at all those irresponsible young yobs on the street fathering children left, right and centre. It won't be them that bring up the babies will it? There are step-fathers in most families these days. This is no different."

"No, I agree," Steph said. "I must go, but it was lovely to meet you. Congratulations again, enjoy her, she's beautiful." She stood up.

"Thank you. I hope I haven't said too much? I don't know if I'm coming or going most of the time these days."

"No, not at all. Goodbye." Steph threaded her way quickly through the tables, her heart still racing. So there were people out there bringing up other men's children. In slightly different circumstances obviously, but Katie had been right, they must be all over the place. She dared her mind to make the logical connection – so, if and just *if*, she ever told Theo the truth, did that mean he could still love the girls the same? Surely, if others loved their non-biological children, so could he. If they didn't tell the girls, if their lives stayed on the same path, surely Theo could bring himself to live a little differently? A vague sense of hope soared within Steph and she felt lighter and more expectant. No more lying, no more hiding from Ed, she could at last lead a normal existence. But then reality crunched into her thoughts; how stupid of her. Of course Theo could never do anything like as maganimous as that lady's husband was doing, because that lady had taken an agreed course of action, for legitimate and soul-wrenching reasons. She hadn't had an ill-thought-out, one-night stand with her best friend and then passed the resulting children off as her husband's. That lady was a good, kind, deserving mother –

not like Steph.

By the time she reached her car, the tears were properly spilling down her cheeks. She jumped in and slammed the door hard behind her. Any confession to Theo would reveal her as a liar and their entire marriage as a deception. It would make a mockery of the last ten years, and that was the bit that Theo would struggle with. Possibly more so than the discovery that he wasn't the twins' natural father. Which was the bigger issue here? Misuse of one persons DNA or exploitation of now three innocent victims? Steph slumped lower in her seat, feeling the black cloud resettle itself above her.

****

Julia watched Steph from a distance. She was shivering in what appeared to be a very thin jacket. And – good grief – were those knee high boots? On Steph, in the middle of the day? How bizarre. Julia wondered where she'd been, and more importantly, who she'd been with. She hadn't quite worked up the courage to speak to Steph since the disastrous dinner. And actually, she felt a bit miffed about the whole debacle too. She'd been drunk, sure, but no more drunk than anyone else and all she'd done was ask about the years gone by so she could catch up a bit.

"Except that wasn't all, was it?" Ed had said, quite gently in retrospect.

"What do you mean?" Julia had snapped. It was the morning after and her headache was abysmal.

"You more or less insinuated that their friend was their employee, and sneered at the fact that they may have reimbursed her for babysitting."

Julia stared in horror, "How?" she demanded finally. "How did I do that?"

Ed repeated the conversation verbatim.

"Sorry, I don't agree. All that means is that I was surprised she was babysitting, and come on, it's not exactly a common pastime for a married, mother of one herself is it?"

"And the word 'nothingy'?"

Julia flushed, "It wasn't meant as an insult."

"That's how it was taken."

"And you agree with them?"

"I'm afraid I do, I think you came across rather badly. I think you should apologise, I would in your shoes." But Julia's pride did not permit that. Instead, she allowed herself to think that it was Steph in the wrong because she had overreacted. And let's face it, Steph not talking to her wasn't the worst thing in the world. It just made things more difficult with Ed; he'd made it quite plain he was unimpressed by her drunken performance at Saturday's dinner. It was hardly her fault, she was just curious. And they were so tight, as friends, it made her feel left out. Or at least, they had been tight, and something had gone on, she was sure of it, Steph and Ed were so peculiar towards one another. The way they'd all clammed up had confirmed it to her. She watched Steph greeting the twins with huge hugs through narrowed eyes. The woman was up to something, she was sure. There were just two questions: firstly, what and secondly, how she, Julia, could find out.

****

It occurred to Steph as she peeled potatoes that evening that she had no idea what Theo's thoughts were on IVF. She didn't think they'd ever discussed it. They'd spoken once about adoption when a friend had adopted two little girls of a similar age to Tilly and Mia, but only to say that neither of them thought they could do it.

"I'm such an instinctive mother," Steph had said, "that I really don't think I would be such a good mother to an adopted child. I wouldn't know them inside out." Even this topic was flying too close to the wind for her, she had been uncomfortable – and those were the days when the truth didn't buzz around her head every minute.

"They often don't give you a baby either," Theo had said. "That's the bit that would get me. Like having a second-hand child isn't it?"

That comment had stuck with Steph for a while, even though it was nothing like the same.

The front door clicked shut and Steph heard the familiar sounds of Theo dropping his keys into the enamel bowl and pausing at the foot of the stairs to see if he could hear the girls. Then on to the kitchen.

"Hi," he always looked slightly wary these days Steph had noticed, and it made her sad. He seemed to have lost the joyful anticipation of seeing her.

"Hi darling."

"Blimey, you look – different. Been somewhere nice?"

"Shops. School. Not really."

"Why the clothes then?"

"Do I need a reason?"

"No. I just thought – never mind." He gave her a dutiful peck on the cheek. "Good day?"

"So-so. I think the girls might be awake if you want to say goodnight."

"I think I will. Mine's a glass of red when you're ready – ha ha ha."

Steph turned as she tossed the potatoes into a pan, "Not funny."

"See you in a second."

The girls had been unusually well-behaved after school today. None of the normal complaints about school or tea, they'd been chatty and happy all evening. And the curly kale that she had served up as part of their meal had been received without comment. Could it be that the lessons were finally sinking in? Steph had a sneaking suspicion that Tilly would have behaved better long ago were it not for the wayward influence of her sister.

Theo pushed open the door to Tilly's room and peered in, "Tills? You awake?"

"Mmm. Just. Hi Daddy."

"Hello darling," he gave her a hug and breathed in deeply, smelling the nutty smell of their shampoo and floral scent of fabric conditioner. It was impossible to quantify how much he loved these girls. "Did you have a good day?"

"Yeah. Mum was in a bad mood though."

Theo's heart sank, "Really?" He noticed 'Mum', not 'Mummy' too.

"Yeah. Don't know why."

"Were you and Mia good?"

"Yeah, we really were! We said in school that maybe if we were really well-behaved that she wouldn't be so cross."

"Why was she cross? What did she say?"

Tilly hesitated, "It isn't so much what she says, it what she doesn't say. She used to chat and be happy and now she isn't. We talk to her and she just says 'mmm' like she isn't listening."

"She's probably tired darling."

"From what? She doesn't do anything."

That silenced Theo. "I don't know," he said finally. "I'll ask her. Don't worry, I'm sure she's fine."

"Night Daddy."

"Night princess."

He stood outside Mia's door and listened, there were deep snores from within. Good, he didn't think he could take Mia's acerbic comments on her mother tonight. At least Tilly was fairly docile and malleable; and if she were cross, then Mia would be raging with injustice. Instead he crossed the hallway to his and Steph's bedroom and slowly took off his suit and shirt to hang up the former and throw the latter towards the laundry basket. This had to stop with Steph, it really did. If the girls were affected then it was serious. Poor girls; fancy discussing how best to get a good evening out of your own mother. The pathos was awful. And the worst of it all was that Theo had literally no idea what the problem was. Nothing had changed, well apart from Ed, and she seemed to be over that now. Julia, possibly? No, she'd been angry, not upset about that. Could it be him somehow? He doubted it, his sense of self-worth was strong. He'd know if he'd upset her, and he hadn't. It was nothing that he could guess. Unless… it was something that she was hiding from him. Something that she didn't want him to know. But there was nothing on earth he could think of that she would hide from him. It was possible that she was generally unhappy with him, Theo supposed. He sat down heavily on the side of the bed. Maybe she'd had enough of him, outgrown him or whatever. The thought filled him with unbearable sadness. Steph couldn't – wouldn't – do that to him. This was no good, he couldn't speculate forever, he'd have to ask her.

****

"What do you think about IVF?" She'd waited until they were sitting at the dinner table and she'd served the food before she asked him.

Theo struggled to fit that into his current picture of Steph. Nope, it didn't feature anywhere. IVF? What the hell? "IVF?"

"Yes. In-vitro fertilisation. You know, petri dish stuff."

"Yes, I know. Um, I'm not sure. It's fine, I suppose. I've never really thought about it. You mean in a gene-selection way? Avoiding cancer?"

"I didn't actually, I just meant for couples who can't conceive." She'd wait a little longer before biasing his perspective.

"Well… if there's no other way then what's the problem?"

"None, I don't think. But, the thing is," she hesitated, "it sometimes ends up with the father not being the biological father. They use donor sperm."

Theo lifted his eyebrows, "That would be tough, I guess. But if that was the only way that you could have a child to raise with your partner, then it would be easier. After all, it's all about the environment isn't it."

"Is it?"

"Yes. I think so. It's the nature versus nurture argument. Whose the one the baby is going to grow up with loving them? That's the one that counts." He wasn't sure that he could be so accepting of such a situation, but he didn't want to reveal that in case it made him some sort of bigot in Steph's eyes.

"Really?"

"Of course." In reality the idea of another man's sperm fertilising your wife and creating a child for you to share was abhorrent, but he didn't need to say that.

"Do you really feel like that? That genetics aren't everything?"

"Yes, I really do. Why?" He laid down knife and fork to look at her. "What's this all about?"

Steph relayed the conversation she'd had earlier today to him.

"Jesus, that's really sad," Theo said when she'd finished. "Twenty years?" He shook his head. "And then you think how many people take fertility for granted."

"I know, I know, it's awful. And I thought what they'd done was so brave and wonderful, but I didn't know if you'd agree."

Theo reached out and took her hand, "Why is this so important to you?" Her cheeks were flushed and her eyes were shining.

"It wasn't. It isn't. I'm just interested, that's all."

"In IVF?"

"In the ethics behind it. The idea of a family raising a child who belonged genetically to one parent but not the other."

"I think it's laudable, I really do. It should be encouraged. The world isn't a fair place at the best of times but at least this helps redress the balance."

"I love you Theo Hammond, I really do."

"Really truly?"

"Really truly."

He gazed at her very seriously for a second before asking: "Then will you please tell me what is going on?"

CHAPTER SIXTEEN

Ed looked at the piece of paper in his hand and gently tapped his mobile against the desk with the other. His gold cufflinks glinted in the sunlight. Good idea or bad? He couldn't tell. And he'd been thinking about it now for about fifteen minutes. And in another ten he had an important meeting with Jack Higgins so he had to decide quickly. Jack was relocating to Boston, the firm were opening a new office over there, and he needed to get things organised before he went. His mind wavered between ringing and not ringing. It seemed like a good idea to him, but Steph was so unpredictable that he couldn't be sure what she'd say. It was only an invitation to lunch, for God's sake. He dialled the home number before he could change his mind.

"Hello?" she answered instantly.

"Steph, hi, it's Ed."

"Hello, how are you?" she sounded guarded, as always.

"I'm fine, fine. Listen, I thought after the debacle of that dinner, well, the latter part anyway, it might be nice if we got together for a Sunday lunch. What do you think?" Ed felt confused, and intrigued; he wanted to get to the bottom of Steph.

"I think no, thank you."

"Oh Steph, why?"

"Do you actually need an answer to that?"

"Look, I know that Julia wasn't the best-behaved person in the world that night, but I wasn't going to suggest that she came with us. It would be just us three, and the girls of course." He held his breath, wondering what she would say to that. Would she openly raise objections to having him near her daughters or was she going to be more subversive than that?

"I don't know, I'll have to ask Theo." Ah, middle ground.

"That's fine. You can get back to me."

"OK, I'll speak to you later then."

Ed smiled as he put the phone down. That sounded more promising. He honestly couldn't work out where Steph was coming from these days. To listen to Julia you'd think she was a malicious bitch, but whenever he spoke to her she sounded so nice and normal. Ah well, that was women for you. Quickly, he gathered his papers and headed towards the conference room.

****

It was unusual for the phone to ring twice in one morning, but apparently it was going to today. Steph was standing at the hallway mirror trying to tame her hair into a neat chignon like the ones she'd lusted after in Paris all those years ago, when it trilled out its familiar tune. It surely couldn't be Ed again.

"Hello?"

"Steph darling, it's Julia."

Worse than Ed. "Hi Julia."

"I'm just ringing to catch up on some Cath's Committee stuff. You've been missed at the meetings." She sounded cautious.

"To be honest I'm wondering whether I actually have the time to dedicate to the committee any more. I have an awful lot on at the moment." Not true, of course, but she couldn't face being all pally with Julia.

"Oh that's disappointing. Ian and Marian have been asking after you. Is there anything I can help with?"

"I doubt it."

"I'll email you a copy of the minutes anyway, just in case you change your mind, you never know."

"That's fine. Or perhaps just give them to me on Sunday?" It was a deliberate dig, but one she couldn't resist.

"Sunday?"

"Yes, you know Theo and I are going out with Ed for lunch? I assumed you'd be there as well."

"Oh. No. He hasn't said anything to me," she said stiffly.

Steph smiled, "Never mind. Thanks for the call Julia."

Steph felt that she had to mention Ed's offer to Theo, she had no other choice, much though she would love to ignore it. It had been an awkward conversation at the dinner table, it made her cringe to remember it. When she'd asked what the hell he was talking about Theo had launched into a litany of criticisms against her, saying how much she'd changed, how the girls felt she didn't listen to them any more – that one hit particularly hard. But she'd been unable to explain that it was because she wanted to protect the girls that she was on edge all the time. She hadn't realised how much it had affected her family though. She'd gazed down at the linen tablecloth for ages while Theo went on and on, ramming home his point. The anger that she'd felt was completely irrational and she'd tried to hide it, but failed.

"You make it out like I'm some sort of Stepford wife most of the time and now I've slipped off my pedestal, how dare I!" she remembered shouting at him.

"No I don't. That isn't true. I'm saying that you've changed, Steph. No one expects you to be the perfect wife and mother but when you fundamentally alter as a person that's when we begin to worry."

"I have not fundamentally altered, as you put it. I've had a little more on my mind as of late, that's all."

"That's all? That's why you're snappy, bad-tempered and can't sleep? I just want to know if you have something seriously worrying you, that's all."

His concern brought tears to her eyes, he would never know how much she desperately wanted to share with him, but she was trapped alone in this. Neither did she think he had noticed her lying awake for endless hours in the night.

"No, there's nothing," she had said finally.

"No baby stuff?"

"Definitely no baby stuff."

"Then why the IVF conversation? You don't think we'll have problems conceiving do you?"

"No. Not at all." She looked at Theo in surprise. "Why on earth would you say that?"

"It just seemed to tie in for a second. You being so – different, not sleeping, saying you're not sure about trying for another one. I just wondered."

"No, Theo, you're way out there. I'd stop speculating if I were you, you're wasting your time." Steph stood abruptly and began clearing the table.

Theo put a gentle hand over hers, "You would tell me, wouldn't you? If there was anything the matter?"

"Yes Theo, I would tell you." What else could she say?

And when she did mention the lunch to Theo, he looked both relieved and delighted. Steph didn't feel that she could not tell him, Ed would be bound to mention it himself. And after Theo's outburst she couldn't approach the issue negatively, she needed to be so careful. Steph waited until the twins were in bed and there was no chance of them overhearing before she raised the subject.

"Do you want to go?" was Theo's immediate question.

"Um, yes."

"You don't sound too sure."

"No, it would be lovely." She had her back to him sorting through the twins' school bags and he couldn't see her face.

"Seriously?"

"Seriously."

"That's a big change of heart."

"Maybe I should avoid that then."

"Sorry?"

"You were complaining that I'd changed so much."

"Stop it, Steph. If you don't mind going, we'll go, and if you do then we won't."

"I don't mind."

"Great. The girls will like it."

Steph wheeled around, "We're not taking them?"

"Why not?"

"They'd be bored."

"Steph, they are well past the age where they'll be bored at a lunch. They have books, they have their DS, they're capable of behaving. They'll be fine, they're not toddlers."

"We could leave them with Katie, they'd prefer it."

"Maybe they would but they're part of our family, not Katie's. Stop being silly, let them grow up." He was short on patience, Steph could see.

"OK. Fine." She was the only one who was going to suffer, after all.

Katie rang later in the evening to enquire whether she'd thought any more about that information she'd given Steph.

"Information?" Steph wondered out loud.

"The interior design courses?"

"Oh. Yes. Them. Er, no, I haven't."

"Surprise, surprise. I'd forgotten about it myself, but I took some stuff over to the shop earlier and Graham asked how it was going."

"Graham? He was asking about my interior design course?" Theo walked past and gave her a strange look. "How did he know?"

"Only from what we mentioned when we went. He obviously has faith in you."

"If he does it's misplaced," Steph muttered.

"Rubbish woman, you should get on with it before you get properly old and regret it."

"Mmm. Oh, I have some gossip for you. Ed rang earlier and invited Theo and I to lunch," she kept her voice deliberately casual, well aware of Theo's presence.

"Really? That's nice."

"Mmm. Anyway, then Julia rang me."

"I didn't realise she had a death wish."

"I know – the audacity is amazing. Anyway, she isn't invited to this lunch."

"Ohhhh, is it all over then?"

"Who knows? We can but hope. I took delight in telling her about it all the same."

"You just couldn't make this up, this is News of the World stuff, it really is," Katie chuckled. "So the gloves are off then?"

"After that dinner? Oh yes. She was even asking for my help on the committee would you believe?"

"Yes, actually I would. What did you say?"

"That I was too busy."

"She can't argue with that."

Steph said goodbye and put the phone down, feeling more cheerful. A chat with Katie always did her good, made her feel somehow more normal. Katie's no-nonsense approach was soothing.

"Are you coming to bed?" Theo came up behind her, carrying his book.

"In a minute."

"Don't be long."

"I won't."

Theo placed his hand on the back of her neck but Steph shrugged him off and walked away.

****

Her plan, when she thought about it, was surprisingly simple. Julia wasn't someone who went in for a lot of ground work but she'd thought she would be doing so on this occasion. Apparently not. It was going to be remarkably easy.

It had been the argument with Ed that started it all off. She'd gone round in the evening on the same day that she'd spoken to Steph and yelled at him for not telling her about the lunch. He'd responded with the fact that not only had he not told her, but that she wasn't invited either.

"Why not?" Julia had been totally indignant.

"Because of your behaviour at the last social event we went to."

"Oh for goodness sake, we were all drunk and they'll have forgotten about it by now."

"I don't think so." Ed had seriously thought about finishing with her after that night, but he hadn't. Julia was a little different to his other girlfriends and he liked it. She was older, but she also had a career, a direction in life, she was intelligent and ruthless in her aims – all qualities which appealed to him. Plus she was very sexy and always willing to please. He'd been wondering recently if Steph was as compliant.

"What are you hiding from me?"

"Don't be ridiculous." Ed stood up and threw the newspaper onto the coffee table.

"There must be something Ed, or you wouldn't mind me coming along." Julia stayed sitting on the sofa, gazing up at him with her hard, glittering eyes. "What is it that's so important to preserve? What do I have to do to be accepted into your little clique?"

"Do you have any idea what you sound like? There's no clique. I hadn't even seen them for ten years until recently."

"That doesn't stop there being something that you don't want me to know. There must be something going on, look at the comment Steph made about you being near the girls."

Ed sighed deeply, "There is nothing that I don't want you to know. I don't know why she said that. Nothing significant has happened that you don't know about." He was still a little hurt by what Steph had said, and Julia was getting very heavy for their short relationship.

Julia sensed his mood and backed off a little, it wouldn't do to annoy him too much. He was too good a catch. So good in fact, that she could probably forgive him for almost anything. But if he was going to start seeing Steph independently of her then Julia would have to be very careful about the lines that she fed him in the future to put him off her. He'd swallowed them all so far but that might not continue.

"Right," she picked up her coffee cup and drained it. "I'm off. I've got a second meeting with a new client in the morning and it looks promising."

"Oh, that's great." Ed took her coffee mug through to the kitchen, marvelling how she could swing between needy and businesslike so easily.

"Speak to you soon, darling," she gave him a quick air-kiss when he returned that barely brushed his cheek and pulled her coat on. "Ciao." If he was going to be offish, then so could she.

Ed watched her walk down the street to her car in the darkness. Considering her mood it hadn't seemed like the greatest idea in the world to tell her that earlier on in his meeting Jack had offered him a good position, and salary increase, to come out and help him set up the Boston office. It was an offer he was mulling over and was sorely tempted by. Great place, great experience and complete change of scene. It was very appealing. But he thought he'd prefer to tell Julia when he could present her with a fait accompli – one way or the other. He rather thought that he might discuss it with Theo; there was no way he could alert any of his internal colleagues to the offer, that could only lead to fisticuffs at dawn.

Julia snapped her seatbelt into place and stashed the filched address book in the glove compartment, quietly impressed at how easily she'd managed to remove it from his little telephone table. There was no way he'd give her his mum's phone number of his own volition so she'd had to resort to dirty tactics. And hopefully there would be more numbers than one that she would find interesting.

"Oh Ed," she said aloud. "If there are any skeletons lurking in your closet, I am going to pull them out." She would piece together his past by hook or by crook.

****

It had seemed logical in the end to arrange the visit on Sunday afternoon. Ed was well out of the way then and it gave Julia a curious satisfaction to think she was going behind his back while he went behind hers.

"I was just wondering if I could come and visit," she had explained on the phone. "Obviously it's coming up to Ed's birthday in a month or so and I was thinking about organising a get-together but I wanted you to meet me first." That idea had been inspired, she thought. Perfectly plausible, objectively polite and with a good reason for not telling Ed she'd been round. She could organise the actual event later.

Mrs Osborne had sounded faintly shocked, "I must be honest dear, I didn't know he was even seeing someone else," she'd said apologetically. "It was a girl called Jenna, the last I heard."

"We haven't been together that long, but we go way back. We met at Uni."

"Oh that is nice. He had such a good time at University. He's always talking about it."

"So if we said Sunday, perhaps? About two o' clock?"

"I shall look forward to it."

And now here she was, outside Ed's mothers house, preparing to grill her, not that she would know that of course. Julia planned to present her questions as gentle interest for creating a good party. She'd dressed carefully in flattering trousers and a tailored Per Una jacket. She wanted to look respectable without being dowdy. She may be older than Ed but she certainly didn't want to look it. She carefully applied a thin layer of lipgloss before she snapped her bag shut and hopped out of the car.

The door opened before she'd knocked, "Hello, you must be Julia. Do come in." Julia followed her into a hall that smelled of lemons and cake. Nice, homely.

If Mrs Osborne was surprised at Julia ringing up out of the blue, she didn't show it. She was a small lady wearing a white blouse and a long skirt. They went into the living room and Julia accepted an offer of tea and cake.

"It's so good for him to have a nice girlfriend," Ed's mother confessed when they were sitting with their cups. "I don't think anyone's organised a surprise party for him before." She had Ed's blue eyes and strong jawline.

"I thought it would be a nice idea. And then I thought it was probably best if we met beforehand so we could get to know one another."

"Oh yes, I agree," Mrs Osborne nodded approvingly. "So do you work in Law too?"

"No. I'm an events manager."

"I see. And what does that involve?"

"Lots of organisation mainly!"

"I see. And do you enjoy it?"

"Mostly." Julia endured a further ten minutes of polite smalltalk before she could steer the conversation the way she wanted it to go. She reached down and drew a paper pad from her handbag.

"So, Mrs Osborne."

"Call me Jenny dear."

"OK then, Jenny, shall we make a rough list of who we should invite to this party?"

Jenny looked slightly taken aback, "I didn't realise it was a joint effort. I'm not sure I'm up to date enough with many of his friends to know who he'd want there."

"I meant old friends. Schoolfriends. I can take care of the current ones."

"Oh. Right. Schoolfriends..." she mused. "Hmm, well there was a lad called Mark, I remember him from sixth form. A girl called Kirsty he was seeing for a while. Gosh, this is difficult, we're going back quite a way here."

"Who were his best friends? Closest friends?" Julia pressed.

"That would have been – um – oh – Theo. Theo Hammond his name was, they were good friends for quite a long time. He lived here in the village as well, you know. And a girl. I can't remember her name now. How stupid of me, they saw a lot of each other."

Julia's heart quickened, "Really?" she asked, ultra-casually.

"Oh yes, those three were always together. From when they were tiny," Jenny smiled fondly. "I think they might have all started school together, but I can't remember now. S-something, I think her name was. Perhaps you could ask one of the others if you get hold of them."

"OK." Julia pretended to scribble down the information on her pad. "And anyone else you can think of?"

"There were some other girls, Kirsty's friends, Grace and Poppy I think their names were. Now, Kirsty I can tell you about. She runs the local riding stables here in Tinford. She always was a horsey girl. She would know more than me."

"That's interesting... all right. But the girl you can't remember the name of, was she Ed's girlfriend? Should we track her down?"

"Girlfriend? I'm not sure. They were very close, they saw each other a lot but then she lived in Tinford too. Actually, now you mention it," she hesitated, "there was a bit of a scandal with her and that boy Theo. I wasn't going to say anything but I can't see what harm it could do."

"A scandal?" Julia feigned surprise.

"Oh yes. They practically eloped together one night. It was very sudden, their parents were devastated. They hadn't even finished their exams."

"Oh. Goodness. Why did they elope?"

"I don't know. No idea. It came out of the blue from what I remember. Ed was very upset, they were his best friends. Now that I think about it, perhaps he wouldn't want them to come to the party? Do you think?" Her forehead creased with concern.

"I should think it's all long forgotten," Julia said smoothly. "He may be in contact with them now, who knows? Are they still together?"

"I believe they got married. Quite early on. Now that did surprise me and I'll tell you why – just before they ran off the girl – Stephanie! That's her name. Stephanie Oakton. There now!"

"Well done."

"Anyway," Jenny leant in conspiritorially towards Julia, "just before they left, and it may even have been the night before, Stephanie spent the night here. With Ed. I wasn't sure what was going on but it seemed a little odd to spend the night with one boy and then run away with another."

"It certainly does," Julia murmured, lowering her face to hide the angry red blush she could feel spreading across it. Ed must have taken her for a fool.

"I suspected that she might have been his girlfriend, but I was obviously wrong."

"Why wrong?"

"Well she went off with someone else, dear."

Julia decided not to enlighten her as to loose, teenage morals.

"It was strange, one night they were here, drinking wine together all night and the next she'd vanished. With that Theo. Very odd behaviour." Jenny shook her head.

"Drinking wine?"

"Oh yes, they pinched it from my fridge."

"And she was there all night?"

"I saw her with my own eyes when I went in. She hadn't folded her clothes either."

"I bet," Julia said grimly.

"Anyway, that doesn't matter now. Where were you thinking of holding this party?"

"I hadn't got that far yet. I needed to confirm numbers first. So thanks very much for all your help, Jenny."

"It's no problem. Are you leaving?"

"I think I'd better. I might head down to the riding stables and try and catch Kirsty." Julia pulled her coat around her shoulders. "It was lovely to meet you. Thank you for the tea."

"You're very welcome. Pity you can't stay and meet Edward's father. He's on the golf course at the moment, he'll be sorry that he's missed you."

Julia smiled tightly, "Another time perhaps." She edged towards the front door, trying to curtail talk of cakes and arrangements as she went. Bastard. What a bastard. He *had* lied to her. There was clearly a lot more to his and Steph's relationship than either of them had let on. Teenagers do not innocently spend the night together drinking wine and then take their clothes off. It had been very indiscreet of Jenny to let that bit slip.

Julia waved goodbye and climbed back into her Saab. She pulled her sunglasses on and followed the directions Jenny had given her of two miles down the road on the left to the stables. Her heart was thumping loudly. What she was hoping to uncover, she didn't know. It was just so bloody mysterious. They were both odd and awkward with one another, for no apparent reason, except that Steph had spent the night with Ed before running off with Theo. Julia wondered if Theo knew about it. *Shit.* Her hand thumped the steering wheel. That was it! Steph had been with Theo when she'd slept with Ed. She'd cheated on him! It was so obvious. A cosy, three-way teenage friendship had led to some drama, it seemed. No wonder Steph and Ed couldn't look one another in the eye. Naughty Steph, Julia would never have thought that of her in a million years. She had well and truly judged the book by its cover.

Julia drew up outside a rickety-looking yard and parked her car. She considered briefly whether or not to bother hunting down this Kirsty girl, now that she'd worked it all out. Then she decided it would do no harm to have some more ammunition. And as a friend, she would surely have been privy to a lot of information that Jenny wasn't. She picked her way across the mud and horse muck, cringing at the thought of her Nine West heels being coated in whatever disgusting crap was on the ground, and pushed the door open to the tiny office.

"Hi," a girl of no more than sixteen looked up.

"Hello, I'm looking for Kirsty?"

"Oh she's in the school, lunging Toffee."

"Right."

"Can I 'elp?"

"No, I don't think so."

"You wasn't wanting lessons then?"

"Not today. Is it all right if I…?"

"Yeah, go for it."

The school was a large, enclosed area with a five-barred gate at one end and a woman with a horse on a long rope at the other. Julia leant across the gate and shouted, "Hello!" The whippet-thin woman swung round and shaded her eyes to look towards Julia.

"Can I help?" she called.

"I think so." She waited until Kirsty came over, leading the horse behind her. She watched closely; Kirsty was very slender but tall with long, dark hair. She had a wide mouth and big eyes. There was a smear of dirt across her cheek. So this was Ed's teenage girlfriend. Julia ran her eye critically up and down.

"Hello, I'm Kirsty, are you after some lessons?" she asked, with a friendly smile.

"No. I'm Julia, I'm Edward Osborne's girlfriend."

"Edward…? Oh! Edward Osborne, from school?"

"That's the one."

"Oh right, yes I remember him. How can I help?"

Julia launched into her party story, fervently hoping that Ed didn't keep in contact with Kirsty any more.

"Ah – OK. That sounds good. I haven't seen him in a year or two. It would be good to catch up."

"But the thing is, I was hoping that you could give me a bit of a clue as to who else he might want there, from school I mean. I've spoken to his mum but she didn't really know. Who were his close friends?"

"There was just a group of us really. Me, Ed, Steph, Theo, Poppy and Grace. That was mostly it. A few others but not as close. I could give you numbers for Poppy and Grace if you wanted, they both live nearby still."

"That would be great. And Steph and Theo? Mrs Osborne was saying something had happened there?"

A cloud passed across Kirsty's face, "Oh. Yes. They ran off together. Literally a moonlight flit. Very weird, we didn't even know they were together."

Julia pulled a surprised face, "Really? How strange."

"Yeah, it was. One minute we were all friends together, well to be honest Steph was always more friendly with Ed than anyone else was with him, he could be quite – sulky, at times."

Julia laughed politely.

"It was definitely for the best that they left, he was different after that. Happier. That's when we got together. It was just a casual thing though," she added hastily.

"Was he upset?"

"Oh my God – devastated. He took it really badly, worse than we'd all thought. I don't know why. It's not like she was his girlfriend or anything."

"Wasn't she?"

"What, Steph? No, not ever. They were really close, but just as friends. At least, that's all I know." She shrugged, "it was such a long time ago. About twelve years I would have thought."

"What do you think about inviting them to the party? I don't want it to be full of people with old scores to settle if you know what I mean."

Kirsty shrugged, dragging the toe of her boot in the dirt, "To be honest, it was all so long ago, I doubt anybody cares. I wouldn't know how to get hold of either of them though. I heard they got married, but they never stayed in touch."

"Strange."

"Yeah, it is a little, the rest of us do. Some more sporadically than others but we're all in contact. Each to their own though."

"Quite. OK, well if you give me your number I can keep you updated." Kirsty scrawled it down on a piece of paper Julia held out.

"Cool. I'll look forward to hearing from you. And I'll chase up the others too." She grinned at Julia.

"Thanks."

Julia hurried back to her car before the dirt could get into her hair and under her manicured nails. God, what a ghastly, incestuous little place this was. Everybody living in each others pockets eleven years down the line; it wasn't normal. And yet – for all their closeness – Kirsty hadn't known that Steph and Ed had slept together. It really was a secret. Why could it be so important? She must have been cheating on Theo; there was no other reason. What a sordid affair. Quite why it mattered eleven years on Julia couldn't see. But then, if Steph had lied to Theo for all these years she probably would prefer that it remained hidden. And as for Ed, Julia gripped the wheel tightly, he was going to hear about this one, that was for sure.

CHAPTER SEVENTEEN

The restaurant they chose for lunch was more of a gastropub than anything else, and set very nicely on the banks of a river midway between Churchwell and Tinford. Sunday turned out to be a glorious day, sunny and cloudless, but cold.

"Girls, you will need your coats," Theo said sternly.

"Why? We're having lunch inside aren't we?" Mia pouted.

"They may be opportunities to explore outside and things like that, and you wouldn't want to miss out would you?"

"OK Daddy," Tilly scrambled to her feet.

"And don't wear your Lelli Kelli's," Steph added, applying lipgloss in the hall mirror. "Wear your Daisy Change ones."

"They're just as nice," Theo pointed out.

"Yes, but then they can play with the little dolls, you see."

"You're worrying about their entertainment far too much."

"Shut up Theo. You won't be saying that when they're whining and nagging at you to take them outside."

Theo held up his hands, "OK. Point taken. Are you ready?"

"Two minutes." Black sandals or black boots? Sandals were maybe a bit OTT for lunch. But they looked nice with her Monsoon skirt. She hovered at the bottom of the stairs in an agony of indecision. Her hair was done, nails painted, gorgeous lacy top chosen; boots would look too clumpy she decided. Sandals it would be. She slid them onto her feet and fastened the straps quickly.

Theo frowned at her choice, "Are you sure? Your feet will be cold."

"Not inside they won't be. Girls!" She grabbed her pashmina wrap. "Come on." Steph stood and watched proudly as they hopped down the stairs. She had reverted to their infant days and dressed them identically in Monsoon dresses that fell in waves to their knees and little shrugs over their shoulders. Their blonde hair had been brushed and blowdried and secured with an Alice band. They looked adorable, a picture of perfection, Steph thought. "Come on, we're going," she said. "Got your books and things?"

Tilly held up a little rucksack, "Yes, Mummy."

"Good girl."

Theo was driving – "So you can drink," – and Steph settled herself into the passenger seat and slid her sunglasses on. She was using her Lulu Guiness bag again. She felt nervous, but also curious. What would Ed think of the twins? She badly wanted him to think well of them.

"Is he here?" Steph asked as they pulled into the pub carpark. It was a staggered affair, with the lowest level directly next to the river. Theo drove down almost to the waters edge and stopped.

"I've no idea. How would I know?"

"Well what car does he drive?"

"An Audi something. A4 maybe."

Steph scanned the carpark, there were no Audis. She flipped down the vanity mirror and checked her reflection quickly. Her hair looked a little limp and she took a tiny hairbrush from her bag and backcombed it slightly.

"Come on, you look fine. Shall I take this for you?" Theo held up her bag.

"No," she snatched it back. The colour complimented her skirt beautifully. Strangely, she also wanted him to think well of her. The mother of his children. It could all have been so different. Steph thought of the different set of family the girls would have if she'd been honest from the start. But not only that, she realised, but the different family she would have had. It was too strange an idea.

The pub was one they had frequented a couple of years ago. It had been different back then, much more of a relaxed country pub where you could have a quick pint or glass of wine. These days it had been taken over by Heston Blumenthal-esque chef and most of the decent seating overlooking the river had been cordoned off for diners only. The bar area had been restricted to a small back section of the pub that was boiling in the summer and freezing in winter.

"Hi, booking under the name of Hammond," Theo said pleasantly to the girl waiting to seat them.

"OK, come this way," she picked up five menus.

Theo went to take Steph's hand but she pulled it away, "Don't. You'll smudge my nail varnish." They followed the girl to a large, round table in the window with a beautiful view of the moored boats.

"Thanks," Theo smiled.

"Do you have to be so sycophantic?"

"What? What's wrong with that? I don't want them to spit in my food."

Steph sat down two chairs away from Theo and wondered if Ed would think the waitress was attractive. She was young, slim and blonde – objectively ideal.

"Why are you sitting there?"

"So the girls can go between us."

"Why?"

"They'll prefer it." Steph busied herself pretending to search for something in her handbag.

"Are you all right?" Theo frowned.

"Yes, why?"

"You're being very odd."

"Can I get you any drinks?" The girl reappeared.

"Actually, we're still waiting."

"I'll have a glass of wine please," Steph said. "Dry white."

"OK," she scribbled on her pad.

"Oh – ah – pint of bitter then for me please. Girls?"

"Coke!"

"And two cokes."

"Good afternoon everyone."

Steph almost literally jumped; she hadn't heard him approach at all and her heart started hammering, "God you made me jump."

"Sorry," Ed bent and kissed her cheek lightly. "It wasn't intentional. How are you all? Hello girls."

They looked up, "Hi."

"Ed, we were just ordering drinks – what do you…?"

"Dry white wine for me please." He slid into his intended seat next to Theo, to Steph's immense relief.

"Shall we get a bottle then darling?"

Steph nodded.

"Well, nice to see you all." He looked a little nervous too, Steph noticed.

"You too, mate. Girls, are you going to say hello properly?"

Mia slid Theo a sideways glance, "What's properly?"

"Look up, smile, be interested."

Ed was immediately presented with two smiling faces; he burst out laughing, "It's OK, you don't need to be polite on my behalf."

"Cool!" Mia grinned.

"So how have you guys been?" Ed asked, settling into his seat.

"Fine thanks," Theo replied. "My wife is currently restraining herself from redecorating our entire house."

"Your house is fine." Ed said.

"*I* know that."

"There's no harm in dreaming a bit," Steph said, not willing to be mocked. "And fashions change."

"You cannot keep our house up to date with fashion," Theo pointed out.

Ed grinned and shifted in his seat to face Mia, "What are you playing on?" he asked.

"My DS."

"Your what?"

"My DS. DS Lite. You know…" Mia held it up so he could see.

"Ah, yes, I do know those. And you two have one?"

"We have two. One each. It would be rubbish to just have one, wouldn't it Tilly? We couldn't send messages then."

Ed shook his head, "The technology they have these days, it's just amazing. Do you remember our Gameboys?" he asked Theo and Steph. "And we thought those were the bees knees. Look how far it's come now. I guess these guys don't even know what a non-digital camera is."

"Probably not," Theo agreed.

"Do they have mobile phones yet?"

"No way!" Steph said vehemently. "Not a chance."

"Muuuum," Mia said, without looking up from her game, "but Sasha's got one at school."

"I don't care, that's up to Sasha's mummy. You're not having one."

"When can we?" Tilly asked.

"When you have your ears pierced."

"When's that?"

"Sixteen."

"Oh that's not fair Steph," Ed said easily. "You were twelve when you had yours done."

"Mummy!" Tilly breathed, eyes wide. "You never told us."

"Thanks Ed," Steph took her first sip of wine.

"Sorry, I don't know what to say to kids."

"Clearly." But she smiled.

The wine did a lot to soothe her nerves. She tried to absorb what Katie had told her, just to smile, be herself and block any other thoughts. Apparently if she did that, it would be easy. Steph thought that she'd underestimated Katie as a friend, a lot of people would have run screaming from such a complicated situation, but Katie had stoically stood her ground. Steph had once asked her whether she felt guilty knowing such a huge secret when she was around Theo, and Katie had replied, "I don't think about it. As far as I'm concerned, he's their father." Which there was a lot of truth in.

Steph flicked her eyes up and across, over Ed and then back to the girls. It was almost mesmeric. There had been so few occasions when they were side by side, she was hungry to see whether there was any physical resemblance. And of course there was. He was their father. Steph gulped anew at her wine as Theo and Ed discussed various golf techniques. It was probably Mia who was most like her father, she had the same slant to her jaw, like she was constantly battling against what was best and striving for what she wanted. Her personality fitted his to a T. Tilly was far more reserved, gentler, softer in her approach to life. Mia just bowled on in, regardless of what others would think. It was hard to say which was the best method.

"Steph?" she was jolted from her intensely private thoughts suddenly, and blushed. "Just wondering if you were ready to order? The girls are hungry." Theo said.

"Oh, yes, I am. I'm having roast beef."

"You look miles away, you OK?"

Uncomfortably aware of Ed's gaze, Steph nodded quickly and frowned at Theo.

"Hey Ed," Mia said conversationally. "Were you any good at playing your – you know – game thing?"

"My Gameboy? I wasn't bad. Why?" Ed set down his wine glass to give Mia his full attention.

"Because I'm stuck on this level. I need to find the doorway for the princess and I can't do it. Can you have a go?"

"Mia darling – I don't think Ed wants…" Steph began, but Ed shushed her.

"No, no, it's fine. Don't worry. Let me have a look then." He slid out of his seat and went to stand behind what was, after all, his daughter. Steph held her breath, watching. He leant forward to squint at the screen and familiarise himself with the buttons.

"OK – here, press this – yes, that's it. Go along there – mind that spider! Yes, keep going, OK jump up there, see that key? That's the one, go along that bit and try that green light. Yes! That's it."

"Wick*ed*. Thanks. Look Tilly, now I've beaten you on this game."

"Yeah but you cheated." Tilly didn't even look up.

"Did not!"

"Did so."

"Er girls, not here please." Theo hissed.

"Sorry, have I caused complications?" Ed asked.

"No, not at all. It's a daily minefield, don't worry, just consider yourself well out of it. How's Julia?"

"Is Julia Amy's mum?" Mia looked up suddenly, her blue eyes fixed on her mother.

"Yes, why?"

"How does Ed know who Julia is?" There was an awkward pause.

"Well, they're friends." Steph said eventually.

"Ed…" said Tilly. "Can you help me with *my* game now?" she shot a challenging look at her sister.

"I can try. What's yours?"

"Imagine Fashion Designer."

"Like your mother," Ed remarked, shifting his chair so he could sit next to Tilly.

"What? Why's that like Mummy?"

"You always wanted to be a fashion designer didn't you Steph?" He took the DS off Tilly and pushed at the buttons.

"No. I did use to think about being an interior designer, but that was a long time ago."

"Didn't I hear you mention that the other night?" Theo remarked. "You were on the phone to Katie, I think."

"Sort of. She'd printed some information for me, courses I'd need to go on to become qualified and that sort of thing."

"Why?" Theo pulled a face. "You aren't thinking about it are you?"

"No. But nice to know that I have your support if I were thinking about it," Steph replied sarcastically.

"I was only asking."

"What stopped you Steph?" Ed asked.

"Life. Marriage. Children."

"Just the few obstacles then."

"Quite."

"You could always retrain, you know. If you wanted," he added.

"But she doesn't want to. Why would she want to? She has everything she could need and she's got her hands full being a mum."

"Theo, I can speak for myself." Steph poured some more wine into her glass. "I do think about it from time to time," she confessed.

"But it's always too difficult, practically speaking. And Theo's right, that sort of thing isn't really my role in life."

Ed shrugged, "I'm a firm believer in getting what you want out of life. And if that's it..."

"No. It isn't. Not really. It was just an idea once."

Predictably, after lunch the girls begged to be taken outside to feed the ducks.

"I would come, but look at my shoes." Steph extended a foot for the twins to inspect.

"She's right," Mia muttered. "Can you come Daddy?" They took him by the hand and dragged him out of the door and down to the waters edge, where there was a tiny jetty and a slope down to the water. A handful of ducks swam about lazily and more appeared as Mia and Tilly threw broken off bits of bread into the water.

"They're gorgeous girls," Ed commented, looking out of the window.

"Thanks," Steph shifted uncomfortably on her seat.

"They're a credit to you both." Ed sipped at his coffee. Steph didn't say anything. "You never know, it might be my turn one day!"

"I didn't think you were very child-orientated."

"No, I never have been. If it had been me in that situation at eighteen instead of Theo, I dread to think how I would have handled it."

"Really?" Steph asked softly.

"Really. I don't think it would have been very well." The desperation to know more was nearly overwhelming but it would have felt obscene to question him further. But somehow, it was nice to hear. It made her decision all those years ago a little easier. She looked at him speculatively for a moment; what would Ed be like as a father? He might claim he'd be no good, but he'd made an effort this afternoon with both girls and he'd done well. There had been something of a natural rapport there. Steph didn't dare try and think why.

"How are things with Julia then?" she asked.

"Hmm. Yes, they're OK. We don't see as much of each other as we would like, but they're all right. Moving along nicely."

There wasn't a lot Steph could say to that, not knowing him well enough to know what his ideal girlfriend would be like.

"Isn't she quite a bit older than you?" she volunteeered.

"Ten years. But – you know – I've been there and done the bimbo thing. It's all very well for a few weeks to have some pretty, young girl hanging off your arm, but when it comes to wanting to have a conversation, they can't. Unless it's about Botox or Heat magazine."

Steph laughed, "You'll have to get used to kids if you and Julia are going to get more serious."

"The thought had crossed my mind. I don't know. Maybe. Actually…" he hesitated. "There was something that I was going to discuss with Theo."

"Oh yes?"

"I've been offered a new job."

"Congratulations," Steph said politely.

"In Boston."

"Boston, USA?"

"Yep, that one."

"Wow. Are you going to go?"

"I'm not sure yet. Maybe. It's only for a year and it's a very good offer. It would look good on my CV, I'd get some valuable experience – it's very tempting."

"What did Julia say?"

"She doesn't know yet."

"I see."

"I'm going to wait until I've made a decision I think. I need to be upfront with her about it and I don't know myself where I stand yet. I need to think about it a bit more so I can be honest when she questions me – which she will."

"She will," Steph agreed. "The USA must be amazing, have you been?"

"No. Never. I haven't done that much travelling."

"Neither have we, just Europe – Italy, Spain and France of course. But that was ages ago."

"Oh yes." France; the source of that hideous, hurtful postcard. Ed dropped his eyes.

"Well, what an exciting time in your life," Steph commented after a couple of minutes.

"I guess so."

"Do think of those of us left behind won't you?"

It was meant in a light-hearted way but Ed looked at her seriously, "You can do whatever you want Steph," he said. "You do know that don't you?"

"Yes, I do. But I'm just grateful for what I've got. I count my blessings every day." She met his eyes in a deep stare. From the doorway where Theo was standing it looked like a loving, trustful gaze, and it troubled him. He felt it would be intruding to break the moment so he stepped away quietly and went back outside to his girls.

Steph updated him later about Ed's job offer, as they sat on the sofa with bowls of soup for supper.

"I'm not surprised," Theo said. "He seems a very driven chap."

"Do you think he'll go?"

"I don't know. It depends how much it appeals to him, compared to what he's got here."

Theo laid a hand on her arm, "Fancy an early night?"

Steph turned away, "I don't know. There's a few bits and pieces on the TV that I want to watch." That was the bad thing of course, the guilt that stole over her every time Theo was his normal, loving self was making her push him away. How could she love him and lie to him at the same time? Her behaviour of the past ten years seemed to have been swept away all of a sudden and her morals and conscience exposed once again. Where had this new Steph come from?

"You go up," she said. "I'll clear this up and follow you. Maybe I could watch TV in bed." Compromise was the watchword of marriage, after all.

****

Ed should have known that this would be a bad idea. He'd thought it would be a placatory gesture to invite Julia round in the evening after Sunday lunch so she didn't feel completely left out, but judging by the black expression on her face he had got that wrong.

"Did you have a nice time?" she enquired, in a tone dripping with sarcasm. She stalked ahead of him into the living room but did not remove her coat and did not sit down.

"Yes. It was all right. Nothing special. Nice to meet the girls properly."

"I bet."

Ed sighed loudly, "What's the matter?" He had a headache and Sunday nights were never his favourite time of the week anyway.

"The matter? Where shall I start? The way that you've lied to me, the things you've hidden from me, the parts of your life you've kept secret from me. And not just once, but over and over and over again."

Ed flopped down on the sofa, "Julia, what are you talking about? Are you going to sit down?"

"I went to see your mum today." That got a reaction, he looked shocked.

"My mum? Er – why? And how do you know where she lives? What the fuck were you doing?"

"Oh – I was doing something nice for you." He could believe the same as the rest. "I was planning a surprise party for your birthday."

"Right… and that led to this mood?"

"Only, when I started asking your mum which old schoolfriends she thought you might want there, that was when I discovered the extent of your deception."

"Elucidate."

"Apparently you and Steph were very *close* as teenagers," her eyes looked at him accusingly. "And it wasn't just your mum who told me that, Kirsty backed her up. You spent a lot of time together."

"Kirsty too? Jesus… I've never tried to hide the fact we were close. I told you we were all best friends."

"No, not *all*. I'm talking about you and Steph. Apparently she used to spend a lot of time at your house."

"Possibly…" Ed said slowly. "Does it matter?"

"It does when she was in your bed."

"*What*?"

"Don't lie to me! Don't pretend you didn't – your *mother* knows."

"Are you talking about the night before she went away?"

"So it was then. That's just charming. Spend the night with one man and run away and marry another the next day."

"It wasn't quite like…"

"Spare me the details. So you slept with her?"

There was a long pause, "Yes. Just that once," Ed said in a low voice, not looking at Julia.

"So you've been lying to me?"

"It depends what you mean by lying. Look, Julia, it was only one night, a long time ago, we were teenagers, that was it. Nothing else. We weren't together."

"How can I believe you?"

"Just trust me. And even if we'd been engaged, what the hell would it matter now?"

"Well it's a bit odd how you've suddenly got back in touch, go to any lengths to see her – how do I know that you don't still have feelings for her? She's young and pretty after all," Julia spat.

"Please – be serious. She is a married woman. We had a teenage fling once, ten years ago. That's it. I had no feelings for her then, or now."

"What did Theo think of your little night of passion?"

"I don't know," Ed said quietly after a minute.

"You did tell him?"

"I didn't, no."

"But Steph?"

"I don't know! I didn't speak to her after that."

"So he doesn't know? Why wouldn't she tell him?"

"She may well have done, I don't know."

"I don't think she would have done."

"Why not?"

"Because I think she was cheating on him. I think old goody-two-shoes Stephanie Hammond was officially with one person and unofficially shagging you," Julia announced.

"No, she wasn't with him."

"How the fuck do you know?"

"Because she told me. That's why she was there at my house that night. She was upset because she liked Theo and he didn't like her." Ed didn't add how much of a chance he thought he'd been in with.

"How very convenient. I'm afraid I don't believe you." Julia picked up her bag. In fact it went beyond disblelief, his denial made her even more suspicious.

"Where are you going?"

"Home."

"Oh Julia, come on, this is ridiculous."

"Bye Ed." She slammed the door behind her as Ed stared after her in disbelief. Shit. What was she going to do next? Storm round to Steph and Theo's and reveal all? Ed sincerely hoped for Steph's sake that she had confessed to Theo all those years ago.

CHAPTER EIGHTEEN

Ed glanced at his watch, ten o' clock, too late to ring? Quite possibly. On the other hand, if he didn't and Julia did storm round there he would sorely wish he had. He stood in front of his phone for a few moments, chewing on his thumbnail. This was all so ridiculous, teenage dramas revisited ten years on. What possible relevance could his night with Steph have now? She was a very happily married woman with two gorgeous children. He had been nothing to her, not even a fling, she'd made that very clear to him. He sometimes wondered how much of a different person he would have been if she had rung after that night. It wouldn't have taken that much effort, from anywhere in the world she could have picked up the phone, dialled his number and explained the circumstances herself. He'd deduced pretty quickly that any relationship with her was out of the question but a simple 'sorry' for buggering off wouldn't have gone amiss. Ed shrugged off the memory and picked up his phone and dialled Steph's number. It rang and rang but there was no reply. Shit. What now? He waited, Ed supposed. There wasn't anything else he could do. He waited and wondered whether it was best to extricate himself from this relationship with Julia; the woman was clearly barking.

****

She did actually drive and park her car outside Touchstone, but there her courage failed her. It was Sunday night, it was half past ten and all the lights in the house were off. She could go storming in, accusing Steph of all of her suspicions, chief among which was that she had designs upon Ed, but that would look desperate. And she mustn't forget that Steph and Theo were fellow parents at St Catherines, she had to face them in the playground, at parents evenings, sports days and on the committee. She must be very, very careful how she acted.

Julia sat there for a few minutes, looking up at the greystone façade of the house, it was a beautiful property. It had big sash windows, a good-size plot around it and little dormer windows peeping out of the attic roof. She'd never been inside but she wouldn't mind betting it was very tastefully decorated. A surge of irritation ran through her. How was it fair that Steph had all this and she, Julia, had so much less? When, let's face it, she'd tried so much harder. All those years of diligent study, applying for job after job, dealing with rejection, juggling a full-time career with bringing up Amy and now – a single parent. And Little Miss Lucky strolled out of college without bothering to sit her exams, walked straight into the waiting arms of Mr Fabulously Wealthy and promptly had perfect twin girls whom she could stay at home and look after. Her determination to bring Steph down a peg or two strengthened. She started the engine and drove away. How perfect if she had cheated on Theo with Ed. How marvellously complex. Who cared if it happened eleven years ago or however long, it would still prove that Saint Steph didn't exist.

****

"Right. Do you have your violins?"
"Yes Mummy."
"Spelling books?"
"Yes Mummy."
"Water bottles? You'll have a cross-country run today."
"Yes… we do."
"Good. Get into the car."
"Why is your hair in a ponytail Mummy? And why are you in a tracksuit?" Tilly asked curiously.
"Because I'm going to the gym."
"Oh, I thought so. You never normally wear your hair in a ponytail."

It was time, Steph had decided, to take back a little control over her life – and figure. She hadn't put on weight, exactly the opposite in fact, but her muscles had withered and once shapely thighs had dwindled to almost bird-like proportions. And besides, she missed the exercise-released endorphins – they were mood-lifting, and God knows she could do with some of those right now. Perhaps a little more running would make her tired enough to sleep at night which in turn would make her feel more rested and she would be able to shake this perpetual lethargy that hung over her. She must think positively, be brighter and more alert. Poor Theo, he must be wondering where his happy, sunny wife had disappeared to of late. Steph smiled to herself; now that she knew she didn't have to worry about Ed, things could be different. She could go back to being the perfect wife and mother that she'd always aspired to be. Lunch yesterday had been good, worth going to. Ed was sweet. He deserved to be happy too. Steph wasn't convinced that Julia was the person to make him so but that was up to him.

Damn. After dropping the girls off, Steph rummaged through her purse and realised she'd forgotten her gym membership card. She'd have to go home. Never mind, it was only a five minute detour. She parked hastily on the pavement outside the house and jogged up the front steps to the red-painted front door, inserted her key and without bothering to shut the door behind her she went on through to the kitchen to the shelf where she would have left the card. She located it, shoved into her tracksuit pocket and turned to go.

"Hello Steph," Julia stood in the doorway. She looked tired and dishevelled, her normally neat hair was scruffy and her face bare of make-up.

"God! You made me jump."

"Sorry – the door was open so I just came in. Don't worry, I shut it."

Immediately Steph had the feeling of being trapped. "Er – what are you doing?" she asked.

Julia stepped forward and placed her handbag on the breakfast bar, "What am I doing…" she repeated slowly. "That's a very good question. Essentially wasting my time, I think."

"Sorry?"

It was irritating, Julia thought, how Steph was one of those people who even looked good dressed to go to the gym. Some women looked flushed and flabby and vaguely unclean while they were striding out their kilometres on the treadclimber, and some looked fresh-faced, slim and competent. Steph was one of the latter.

"Julia, I don't mean to be rude, but why have you just walked into my house?"

"I came to talk to you."

"Ok, well, can you be quick? I'm supposed to be somewhere."

"You have an important meeting with a treadmill do you?"

"What's that supposed to mean?"

"That you don't have anything better to occupy your time."

Steph stared at her in shock. "What's going on?" she asked eventually.

"Well, I did come to build some bridges with you."

"Build bridges?"

Julia sighed, "That dinner we had didn't go too well did it?"

"Oh – no."

"That's what I meant. Apparently I was rude and I came to offer an olive branch." She made a vague attempt at a smile.

"Don't worry about it," Steph said uneasily. "We'd all had a little to drink."

"Nice of you to say so. Actually, I didn't think I was that rude, but Ed disagreed with me."

"Really?"

"Oh yes. He came down heavily on your side."

"Did he?"

"Yes. Why, does that surprise you?"

"That sounds like a very loaded comment to me, Julia. What are you trying to say?"

"What I'm trying to say is that I've found out about your sordid past. No point beating about the bush. You're not quite as perfect as you make out are you?" Even Julia couldn't have hoped for the reaction that she got.

The colour fell away from Steph's face, she gasped and sank backwards onto a kitchen chair, "What do you mean?" she asked.

"I mean that I know about you. I know about your past. I know what happened in Tinford before you left."

Steph tried to swallow; her throat was dry. "What are you talking about?"

"Don't play the innocent with me, it doesn't become you. I don't know why I didn't guess sooner. He's attractive, isn't he?"

"Who?" Her mind felt like it had shifted into a lower gear.

"Ed."

"Attractive?" Steph shook her head in confusion. "Yes, I suppose so. Why?"

"Have you always been waiting for him?"

"Waiting for…? No. No, Julia, I have not. I have never waited for Ed."

"Are you sure? Are you sure you didn't make a terrible mistake all those years ago and choose the wrong man?"

The blood roared loudly in Stephs head and stomach flipped over. I'm going to be sick, she thought, and bent her head towards her knees.

"That looks like the pose of a guilty woman to me. You've been waiting all these years haven't you? You just couldn't leave the past behind and you've been living a lie, waiting for him. And now he's here, so you thought you'd call time on the waiting and snatch him from under my nose."

"Julia," Steph said desperately. "I don't know what you think you know –"

"Oh there's no 'think' about it. I've had it straight from the horses mouth. I've done my homework. I've spoken to your friend Kirsty and she told me exactly how close you and Ed were at school."

"Well yes, we were –"

"And how he didn't have eyes for anyone but you." That was an embellishment, but Steph wouldn't know that.

"OK. Fine."

"You don't even deny it!" Julia gave a sharp, harsh little laugh.

"I can't deny it. Ed was keen on me at school, everyone knew it. Especially Kirsty. I wasn't so keen on him, Theo was always the one for me."

"Is that right?" Julia asked smoothly. "In that case, why did you sleep with Ed?"

"I didn't –"

"Don't deny it, I've spoken to his mum and she knows. She *saw* you. The whole village must know that you slept with him and your horrible little secret."

No, no, no. Steph hoped fervently – prayed, even – she could take anything in life but not that. Not anybody knowing. Not even if they were the spitting image of Ed, please no, don't let *that* be true. No, no –

"And now he's back in your life, it must be a dream come true for you isn't it Steph? After all, he's waited a long time to claim what is rightfully his. And you want it just as much, don't you? Poor Theo. Does he have any idea?" Julia gave her a sorrowful look.

Steph closed her eyes briefly, "No. Theo doesn't know a thing."

"I knew it!" Julia chortled. "I didn't think Theo was the type to be so magnanimous and take on something that wasn't truly his."

"Julia – please – you have to listen to me – no one knows, this is…"

"Are you asking me to keep your secret?"

Steph gazed at her through huge, terrified eyes, so much adrenalin pumping round her body that she could hardly think, "Yes, yes, I am. Please Julia, I can't tell you."

"Morning dears." Like a rainbow onto a battlefield Mrs B wandered through the open kitchen door. "Sorry I'm a bit late, there was a terrible accident on the A36. A Ford KA, squashed flat it was, I can't think anyone got out of there alive. Where do you want me to start today Stephanie?" Of course. It was Monday.

"The playroom," Steph said in an almost whisper. "The playroom, please." It was the furthest room from the kitchen.

"Righty-ho. No problem. We're nearly out of Pledge dear, I'll pop it on the list shall I?"

"Yes, that's fine." Steph held Julia's gaze; she looked triumphant. They waited until Mrs B had left.

"I'm very surprised at you Steph," Julia said casually. "I would never have thought it of you."

Steph dropped her head, "I know."

"Is that the worst bit? That the perfect façade you present to the world is completely fake?" Steph stayed silent. She could not bring herself to discuss this with Julia. "The thing is Steph, that if you and Ed continue with this pretence then there's no room for me in his life. And we're good together."

"Ed doesn't know," Steph whispered.

"Oh but he does. How could he not? He's part of it. He's wanted this for years."

So it was true. Steph felt suddenly faint. That was why he'd popped back up, why he'd been in touch. He'd known all along and now he'd come to reclaim the girls – panic swirled over her in a debilitating mist. He'd done a good job of pretending otherwise, but then he was a lawyer wasn't he, and they said lawyers were good at lying. And then look at how good he'd been with Tilly and Mia yesterday, really making an effort. She'd thought it was odd at the time, perfectly obvious now.

"He told you?" Steph asked.

"No. I worked it out and asked him. He didn't deny it. All the pieces of the puzzle just fell into place like that," Julia clicked her fingers. "It wasn't difficult when you know the relevant bits – close friends for years, closer as teenagers, the way he felt about you, the night you spent together – that's the crucial bit, clearly. Tell me Steph," she leant in closer, "did you actually think that you'd get away with it?"

Behind the kitchen door Steph heard Mrs B move into the hallway and begin polishing. "Playroom didn't need touching Stephanie, them girls have been good in there I see. Thought I'd move out here," she called.

"You have to go," she said to Julia.

"Yes, I think I should. I need time to think about this."

She watched Julia's exiting back in a daze, heard the click of the front door as it swung shut behind her. She scrabbled for her mobile with shaking hands and ran upstairs to the privacy of her bedroom.

"Hello? Katie?"

"Hi Steph, hang on, just let me switch the radio off – there we go. You OK? What's up?"

"She knows Katie, Julia knows. Everything." Tears rose unchecked in Steph's eyes and she swallowed a huge sob.

"What's everything?"

"About me sleeping with Ed, about the girls being his."

"How do you know this?" Katie's voice was suddenly sharp.

"She's just been here, she's told me."

"Hang on – I'm coming round."

"No, Mrs B's here. Too risky. I'll come to you."

There was a glass of wine waiting for her on the kitchen table when she arrived. Steph bit back another half-sob when she saw it, "Is that what I'm reduced to?"

Katie steered her to a chair, "Desperate times, desperate measures and all that. So, tell me, what happened? How the heck has she found out?"

Despite herself, Steph took a sip of wine. "She's been to talk to Ed's mum."

"And...?"

"And she told Julia that Ed and I slept together."

"How does she know that?" Katie's face was a picture of confusion.

"She walked in, when we were asleep. I wasn't in the bed, I was on the floor and she told me the next morning. I thought we'd got away with it, but apparently not."

"And she told Julia? That doesn't seem like the smartest move."

"You know what Julia's like, stones would volunteer their blood for her."

"But it doesn't make any sense, why would she just come out with it?"

"Julia would have been asking. From what she was saying she's put two and two together and – I can't quite believe this – Ed *knows*. He probably told her when she confronted him."

"*No!*"

"Yes. That's why he got in touch. He's been waiting for years apparently. Julia told me. She kept going on about my 'sordid' past and my 'secret', telling me that she knew everything."

"What's she going to do?"

"That's the worst bit, she left the house saying that she needed to think about it." Steph felt dizzy and sick with panic. "What if she tells Theo?"

Katie didn't know what on earth to say. It wasn't beyond the realms of possibility, that was the problem. She poured Steph some more wine. "Are you sure Julia is talking about what you think she's talking about? Are you sure she does know?" she said finally. "It seems very peculiar that she's suddenly just guessed."

"She hasn't, she said as much to me, she's put the pieces of the puzzle together, that's what she's done. And to be honest, if Ed knows then he probably told her."

"How would Ed have found out?" Katie asked sceptically.

"We slept together at exactly the right time, I leave Tinford for good, and the next time he hears about me I've got twins that look like him. It doesn't take Einstein."

"No – hang on – he didn't know about the twins."

"So he said. He's been lying to me Katie, lying for ages. God knows what he's heard. We still have friends, family in the village. It's filtered back to him that they're the spitting image of him and he's worked it out that there's a very good chance that they could be his."

Katie shuddered, "It's creepy if he's been waiting all these years to make a move."

"Well he wouldn't have wanted two babies would he?" Anger and fear filled Steph in equal measure. "He told me that yesterday. You don't think he'll take them away from me do you?"

"No, of course not. No court in the land would send two little girls to live with a father they've never known about." There was a long pause.

"I cannot believe that I am discussing this," Steph dropped her head into her hands, face ashen. "Just a couple of hours ago I was happy, in control of my life and off to the gym and now I'm thinking about if I can retain custody of my children. It's absurd."

"Don't be silly. There's no question of that. But what you do need to do is find out from Julia what she's planning to do."

"What do you mean?"

"Well," Katie hesitated, unsure how to phrase it, "if she's going to approach Theo you need to get in there first."

"Fuck. I can't tell him."

"Cross that bridge when you come to it. Think, Steph, what's

Julia likely to do?"

"She's not happy with me," Steph took a deep breath. "She said that I was in the way of her and Ed. That if we kept up this pretence then there was no point her being around, and she wants to be. She said they're perfect together."

"So she wants you out of the way?"

"I guess so. She doesn't want me near Ed."

"And what's the quickest way of achieving that?"

"God – Katie, I don't know," Steph looked appalled.

"I hate to panic you, but I think you need to speak to Theo."

I can't, I can't, I can't was all Steph could think. Every time she had tried to imagine releasing those awful words her mind just blanked it as a concept. It wouldn't let her imagine the likely consequences. And, deep down, she'd always thought that as long as it was just her who knew the truth, there was no way Theo would ever need to know. But she'd told Katie of course – the first sign of her defences weakening. And she had never counted on Julia being in the position she was and being so vindictive. The trouble was, when the truth surrounded you, engulfed you, left you gasping for breath it was very hard to fight your way out of it any more. And that was what Ed's reappearance had done. His presence meant that she was unable to live a lie any longer. Her previous life was over, done, finished with. And if that was the case then what did she have to lose? She could only go forward from here, and she was certain of one thing, both she and Theo would have the twins' best interests at heart. They wouldn't suffer through all of this.

"Right," Steph stood up decisively. "I'm going to talk to him."

"Him?" Katie looked up anxiously.

"Oh – Theo. Not Ed. He can wait."

"What are you going to say?"

"I don't know." Her head felt all funny and swimmy. "I don't know yet. But I'm going to get through this. I am going to come out the other side."

She drove home in a daze and to her great relief, Mrs B had gone. Steph wasn't sure that she was up to being sociable at the moment. She paced up and down the length of her kitchen, arms folded tightly across her body. She had no choice but to do this, she really didn't. If she left things as they were then either Julia or Ed would get to him first and at least this way she could retain a shred of self-respect. It would be withered by eleven years of neglect, but it would be there. She grabbed the phone and dialled a number, "Hello, Mum?"

"Hello Stephanie," her mother responded cheerily. "How are you? It's been ages since I heard from you."

"Fine. Absolutely fine. Mum, I need to ask a favour," Steph said urgently.

"Oh yes?"

"You're not going away anywhere this week are you?"

"No, why?"

"I need you to have the girls for a couple of days if you wouldn't mind. I need some time with Theo. I can't explain right now but…" to her horror, she heard her voice crack.

"Stephanie? Is everything all right?"

"No. Not really. Can you do this for me Mum? I'll pack everything they need for school and things."

She managed to focus while she packed their bags but it felt like she was packing their life away. Tears dripped down her cheeks, soaking her face and spotting their colourful, ironed pyjamas and neatly folded vests. But she let herself cry because they wouldn't see it. Her beautiful, gorgeous girls – what had she done to them? Then the tears grew stronger and became sobs and she could feel grief overwhelm her entire body, shaking up through her relentlessly. This was it, it was all over, her whole life. Everything she'd known and loved for years was fractured and cracking and falling around her. She would lose Theo, she knew that, but what of the girls? Images of weekends spent alone while they saw their father flashed through her mind. She would have to share them with another woman, Theo would remarry and they would grow apart from her. They would hate her for what she had done, especially Mia, and they wouldn't want to live with her. Everyone would find out and all her lies would be exposed. Steph slumped against the wall, hands gripped tightly over her mouth. Her entire life was going to fall apart. The wave of panic that washed over her was tangible. She struggled to regulate her breathing and pushed sodden strands of hair behind her ears. Her hands were shaking badly. And she still had to speak to Theo.

Minutes later, she didn't know how many, she heard the slam of a car door and then a knocking on the front door, "Stephanie? Stephanie, are you there?"

Steph rubbed at her eyes, picked up the two pink holdalls and opened the front door slowly. Her mother rushed into the hallway, cardigan flying out behind her, "Stephanie, whatever is the matter?" She enfolded her daughter in a hug.

"I can't talk to you right now Mum," she said into her mother's shoulder. "I'll ring you later. I'm fine, I really am."

"You'd tell me if anything serious was the matter?" Doubtless she meant cancer and death, not a life constructed out of nothingness.

"Yes. Yes, I would."

"OK, well, you leave those girls to me and we'll speak to you later. I love you." She dropped a kiss on Steph's forehead.

"Tell the girls I love them," Steph said and tears welled up once more. She waved goodbye and picked up the phone to call Theo, dialling his number with white, trembling fingers. She didn't think she'd ever cried so much before in her life, the tears just flowed and flowed. Was there an infinite amount? The screen blurred in front of her, had she dialled the right number? Please don't let Julia have got to him first, please, anything but that. She'd know when he answered, she'd be able to tell from his tone of voice. Literally biting on her knuckle she waited for him to pick up the call – "Hello? Theo?"

"Hi darling," he sounded happy and relaxed. "You OK? What's up?"

Before she knew it, Steph was crying hysterically into the phone, "I need you to come home Theo, right now, I need you. Please come."

CHAPTER NINETEEN

He arrived fifteen minutes later, swinging into the driveway through the open gates and not bothering to park properly. Steph was watching him from the sitting room window. He'd tried repeatedly to call her on the way home but she ignored them all, just stayed staring and watching and waiting. She'd even tried to rehearse some form of speech but her brain wouldn't let her; couldn't cope with the magnitude of what she was about to say. Deep down, she had never thought it would happen. Like a child, she'd expected the danger to recede with the amount of time that passed. If she hadn't been caught instantly then she never would be. But she had been wrong. She'd grown up very suddenly.

Theo burst into the living room, "What the hell's going on? What's happening? Where are the girls?" His eyes were wild with fear.

"It's OK, it's all right," Steph managed to say. "They're fine. They're fine."

"What is all this about?" He crossed the large room in three strides and put his hands on her upper arms, "Tell me Steph."

He thought someone had died, she could see that. It was like watching some terrible play unfold in front of her eyes. She was the audience and also the main protagonist. She could see and understand what he felt but it was her job to convey the truth to him.

"No one's dead Theo."

His relief was palpable, "Then what?" He still had his shoes on. He had his car keys in his hand. It felt all wrong and awkward.

"Sit down, relax a minute."

"I don't want to relax, I want you to tell me what's going on, you look terrible!" And she did; her hair was messy and knotted, her face was white with tears tracks imprinted under each eye, her nose was red and swollen and her eyes were bloodshot. She looked about eighteen; grief had stripped away the years.

"I – you need to sit down. You need to listen to me," she was crying again. The urge to justify before she had explained was intense.

Her feelings were running riot.

"OK, OK, fine, I'm sitting," he backed slowly to the sofa. "Now tell me."

Steph looked at him wordlessly – where to start? The beginning. That was always a good place.

"You remember when we were teenagers and at school and living in Tinford?"

"Yes."

"And you remember who all of our friends were?"

"Yes."

"But it was always you and me and Ed who were closest, right?"

"Yes." It was disjointed, but at least she was speaking.

"Ed and I were closer than you realised."

"OK."

The tears were spilling over once again, "We were very close. For just such a short period of time. It was all wrong, it should never have happened, I don't know what we thought we were doing."

"Does it matter now?" he interrupted suddenly. Guilty though she might feel for having a relationship with Ed, or whatever it was that had gone on, Theo couldn't for the life of him see how it could matter now, eleven years on. But he was unpleasantly reminded of how close they'd seemed recently. Steph nodded with streaming eyes and nose, she swiped a hand across her face desperately, it was pathetic to see, she looked like a child, all small and shrunken. Theo longed to take her in his arms but alarm bells were ringing. He'd never seen Steph like this before.

"It does matter. It really does. I always loved you Theo, it was always you. It's only ever been you, which is why this is so much worse. This isn't the way I want it to be."

"You aren't making any sense." He felt well and truly alert now, with adrenaline thudding through every part of his body. Outside in the hall the phone rang, but they ignored it.

"It was the night that you came round to talk to me. The night of the village event, everyone was out and I told you I loved you and then you ran off." Theo nodded soundlessly. Steph took a deep breath, "After you left, I went to Ed's house. I was distraught. I adored you, I thought I'd made a fool of myself. I thought you would never speak to me again. Actually, I didn't, I thought you would pity me, which was worse." Her voice became softer and calmer. "Don't underestimate how I felt about you at the time and how I feel about you now Theo." She met his eyes in an intense, anguished gaze.

"Carry on."

"So I went to Ed's. We drank wine and talked and everything seemed better. He persuaded me that I didn't need you. He had a thing for me then, a crush or whatever you want to call it. He liked me more than I liked him, and I didn't properly realise. I knew he was a good friend but that's it. But, that night, we got properly drunk and – and – we slept together. Just once, I swear, just once. It was meaningless sex. We were friends. We were silly to have done it. We didn't know what we were doing. And because we didn't know, because we were drunk, we did the most stupid thing," she paused briefly before plunging down the precipice. "We didn't use any contraception."

"Right," Theo looked confused. A jumble of thoughts were struggling to untangle themselves in his mind. What was she telling him? They'd had sex – OK, fine. Well not fine, but not a disaster. Did she have HIV? Herpes? "So – what, Steph? What is it? A disease? A termination?"

"No. I don't have a disease. And I didn't have a termination."

"Then what?" What else could come from unprotected sex?

"Theo – I fell pregnant. From that one night," she was crying again. "I didn't realise for ages, I never thought it could happen, I barely knew my own body at that age and I didn't realise until we were in France."

"And? So?"

He still wasn't there, Steph could see, he still hadn't made that heartbreaking link.

"The girls, Theo," she sobbed. "The twins, Mia and Tilly. Ed is their father."

Actually, he had made that improbable link, a split second before she said it, but he hadn't been able to react quickly enough to stop the words coming out of her mouth. His whole body turned icy cold and began to tremble, "What? What did you just say?"

She just sat there and stared at him, unable to reiterate. She waited for him to react.

"Ed is their father?"

Steph nodded wordlessly; a brief hiatus in her emotion.

"My God." Theo tilted his head back to look at the ceiling and brought his hands up to cover his mouth. He felt sick. The twins. His precious, perfect twins – they weren't his. How could they not be? He stared at his wife in confusion, "No, you must have made a mistake."

"I haven't. I wish I could have. I calculated it time and time again but I was pregnant before we even had sex, Theo. There is no way they can be yours." It sounded brutal; it *was* brutal.

"Are you sure?"

"I'm sure."

"My God." Somewhere inside himself an unexpected furnace opened up, a horrible, deep, churning well of rage. Theo stood up with clenched fists and turned, blind with anger, towards the nearest wall. He thrust his hand so hard at it that the paintwork cracked; Steph heard the crunch of his knuckle and cowered into the chair. She hid her eyes while Theo roared in pain and anger, he wheeled around the room, grabbing photoframes to throw them onto the floor and stamping on them. Each crunch of glass sent shockwaves through her.

"No!" he kept yelling. "It can't be. I won't let it. No, not my girls, not my girls."

Steph tried to speak but he didn't hear her. She stayed, curled in the chair, absolutely still until it had passed. When the noise stopped she opened her eyes and flicked them around the room until she found Theo, leaning against the wall, weeping. Blood ran from his hand and dripped onto the carpet.

"Theo." She was halfway to him before he looked at her. Anger and desolation burned in his eyes.

"Why now Stephanie? Why tell me now?"

"I had to, or Julia would have done."

"Julia?" he repeated dumbly.

"She knows. She worked it out or Ed knows – or..." she didn't know what to say.

"Ed knows?"

"I think so. I don't know what's been going on. Julia came round this morning and she told me that she knew. She said she'd been speaking to Ed's mum and Kirsty and," she rushed the words out, desperate to recount something that wasn't her fault, "she told me that she knew my secret. She knew all about my past."

"I just can't quite believe this," Theo said slowly. "It doesn't make any sense. How can what you're telling me be true? Those girls are my own flesh and blood."

Steph closed her eyes.

"But they aren't, are they?"

She opened them, "No. Not flesh and blood Theo, but they are yours. They are your own. You're their father. You love them, they love you. You're all they've ever known. It doesn't need to change. Like IVF."

"Don't patronise me!" he roared.

"I'm not, I'm not."

"But they aren't mine."

"No." Steph forced the word out. Theo looked at her for a second before he pushed his way out of the room and ran up the stairs. Steph followed him, she found him flinging clothes into a bag. "What are you doing?"

"Leaving."

"Where are you going?"

"I don't know."

"When you say leaving, do you mean?"

"How could you do this to me? How could you spend ten years of your life being married to me, living a lie? I don't know you at all."

"Theo you have to understand what was going on at the time. I didn't know I was pregnant for about two months. We were so in love, we were travelling, I was the happiest I've ever been."

"I don't want to hear your sob story Steph," he spat.

"It's not a sob story. I'm trying to explain."

"So why not get rid of them? When you found out?" It broke his heart to speak of his girls like that. His chest tightened as grief rose inside him.

"I couldn't do that. After seeing how mum…."

"You're blaming her?"

"No! I'm trying to explain." But he couldn't listen. The words didn't stick. The sentences didn't make sense. Theo tried to concentrate on his clothes. Two pairs of jeans, five shirts, two jumpers, t-shirts, socks, pants. Then razor, comb, hair gel, jacket. Tears blinded him as he shoved everything into his bag.

"See you Steph." He pushed past her to get out.

"No, Theo, don't go. Please listen to me." But the door slammed and he was gone.

****

Steph stayed lying on the bed, watching the day outside gradually darken and the sun go down. Occasionally she heard footsteps going past, or cars hooting their horns down the road. She felt completely displaced. It was hard to believe that the world was still the same, that out there were people going about their normal days, driving home, putting the kettle on, taking their shoes off. Somewhere her girls were having tea, chatting and laughing, probably excited to be at Nana's house. Downstairs, the phone rang over and over again, but Steph ignored it, it wouldn't be Theo. Listlessly she tried his mobile again, but it went straight to voicemail. She'd left five messages so far. She was too ashamed to ring his family.

She stayed on the bed until it was completely dark, both inside and out. Then she got up, pulled her clothes off where she was standing, and put her pyjamas and dressing gown on. Then she went downstairs, put the kitchen light on and gazed around. It all looked so normal. Everything was in its place. How could that be? How could her inner turmoil not be matched here? She looked at the empty spaces at the table where Mia and Tilly should be eating tea. She looked at the floor where their school bags should be lying, the area around strewn with bits of paper and recorders. What should she do? What was there to do? She felt empty and lost. Worthless. She walked to the patio doors and looked out over the garden. It was still. Then the phone rang again, making her jump. Her mind confused, she answered it after a single ring, "Hello?"

"Steph, thank God!" Katie's voice was full of relief. "I've been trying to get hold of you all day, I was so worried."

Silence.

"Steph, are you there?"

"Yes."

"Listen, have you said anything to Theo?" Katie asked urgently.

"Yes."

"Oh God – what did you say?"

"I told him. Everything."

"Oh God, Steph. Shit. I talked to Julia, she doesn't know anything!" Katie had practically put a gun to Julia's head to get the information.

"What do you mean?"

"She doesn't know anything Steph. She has this weird idea that you and Ed have been madly in love for years and years and have just been waiting to get together. She thinks you cheated on Theo with Ed, that's what all the 'sordid past' stuff was about. She doesn't know anything about the girls."

"Nothing? Are you sure?"

"Positive." There was a pause while Steph wondered how she felt. Strangely, she didn't feel a thing. It didn't matter now. Retrospect was all very good but it didn't save lives. Not hers and not Theo's. "Steph, what did you say to him?"

"I explained exactly what happened."

"Where is he now?"

"He's gone. He's left me." Her voice sounded flat and empty.

"I'm coming round."

Katie arrived with a bottle of wine in one hand and a bag of Indian food in the other. She took one look at the sitting room and closed the door, and went round the house pulling curtains and switching lights on. Steph sat silently in the kitchen, looking crumpled and pale. Katie made her a cup of strong, sweet tea which she drank obediently.

"Where are the girls?"

"With my mum."

"Good. They'll be fine."

"Theo won't answer my calls."

"No," Katie hesitated. "I'm not surprised. He needs time, sweetheart. Give him time and space. He'll talk to you."

"He's left me, Katie. He's actually left me."

"You don't know that. Things that are said in anger often don't stick."

"But I've destroyed his life, haven't I? He dotes on those girls, they're everything to him."

"That doesn't need to change."

"Yes it does. I've been so stupid, thinking that we could all live happily ever after. Thinking that DNA didn't count for anything, that it was just like IVF when all along it was so different. I've lied to him for years, lied by omission. I've let him build up a totally false picture of his life. Everything that he held dear doesn't exist. He said as much, he said he didn't know me. And he doesn't. He didn't marry the girl he thought he did, that girl wouldn't have done this. But I didn't mean to, I know it sounds pathetic, but I really didn't. I got caught up in a mess and I loved him so much and there was never a good time so I let the whole thing run on and on. And deep down, I thought I was safe. I thought my guilt was punishment enough, I never thought I'd have to confess. It scared me, I imagined it happening sometimes, but I never could picture it *actually* happening."

"I don't think you've been quite happy with your life for years," Katie commented quietly, removing the teacup and pouring the wine. "If you want my honest opinion."

"What do you mean?"

"You seem to have so much more to you, Steph. You're so clever and focussed, you could easily have combined a career with your children. I think you feel that you missed out."

"Maybe. What difference does it make now?"

"That you acted through unhappiness, not malice?"

"It doesn't change anything."

There was a small silence. Katie cleared her throat, "Um – there is one thing we do need to do."

"What's that?"

"Talk to Ed. No, listen to me - one of three things will happen, either we talk to him first or Julia or Theo will get to him. I think you need to speak to him urgently. Now."

"I can't face it. Not tonight."

"Steph, you need to, this is important."

"Tomorrow, then."

"Tomorrow might be too late and he'll be at work. It's only nine o' clock. Ring him, ask him to come round."

"I can't do it, it's too much."

"I'll do it then."

Steph said nothing. She wasn't thinking about Ed, of course she wasn't. She had far better things to think about, but Katie was dreadfully afraid of someone else breaking the news to Ed, and Steph losing control of that situation. She needed to be the one to tell him, to explain properly and to ask him whatever it was she wanted him to do with the information. She took Steph's silence as acquiescence and slipped out to the hall. Steph didn't appear to notice. She found Steph's mobile and thumbed through until she found Ed's number. She hoped fervently that she was doing the right thing.

"Hi, is that Ed?"

"Yes." He sounded guarded. "Who's this?"

"Sorry – it's Katie, Steph's friend. Look, I'm sorry to bother you and I know this is going to seem out of the blue but could you come round to Steph's house now? It's really, really important." Katie felt about fourteen.

"What?" he didn't sound too pleased. "What's this all about?"

"I can't say, it isn't for me to say, but please? Can you?"

"Is Steph there?"

"Yes, but you can't talk to her, she's not in a good frame of mind."

"Okaaaaaaaay… are you sure you can't tell me over the phone? I've got to be honest, it all sounds a bit weird to me."

"I'm positive I can't tell you. Just get over here as quickly as you can. And don't answer your phone until you get here," she added as an afterthought.

Katie went back into the kitchen, "Come on," she urged Steph.

"Go and put some clothes on and comb your hair. How far away does Ed live?"

"About half an hour. I'm not getting dressed."

"Don't be ridiculous. Go and get dressed, brush your hair and clean your teeth and then you'll be ready to face him. Steph – you are about to tell this poor guy that he has two kids he knew nothing about. It's a pretty big conversation. You can't have it in your dressing gown."

With a mammoth effort Steph dragged herself upstairs and found some jeans and a jumper. Katie was right, she looked awful. But she couldn't bring herself to care. Listlessly she ran a brush through her knotted hair and tied it in a ponytail. She brushed her teeth and splashed a bit of cold water on her face and went back through to the bedroom. It was full of Theo; his things were everywhere. A discarded jumper, an odd sock, his iPod. His night table even had his glass of water on it still. Steph wrapped her arms around herself and felt the tears fall anew. He would never come back, he would never forgive her. She had spent her last night with his arms around her in bed. How could she have done this to him? How could she have deceived everyone like this? It seemed impossible now that she thought about it. And no one would believe her that she hadn't meant to. Everyone would think that she'd hung onto a good thing, that she'd been ruthless and conniving, when actually she'd just been young, scared and confused. She'd made a bad decision, but that didn't make her a bad person.

"Steph?" Katie's head poked around the door. "Oh come on sweetie," she pulled her into a hug. "Come on. This is as bad as it gets, it can only get better from here."

"How can I live without him? How can I? I can't, I love him so much. And the girls, I love all of them. I want it all back the way it was."

"That can't happen." It was brutally honest, but Katie felt Steph didn't need false reassurance now. There was a chance that Theo would come home, but it wasn't a strong one. He was such an honest, straight-down-the-line kind of guy that anything like this would appal him. And the fact that it had come from his wife... Katie honestly didn't know where Theo was going to go from here.

It wasn't long before there was a knock at the door.

"You go." Katie said.

Steph shuffled through to the front door, feeling exhausted. It seemed impossible that she had yet more of this day to get through.

She felt numb.

"Hi, Ed. Come in."

He looked nervous, "Hi Steph. What's going on?" His eyes moved past her into the hallway. "I had a call from your friend."

"Yes, I know. She's in the kitchen."

"Where's Theo?"

"Who knows? No idea." She felt the tingling of tears in her nose but they didn't fall this time. They'd probably run out.

"Er – what is going on?"

"You have to sit down for this. I'm sorry Ed, I really am. I am sorrier than it is humanly possible to be. I have seriously messed this up."

"Ed?" Katie appeared. "Hi, thanks for coming. She's right, come and sit down. You'll need a drink." Even Katie looked white, Ed thought. This was going to be interesting.

They all sat awkwardly around the kitchen table. Katie had offered to leave but Steph wouldn't let her. "I will do the talking," she said, "but I want you here."

"I have my drink," Ed said. "Can we get on with it now?"

Steph took a deep breath and looked him straight in the eyes, "Do you remember that night back in Tinford?"

CHAPTER TWENTY

Ed just looked blank. Steph scanned his face.

"They're yours," she said quietly. "Your girls. I fell pregnant that night."

"That night... from that night?" He didn't sound like he believed her.

"Yes."

"How can you be so sure?" his eyes narrowed.

"My dates. I didn't have sex with Theo for a long time. He'd never done it before, he didn't want to until he was certain that we had something serious. That was fine by me, but it made me sure they couldn't be his." She started crying again. "Believe me, this is the last thing I wanted to have to tell you."

"Holy shit Steph, I can't believe this. What – how – are you being serious?" he hardly needed to ask.

"Deadly," she replied.

"Why didn't you tell me at the time for God's sake?" he leant forward to her, his eyes angry.

"It wasn't you that I wanted. I wanted Theo, we were so happy. I just – blocked you out. It was so bad I couldn't take it in."

"And you didn't think to mention it since?"

"No."

"Jesus Christ," his hands gripped his head. "Do you have any idea what this means? This changes my whole life. Why now Steph?"

"Ah well," Katie interjected and brought him swiftly up to date with Julia.

"This gets more unbelieveable every second. I have two – daughters. Oh my God. Daughters." His face turned to the huge portrait of them all on the wall, "Those girls..." he stood and moved over to it, his hands shoved in his pockets and he turned his face this way and that, taking in every tiny feature. "They're mine."

Steph was exhausted. It was beyond her to help him understand, to explain, to care, even. She had nothing left to give.

"I'm going to bed," she announced, and stood up from the table.

"Steph," Katie said pleadingly, but she was ignored. Steph moved slowly towards the kitchen door, like she was weakened from a hundred years of living. She turned and looked at Ed briefly, before going into the hallway and shutting the door behind her.

****

Looking back even two weeks later, Steph couldn't remember how those next couple of days passed. She knew only one thing for certain and that was that Theo neither rang nor answered her calls. She left message after message, but she heard nothing. The rest was a blur of sleeping, watching aimless, daytime TV, wandering around her house and dealing with Katie when she popped in. She had never felt so low in her entire life. She didn't eat properly, just the odd bowl of cereal here and there when hunger pangs got too much, and she only slept thanks to the bottle of wine she drank every night. Then she would sit, sobbing in her pyjamas, looking through old photos. Such a cliché, but she would have walked over broken glass or molten lava or *anything* to go back to those old, happy days. Matt rang from the stables one afternoon to tell her rather apologetically that Archie was being sold, and she didn't care. She was completely disorientated without her family around her and struggled to perform even basic household routines. It was Katie that held the house together and loaded the washing machine for her, stacked the dishwasher and checked that there was enough milk for her endless cups of tea.

Steph spoke to the girls once and explained that Daddy was away working and Mummy didn't feel very well so that's why they were with Nana and then she listened as the girls blithely described their days at school and who had said what to whom.

"They're fine, Stephanie," her mother reassured her. "Better than you by the sound of it. What's going on?"

"Just a few problems with Theo," Steph managed to say.

"Oh no. What a shame. You two are so solid normally."

"I know." They agreed that she would keep the girls over the weekend and then Steph would collect them from school on the Monday. "A week is long enough, I think," said her mother.

And on the third day, Ed turned up. And he didn't look exactly friendly.

"Hello," Steph said warily on the doorstep.

"Hi."

She'd thought a lot about ringing him to follow-up on that

ghastly night, but she hadn't been able to. He'd want all sorts of things from her which she wasn't able to give and then she would look weak and uncaring, so on the whole she'd thought it was best if she waited for him to approach her. And now, here he was. And at least she was dressed, it was only a tracksuit, but better than nothing.

"I suppose you'd better come in."

"I suppose I had." He followed her through to the kitchen where she made him a coffee and put it in front of him. She looked absolutely terrible, he thought, white and drawn and as thin as he had ever seen her.

"So – where do we start?"

"At the beginning." And she took him through it all. Their stupid mistake that night, how she'd got it wrong with Theo, how they'd run away as they felt that was their only choice. How trapped she'd felt in Tinford, what a mess she'd made of her friendship with Ed and what a relief it was to find herself clear of everything. Their decision to go travelling, what fun they were having and then – that discovery. The one that had shattered both her day-to-day life and her life with Theo.

"But why pretend?" Ed leant forward. "Why not come clean? However bad, that's always best."

"Ed – I was eighteen, I was frightened. I didn't know what to do. I was hiding from myself. Theo and I meant everything to each other, even back then, and I knew if I owned up then I would lose him. I thought anything was better than that, even deceiving him."

"But it was hardly a momentary deception, Steph. There were serious repercussions."

"I know, and that's the bit that I didn't understand at the time. In the beginning I thought I could tell him one day, a few months down the line, but he was so excited at the thought of his baby, and the pregnancy went on and when I gave birth and saw his face I knew I couldn't. I knew I had to live the life I'd chosen."

"And what about me?"

"There was no place for you Ed," Steph said softly. "I loved you as a friend, but we took it further, we should never have done that. Neither of us ever felt like that about the other."

"I did. I felt like that about you."

"What?"

"I don't think you'll ever understand how much you screwed my life up, Steph. I adored you, I thought the world of you. And after that night I thought you adored me too, I mean – you must have done to have slept with me, that's pretty special isn't it? I trusted you totally, I was so secure in your affection. It literally never even crossed my mind that we wouldn't get together properly then." He gave a short, harsh laugh. "I can't believe how wrong I was. You left not only my bed, but my life, without even a note or a phonecall to soften the blow. I didn't trust anyone after that. I don't think I ever have, no girl, not ever. I couldn't go through that heartache again. It was far better to keep it simple. I always knew I was missing out," he shrugged, "but it was better than the alternative."

"Ed, I'm sorry, I really am."

"And now you tell me that I have two children! I mean, how do I deal with that Stephanie? Seriously? What do I do? I haven't got a clue about kids, I don't know these guys – I don't want kids. That isn't my scene. And yet you've thrust them upon me in your own fucking selfish way. You have ruined my life. Just what the fuck did you think you were doing?"

Steph was crying again, "I wasn't thinking – I wasn't even doing. I just reacted. I *know* I was wrong, but I didn't know what else to do. I'm sorry."

"And would you have told me, ever, if it wasn't for the circumstances?"

She bit her lip and looked down, "No. Probably not. Not now. What good would it do?"

"It will do no good, except ease your conscience."

"At the cost of losing my husband? I'd rather have the conscience if it's all the same to you," she replied bitterly.

"Why did you tell him?"

"Because I thought Julia was going to. She told me you knew, she told me that she knew – the obvious next stop was Theo. Julia adores you Ed," Steph said tiredly. "She'd go to any lengths to keep me away from you. She has this bizarre fixation that you and I are star-crossed lovers or something."

"Julia and I are over."

"Oh." There wasn't much to say to that.

They were silent for a moment and Ed gazed at the portait on the wall; how could those children be part of him? It was so strange. Little pieces of himself had grown into those two, identical, beautiful girls. He was awed. And loathe though he was to admit it, he could see the resemblance. They were blonde for a start, when both Steph and Theo were dark. They looked remarkably like their mother, which he supposed they would, as girls, but their eyes were his. He'd always recognised the eyes, he had thought they were Steph's but they weren't, they were his own. Startlingly blue, strong eyes. And in another photo he could see a turn of expression on Mia's face which he recognised as his. And Tilly, quieter, more like his younger self. Ed got lost in his thoughts as his eyes worked around the various photos dotted around the room. They were two much-photographed girls. He felt a rush of something, suddenly. Not love, but something akin to that. Recognition of something that belonged to him. But at the same time, it really didn't. Jesus, what a mess. He buried his head in his hands, "I don't blame you," he mumbled. "Not really. I can understand what you're saying. I don't accept it yet, but I sort of understand. I don't think everyone would have made your decision, but I see why you did."

"Thank you." The slight sympathy brought more tears to her eyes; it was so unexpected.

"But Steph – what do you want from me?"

"Nothing. I don't want anything. I don't want anything to change."

"I mean – I have my own life, my dreams, my ambitions, a family of my own one day. I'm meant to be going abroad. I hadn't planned on –"

"I know. And I mean it, I don't want anything, not time, not money. You should still go to the States."

"I can't now. It would feel wrong. I have," he took a deep breath, "*responsibilities* here. I can't just piss off and leave them."

"You can."

"I *can't*." It was said through gritted teeth.

"Where's Theo?"

"I don't know."

"Right. What are you going to do?"

"Wait until he rings me or comes home, what else can I do?"

"I guess he wants to be left alone."

"I guess he does," Steph said in a small voice. Ed reached across the table and took her hand, bizarrely enough, he felt sorry for her. She was so obviously utterly lost and alone in this. He believed her when she said that she'd acted out of ignorance and panic, the Steph he'd known wouldn't have been able to do anything but. Except, he'd been tortured by thoughts during the last three days of what life would have been like if she'd owned up. Would he be her husband now, instead of Theo? Would they have lived happily ever after, just like he'd wanted? Or at least, his eighteen year old self wanted, before he knew about the children. Kids changed everything, Ed could see that now. Steph might have said that she didn't want anything from him but that didn't stop him being ultimately responsible for two, small, girls. And he would be, if he needed to. He'd sworn that to himself.

"When was the last time that you ate?"

"I had some cereal at lunchtime."

"I meant properly."

"I don't remember."

"I'll make you something then."

Ed stood and began to rummage through cupboards and the freezer. They had a very well-stocked kitchen, which was no surprise. Steph and Theo were clearly the type of people who could throw a dinner party at a moments notice. Or at least, they had been.

"What do you feel like?"

"I'm not hungry."

"Do you realise I haven't been to work for three days?"

"So?"

"I have never taken a day off sick in my entire career."

"Am I supposed to be impressed?"

"No, you're supposed to realise what this has done to me." Ed pulled out a packet of pasta and a tin of tuna from a cupboard. "Do you have any mayonnaise?"

"In the fridge. I tried to ring you."

"When?"

"From Paris. We were in Paris and I rang you but it didn't connect. You said hello and that was it. And Theo came back and I lost the chance. I wanted to say that I was sorry, that was all. But I did try Ed."

"So you mean that I've spent my whole adult life thinking that all women couldn't be trusted and actually, you'd tried to behave decently after all?"

"I tried to apologise, yes."

Ed rested his head against the cupboard door briefly, "That makes it worse. I've spent ten years thinking that you're something you're not." It was almost comical. Almost.

"It was only a missed phonecall."

"It would have meant the world to me."

"So why did you get back in touch with us if you were so bothered?"

"Curiosity. Partly because I wanted to get to know you both again, and partly because it should have been water under the bridge by now."

"Should have been?"

"Was. Mostly." Ed busied himself chopping an onion as an awkward silence pervaded the kitchen. "Do you ever think of how it could have been?" he asked, conversationally.

"What do you mean?"

"How things would have been, if you'd told me at the beginning. Ten years ago – fuck, ten years is a long time to be on this earth and not know you have kids, it really is."

"Theo and I have been good parents," Steph's lip trembled.

"I know you have. I don't doubt it. From what I've seen, you guys are the best. But do you ever think of how it could have been?"

"No. Never."

That was pretty decisive. "What are you going to tell Mia and Tilly?"

"Nothing. That's up to Theo. I need to know what he wants to do."

"Fair enough." Ed laid the knife down and turned to Steph, "I'd like to see them."

"What do you mean?" she asked warily.

"I'd like to see them. As in spend some time with them. Just once, perhaps an hour or so. I'd just like to know something of them. Not for any reason other than my own, selfish interest. Even if I just came here, had a cup of tea with you and they were around, doing whatever they do."

"I don't know about that."

"Please, Steph. It's pretty obvious that I'm never going to be a father to them, the least you can do is let me see how they walk, how they talk, what they say, the things they do, the mannerisms they have. Please." He had a deep, burning, curiosity inside him to know something – anything – of his daughters.

"I'd have to ask Theo." The ultimate get-out clause.

"Fine."

The pasta was ready within half an hour and to her surprise, Steph was almost hungry by the time Ed served it to her.

"Thanks."

"It was nothing."

"I appreciate it."

They turned the TV on while they ate and sat side by side on the sofa in silence. It felt like a parallel universe. And then they drank some wine, Steph vaguely aware that this was all wrong but so much of her was so grateful to have some friendly company that she let it happen. She was lonely; one evening couldn't hurt. After the first bottle they opened a second and Steph's head fell back against the sofa, she spoke with her eyes looking up at the ceiling. They chatted about neutral topics, their shared childhood mainly. Old memories, old friends, old events. Life before it got complicated.

"I forgot how well we got on," Steph commented.

Ed turned to look at her, "We got on very well. That's why I always thought there could be more."

"I was only aware because people told me. Really, Ed, it was never like that between us. It was always Theo I wanted, when I started wanting someone."

"I can see that. Teenagers, hey, they shouldn't be allowed." Ed yawned and stretched up his arms. "You realise I've had too much to drink to drive home?"

"Stay here. There's no one else in the house."

"Is that wise?"

"Why not?" Steph shrugged. "Mia's room has a double bed." The discussions surrounding that bed shot painfully into her mind. It seemed like another lifetime that she and Theo had been talking cots and beds and more babies. A rose-tinted lifetime.

"Well, if you're sure." He leaned over and pecked her cheek. "I'm going up then, I'm shattered."

"Good night. Thanks for dinner."

And after he'd gone, the space seemed emptier than ever.

****

By Saturday Steph knew that she seriously had to pull herself together. Children required clean, tidy houses, food in the fridge and a mummy that was sane. So she stripped her bed, flung the windows open wide, did a whole load of washing and vacuumed the house. Then she showered, dressed properly for the first time in days and blow-dried her hair. After that, she ventured out to Waitrose and filled a trolley full of food, defiantly not thinking about feeding three people instead of four. But by the time she got home and unpacked, the sadness and loneliness had crept back again. She'd done the boring stuff, but there was no one to appreciate it and no one to now have fun with. She wished momentarily that she had a dog, but Theo had never permitted one. Without hope, she dialled his number again, as she did daily and left him a brief message, telling him that the girls were coming home on Monday. Then she wondered if that was insensitive.

Ed had rung her four times since that night but Steph hadn't returned his calls. She needed to be stronger before she could talk to him. She owed him a lot and she didn't have it to give yet. But then looking round her empty house, she thought maybe she should talk to him. She did owe him.

"Hi Ed," she stood in the hall and looked out of the small window onto the driveway. "It's Steph. Just wondering how you were doing?"

"I'm OK, thanks."

"Good."

"And you?"

"All right."

"Heard from Theo?"

"Not yet."

"Have you tried his parents?"

"No. I can't face it."

"I know how you feel. I can't face my mum."

"Why?"

"I don't know what she knows. And I might have to tell her that she has two granddaughters that she knew nothing about."

A fresh wave of horror broke over Steph, "I don't think that's a good idea," she said quickly.

Ed sighed, "None of this is a good idea." Steph stayed silent. "What are you up to tonight?"

"Nothing."

"I might come round. I need to talk to you."

"What about?"

"Nothing new. I just have… a few questions that have come to me." Ed had wondered periodically over the last few days whether he was behaving as a man should in his situation. He thought perhaps he should be a bit more caveman about the whole thing, beat his chest and de-cry womankind and rush in to claim what he'd sired. But he had enough detachment from the situation to see that actually, nothing really changed. He and Steph weren't about to set up house together and no one was going to acknowledge him as the biological father of these girls. He'd seen enough cases during his training seat in family law to know that there were hundreds, if not thousands, of families who had this exact situation. It wasn't exactly familiar, but Ed thought that he probably had the sense and intelligence to deal with it how it should be dealt with – respectfully and from a distance. He just wished that Theo would put in an appearance, he could do with talking to him.

"I'm fine. I'm not exactly overrun with visitors," Steph said sadly. Kate continued to pop in but her tea and sympathy routine was wearing thin.

Ed arrived with a bag full of convenience food, "I thought I'd pre-empt dinner this time."

"Thanks but you needn't have. I've re-stocked the fridge for the first time in a week."

"You can save it now for an emergency."

"Like Theo coming home?"

"That wasn't what I meant."

Once again, she made him coffee and set it in front of him.

"You look better," he commented.

"I can't wallow in self-pity forever."

"That's the spirit."

"Besides, Theo might come back and then what would I look like? He'd think I'd morphed into a tramp on top of everything else." Despite himself, Ed laughed. "So what was it that you wanted to discuss?"

"I just want to understand everything. Take me through it again, so I can make sure that I have the right jigsaw pieces in the right place." And he'd wanted to see the photos again, the photos of his daughters. He was hungry for information, to know what sort of characters they had, what activities they enjoyed, what they wanted to be when they grew up. But that was private information; he wasn't sure that he would be privy to it yet.

So Steph took him through it again, gently this time. She emphasised the young, drunk and silly bits and how much she had loved Theo. She admitted fault, but backed it up with only being human and therefore being fallible. And she confirmed that she wanted the girls to know nothing. "Obviously it's up to Theo, but if I could choose, I would choose that they know nothing."

"Is that for your benefit or theirs?"

"Both. If I'm honest."

Ed met her eyes and smiled. "Is there any chance that I could see more photos?" he asked hesitantly. "Tell me if I'm jumping the gun here, but I've been at home for the last week just wishing that I knew some more about them. Just what they looked like when they were born, when they started walking. Just a few snapshots of their life."

Stephs heart went out to him and she grabbed his hand, "Yes, all right." She couldn't deny him any more than she already had.

She selected a few, bound, photo albums to show him. There were tins stuffed full of photos, especially from when they were tiny, but she concentrated on the best ones. And it felt just like showing off her daughters to a friend.

"See this one," she exclaimed from time to time. "Here was the first time they saw snow, it was priceless. And this, the first time we went abroad," it was a photo of the twins, in matching sunhats and sandals, their backs to the camera, looking out over a beach.

"Looks amazing," Ed said. "The beach, I mean," and he grinned. They went on and on, through Christmases and birthdays, riding lessons, ballet lessons and their first day at school. Steph had saved locks of hair and teeth they had lost and she showed them to him, bit by bit building him a picture of their lives.

"Wow. You really are a dedicated mother. Not many mums would have saved their first spelling test."

"Why not? It was so funny, Mia was determined to beat Tilly, by fair means or foul and she ended up getting two marks lower. Don't ask me how. I think the determination affected her concentration. She was so cross. Really stroppy."

"I wonder where she gets that from." The words were out before Ed realised what he was saying. "Sorry – I didn't mean…"

"It's OK." Steph looked at him. "She's like you, you know," she said softly. It felt cataclysmic to utter the words, but she couldn't resist. "Just like you. She's got a streak of steel running through her – what Mia wants, Mia gets."

"She'll go far in life."

"I hope so. Tilly's quieter, more like me. Pensive, sometimes. She loves reading and creating, Mia loves doing. She's proactive."

"Do they have lots of friends?"

"Oh yes. I'm never sure if it's the novelty or not but they're popular girls."

"Good. Friends are important."

They sat, heads close together, looking down at the photos of their children spread across the table. For the first time ever, Steph felt a sense of loss, not for her sake but for his that Ed would never get to be a real father to them. She couldn't ever see Theo letting that happen. And even if Theo vanished off the face of the earth, Ed couldn't be a dad. He wasn't ready for it yet and he didn't know them. She refused to allow herself to think of what it might have been like; it was too dangerous.

"Shit." Ed said suddenly.

"What?"

"Paper cut." He held out his thumb, the edge of one of the photos had nicked him. He stood up, "Do you have any plasters?"

"Yes, in my bathroom upstairs, I'll get them."

"No, it's fine, I'm already up." He walked away and up the stairs.

Steph stayed staring at the photos on the table. Here was their whole life in front of her, everything that made them up as people. A stranger would know what kind of girls they were just by rummaging through all the things that she had saved and collected. A dedicated mother, that was what Ed had called her. It was nice when an impartial observer said something like that. Well, not impartial, but someone who did not have a vested interest in paying her compliments. Maybe she had been doing all right in life before this. As she pondered that thought, two things happened simultaneously; the toilet flushed upstairs and a key clicked the front door open. Steph was immobile, frozen in horror. She couldn't move. And then Theo appeared in the doorway; her heart leapt. Her precious, precious Theo. He looked very tired and very sad.

"Hi," he said quietly.

"Hi. Um…"

"I've come to talk."

"OK. But…"

Theo's eyes fell to the photos spread out across the table and Steph saw him visibly wince. "What are you doing?" he asked.

"This is a bit awkward, I'm…" and then the dreaded footsteps began down the stairs.

"Steph," Ed called. "Thanks for a great evening but I'd better be off. I found the plasters." He reached the living room door and literally jumped when he saw Theo. His face paled, "Er, mate, this is not what it looks like," he said quickly.

"Oh, I see. Firstly, I am not your mate," Theo spat at him. "And secondly, what this looks like is a cosy tête-à-tête between two people who know each other very well. Are you going to deny it?"

"No, no, it isn't," Steph said wildly, leaping up. "Ed came round – we needed to talk, that was all."

"Three guesses what about." Theo looked unshaven and his hair seemed thinner. His glasses dwarfed his face.

Ed flushed crimson, "Theo, I'm going to go. Steph's been waiting for you to call, waiting for you to come home."

"Yeah, so she can make more of a fool out of me," Theo replied bitterly. "Well you're not going to!" He yelled at her. "I came here to talk to you, to try and understand what you did. No promises, I was going to say, but let's talk. I even brought my bag," he held up his black holdall. "How stupid of me. Only gone two minutes and already holed up with your lover." His face was rigid with pain.

"Theo! I swear it isn't like that. You have to listen to me," Steph begged. "I need you so much."

"Save it. I am not interested. You must think I'm a complete idiot if you thought I would be happy with you two having a nice little dinner together in my absence. I'm surprised he wasn't planning to stay the night." Their ashamed faces said it all. "So he *has* stayed? Oh this gets better and better. Well, tell you what, how about I leave you two lovebirds to it and you can catch up on your lost years and discuss the children you have together. How does that sound?" Without waiting for a response, he turned and stormed out, slamming the front door behind him.

Steph heard his car engine start two seconds later, and fell back against the wall. "I've lost him," she sobbed. "That's it, I've lost him. He won't come back now."

CHAPTER TWENTY-ONE

"So girls, if I were going to let you choose your own dinner, what would it be?" Steph glanced in the rearview mirror at the twins, neatly belted into the back seat.

"Pizza!" they said in unison.

"Bought or homemade?"

"Homemade, definitely," Tilly said. "With ham and sweetcorn on mine."

"And pepperoni on mine."

"Well how about we do that then, as a Friday night treat? I may even have some garlic bread in the freezer."

"Yummy!" said Mia. "Will Dad be back?"

"No, I don't think so darling."

"Oh good. It's more fun without him," she said contentedly.

"What do you mean?"

"You're more fun, you play with us more, don't make us go to bed early, stuff like that."

Mia was referring to a couple of things; Steph's determination to make it up to the girls after the recent weeks, and her fear of being alone in the house where her thoughts could crowd her. She preferred to be distracted and the girls were definitely the best way to do that. She put endless time into talking to them, cooking with them, doing their homework with them, even watching TV with them. For the last five days she had catered to their every whim. On Monday morning, Steph had had literally no idea how she was going to function enough to be a mother to the twins. She was still crying almost constantly, she hadn't dressed all weekend and she slept sporadically through twenty-four hours, not keeping to set days and nights. She'd thought it would be far harder with them at home, having to get up and dressed and out of the house, being forced to keep sociable hours, not being able to sleep off hangovers if necessary, but actually it had been easier. Having an imposed timetable and expectations made of her helped to keep Steph on the straight and narrow. She had less time to think, less time to wallow in self-pity and she did draw a lot of pleasure from spending time with the twins. She'd been a little afraid that they may have altered slightly in her eyes, that Ed's genes would have loomed at her overwhelmingly, but they hadn't. They were the same Mia and Tilly as they'd always been. Steph had always known the truth within herself, she just hadn't always admitted it.

Her most surprising discovery of the week had been that Julia had removed Amy from St Catherines. She had prepared herself to face Julia in the playground on Monday afternoon, but she hadn't been there. Nor on Tuesday, nor on Wednesday. And that was when another mother had explained that Julia had taken Amy out and moved fifty miles away to be closer to her parents, apparently. The shock in the playground was not that Amy had gone, but that Julia hadn't given the statutory term's notice.

"That means she'll have to pay a terms fees in lieu," they gossiped. "Do you think she will?" There were arched eyebrows and pursed lips. "Hmm. I don't know. Everyone knows it was Him with the money, not Her. My guess is that she couldn't afford it, that's why she had to leave."

"Do you think?"

"Oh yes, why else would she go?" Steph, standing alone, listened to this exchange with interest. She knew exactly why Julia had gone, but she wasn't about to explain. The relief she felt was overwhelming. The fact that she'd gone made it a lot easier, and therefore made Steph happier. One link broken.

The girls when they came running out had no idea why Amy had left, "How would we know?" Mia scrunched up her nose. "She's not in our year."

"I just thought you might have heard something."

"No. But – guess what mum!"

"What?"

"We're going to have some new pupils at the school."

"Oh yes?"

"Yeah," Tilly grinned, "there are going to be eight."

"Eight?"

"Yes, because they're chickens!"

"Oh wow, chickens, that'll be good." The school had large grounds and Steph could quite picture a chicken coop sitting happily in some corner or other. There would be feeding duties to share out among the children, eggs to be collected; it would be fun, and good for them to learn some responsibility. "They'll like living in that big garden."

"Oh no, they're not in the garden, they're in the science lab."

"What?" Another – entirely different – possibility flew into Stephs mind.

"Yep, in the lab, in an incubator and they will definitely hatch by next Wednesday."

"They're still in the eggs?"

"Yes, and mum, you can hear them cheeping inside, it's so *cute*!"

"Ah, bless."

"And, mum?" The girls climbed into the car and strapped themselves in.

"Yes?"

"We were going to ask you something," Mia and Tilly exchanged a knowing glance, "but then we thought you'd just say no, so we won't." Their little faces looked mournful and Stephs heart sank; was she really that distant to them that they didn't dare ask her for anything any more?

"Oh no, do ask me. What is it?"

"Weeeeellll…" Mia began, "when the chicks are hatched…"

"Mrs Ivory says that if we're allowed we can take them home!" Tilly finished. "And keep them as pets. The school are going to let us all handle them especially so they're good pets. But we knew you would say no, that's why we didn't ask."

"Well, we haven't got a chicken run or cage for them or anything."

"But we could easily fit one in the garden. We could buy one."

"I…" she was on the verge of giving a standard, 'not right now' mummy answer when she thought, actually, why not? The girls wanted them, chickens couldn't be much trouble could they and Mia was right, they could get someone to build or sell them a chicken coop. And there was space in the garden, maybe down at the bottom by the trees…

That had been Wednesday, and today the girls had come bouncing out of school saying that Mrs Ivory had promised them first pick of the chicks, on the proviso that Steph was prepared to go into school and validate their claim that they were allowed to have them.

"Have they hatched yet?"

"Two have," Tilly said. "And one while we were there. It was so cool, wasn't it Mia?"

"Yeah. It took, like, five minutes and then nearly straight away it was up and walking around."

"Sounds like a strong one to me," Steph remarked. "Maybe you could pick that one. Have you thought of names for them yet?"

"Yes, Sharpay and Gabriella." Mia stated.

"Or Abigail and Crystal?"

"How do you know they'll be girls?" Steph smiled at them as she lugged their sports kit and book bags out of the boot. The twins ran on ahead up the steps to the front door. Steph took a deep breath, this was it, first weekend without Theo. She alone was now responsible for the girls from now until Monday morning. It was a sort of challenge, and Steph was prepared to rise to it. Katie had said that she and Mia and Tilly were welcome for Sunday lunch, and Steph rather thought that she might take her up on it. She would never have agreed had Theo been around, he was adamant that Sundays were family time. But the idea of going to Katie's happy, messy, little house and sitting back while she cooked appealed to Steph. And it was certainly better than sitting at home, alone.

And then, tomorrow morning a local craftsman was coming to measure the space she had set aside for the chickens.

"You'll need a coop and a run with wire round the lot," he'd said on the phone. "Them foxes will get in wherever they can if you don't. Shut 'em up at night and let 'em out in the mornin'. How many you 'avin?"

"Just the two."

"You'll end up with more. I'll build you a decent run for 'em, anyway." Steph hadn't enquired how much the decent run would cost and it hadn't occurred to her until now that Theo might cancel some or all of her cards. No, she decided, shutting the front door behind her, he wouldn't see her penniless, though he was quite within his rights to do so. That wasn't how Theo worked at all.

As promised, she made the girls their pizzas and then sat with them on the sofa while they ate and watched High School Musical for the thousandth time. Steph sipped at a glass of wine and picked at their crusts when they were done. She wasn't sure that she would bother cooking for herself. And later, when they were in bed, she sat alone in the sitting room, scanning through what was on TV and realising how quiet the house was without Theo. You didn't realise a person's noises until they weren't there. There was no rustle of newspaper pages turning, no click of keyboard keys, no footsteps or low cough as he cleared his throat, no opening and shutting of cupboards as he foraged for snacks. With the twins asleep there was just her for noise and the silence was loud. She looked around the house and wondered what to do. A pang of pure terror shot through her – was this how it was going to be every day, every night? That she would be living her life vicariously through the twins? That was where her day ended at the moment, once they were in bed then time may as well stop until the next morning, Steph wasn't going to achieve anything in those intervening hours. She let her head fall back against the sofa and tears came to her eyes once more. This was pathetic, she rubbed them away angrily. She was a grown woman crying because she was lonely. The trouble was, in all of her adult life Steph had never had to fend for herself, she realised. She'd had Theo leading her every step of the way. OK, go back ten years, what would she have done if she'd have been feeling like this? She would have been more proactive, that was for sure. She would have been looking for ways to solve the situation. What was she trying to solve? Her own direction in life, that was what. She needed something to do for herself. Like Katie, with her sculpting. That was purely and totally hers, unaffected by anyone else. She did the work and she reaped the rewards. Steph knew what Katie would say if she were here, she'd say "Go on then, get started, are we going to make a designer out of you or what?" It was just all so daunting. People did not sit in their living rooms of a night and think I'm going to become a designer, and then get up and do it. Except – except – Steph stood up and wandered through to the little study. There, in the drawer, were the printouts that Katie had given her. Consumed by curiosity as to exactly how difficult it would be, she sat down and began to read.

Hours later, she finally shut the computer down and sat there, feeling her head buzzing with information. It was far more of a possibility than she had ever believed it to be. It served her right for not doing some more research before now. There were various institutes offering interior design qualifications, courses she could go on, lectures she could attend. There were flexible payment plans and money back guarantees. There were even internet courses, distance learning in 12-24 weeks or at your own pace, and all you needed was basic computer skills. There were ways of making this happen. All she needed was some spare time, some money and a positive attitude. Steph was sure that she would be up against the college hotshots but so what? Maybe they wanted to shoot straight to the top; she didn't. She wanted to take her time, to explore, understand and enjoy the subject and work out which bit of it appealed to her most. Maybe then she could finally make a long-overdue move along her own career path. She'd imagined the twins being able to say, "My mummy's an interior designer," and this inspired such a reaction in her that she'd almost signed up for a course there and then. No, Steph, she thought. Take your time, don't rush, you've waited eleven years for this, another few weeks won't make a difference. For a moment she wished Theo were there to share her burgeoning excitement, but then she remembered that he wouldn't have done. He would have – very nicely – scoffed at her ambitions and told her that she didn't need to work, that she had everything she could ever want. Which was true, apart from personal pride in a job. Steph thought that she was beginning to understand that actually, she wasn't happy to be a housewife forever and a day, even if she should have that chance.

****

The chicken coop man was called Dave, and turned up on time the next morning. Steph had just finished hanging out her washing in some unseasonable sunshine, when a man rapped loudly on the back gate.

"'ello?"

She hurried to unlock it, "Hi, come on in." The twins were inside, but Steph explained what they wanted, "An all-encompassing thing so we don't have to move them around too much. With a coop for sleeping that we can lock up and space for them to peck at the dirt or whatever it is that they do. And it must have a wire mesh roof too."

"You've been doin' your research," Dave said.

"I certainly have. I don't want to be running a takeaway for foxes in two weeks' time," she grinned at him. "Excuse me, that's my phone." Steph ran back up the garden wondering if the chickens were living in the right place, perhaps they would be better off nearer the house. But from what she'd read online, they had a tendency to smell so in that case they would be better at the bottom of the garden. Three guesses who'd be donning wellies and a coat in the middle of winter to go down and feed them, she thought, picking up the phone, "Hello?"

"Steph, it's me," said Theo's voice.

"Oh." Steph sank down onto the stairs, feeling her heart rate treble suddenly.

"Are you free to talk?"

"Yes." This must be good, if he was ringing her. She had half-expected never to hear from him again.

"I wanted to talk to you about access to the girls."

"Right."

"We'll need some sort of formal arrangement. I've spoken to my solicitor and he's advised that I speak to you as soon as possible so we can get things firmed up as far as they're concerned. I had more or less thought every weekend and a night during the week?"

"For what?" Steph felt confused.

"For them to visit me."

"Visit you where?"

"I'll be moving into a flat just outside Churchwell in the next few days, it's a temporary measure until the house is sold. But I'll be close by and I can take them to school and things on the nights that they stay so you don't need to worry about that."

"Theo – aren't you jumping the gun slightly? I mean, we haven't even *talked*?"

"I don't think you have anything to say that I would want to hear Stephanie," he said coolly. "And I know they may not be biologically my daughters but I still feel as if they're mine and they're the only issue that I want sorted out immediately. We need to think about the house, of course, perhaps you could arrange some valuations?"

"You don't even want to come round and talk to me?"

"No. I'd prefer it if we could mostly communicate through our solicitors. You'll need one but you can use our usual one if you want, I've employed a different chap. Or perhaps you might see if Ed has any recommendations?" he said sarcastically.

Steph felt like she'd been hit by a train, and nor did she understand; how could he sound so cold and detached? This was her husband of ten years, was there no emotional link to her?

"Yes, I'll – er – get on to it." She felt faintly dazed.

"Good. We also need to think about what we're going to tell the girls and when."

That did fill her with panic, "Actually, I hadn't thought that we would tell them anything."

"I meant about us separating, not the other issue. We can discuss that some other time."

"Oh. I see. I don't know, I hadn't realised that we – never mind. I don't know."

"Have a think. As for this weekend, what are you doing?"

"Bits and pieces, um, sorting something out in the garden today and then lunch at Katie's tomorrow."

"Perhaps I could see them tomorrow?"

"Well Katie's expecting us for lunch, it'll look rude if we all cancel."

"I meant just the girls, I don't care what you do."

That hurt. "OK," Steph said stiffly. "Come round tomorrow."

"Fine. Eleven?"

"Yes, eleven's fine."

"See you tomorrow then. Bye." And the phone went down with a click, Steph staring at it in disbelief. How could he sound so blasé? He hadn't even told her where he was staying. They had so much to discuss, he couldn't just wipe it all out. But a nasty thought crept into her head – he could if it didn't matter any more. If he really was preparing to move on then nothing from their past need bother him.

A voice jolted her from her thoughts, "Hello? Mrs Hammond?"

"Sorry," Steph stood up with an effort and shook her head clear. "Are you finished?"

Dave rattled off a list of what he thought would suit them and estimates for cost and completion, but Steph wasn't really listening. If Theo was going to make her sell the house was there a lot of point to start with? Then a sudden, unexpected anger filled her, how dare he call all the shots? He might pay the mortgage but it was home for her and the girls. And him, if he wanted it. He couldn't just demand it was sold from under her feet. In fact, she was fairly sure that he actually couldn't. Legally couldn't. There was something called a Mecher Order she knew, where the wife was entitled to keep the family home until the children grew up and left it. Unless Theo could not afford to run two homes including this one. How strange to have to think about money after all these years of having not plenty, but enough for a reasonable standard of living. If that were the case then Steph had little reason not to go to work. She would have to manage her studying in between working and the girls somewhere; the idea was daunting. Life had the potential to get very busy. But she would cope, she would have to.

Dave left a copy of his estimate of £400 on the side in the kitchen, but Steph told him to go ahead and get started anyway. She'd pay him in instalments if necessary, she was not prepared to let the girls down over this. But lesson learnt, all the same, she should have investigated the whys and wherefores before she agreed.

She made the girls pasta for lunch and then phoned Katie to apologise. A short silence greeted the news, "So it's all looking pretty final then?"

"He won't talk about it. He just wants to see the girls. But yes, he's talking as if we'll be – divorcing." It cost her a lot just to say the word.

"Tell you what, how about we scrap lunch tomorrow and I come over this afternoon instead? Jack will be disappointed not to see the twins."

For a long time after Katie arrived Steph couldn't bear to discuss Theo. She hadn't quite made her mind up yet what she thought, or how she was going to tackle it. So they sat in the kitchen and drank coffee while the children ran off outside, and made idly, chatty conversation for a while. It felt good. It felt normal. Then Steph concentrated on telling Katie about the chicken plans, for which Katie thought that she was quite frankly mad, and about her tentative job thoughts. Katie was predictably delighted at this. "I told you!" she exclaimed. "You'd love it Steph, you really would. It would be like you're finally living the dream."

Steph laughed, "That's a bit of an exaggeration. And I'm also not sure whether I'd be able to train in the career that I actually want. I might not have that luxury." If that were the case then she would truly regret not doing it earlier.

"What do you mean?"

Slowly and sadly, Steph explained about Theo selling the house, "Which leaves me wondering if he's doing it out of spite or necessity. If it's the former then maybe I could somehow work and earn enough to buy him out." Katie looked around doubtfully at this. It was a pretty spectacular house. "And if it's the latter then again, maybe I could finance it. I would never make financial demands on him that he couldn't meet."

"He does have a responsibility towards, well, certainly you…." Katie stopped suddenly; the girls were a thorny issue.

"I don't see it like that, to be honest. I'd hate to sit here and be 'kept', I don't feel that Theo has any obligation towards me at all, I'm a grown woman with my own earning capacity. It's up to me to look after me."

Brave words, Katie thought. "And what about the girls?" she asked gently. "I don't know quite how things stand with them, are you going to ask Ed for any contribution?"

"No!" Steph looked horrified. "I would literally rather live on the streets. I don't see him as having any responsibility at all. I would never, ever, ask him for money." The idea was abhorrent.

"I can see that." And Katie could. Though the girls were Ed's girls, he didn't have any involvement with them. It would be almost obscene to ask him to start contributing financially. "Though I can see that there would be plenty of others behaving differently in your situation," Katie sighed. "Meal ticket and all that."

"I'm not like that." A fierce pride burned within Steph. "I wouldn't have people thinking that of me."

"No, I know you're not. Have you spoken to Ed?"

"No. Since – that night – he's rung once to see if I'm all right and that's it. He said to ring him if I needed him, and I don't. I don't blame him for that night, I really don't, it was just a terrible coincidence. It looked so bad."

"It would have done from Theo's point of view, and I suppose he doesn't have enough perspective yet on the whole thing to see beyond what it looked like."

"I could kick myself for being so stupid now. But I never, ever thought he would just turn up like that. The bit that kills me is not knowing what he was going to say. I'll never know now. He won't feel like he did that night ever again," Steph said sadly.

Katie was silent. "Hindsight is a wonderful thing," she said finally.

They sat, looking out over the garden as the sun slid from the sky. "I wish it was warm enough to sit outside," Steph remarked. "Evening sunshine and a glass of rose wine – that would be perfect."

"Can't do you evening sunshine, but I can do rose wine," Katie announced. "I saw some in your fridge earlier. Shall I open it?"

"Why not."

Steph seemed a little different, Katie thought. She'd watched her over the last few months go from being fabulously happy and positive and with her life on full steam ahead, to petrified and miserable and having a hunted look about her. Then the swing to barely functioning in those first few, low, days when she'd told Theo, Katie had been really worried then. Almost worried enough to consider calling a doctor out, but the ramifications of explaining the situation had made Katie shrink from that possibility. And then Steph had seemed to rally again, for the sake of the twins, she supposed. Steph had coped a lot better with having them home than Katie had ever predicted, and now she was different again. She seemed – harder, somehow. Like she'd grown a shell. She was obviously aware that her life looked set to change completely and that she wasn't going to be the cosseted wife any more, but she hadn't fallen apart at this concept, instead Steph seemed to have taken it in her stride – bitten the bullet – whatever simile you wanted to use. Katie twisted the corkscrew deeply into the cork and felt a quiet admiration for Steph. She was doing well. The only thing that remained to be seen was which permutation of Steph would eventually emerge from this chrysalis of change.

"Mummy?" Tilly came into the kitchen and laid her head on Steph's shoulder. "I don't feel very well."

CHAPTER TWENTY-TWO

Steph planned for Theo's arrival very carefully. It was a long time since he'd spent any time in their family home, and part of her thought that perhaps if she made everything perfect and welcoming he'd see what he was missing and have second thoughts. It was a vague hope, but she clung to it all the same.

She made sure everywhere was clean and tidy, filled vases with scented flowers and allowed a fresh breeze to drift through the house. She bought his favourite Danish pastries and checked that there was plenty of coffee in the cupboard. She even thought about what to offer him for lunch. Tagliatelle with a spicy sauce, he loved tagliatelle.

"What time will Daddy be here?" the girls demanded impatiently. Even they were beautifully dressed in their matching dresses from the day of the Sunday lunch with Ed. Steph hoped that the move might inspire fond memories. She dressed carefully herself in a long, flowing cream skirt and fitted, turquoise, lacy, Alice Temperley top and wore matching beads around her neck.

She was tense and jittery all morning until the doorbell rang at five past eleven. Doorbell? Steph opened the door, "Why aren't you using your key?" she asked with a small smile.

"I don't live here any more," Theo responded gravely.

"Oh. Come in."

"Actually, I won't. We'll go straight off if it's all the same to you."

"Straight off?" Her heart plummeted.

"Yes. I'm taking them out for lunch and then swimming. Not David Lloyd, we'll go to the waterpark."

Before Steph could respond the girls came tumbling out of the house, "Daddy!" they squealed, wrapping themselves around him. "Daddy! Daddy! We missed you!" Theo closed his eyes so Steph couldn't see the expression in them.

"Hello my darlings, I've missed you too. Are you ready to go?"

"Where are we going?"

"Lunch, then swimming, to the Rapids. How does that sound?"

"Is Mummy coming?"

"Not this time. I don't know if these dresses are the best thing to wear, either. Do you two have something a little more robust?"

"What does robust mean?" Mia asked.

"Something like jeans and t-shirts. Can you go and get changed?"

They scampered off and Steph and Theo were left on the doorstep.

"Are you sure I can't offer you a coffee or something?" Steph tried again.

"No, I'm fine thanks," Theo replied formally. He wouldn't even meet her eyes.

"How are you?"

"Fine."

"How's work?"

"Fine."

"Good. Oh, Tilly was complaining of a headache last night. I gave her some Calpol and she hasn't mentioned it this morning, but just so you're aware…"

"OK, I'll keep an eye on her." They didn't exchange another word until the twins came back, shrieking with excitement and demanding burgers and chips for lunch.

"I'll bring them back at about five, OK?" Theo said casually over his shoulder on the way to the car.

"That's fine." Steph said, but it hadn't really been a question.

She wandered back inside the house and shut the front door. Her careful preparations slapped her around the face; her flowers, her coffee, her pastries. Steph angrily ripped the beads from around her neck and they split all over the varnished floor. She was an idiot, a fool. Why had she ever thought that Theo would want to come and spend the day in their formerly happy home? She was stupid and she deserved everything she got.

****

Mia was clearly more tired out by the day than Tilly was because she lay down on the sofa when Theo brought them home, later than he'd intended. He'd actually carried them inside as they lay their heads on his shoulder, which they hadn't done for years.

"Mia's got a headache," Theo said immediately. "I told her she could have some Calpol at home."

"Of course," Steph fetched it from the kitchen. "Are you OK

darling?"

Mia nodded, looking tired, accepted the Calpol without complaint and then lay down on the sofa.

"Did you have a nice time?" Steph asked. Gone was the pretty skirt and Alice Temperley top, they'd been replaced with jeans and a wool sweater. Her hair was pulled into a haphazard ponytail, she'd spent the afternoon in front of the computer.

"We had a lovely time, didn't we girls?" He kissed each of them tenderly. "Tilly's been fine, she said she had a sore throat at lunchtime but we cured it with ice cream."

"Daddy let me have two bowls," Tilly added sleepily.

"They've obviously got a cold or something," Steph said. "With these headaches and sore throats."

"I'm sure they'll be fine. Are you two going to get undressed?"

"I'm tired," Mia moaned.

"All the more reason to go upstairs and get changed. The quicker you do that, the quicker you can go to bed. Go on, get changed." He waited until they were gone before turning to Steph, "I'm moving into my flat on Tuesday, so it's probably best that I don't have them overnight this week. Give me a week to get things sorted for them."

"Theo – please – can't we talk?" Steph asked desperately. It was all she could do to not fling herself against him and cling on.

He looked at her blankly, "What about?"

"Us! This," she gestured around herself, "the house. I hate this. I want to talk to you."

"Too little, too late. As I said, I'd prefer it if most of our discussions were done through solicitors. It's better if it's all written down."

"Theo, this is me," Steph pleaded in a low voice. "Come on, we've been married for ten years, you've known me all your life. *Please*, how can you not talk to me?"

"I think you know the answer to that." He turned to go. "I'll speak to you in the week."

Steph caught at his sleeve, "Please Theo, please stay and…"

"No," he snatched his arm away. "And don't ring me either, I'm going to be very busy. I'll call you when I'm more sorted."

Steph watched him walk away with a rising sense of frustration and anger; she only wanted to talk to him. She was sure if she could just explain – but he'd gone. She stayed where she was as he said goodbye to the girls and let himself out of the front door. It shut softly behind him. And in the instant that he walked away, all the antipathy drained out of Steph. She suddenly felt exhausted, miserable and totally lethargic. She could quite well understand how depressed people just went to bed and stayed there for days. But she was made of stronger stuff, she told herself. She took five minutes to re-invigorate herself before she went upstairs to the girls, and then felt guilty because Mia was already undressed and fast asleep in bed. Steph switched her bedside light off and kissed her gently on her cheek, "Sleep tight darling," she whispered and tiptoed from the room.

Tilly was sitting cross-legged on her bed writing something in a little book, she looked up when Steph entered.

"Look Mummy," she held up the purple notebook. "I'm going to write a diary. It's Daddy's idea. I told him that I missed him not being at home at the moment and he said I could write a diary for him so he didn't miss out on anything. Then when we see him, he can read it." Steph's heart nearly broke and she swallowed a big lump in her throat.

"That's a lovely idea darling." The guilt was overwhelming and Steph wondered in that instant how she would stand even a second more of it.

"Is Mia doing her diary?" Tilly asked.

"She's already asleep darling, as you should be." She took the pen and paper off Tilly and laid them on her desk. "Come on, lie down now," she tucked her up under the duvet. "So did you have a good day with Daddy?"

"Yes, it was fun." Tilly yawned widely. "Night Mummy."

Her sore throat obviously wasn't bothering her too much, Steph thought shutting the door behind her and going downstairs to check that the sports kits were in order for the morning. It was quite early, not yet seven-thirty, and Steph saw the evening stretching out before her, long, tedious and lonely. She busied herself tidying the kitchen and sorting through some old letters, before she poured herself a glass of wine and found a detective drama to watch on television. She wondered vaguely about attempting to write her basic CV, as she knew she would need to in order to apply to the courses she was interested in, but it seemed too much of a mammoth task at the moment. All the help she had was a template that she'd got off the internet which looked a little dull. Steph had an idea of adding a photograph of herself into a corner at the top, surely if people could see what she looked like then they were more likely to remember her credentials. If you could even use that word, she thought glumly. But she would get there.

Later, when she was desperately trying to remember the order of events, Steph thought that she'd gone up to bed at about nine-thirty. She'd been bored by the TV drama and had closed up the downstairs of the house early. It wasn't too early because she would be getting up at six-thirty to get the girls ready for school, but it was definitely before her usual time. She'd collected a glass of water and her book and gone upstairs. It was from that point that she couldn't remember exactly what had happened. She knew that she'd put her water and book on the floor at the top of the stairs, but she didn't know why because she would normally have turned right and carried them straight into the bedroom. In retrospect it felt like sixth sense. She never normally checked the girls, they were too old now, they weren't babies but this evening, for some reason she did. Perhaps it was because they'd been out all day and she subconsciously felt that she hadn't seen them enough, perhaps she really had been guided by instinct. Whatever – it had been near enough nine forty-five exactly when she'd pushed Mia's door open and heard the harsh, horrible sound of her laboured breathing. In the darkness Steph stopped, confused. It took two seconds for her brain to decipher the unfamiliar sound and identify it as Mia's breathing. She went to the bed and looked down, but it was too dark to see anything and she reached out to touch Mia's head; that was when the worry started. She was boiling hot, her face flaming with heat, and when Steph sought her hands they were ice cold. She turned the light on and Mia didn't stir.

"Mia darling?" No response. Steph again laid a hand firmly over her forehead and touched her cheeks, she was burning hot. But she shouldn't have a temperature, she'd had Calpol just over two hours ago. And there was something else that Steph didn't like in that instant; Mia hadn't moved. She shook her shoulder gently and said her name again, "Mia? Mia, wake up darling." There was no response. Steph pulled her from her side flat onto her back and Mia stirred gently but didn't open her eyes.

"Mia!" she said loudly and shook her harder. Nothing. Frantically, she pulled the duvet off and a vivid, red rash glared up at her from Mia's arms and legs.

"Oh my God," Steph said and felt her whole body begin to tremble. "Mia?" She stared at the rash and with all her heart she wished that Theo were there, she had no idea what to do. Doctor? Ambulance? Hospital? She turned and raced out of the room and down the stairs. She grabbed the phone and dialled Katie, "Hi, I'm sorry to bother you but can you come over?" she gabbled. "Now? I'm really sorry but Mia's ill, she won't wake up, she's got a rash and I need to take her to hospital."

"I'll be there in two minutes," Steph heard her grab her car keys and flinging the phone down she ran back upstairs, shaking.

Mia hadn't moved. "Mia? Oh God Mia, wake up, wake up." Mia moaned softly but still didn't open her eyes. OK, don't panic, Steph thought wildly, stay calm and think – what do you need? She looked around. What would Theo take? Money, keys, phone. They were all in her bag. Tilly was asleep, Katie would be fine with her. A coat or – or – her dressing gown or something – Steph snatched the dressing gown from the back of the door and by the time she'd thrown it onto the bed, Katie was banging at the front door.

"I drove like a lunatic to get here, what on earth's going on?" She burst into the hall, wearing her pyjamas and a coat.

"It's Mia – I can't wake her up, she's got a rash and a really high temperature," Steph felt tears of panic sting her eyes.

Katie laid a hand on her arm, "Don't panic, stay calm, she'll be fine. Do you want me to ring an ambulance?"

"No, I'll drive her to the hospital, it's only ten minutes, it'll be quicker." Steph shoved her feet roughly into her trainers and jumped up, "I'm going to get her."

Upstairs, she pulled Mia into her arms and wrapped the dressing gown around her. Mia roused briefly but when Steph stood up, her head flopped against Steph's shoulder. How the hell had this happened? She'd been fine all day, apparently. How had she gone from fine to practically unconscious in two hours?

Steph carried her out to the car and Katie followed with her handbag, "Don't worry, it's probably just a virus or something," she said comfortingly. "You're right to get it checked out but try not to worry."

"OK." Steph's face looked almost luminous in the moonlight. She hadn't even got a jacket. "Thanks so much for this Katie, I really appreciate it."

"It's no problem. Let me know what happens. I'll just stay here till you're back."

The A&E department of the local hospital was a short hop down the motorway. Steph drove as fast as she dared to get there, perfectly prepared to argue with any police that stopped her. She tried Theo's mobile twice from the car phone, but there was no answer and his answering machine was switched off. Mia's head lolled back against the seat and her breathing was fast and laboured. Steph swung into a space, pulled Mia over her shoulder again with aching arms and carried her as quickly as she could into the hospital.

"Hello," she approached the reception desk, "it's my daughter, I can't wake her up, she's got a temperature and a rash."

"Hold on a moment," the receptionist turned and picked up a phone. "Emergency, child, unconscious," she said softly into a receiver and the next moment a doctor in green scrubs appeared from Steph's left.

"Hello, I'm Dr Brennan, who do we have here?"

"Mia. She's called Mia."

"OK, come through here," he gestured through some double doors. "If you could lie her down on the bed. What are her symptoms?"

"The breathing you can hear, she said she had a headache earlier and she has a rash on her arms and legs."

"And you're Mum are you?" he asked over his shoulder.

Steph watched anxiously as he poked and prodded at her body and held a thermometer up to her forehead, "Yes, yes I am," she said.

"And what's been going on with Mia?" he asked Steph. "Mia? Can you hear me?" he spoke quite loudly and shone a small torch into her eyes.

"Um – nothing. She's been fine all day, she was out with her father and her sister – she's a twin – she said she had that headache when she got home."

"What time was that?"

"About half past six, she had some Calpol then, she went to bed and I found her like this just before ten."

"Right…" The doctor scrawled something down, and then suddenly Mia's eyes flickered open.

Steph rushed to her, "Mia, darling, can you hear me?" Mia nodded slowly, shutting her eyes again.

"Mia," said Dr Brennan. "Can you open your eyes for me?"

"It hurts," she whispered. "Too light."

"Too bright? OK." He turned to Steph. "She is pyrexic – she's got a temperature – it's forty degrees so I'm going to try and bring that down for her first of all and then ask my colleague to have a look at her. What time did you say she had Calpol?"

"Er – six thirty I think."

"So we'll give her some Ibuprofen. I'll get that sorted out. Does she have any allergies or any other medical conditions?"

"No."

"Is she taking any other medication at all?"

"No, nothing. Forty degrees is quite high isn't it?"

"It's a little higher than we'd like, but it's not a problem. We don't worry about the temperature on its own, but she'll feel more comfortable if we can get it down a bit. Mia, how do you feel?"

"A bit sick," she was still whispering. "And it hurts to breathe. And cold, I'm cold."

"OK…" He wrote more things down. "Right Mia, we'll get you a blanket. The nurse will come in a moment," Dr Brennan said to Steph. "And you're her next of kin?"

"Yes, I am." It felt totally surreal. Almost like it was really just a dream, it was so sudden and unfamiliar.

She waited until he'd left the room before digging her mobile out of her bag, watching Mia like a hawk the whole time. She just lay on the bed, shivering, with her eyes closed. Steph sat next to her, uncertain whether to hold her or whether that would push her temperature higher. She tried to call Theo again but it rang out and she couldn't leave a message. In desperation she typed him an urgent text. He wouldn't ignore that, surely. She needed him here, she was way out of her depth.

"Hello, Mia Hammond?" A nurse came in.

"Yes, that's right."

"Ibuprofen, I hear and a blanket. Dr White will be round in a minute," she said to Steph. Before she could respond, Mia turned slightly and vomited onto the bed.

"Oh God!" said Steph frantically.

"Oh dear. Never mind," the nurse went to her swiftly and helped her upright. "There we go," she reached for a small cardboard bowl and handed it to Steph, "do you want to hang on to that mum? Good job that was before the medicine, not after."

She found an operating gown for Mia to wear and put the soiled things into a plastic bag. She administered the Ibuprofen, and told them to wait. Steph sat by her small, shaking daughter whose face was nearly translucent, it was so pale and held her hand. Mia just lay there with her eyes shut, not moving or speaking, cheeks fiery and hair matted with sweat. Steph kept her mobile by her side and checked occasionally that it had a signal; it always did but it still didn't ring. Where could he be? What was going on? Various, nasty, possibilities filtered through Steph's mind. That he'd crashed the car, that he was with another woman (she nearly vomited herself at that thought) or worst of all – that he was deliberately ignoring her because he didn't care because Mia wasn't his daughter.

Steph sat on the edge of the bed, feeling her whole body tense. She hated not knowing what was wrong, she was petrified in case it was something serious. She wished fervently that she had someone with her, someone to comfort her, hold her. The door opened suddenly, "Hello, is this Mia Hammond?" A tall, grey-haired man walked in.

"Yes, that's right."

"I'm Dr White." He leant forward and shook Steph's hand before running through Mia's history quickly and retaking her temperature.

"Hmm. It hasn't really gone down at all. My colleague and I have agreed that we'd like to run some tests on her, it looks like an infection somewhere. And in light of her symptoms we're going to test for meningitis."

"Oh my God," Steph whispered.

"But we can't do that here, we have no paediatric facilities, so we'll have to transfer her to the nearest paediatric centre."

"OK. Do I take her?"

"No. It sounds stupid but in case something happens on the way we'll need to transfer her by ambulance. We've got one waiting, we just need a porter to take her down. You can come with her or follow on by car. Is there anyone else on the way?"

"What do you mean?"

"Your husband or anyone who we'll need to redirect?"

"No. No, there isn't anyone." She glanced again at Mia, lying on her side, breathing heavily.

"Don't worry, she'll be in good hands there. But we do need to get on with these tests, as you probably know meningitis needs to be treated promptly."

"Is that what you think she's got?" Steph heard her own voice shake through fear.

Dr White hesitated, "I can't say and I'd hate to speculate, but she is displaying some symptoms consistent with that diagnosis. We really just need to get on and find what's making this little one so poorly, the sooner we get her to St Marys, the better." He spoke very calmly.

"OK, fine." Steph bit her trembling lip. She decided to go with Mia and leave her car where it was; sod the parking fines. She rang Katie as they walked down to the ambulance and told her what was going on, "I'm sorry," she said. "I didn't expect this. Are you all right to stay?"

"Absolutely fine. Don't worry about us, I'll explain to Tilly what's going on in the morning and get her off to school if you're not back. Just keep me updated, all right?"

"I will, I will. Oh and Katie?"

"Yes?"

"Could you do me a favour? I can't get hold of Theo. I've tried and tried and he's not answering his phone to me. He told me not to ring him earlier – I wanted to talk and he didn't – I've text but still nothing. Could you try him for me please and tell him where we are if you get through?"

"Of course I can." Katie's heart went out to Steph. "Just look after yourself."

"Thanks. Bye."

The ambulance ride was calm, but quick. Mia was monitored constantly along the way and the paramedics had murmured conversations and studied printouts from computers. Steph had little energy to do anything but sit and hold her daughter's hand; she couldn't ever remember being so terrified in her whole life. A cold dread filled her entire body, nothing compared to this. Meningitis – that was serious. There were all sorts of repercussions, she strove to retrieve information read and stored a long time ago. Brain damage and death featured prominently in her thoughts. She pressed a finger against the rash on Mia and it faded, but didn't disappear completely. The only small comfort was that they were in the right place and heading to a better one.

"They're tough, these little ones," a female paramedic said with a sympathetic smile. "Stronger than they look."

Steph nodded sadly. She thought she would have given up any belonging, any privilege to have Theo by her side right now, holding her hand and telling her it would be all right. She felt completely alone. But if he didn't want to be here, then there was nothing that she could do. To her horror, she felt tears rise and spill over, dripping into her lap. The paramedic handed her a tissue, "She'll be all right," she said. "I've seen plenty worse in my time." Steph knew she was trying to be kind but it wasn't helping. They obviously did not know that she would be all right. Limbs could go gangrenous with meningitis, she remembered. How would she feel if Mia lost an arm or a leg? More importantly, how would Mia feel? Steph closed her eyes to that terrible thought. She wouldn't care of course, nothing could ever change how she felt about Mia, but the thought of her strong, bright daughter being disabled was awful. This was divine retribution, she knew it. Mia was going to die and it would all be her fault for what she'd done. She'd enjoyed the fruits of her deception for too long, it was time to take them away from her now. She saw it as clearly as though God's eyes were her own.

A paediatric team was waiting for Mia upon the ward when they arrived at the hospital. They strapped a tag around her wrist, examined her again, repeated the tests that had already been done, and made lots of scribbled notes. No one seemed able to tell her anything. The light on the ward was bright and dizzying, Steph's eyes felt gritty, she had no idea what time it was and looked round for a clock. Eleven o' clock. Mia mumbled responses to questions but kept her eyes firmly shut, Steph had the impression that she was drifting in and out of sleep. She looked tiny lying on the bed, tiny and thin. Her vibrance was all but gone. She looked more like Tilly than she did herself at that moment. A doctor in a white coat this time approached her, "Mrs Hammond?"

"Yes."

"Mia needs to have some tests done urgently. We're going to run some blood tests and do a lumbar puncture."

"What's that?"

"A test on her spinal fluid that will help us confirm or rule out meningitis. It's not a very nice test and she'll need to be sedated. I recommend that you wait here, it's not something that you want to watch."

"But I want to stay with Mia."

"Mia will be better on her own for this. It won't take long, perhaps twenty minutes. Go and get a cup of coffee or something, one of the nurses will show you where the kitchen is." Steph stared after the doctor, should she go anyway? Or was it best to stay here? Mia didn't seem to notice whether she was there or not at the moment. She watched as they wheeled her daughter out of the room, fighting back panic. What if she never came back?

The room slowly emptied and Steph saw that she was in a small, three-bed ward off the main ward, but the other two beds were empty. Her head ached and she longed to turn down the lights. It was silent, apart from the pump to a fishtank whirring away in the corner. There was a chair by the bed but she couldn't settle, she paced the room restlessly. She'd always wondered whether people actually did that, it seemed so pointless. She pulled her mobile out and stared at the blank screen; no message from Theo. She wrote a quick text to Katie and watched as it sent. Mia had been gone ten minutes, she wondered what they were doing to her, and quickly stopped. Her imagination was not to be trusted. She wrapped her own arms around her body and tried to think about something else.

Suddenly, the silence on the ward was shattered; Steph could hear some raised voices at the other end of the corridor. She listened and tried to distinguish what was being said, "No sir," she heard a nurse say firmly. "We don't have anyone of that name on the ward." And then a more muted discussion, before "I really cannot allow…" Just on a hunch, Steph crossed the room to the door and slowly peered out. Theo was standing at the other end of the corridor by the reception desk. A palpable relief threaded its way through her entire body. He was here. He had come.

"Theo," she walked towards him slowly and as she got close she was able to see the panic written across his face.

"Steph!" He was by her side in two steps and put his hands on her arms, "What the hell is going on? I've had a garbled message from Katie telling me that Tilly's ill and I had to come quickly but the staff are telling me she's not here."

"Not Tilly, it's not Tilly, it's Mia. Mia's ill."

"Oh my God – what's the matter with her?" his eyes searched her face desperately, Steph wasn't able to cushion the blow, "Meningitis, they think."

"Meningitis?" he ran his hands through his hair. "What – how – but she was fine today. Fine." Steph was amazed that it was still the same day, a hundred years seemed to have passed between this morning and now.

"I know, she went downhill so quickly."

"Where is she?"

"Having a test done, a lumbar puncture." She repeated what the doctors had told her. "Come and wait through here." She led him into the small ward and shut the door.

"I don't know what's the matter with her Theo but she's very ill. She looks awful, not like Mia at all. She can hardly wake up, she's got an awful rash, they can't get her temperature down," suddenly the stress discharged itself and Steph was crying. "And meningitis – she might lose a limb – brain damaged – people *die* from it," she sobbed.

Theo looked sober and frightened, "She won't die," he said uneasily. "She's in the very best place. Once they've found out what the matter is."

"How do you *know* that?" Steph cried, rounding on him. "I'm fed up of everyone apart from the doctors telling me she's going to be fine. They don't know what the matter is Theo!" And Steph looked so young and scared standing there that it was the easiest thing in the world to pull her into his arms and comfort her.

"Shh shhh, calm down, it won't do any good for you to get this worked up. Let's just wait and hear what the doctors have to say when she comes back. Where's Tilly?"

"With Katie at home," Steph sniffed, she was both comforted and confused. Theo's bulk against her felt familiar, but forbidden. "Why didn't you answer my calls? She could have died!"

Theo looked wracked with guilt, "I didn't have my phone on me for a long time, and when I saw it, I just thought – well – I didn't want to talk. I'd told you not to ring. I didn't realise what was going on." He looked ashamed.

"But I sent you a text as well."

Theo shook his head, "I didn't get that. When Katie rang for the fifth time, that was when I answered. I came straight away, I swear."

"I wouldn't blame you if you hadn't." Steph mumbled, face buried against his chest. He was a good head and a half taller than her, she didn't need to look at his face but he held her at arms length, looked her seriously in the eye, and said: "You know me better than that."

CHAPTER TWENTY-THREE

They waited for what felt like hours, sitting next to each other, staring at the floor. When they broke apart, Steph wasn't sure if that hug had been an emotional mistake or whether Theo was setting a precedent, but right now, she couldn't care. With every squeak of rubber-soled shoe and every twist of a door handle on the ward they both glanced up anxiously, Steph searching for a glimpse of her small, ill daughter and Theo fearful of what sight would meet his eyes.

It was difficult to describe the emotion that had overcome him when he'd finally answered Katie's calls. He hadn't known what she might want to say to him, but he certainly hadn't predicted that news. He'd spent so long painstakingly building up his defences, refusing to talk to Steph even though it was all he wanted to do, the only thing that made sense to him. Some evenings he had literally had to sit on his hands to stop himself picking up the phone. But he couldn't, because he didn't know what he wanted to do, or what he wanted to say, and some ill thought out, half-baked conversation about something so important was not a good idea.

And Katie's phonecall, in one fell swoop had destroyed those defences and his careful, logical reasoning. An absolute panic had settled over him instantly as a gut reaction, and his immediate instinct had been to get to the hospital. He'd driven very unwisely to get here. And then finding out that it was Mia ill, not Tilly, had made it worse when he'd arrived. Mia was so strong, it took a lot to knock her off her feet – it was impossible to imagine her as Steph was describing. She was a tough old thing, Mia, it was so hard to picture her as actually being susceptible to the same illnessess as other children. It was the first time that either twin had been seriously ill; they'd been lucky he supposed, to have such healthy children, but there was a first time for everything.

Then some insidious, but not entirely unexpected, voice had crawled inside his skull as he bombed down the motorway and shot across the town, asking if he should be doing this now that he knew that Mia and Tilly were not his children. Theo was vastly relieved to find that the answer was yes, despite what common sense dictated. They were no different in his eyes he had discovered; he still knew them the same amount, loved the same, understood them the same. And they wouldn't understand if he wasn't there, this wasn't their fault, they were pawns caught up in something miles beyond their control. And their childish faith in him was something that he neither took for granted, nor was prepared to lose.

His reaction to Steph's admission had initially chopped and changed between sheer, unadulterated anger and intense distress, but eventually settled into a murky quagmire of disappointment and hurt. His mind hadn't quite worked through all the circumstances surrounding the twins conception, it didn't yet want to, but for the moment he thought he could understand his feelings. He shouldn't have gone home the night that he'd found Ed there, that had been a big mistake. It was too soon, he was blinded by grief, everything was too uncertain. He hadn't known his own mind at that point and if the argument had not been sparked by Ed's presence, it would have been something else. He didn't feel guilty, he thought it was understandable, he hadn't known which way to turn at that moment, but he did recognise it as a mistake. And knowing that Mia lay so ill here in the hospital made him see that there was nowhere else he could be right now.

Theo's head snapped up as the door opened and a trolley was wheeled through. A small, blonde girl lay asleep on it. Theo leapt up and went to her side, Steph was right, she looked dreadful. White with feverish cheeks and audible breathing. He touched her cheek gently as the nurse bustled around him.

"How did it go?" Steph asked anxiously.

"Fine. She's been sedated, she'll sleep for a few hours now. We've started her on IV antibiotics in case, so mind her arm." Steph looked and saw the bandage covering a tiny tube. "She needs them every four hours. The doctor will be round in the morning to speak to you."

"The morning?"

"It's only six hours away. I suggest you go home for a bit."

Steph shook her head firmly, "I'm not leaving her. She might wake up."

"We can put a bed in here for one of you."

Theo looked at Steph, "I'll stay," he said. "You look exhausted. Go home to Tilly."

****

She slept badly after saying goodbye to Katie, only falling asleep through sheer exhaustion and opening her eyes at six, wide awake immediately. A cold, hard ball of dread sat in her stomach like an iron fist squeezing her whichever way she moved. There was a text from Theo sent at five, *'no change x'*.

Tilly sat at the breakfast table, swinging her legs and eating cereal. She demanded to know time and time again exactly what happened, she didn't seem able to believe that all this had happened in the space of one night while she slept. It felt odd to Steph, to see one small daughter sitting happily at the table, looking a picture of health and dressed correctly in her uniform, while the other lay in who knew what state in the hospital.

"Can I come and see her?" she asked, but Steph didn't dare. Grotesque images of withered black limbs floated periodically through her mind. She knew she was probably being over-dramatic but lack of sleep and fear had made her paranoid. She couldn't cope if anything happened to Mia, she knew she couldn't. Loss of a child – that was the worst thing she could ever imagine. It was so wrong to outlive a child. Her hands clenched tight around her coffee cup, and she quite literally prayed that Mia would pull through. But if she didn't, she had only herself to blame. Tilly watched her mother's dark hair swing across her eyes and wondered why she was being so quiet.

"Mummy, is Mia going to die?"

Steph's head snapped up, "No darling, of course not," she said automatically.

"Then why can't I see her?"

"Because you've got school. Maybe afterwards."

"What's wrong with her?"

"They don't know yet. They're doing tests to find out."

"I might want to be a doctor when I grow up."

"You could be whatever you want darling. Are you almost finished? Go and clean your teeth and we'll get you to school."

By the time she walked onto the ward, feeling wobbly through lack of sleep, the hospital was buzzing with activity. It was completely altered from the quiet, still place of midnight, the corridors were full of children and doctors and people being wheeled along on trolleys. She'd had no more communication from Theo, which she took as a positive sign. And up on Mia's ward when she walked through the double doors, Theo was standing by the bed, hands thrust into his pockets, talking earnestly to a doctor. Steph went to his side and touched his arm gently, "Hi," and her eyes flew to Mia, who lay in the bed, awake. "Hello darling," Steph perched on the side of the bed and covered Mia's hands with her own. "How are you feeling?"

"Tired." She smiled weakly.

"She hasn't got meningitis," Theo said, and when Steph looked at him she could see that the tension had drained away. He looked tired, and older than he had, but his eyes were clear.

"No, the test results came back negative for meningitis," the doctor said as Steph scanned his face. "We think she has pneumonia."

"Pneumonia?"

"Yes, we can hear some congestion in her lower left lung and that would explain the breathing and the temperature."

"But she doesn't have a cough."

"She doesn't need one to have pneumonia. We see a few cases present like this. Mia will need an X-ray to confirm the diagnosis but we're happy that she's on the correct treatment."

Steph let go of her breath that she had unwittingly been holding, "Thank God," she said gratefully. "Thank God."

"It's been a nasty few hours for you hasn't it," the doctor said sympathetically.

"Just a bit," Steph smiled at him.

"Well, as I said, we'll get that X-ray organised and that should give us a few answers."

"Thank God," Steph breathed, feeling tension drain out of her. "Thank God."

In a clichéd way it felt like a load of old iron had been lifted off Steph's shoulders. If Mia was fine then nothing could be wrong with the world, nothing. A glance at Theo's face told her that he felt the same way.

"Do you want anything?" he was asking Mia. "A drink or anything?"

"Yes, I want Coke."

"Coke?"

"Yes."

"OK, you can have Coke." He really did feel the same way.

Mia spent the morning after her X-ray alternately sleeping and watching television. Neither Steph nor Theo left her side and just after lunch another doctor appeared to confirm that Mia did indeed have pneumonia and would need some strong antibiotics to treat it. But the good news was that she could go home in the next couple of days.

Steph felt like she was walking on air. To be thrust from such deep horror to absolutely none at all was an incredible experience.

"What if they've got it wrong?" she asked Theo at one point in panic.

"They haven't," he said. "Look at her, she's better already." And she was, sleeping soundly, her cheeks were less flushed and she was definitely less hot. She looked peaceful.

Steph found that she didn't quite know what to say to Theo as they sat there during the afternoon. The situation between them had been temporarily suspended while they thought that Mia's life lay in the balance, but what would happen now that she was fine, Steph had no idea. She did realise that it had never occurred to her to phone Ed during the whole drama. It had never even entered her mind. Presumably that was her subconscious guiding her. But when Theo left to collect Tilly from school, Steph made sure that Mia was asleep before she slipped outside to make a phonecall. If there was one thing this episode was showing her, it was that she knew what was important and what was not. She stood on the busy roadside and dialled the number, feeling more than a little of deja-vu. The late afternoon sun gave no warmth and a cool breeze whipped around her shoulders. Colder than Paris.

"Hi Ed, it's Steph."

"Oh, hello. How are you?" He sounded more distant than he had in the past. Steph repeated the events of the last twenty-four hours as succinctly as she could, being careful to put no emotion into her voice. Discussing concerns about Mia with Ed was a bizarre experience. She felt disembodied.

Ed sounded shocked, "God, sorry to hear that. Is she OK now?"

"She will be, yes. Listen," Steph hesitated before she ploughed on. "I've come to a decision. I don't think that it's right for me or the girls to see any more of you."

There was a small pause before Ed said "I had more or less come to the same conclusion myself."

"Really?"

"Yes. I don't have anything to contribute to your life, Steph. Look at you, you're happy with your girls, you love Theo, he loves you. I don't know how that will turn out for you but there is nothing to be gained from staying friends with me. The whole thing is too awkward, it feels wrong."

"You do realise that you're turning your back on your children Ed?" Steph enquired gently.

"I do, yes. And believe me I have thought about that in some depth. I'm not a callous man Steph, you know that, but I've lived eleven years with no children and they aren't really mine anyway. If we open that particular can of worms and start telling friends and family, it could be a disaster. Never mind that it wouldn't be the best thing for the twins anyway."

"No," Steph said in a small voice. It was all very well when she had planned what she was going to say to him, but she had at least expected half a fight.

"What I will say is that I'll always be around if you need me. If you get into any troubles or difficulty then I'll make sure that you always know where to find me."

"Thank you." Was that it? A lifetime of friendship ended be a few, swift, words?

"And on that note," he took a deep breath, "I've changed my mind. I am taking that job in Boston."

"Oh. Congratulations."

"Yeah – it's not forever, or at least it needn't be, but I changed my mind about it. I need to get away for a bit, change of scene, calm my life down. I'm still picking up the pieces from the Julia mess."

"Really?"

"Yes, I've already had a phonecall from Kirsty about my birthday. I just don't want to be reminded the whole time of everything that's happened in my past. Finding you again has been cathartic and it's sorted some things out in my own mind so I really feel now that I can move on. I always did have lingering thoughts and questions about you, but they're answered now. And I'm happy with the direction that my life's taking, I've worked bloody hard to get where I am and I'm enjoying it. I want more of the same. To be honest, two kids is the last thing I want. I don't mean that to sound cruel, but they're yours and Theo's children, not mine."

"It's weird to hear you talk like this. I can't believe this is goodbye."

"It isn't goodbye. Nothing's written in stone. I'll be back at some point and maybe we can meet up."

"We won't though. If I stand even a chance of things working out with Theo I think you'll need to be permanently out of the picture."

"The odd email, then." Wisely he didn't ask after Theo.

"Perhaps."

"Listen, I'm in court tomorrow morning and I've got a stack of papers to read through before then so I'm going to have to love you and leave you. Shall we continue this another time?"

Steph recognised it for what it was, goodbye without the goodbye. "Yes. Can do."

"Speak to you later. Bye Steph."

She went back into the hospital out of the cold into the warm and feeling a little strange. That would be her last conversation with one of her childhood friends. Somehow, she hadn't imagined that being the outcome. She'd thought he'd want to stay in touch, that he might want to forge some sort of relationship with the girls, albeit a remote one. She hadn't expected his complete revocation of any form of friendship. He was right though, in everything he'd said. Ed had no place in her life, he never had really, and associating with him could do no good. Steph pushed open the doors to the ward and her heart lifted to see Mia, Tilly and Theo sitting together on the bed. Theo looked up to see her, "Hi, I thought I'd bring Tilly in to see her sister."

Tilly flopped back on the bed, socks crumpled round her ankles, hair askew and chocolate smeared around her mouth, "Hi Mummy, guess what? I made a real kite today in DT. And Mrs Ivory says that the chicks can come home in a couple of weeks," she added.

Steph stooped and gave her a hug before sitting back in the chair, "Have you said hello to Mia?"

"Yeah, course I have. She doesn't look that ill." And it was true, Mia was looking a little brighter. She was sitting up holding a bottle of Coke. "And I've been telling Dad about everything at school."

"Good. Did you have a good day?"

"Sort of. It's boring without Mia. When can she come back?" Steph sat back, allowing the burble of conversation to go on around her.

Every now and then a nurse came by and took Mia's temperature, marvelling over the fact that she was an identical twin. "If no one had told me, I'd have thought you'd made a miraculous recovery," she teased. "Temperature's nice and low, that's good."

The room was warm which was nice after being outside and slowly, Steph closed her eyes, the hard side of the bed against her hand, she could feel the comforting movement of the girls through it. Theo leant forward, "Going to sleep are you?"

"Possibly," Steph admitted. "I didn't sleep that well last night."

"No, you and me both."

"I look forward to being in my own bed tonight."

"Me too." Steph kept her eyes closed but her heart started beating a little faster. Did that mean what she thought it could mean? She didn't dare open them. She couldn't stand for her fledgling hopes to be shattered by disappointment. Then she scolded herself silently for being so ungrateful. She should be pleased that Theo was even here, she could not imagine doing this on her own.

"Steph?" Theo touched her hand lightly, sending a bolt of adrenaline through her; she longed for his touch.

"Yes?" She opened her eyes to find him looking at her very seriously.

"I've got something important to ask you."

"OK."

"What is this I hear about chickens?"

****

Mia was discharged two days later, and surprisingly she requested to share a bedroom with Tilly. "I missed her," she said simply by way of explanation.

Theo had spent the nights at the hospital while Steph had taken Tilly home and done the school run. It had smoothly avoided any awkward situations about where he would stay. But once Mia was home and settled and Tilly had been collected, the pair of them sat on the sofa in the living room watching a DVD. Steph looked at them, thinking that she would probably never take her children for granted again, before she closed the door softly and made her way into the kitchen to find Theo. He was standing with his back resting against the Aga, reading through some post. He looked up when she shut the kitchen door, "Anything important?" she asked, gesturing at the paper in his hand.

"No, just some bank stuff. Girls all right?" He had one hand resting in his pocket and he was wearing a flamingo pink polo shirt that Steph had never liked.

"Yes, they're fine," she looked down at the floor. "Um, Theo, I wanted to talk to you."

"What about?" his expression didn't change.

"Us."

"Mmm. I know we need to talk."

"Do you want to?"

"Yes, I do. I've had time to do a lot of thinking in that hospital, and I can tell you how I feel Steph and I can tell you what I want, but I can't tell you what's going to happen. This – this – thing that's happened between us is so enormous that I'm having trouble getting past it." Steph stayed silent. "The only things that are stopping me from leaving right now are the girls and the fact that I know you, inside out and back to front."

"What's that got to do with it?"

"I loved you way before the girls came along, I fell in love with you totally, completely and deeply. When they were born I loved you more. I've adored those girls for ten years. By telling me that they aren't mine you have shattered my life entirely. I don't know how I'm ever going to find the strength to deal with that. I'm devastated, and I don't use that word lightly." It was a very eloquent speech for Theo.

"I know," Steph whispered, eyes fixed on his chest, hardly daring to hear what came next.

"But at the same time, I understand you, I understand things that have happened to you in the past and I understand that you were very young. I think I also understand that you didn't mean for this to happen. I don't care that you had a fling with Ed."

"It wasn't…"

Theo held his hand up, "Whatever. That bit doesn't bother me. Teenagers do silly things. What I am bothered about is how you have concealed the truth from me for so long, how you could possibly have lived with yourself. I thought I knew you completely and I don't." Steph twisted her fingers inside the sleeve of her cardigan, she had a hundred explanations to make, thousands of justifications, millions of apologies. But she held her tongue. "I want to come back and live here with you and the girls, carry on like before, pretend it never happened, have another child – but I don't know if I can. And that's the honest truth. I don't know yet if I have it within me. But I'll tell you one thing, whatever happens I will always be a father to those girls." He nodded towards the living room.

"Thank you for being honest." She felt worse now than when he had started, but at least she knew the truth.

"That's all I can give you right now."

"OK. That's fine." She twisted her hair into a knot and secured it with a band.

"Have you spoken to Ed?" Theo asked seriously.

"Yes. Once. He's moving abroad, he isn't going to be around. And we've agreed not to speak. There's nothing that we want from each other."

A tangible relief washed over Theo's face, "So he doesn't…?"

"No." Steph confirmed.

"OK. Good. Good." A whole potential conversation rolled away from them leaving the way a little more clear. The room stayed tense and Steph couldn't help but meet his eyes searchingly. He shrugged, "I can't give you more Steph. You can't underestimate what you've done."

"I don't."

"I need time and space."

"That's what Katie said," Steph replied unthinkingly.

"Does she *know*?" His eyebrows shot up.

"Yes. I told her a few weeks ago."

"Jesus, Steph," he looked at her in disgust.

"I had to Theo, I had no one. I didn't know what to do," she said pleadingly.

"Your best friend knew before me that the girls weren't mine?" The hard, angry look was back, like shutters had gone down.

"Theo, please. I told her because I was desperate, almost at my lowest ebb. I wouldn't have otherwise."

"You are unbelieveable." He glared at her before grabbing his jacket and leaving the house.

CHAPTER TWENTY-FOUR

Theo found it amazing how time could pass so slowly. And yet it did pass, and that was amazing too. How could the world still be spinning, the clocks still ticking, life still going on whilst there were so many unanswered questions in his head? He was stuck in a moment and yet no one else was. He needed to move one way or the other, but he couldn't do that either. With each new minute he expected a conclusion – a decision – to hop into his mind, but it didn't happen. The hands moved around his watch as they had always done, and nothing changed.

He glanced outside over the harbour. A strange, unfamiliar view. Good. Nothing there to jolt or remind him of a past life. No hidden memories lying in wait for him. A new view, unseen, unadulterated. But was it better for being that? Because no memories would be made here in this unimposing seaside hotel. It was an escape, a bolt-hole, somewhere to flee to when he hadn't been able to take the pain any more. The façade that he had been presenting to the outside world had well and truly crumbled and it had been time to reveal all or run away. But you can't reveal half a story, there would be too many questions and too many answers demanded. Too many people rummaging through the detritus of the last ten years and trying to help. Family and friends would split into camps and persuade others to take sides. There would be recriminations flung about – the girls might find out... no. It could never happen like that. So cowardly though it seemed, Theo had fled to a hiding place of anonymity. Where he had been able to check-in and the receptionist had barely bothered to look at him. He'd stood there, with his bag beside him, wondering what would happen if he suddenly opened his mouth and poured out his story. How would she react to him then? Pity? Probably. Scorn for being so stupid? Maybe. But most of all, probably just a nervous look of not quite knowing what to say and being glad that all of her problems were immediately diminished in light of his.

It did put everything into perspective. Theo had always been slightly scathing of people who were flung into depressions by money worries and failed relationships – couldn't they see that such extreme emotions should only be caused by extreme situations? Death – injury – poverty. But that was a narrow-minded and naïve view; the ending of situations was a death of a type, and his situation had ended on as as big a scale as Theo could ever imagine. As he'd sat in the chair the sun had shifted across the sky, marking again the passing of time. If he sat here much longer the sun would sink from view completely, night would fall and the clocks would turn on to yet another day. In an instant Theo sprang up and grabbed his jacket. He looked in the mirror briefly – tired, pale, unshaved – before pulling the hotel room door shut behind him and making his way towards the cold outside.

His limbs felt heavy and unused. His shoulders wanted to droop. It was an effort to walk briskly. Despite the place being unknown, it ceased to help as Theo walked along the harbour. The boats moored there suddenly and poignantly reminded him of looking out over the water in Vannes all those years ago. He could imagine the girls running along the wall, throwing chips to the seagulls, shouting out the more interesting names of the boats – **Rajar Goose** – **Ishacoco** – **Aquaholic** – he could almost hear their voices, "*Why is that boat called that name Daddy?*"

"*People can choose what they want to call their boats*," he would reply.

"*Can they call them anything?*"

"*Anything at all.*" Any label they cared to put a boat, they could. Think of a name – bam – done. Imagine that dictatorship over the rest of your life. People thought they had it, but really, they didn't. Your life was always subject to the demands and influences of others. Theo had thought his life was truly his, insulated from the rest of the world by his family, but actually, Ed's teenage desire for Steph had seen to it that that would never be the case.

****

Steph looked around the kitchen. So this was it. This was what single parenthood was like. She'd always imagined that it was loneliness, that it meant feeling lost and alone and excluded from normal life. In the beginning, at least. But it wasn't at all, it was emptiness. And silence. The mess that she had always resented and moaned about, the coffee cups and laptop and ties and Blackberry cluttering up the work surfaces was no longer there, and the lack of it had left a huge hole. Because that mess was Theo – had been Theo. It was the embodiment of him, it was what meant Steph could expect to hear a cough, the sound of a key in the door – and now that was gone. So she might have a tidy house but her life had shrivelled away to nothingness. In that instant she felt utterly exhausted, as though she couldn't manage to breathe through the next minute, never mind live the rest of her life. She was just choosing whether to give in to the lethargy and flop on the sofa or whether to fight it and empty the dishwasher, when the doorbell rang.

"Hello," a huge bunch of flowers obscured Katie's face.

"Hi, what on earth are those?" Steph stood back to let her in.

"I was collecting an order sheet and the garden centre had them at half price so here.-" She thrust them at Steph. "They're for you."

"Thanks." They were beautiful flowers in an artful arrangement, full of vivid blues and pinks and yellows. "They're very lovely."

"You're welcome. Got time for a coffee?"

Steph shrugged, "Sure. Nothing else to do with the rest of my life."

"Don't be like that." Katie moved past her and into the kitchen.

"How are you?"

"Fine. I suppose."

"More importantly, how's Mia?"

"She's bounced back. Quite incredibly when you remember how ill she was."

"That's fantastic. So pleased to hear it." A small pause.

"Have you heard anything from him?"

"No."

"It's only been a few days." *Has it?* "He'll ring."

"I know he'll ring, but when he does he'll be closed and quiet and detached. He'll want to discuss the girls and selling the house. Nothing else."

"You don't know that."

"I can take a pretty good guess," Steph said bitterly.

"Whatever you did, you guys have raised two kids together, that's got to count for something."

"Not in this case I don't think."

"Really? Even after everything he said and the kind of person that he is, you still don't think there's a chance he'll come back."

"No. I don't. How could any man go through what I've put him through and know that it will never ever end for the rest of his life – and still want to be here?"

"A special one." But her words fell flat. Steph could see her whole life stretching out in front of her; as a lone mother to her girls. Finding another man didn't even enter her mind. It would be too incongruous. Soon it would be as if Theo had never even been around, she could see that. Soon life would be normal with just her and the girls and that was a truly terrifying thought. How could that be? How could she have let this happen?

"And that's the worst bit," Steph almost didn't realise that she was speaking out loud. "That coldness that Theo's got about him now. It's dreadful. When he used to be so warm and friendly and open – to have to guess at his moods and his thoughts, to have to watch for signs rather than be told, it's horrible. And difficult. I can't even hope to have any sort of meaningful relationship with him like this."

"He just needs time and gentle persistence, Steph. He's put up barriers, of course he has, but they'll come down." Katie squeezed her hand softly.

"For what purpose?" There was no answer to this so Katie didn't even try.

CHAPTER TWENTY-FIVE

Steph looked out over her garden critically. The weather was perfect, which was an unexpected bonus. Sunny, warm and dry. So warm in fact that she suspected it would actually get hot later, which was a real result for early June. That should keep the guests happy, all one hundred of them. The marquee was erected, the bins filled with ice in preparation for receiving wine and beer, and balloons floated from just about every place that the girls could conceivably fasten them. Steph looked at the ones on the top of Betty and Mabel's coop and dreaded to think how they'd achieved that. The chickens had been tidied well into their corner for the occasion, the last thing she wanted was them running amok during the celebrations, chased by the cockerel. It was bad enough to watch the newly-arrived rabbits mating.

The hog to be roasted had arrived at eleven and had been gently turned on its spit ever since; the girls had been desperate to see what a whole pig being spit-roasted looked like. A fascination that Steph thought bordered on the unhealthy. But what Theo wanted he wold get, after all, you only turned thirty once.

"Steph!" Katie shouted through from the hallway. "Tom wants to know how many burger buns to bring in from the car?"

"Start with thirty. I can't think we'll need that many, but you never know." It was three o' clock in the afternoon and guests would start arriving from six. Steph had invited everyone that she could think of, determined that this would be a real celebration. Theo himself knew something was happening, but not the full, grand plan. He had been banished the day before to stay with his parents overnight.

"I feel like a child again," he'd complained as Steph packed him off with a kiss and a mysterious smile. "Banished home for an early night so I'm not tired for my birthday."

"Well enjoy it, because you won't be able to feel like a child after many more birthdays because you'll be too old."

"Don't remind me," he groaned. "Downhill from here on in, I know. It's amazing how many people have said that to me this week."

"Don't be grumpy. You're young yet and just look what you've achieved in your life. I'm very proud of you, Theo Hammond."

And now, now that it was so close to kick-off time, all Steph could think was how lucky she was to be in this position. To be able to throw the world's biggest party for a husband that she adored. If she cast her mind back just a few, miserable months, she would have given her chances of this happening a big, fat zero. When Theo stormed out for the second time she'd thought that was it, her lives were used up, he wouldn't return. So she'd squared her shoulders and carried on with the evening, every ounce of energy drained from her. She'd cooked for the girls, done Tilly's homework with her and put them both to bed in the same room, relishing the feeling of being able to look at them being so close together again. She'd felt more sure than ever that night that there was a bond between them that existed unseen, and not only that but that she and Theo shared it. And Ed didn't. There had been nothing whatsoever between her girls and Ed, despite her fears. No glimmer of recognition on his part, or theirs. It had been possible to move on forward, the shadows banished. And Steph had waited.

Then, two days, Theo had come home. Sober, calm and determined. He'd left he said because he couldn't handle anyone else knowing at all. It made him feel belittled and like he'd been made a fool of. Steph said that she understood but that it wasn't the case at all. And then Theo had looked at her and told her that he knew that, that he was hanging on grimly to the vestiges of what had once been between them, and that if he was successful they would be able to carry on. Just like that. It had been a long conversation that had continued late into the night, with tears on both sides. Steph repeated again and again how sorry she was, how stupid, how it hadn't been deliberate – until Theo had stopped her. There would be no place in this new life for explanations and apologies, he said. He knew all that he wanted to and now he had to merge desire with reality. He had to stay grounded and focussed. He had taken a month off work, which was a record for him, and they had gone abroad to America and travelled around California and into the Nevada desert to visit Vegas.

"Make the most of it girls," Theo had said cheerily, "because you are never coming here unchaperoned."

It had been a healing time for Steph and Theo. Removed from the stresses and strains of everyday life they had been free to talk and try and mend their relationship. It hadn't been easy, more than once Steph had caught a sideways glance from Theo which had spoken of dislike and distrust, but she had always supposed that to be her lot. She had, after all, done things which would make him dislike and distrust her. They sat by the pool late one night, cocktails in hand, looking out over the shimmering green surface of the water and Theo had said quietly that now he was certain that they could try and salvage their marriage, that his long – and deeply-held feelings for Steph had formed a partial explanation for her actions.

"I know how important a father figure is to you, I know how much you were frightened by your mums miscarriage, what that represented. I know how headstrong you are, how young you were and, above all, I know how much you love me. I've seen it every day since we've been together. I don't doubt it and that's why I can be with you."

"You are everything to me Theo. Most of the time I feel like I'm on the outside looking in, and I can't understand how I can have lived as I have for ten years. But I want you to know that there's always been a part of me that you haven't known which has existed in shame and secret. But not any more. That's gone."

Theo put his hand over hers, "I know." There hadn't been much physical contact between them since it happened. Theo hadn't come near her and Steph hadn't pursued it. He had even slept in Mia's room while she continued to share with Tilly. Knowing how meaningful it was to him to sleep in the same bed as somebody, Steph hadn't said anything. Theo had often told her that he thought sleeping with someone was just as intimate – if not more so – than actually having sex with them. Steph had told him a muted tone that she had never slept in the same bed as Ed, and though he hadn't said anything to that either, Steph thought it had helped.

"So now," Theo swirled the last of his drink around the bottom of his glass. "We need to decide what we tell the girls."

"What do you think?"

"I think nothing," he said decisively. "I think leave them as protected as they are now. None of this is their fault, they won't be able to accept the truth easily and why do they need to? Ed is never going to be a part of their lives – they don't need to know him. He doesn't want it, they won't want it, I don't and I'm presuming you don't?"

"No. I do not."

"Then what's to be gained? I'm their father and they need never know differently."

"Is it fair to keep it from them?"

"Completely. Ask yourself what good it would do? What benefits could come of them knowing?" An uncomfortable scenario of tears, misunderstanding, anger and pursuit of a father who didn't want to know them opened up to Steph. She was desperate to do what was right by her girls, and that wasn't it.

"So we're agreed?" Theo asked.

"Agreed."

It felt like a lid on the affair. Case closed, new chapter opened. Steph felt at long last like she had been helped through the final bit of the hideous situation, like some of the work had been taken away from her. She was newly able to give her arm to Theo for him to lead her along a better path. That night was the first night that he had come back to her bed, and it wasn't until he was there that she realised how much she had missed him. Her tears after sex comforted him slightly; her emotion showed him how much she cared. She wasn't malicious, she never had been. He thanked God that he had been born intelligent enough to be able to see past the immediate issue and have some sense of perspective on it. The feelings of hurt and bewilderment would never leave him completely he didn't think, but they could be buried; he could focus instead on what he had in his life. And he had not said as much to Steph, nor would he ever, but he was grateful that it was Ed who was the father of their children. It was better that way than someone else, someone different, whom he didn't know, whom he had not been friends with. At least he had known, understood and liked Ed. There was no bit of his daughters that he wasn't familiar with. It was another thing that was making it possible for him to rebuild his shattered relationship with Steph.

A call from upstairs disturbed Steph from her recollections. She jumped slightly and came to, looking around herself. How long had she been standing in the hallway? She could smell the roasting pig.

"Mum! Can you hear me?" Mia swung round the top of the banister.

"Yes, I can," Steph started to climb, "what's up?"

"Straight hair or curls? Which do you think?"

"I think that you can have straight hair any day so choose curls."

"OK, cool." Mia shot back into the bedroom she still shared with Tilly.

Steph gave the outfit that she had laid out on the bed a long, appraising look. She wanted to look perfect for Theo, she wanted him to be proud of her. And she wasn't sure that the fussy, flouncy dress she had chosen would do the trick. No more façades. Instead she selected a dusty pink, halterneck dress from her wardrobe with tiny pearl bead detailing around the hem, and a sash at the waist. It was a very 1920s, vintage-style dress, although it had come from TopShop. Simple, understated and yet elegant. Like her new Carvela heels that she adored. She put a black shrug on to cover her shoulders and affixed long, sparkly earrings in her earlobes. Her new sleek, blonde, bob highlighted them perfectly. It had been a dramatic haircut, but the style suited her elfin chin and tiny, slim figure and was a subtle nod towards her new, changed self. Katie had commented that she had chopped all her years and all her worry off, as Steph had gently swung it from side to side when she got home from the salon. She would have to forget about the long-coveted chignon now, but Steph thought that it was a sacrifice worth making. She applied her make-up carefully, squirted herself with the light Prada perfume that Theo favoured, and went downstairs to oversee the last of the preparations.

****

Theo's face when he walked in on the scene had been a photograph worth taking. Steph had done the traditional thing and blindfolded him to walk through the house and out of the kitchen doors, straight into the party that was in full swing. The twins had snapped shots like crazy as champagne corks were popped, streamers released and everyone sang a version of Happy Birthday. Theo's eyes were wide with amazement, "I never thought it was this," he kept saying. "Never."

The party went on all night in an endless whirl of guests, alcohol and dancing. Steph didn't think that she'd ever had so much fun in her life. Everyone that Theo cared about was there, part of the evening, and he was touched that she had gone to so much effort. "I can't believe it," he said at one point. "You've remembered everything."

He burst out laughing when he saw the hog-roast; the image of a whole pig on a spit-roast in his garden was surreal. The twins tried the meat but didn't like it, pronouncing it 'greasy'. "Actually Mummy," Mia said, "I thought I might like to become a vegetarian. I don't like the thought of eating Betty and Mabel."

"You don't have to eat them," Steph said.

"Or any other chickens. We might be eating their friends."

"It's highly unlikely. But we'll discuss it in the morning." She thought any sensible conversation was best deferred until then.

But the best bit of the whole evening had come through Katie.

"Do you remember Graham?" she'd asked Steph.

"Graham...the man who owns the shop and buys all your work?"

"That's the one. I've brought him along tonight."

"Oh, OK. Why?"

"Well, I told him about your course."

"Katie!" Steph cried. "What for? That was supposed to be a secret." She had only recently worked up the courage to get started on the long road towards her goal of becoming a qualified interior designer. Even the thought that she might one day get close made her shiver with anticipation. She had bitten the bullet and enrolled on a two year, full-time HND course for Interior Design at Greater Churchwell College. She'd been so nervous at the interview that she thought they would reject her on the grounds of her shaking hands, but the feedback had been good.

"We get lots of mature students applying," she had been told. "But only a few with your level of confidence and commitment." They had recommended a stint of work experience if she could get it. "It sounds silly talking about gaining experience of work at your age, but it really would give you a valuable insight into the world of interior design, as well as perhaps forming important contacts." It was this that Steph had repeated to Katie.

"Hold your horses girl, and wait to hear what I have to say. So Graham was asking about you the other day."

"Why?"

"I don't know, he remembered you. Anyway, I was explaining your new career venture and he asked if I knew who he was."

"Who is he?" Steph looked slightly fazed.

"He's only the managing director of Raggy Rose! How's that for a coincidence?" Katie waved her glass in the air in excitement. "And – even better than that – he said that you'll have to apply through the formal process but he can almost gurantee you an internship at some stage in Raggy Rose in Churchwell. Apparently he's the reason that the shop even opened here at all."

"Oh my God, are you serious?"

"Deadly." Katie's green eyes held Steph's blue ones, before she shrieked out loud and jumped up and down, "I can't believe this! How incredible! How insane!"

"Who's insane?" Theo came up behind them, grinning and waving a wine bottle.

"Your wife," Katie said, "she is insanely lucky." She repeated the story to Theo.

"Yes, I'm coming around to the fact that I may have a budding designer on my hands."

"She's been budding for years, Theo," Katie replied dismissively. "She's just about blooming now."

And later, when it got dark and cold and Steph wrapped a jacket around her shoulders, Theo put his arm around her and drew her in close as they stood to the side of the marquee, just a few steps away from the fun for the moment.

"You do know that I'm proud of you for doing this?" he said seriously.

"I hadn't, but thank you."

"It won't be easy," he warned. "Expect to be frustrated and thwarted along the way. It'll be hard work and there will be disappointments."

"Nice to see you focussing on the positives," Steph grinned.

"I'm being serious. I want you to know that I will support you every step of the way. I realise that you've grown-up within our marriage Steph, and what may have been right at the beginning isn't necessarily so now."

"I know," she said quietly.

"And I haven't always been receptive to your change of direction in the past, so I wanted to say to you, here and now, that I can see what you want and that I'll help you get it. If you need my help."

"Thank you."

It was left unsaid, but Steph knew that he was talking about her former role as housewife and mother alone. About his release of plans for a third child, his silent admission that it would have to wait. And she was grateful that he could see that she wanted – needed – more. It felt as if her whole life was suddenly rich with possibilities; the way that she had always perceived Katie's life. And now that she had laid open every last, little part of herself to face in a new direction, she had all the energy she could want to throw into it.

Even later in the night, as the party wound down towards a close, there were fireworks that lit up the sky brilliantly and exploded their noise over the celebrations. Theo held his wife close and whispered in her ear, "Thank you for this. It's amazing. The best birthday I could have."

"You deserve it," Steph said honestly. "You deserve it all." She looked out happily over the garden, with its marquee, mess, wineglasses, abandoned plates and guests trickling in and out of the house. It looked like the perfect end to the party. She could see Katie sitting with Mia and Tilly, giggling about something. Probably the rabbits. Where would that saga end? She rather thought that she might put the twins forward to a modelling agency; that had been a good idea of Katie's. After all, they were remarkably pretty.

"But there's one thing that I don't think you realise," Theo said in a funny tone.

"What's that?"

"I've done something I never would have thought possible. And you've given me things I never knew I had."

She tilted her head back to look at him quizzically, "Things you never knew you had?"

"You've taught me that I can do things I never knew I could."

And Steph thought those words would stick with her over the long years of their marriage, through the twins childhood and then adulthood, and through those of the new baby that lay as a shimmering possibility in the distance. 'Things I never knew I had'. She would never know if he was referring solely to qualities he had drawn on deep within himself to cope with her revelation, or whether it was more mundane and prosaic than that. But eventually, Steph always came to the same conclusion – that there weren't many better things to give to someone, were there?